The Hill Ranch Racers

Nick Ienatsch

outskirtspress

DENVER, COLORADO

Outskirts Press, Inc.
http://www.outskirtspress.com

ISBN: 978-1-4787-6415-1

Outskirts Press and the "OP" logo are trademarks belonging to Outskirts Press, Inc.

Author's Note

Nothing in this book actually happened. I made up some of the motorcycle models and all the racing…most of the names used are not real people. The names of the AMA racers are real because they are my heroes.

That said: The heroics and super-deeds and morality described in the next few hundred pages have definitely happened. This sport of motorcycle riding and racing has introduced me to the best people on the planet and it's the traits and personalities of these friends I have included. Consider this novel a thanks to the motorcycling community, especially my family and personal friends, for giving me the best life imaginable.

Bruce Meacock, John Joss and Scott Sexton helped me with the editing and publishing of Hill Ranch Racers, and Jason Disalvo contributed a few pages of copy back when the story was getting passed back and forth between us as a lark. Thanks to all four of these friends for helping push this book to the finished state you now hold.

Thanks to my early critics Bruce, Kennedy and Elsa for encouragement and guidance.

To quote Samuel Clemens (Mark Twain) in his preface to The Adventures of Tom Sawyer: "*Although my book is intended mainly for the entertainment of boys and girls, I hope it will not be shunned by men and women on that account, for part of my plan has been to try to pleasantly remind adults of what they once were themselves..."*

Motorcycle riding…there's nothing as wonderful. I hope that comes through in this book.

-Nick Ienatsch

The Rock and Horse Ranch, Colorado

Fastersafer.com

Ridelikeachampion.com

Dedication:
To my dad the rider, my mom the writer
and my wife the achiever.

Prologue

August 17, 1995. Anaheim Stadium, Anaheim, California

*T*he 83,000 fans *at the 1995 Anaheim Supercross leapt to their feet as the starting gate dropped to launch the 250 main event and for the next twenty-six laps they never sat down. For thirty-nine minutes, Jeff Ward, David Bailey, Jeremy McGrath, Bob Hannah and Jeff Emig bashed and battered each other as the spectators roared themselves hoarse. These five superstars gained a slight gap on the intense battle for sixth, but not one of these immensely-talented riders could pull away and the order changed literally every corner. For twenty-six laps.*

Racing a motorcycle at this pace and for this distance was and is immensely difficult. Even the mental focus required to run flat-out for three-quarters of an hour is beyond the reach of most individuals and pales in comparison to the physical stamina needed. When the gate drops these racers need to be mentally bulletproof and physically prepared.

Anaheim's winner wasn't clear until the last three feet of the race, when McGrath, Hannah, and Ward drag-raced off the final corner to the check-ered flag and a photo finish. It took five minutes to review the film and triple-check the results. McGrath, Hannah and Ward sat together at the top of the first jump, reeling with exhaustion tinged with the knowledge that they'd just done something extraordinary. The crowd let them know that.

Supercross racing sprang to life in America in 1972 and by 1995 the art of the show had been polished to a fine sheen. But television executives can't manufacture what Hannah, Emig, McGrath, Ward and Bailey had just delivered on this Saturday night in southern California.

By the time the podium finishers were sorted out and the champagne started spraying, Tommy Hill had just arrived at Anaheim Memorial Hospital, rushed there in the back of an ambulance, barely conscious. The ambulance had run flat-out from the front straight of Anaheim stadium to the hospital, lights flashing, siren and engine screaming.

As McGrath soaked Hannah and Ward with bubbly, Hill was being swung onto an emergency-room table after being sprinted through the ER doors on a gurney.

As the announcer screamed out "Winner Jeremy McGrath!" Hill's motocross gear was being cut off and the surgical team was scrubbing for an immediate surgery to attempt to repair the young kid's right leg.

As McGrath held a gigantic $120,000 cardboard check over his head just before the press interview, Hill's surgical team worked with millimeter-perfect precision on what they hoped wasn't a lost cause.

As the party in the Honda pit grew to encompass the entire paddock and the clock moved close to midnight, Tommy Hill lay alone and battered in a semi-private room on the third floor of the Anaheim Hospital twelve-hundred miles from home.

Anaheim 1995 launched a young Jeremy McGrath's professional motocross racing career. It ended Tommy Hill's at the age of twenty.

1

Southeast Colorado…15 years later

The two motorcyclists tucked their chins to their chests as the rain turned to sleet, their helmets' visors thwarting the cold wet stuff. Southern Colorado in March could be hot and dry or cold and wet, but ranch work had to be done. This Tuesday morning was no different.

The moods of the two riders couldn't have contrasted more profoundly as the bark of their two-stroke engines echoed across the southern Colorado landscape. Tom Hill led the quick-moving duo, the thirty-five year old rancher's mood as cold as the weather as he mentally tallied the cost of extra hay this storm would cause. The forecast called for six to eight inches of heavy, wet snow in the next twelve hours: his free-ranging herd wouldn't be able to forage from the land. Tom's twin brother Brian was already towing a trailer full of hay to the feed lot and would meet Tom and his son Teddy there, once they got the 274 cows across the mesa.

Tom checked quickly over his shoulder and saw his twelve-year-old son Teddy behind him in the sleet on his faded red Honda 125. Tom had slid his Suzuki 250 onto the Skyline trail in a fourth-gear full-lock slide and the kid was just catching back up, standing on the pegs of his Honda, mimicking his dad as the two bikes careened up the forested trail. Tom rode quickly because he knew the cows would start to panic as the storm approached; the sooner he and Teddy could get them moving toward the feed lot, the better.

Teddy rode quickly because he was having fun, fun, fun.

Teddy could feel the stress his dad was under but that couldn't wipe the smile off his face. He secretly loved the times he and his dad had to save time by riding fast, pushing their dirt bikes across the ranch at big speed. Flying up one of the ranch trails to fix a broken fence the herd was drifting through, hustling to get cows off the road, or taking care of a busted gate before dark…any time his dad had to rush, Teddy thrilled with the speed at which they rode.

"Let's go, it's a rush job," was all Tom would mutter to Teddy before booting his 250 to life. Teddy knew that as soon as the clutch came out his dad would set a pace that Teddy couldn't come close to matching but sure enjoyed trying. Tom would always check over his shoulder for his son, adjusting his pace to bring the two riders closer together before lighting the wick again. Teddy's pace improved constantly but his dad seemed to live in another universe of gravity and motion.

During a few of these 'rush jobs,' as Teddy began to think of them, he'd seen his dad purposefully swerve his 250 to launch off the steepest part of a draw or veer over to the sharpest part of an uphill. The old 250 would soar into the air in slow motion and return to earth in perfect form to vault off into the distance, leaving Teddy open-mouthed and just a little freaked out. But his dad never mentioned the rush-job riding, the jumping, the speed…it was just another day in the life of Colorado rancher Tom Hill.

Dirt bikes on the Hill Ranch were tools, pure and simple. Hammers pounded nails, wrenches turned bolts and bikes moved cows, transported lunch to workers, took Teddy to school and performed a dozen other tasks. Tom Hill treated a motorcycle as a means to an end, period. It was quicker than walking, simpler than a horse and fit in places a truck couldn't go while burning much less fuel than trucks or tractors. If it was ever fun to ride, nobody would sense it because the Hill ranch consisted of two things: work and work.

But as twelve-year old Teddy Hill bunny-hopped his 125 Honda over a tree root in the middle of a third-gear left hander with a little giggle, he said a quick thanks to his dad's dad, grandpa Carl.

<hr />

Carl Hill had been the first to realize the value of a dirt bike on the enormous cow ranch. At fifteen he used his modest chore money to buy a barely-running Harley-Davidson 250. Carl attended high school in Walsenburg but was hip-deep in the workings of the ranch, especially the full-time maintenance of the various pieces of machinery. Getting the two-stroke Harley rebuilt and running was quick work and it wasn't long before Carl was commuting to school on it, running to the store for his parents…even doing a little ranch work.

By the time Carl took over the ranch from his parents, the Hill place was not just getting by, it was prospering. The old Harley 250 was still running and proved to be a great bike for Carl's new wife Elsa, while Carl picked up a used Triumph Scrambler. Teddy's grandpa Carl and grandma Elsa continued to prosper and by the time they had twin boys, Tom and Brian, the elder Hills both realized that having the choice of a dirt bike or a good horse was the reason for the prosperity.

Dirt bikes were louder and smellier than a horse and often frightened cattle too much, moving them too fast and burning valuable pounds. Buyers bought cattle from Carl by the pound so Carl let his boys know that moving cattle late in the summer would always be done on horseback. Bikes were used at other times of the year to position cattle around the ranch but the Hill ranchland was initially too challenging for the young Hill twins and they spent a lot of time on horseback. But by the time they were thirteen their motorcycle skills had improved to the point where no spot on the ranch was out of bounds. Whether on four hooves or two wheels, Tom and Brian ruled the ranch. Tom proved to be especially adept on the bikes.

Carl fed their passion, but the three motorcycle rules had been established early: 1) good grades or no bikes; 2) good attitude around home or no bikes; 3) maintain your bike or lose it. Worked like a charm because the kids loved to ride. To school. To friends' houses. To the store with a backpack to fill Elsa's grocery list.

Bikes were sold to neighbors as the twins outgrew them, each replaced with a larger, newer model from Pueblo and even as far away as Colorado Springs. The boys would sit with Carl and comb the want-ads for their next 'new to them' bike, standing next to their dad as Carl called to inquire about a bike they might like to buy.

Carl knew what to look for and the twins would listen as he asked, "Is the bike complete? Has the engine ever seized? What condition is the seat and bodywork? What about the tires? Are there any modifications?"

Finally, if Carl was satisfied with the answers, "What would be the lowest you could accept for this bike?"

Many times Carl thanked the bike owner and set down the phone shaking his head. "Sorry boys, we just can't swing that one."

Each of these purchases were planned, discussed and agonized over because the money in southern Colorado ranching has never been over-abundant. Carl, Elsa and the boys worked hard to get the most from their land and made do with few of the extravagances money can bring. Ranch profits were poured back into cattle, feed, water tanks, fencing and occasionally land when Carl could put together a big enough chunk of money to buy a few neighboring acres. Those acres would then be fenced and Hill cattle would have a bigger home; through it all the Hill family realized the utility of motorcycles on and around the ranch.

"And let's not forget," Elsa often reminded Carl, "those boys are having a heck of a lotta fun racing in Pueblo. They work harder at school and here."

Carl nodded. He knew what Elsa said was true. Since age thirteen, both twins had been racing once or twice every summer at the track in Pueblo, driven there by Carl. Tom and Brian saved their chore money to buy an old Ford van when they were sixteen and Tom had gone as far north as Colorado Springs and Denver to race, even to southern California once. Carl held little interest in the boys' racing and placed it a distant second in priority to what drove the Hill ranch: work. His interest in racing seemed to be entirely obliterated by Tommy's last race in southern California at a place called Anaheim.

Though the racing bug couldn't be sustained, by the time the twins Tom and Brian married and had kids of their own, the 'bike budget' was firmly set in the Hill financial plan. Bikes were the tools that saved time and increased mobility, but the bike budget was always aimed at five- and six-year old machines that became affordable to a ranch that used its tools hard. A new bike had never touched the dirt of the Hill ranch and the idea of racing a motorcycle around a track for fun was long gone.

2

The freezing weather had jolted Tom and Teddy as they left the barn but half-way up Skyline both riders were warm and breathing hard with the exertion of pushing a dirt bike to its limits. They knew Skyline like they knew the wood on their kitchen floor but the rain and sleet had added an extra layer of challenge as the 250 and 125 careened toward the mesa. Tom's occasional quick checks over his shoulder would affect his throttle hand as he gauged Teddy's speed and comfort level. A trickle of joy crept into Tom's cold mood as he wheelied up and over a fourth-gear rise, pinned and grabbing fifth, holding the wheelie until the last moment before setting the front wheel down and going to the brakes and snapping off three downshifts for the next tight left. But his joyful trickle was quickly squelched: there was work to be done and the snow wouldn't wait.

Teddy's first memory was moving cows with his dad and Uncle Brian, perched in front of his dad on an old Kawasaki KX 250. Teddy would squeeze the tank with his little legs and cling to the handlebar brace as his dad went about his ranching business. The best times were heading back to the valley ranch house after a chore because his dad would occasionally let loose and pull a fifth-gear wheelie, both Hills flying through the air weightless and free.

Teddy would always urge his dad to "Race faster, race faster!" but

Tom's standard answer was, "These aren't race bikes, they're work bikes." But despite the pat answer, there were days when Tom would thrill his young son to speechlessness with speed that denied the laws of physics. Clinging to the bars, eyes wide and bright inside the goggles, Teddy Hill was feeling a dirtbike ridden to and beyond the edge of grip and sanity. They would arrive back at the barn with hearts pounding and Teddy would stumble from the bike awed with the speed and pace of the aging KX. His dad never commented, just rolled the 250 into the barn's shop and gave it a quick wipe-down to ready it for the next day's chores. It was just a tool.

Skyline plunged the two riders into the clouds on the way to the mesa. The storm was starting to take hold of the land, sleet turning to real snow and the flakes starting to stick. Tom muttered under his breath; they should reach the herd in the next two minutes and their pace up Skyline just might beat what Tom knew was on the way: a snow so bad that man, bike or beast would be seriously challenged. These spring snows came down so heavy that cows couldn't paw through them to reach the grass, and that often caused panic. It would definitely take more hay.

Tom popped over the final crest and slid to a stop, Teddy pulling up next to him. The snow and fog made the herd appear like ghosts, but Tom felt the majority of them were still together.

"You wanna round 'em?"

Teddy was peering intently to the left, where the trees began. He nodded, still looking for the edge of the herd. "Are they all out?"

"Doubt it," Tom answered, his mood audible in his voice. He suspected that a few yearlings started running as soon as the fog rolled in and had found safety in the thick junipers Teddy was studying.

"The yearlings?"

Tom was nodding as Teddy looked over at him.

"Get in the arroyo, get behind 'em," Tom growled.

The Hill land was 2200 acres of high-desert mesa, canyons of every size, rock outcroppings and dry waterways cutting through the land. These 'arroyos' carried water during the flash-floods, but otherwise were dry mini-canyons. Tom wanted Teddy to ride along the bottom of the nearest arroyo to get past the cows hidden in the trees, then exit the arroyo and push the cows toward the gated pasture where Brian waited. Tom would shadow the edge of the herd, eliminating their option of heading down Skyline toward the valley floor. Herding cows was a two-man job, three if you had them and more if you could get them.

Teddy booted his 125 to life and slipped it into gear, idling away easily to keep the nearby cows calm. He slipped the bike into second gear and approached the steep edge of the arroyo. His bike, body and helmet disappeared from view and a moment later the exhaust note of his Honda disappeared too. Tom heard a faint cry and then silence. Teddy had crashed into the bottom of the arroyo, his Honda snapping sideways on the snowy incline and tossing him off before landing on top of him.

Twenty seconds later Tom was into the arroyo on foot, sliding down the side like a ski-less skier to arrive at his son's side. The elder Hill lifted the 125 off his son as if it were made of balsa wood, the rancher's sturdy frame packed with muscle and sinew that a college-level wrestler would envy.

"You alright?"

"Yeah," Teddy said, quickly struggling to his feet in embarrassment. "I lost the back end in the snow."

"Yeah, I heard. You're late with throttle. Soon as the rear wheel drops in, you gotta spin it to push the bike forward, not just down. C'mon, I'll show you."

Tom handed the 125 to Teddy and then walked down the arroyo a few yards before finding a place to clamber out. Teddy re-fired his bike and rode it out of the arroyo in his dad's footsteps, circling back around to park at the edge of the arroyo, just above the spot he'd crashed.

For the next five minutes the cows were forgotten as Tom showed his son the technique of slip-sliding into a snowy arroyo. Tom started with a couple of easy trips down the embankment, but finished with a third-gear assault that made Teddy gasp…and doubt that he'd ever achieve that pace and control no matter how many years he rode.

Tom watched as Teddy struggled with the tricky procedure but finally nodded approval with the third attempt.

"Okay. Go."

Teddy, up on the pegs now, crash forgotten and lesson learned, cruised out of sight up the arroyo as Tom returned to the edge of the herd quietly, easily, quickly. Less than a minute later, Tom heard the Honda's engine slow as his son searched for a smooth exit from the arroyo, deep in the forest of junipers and falling snow. Tom heard a quick shot of acceleration and imagined the little 125 scrabbling up the side of the canyon with Teddy standing forward on the pegs, trying to be quiet but needing the power to fight gravity.

Teddy fought the urge to gas it, knowing that hurrying now would push any strays even further from the main pack, doubling or even tripling their morning's work load and adding to his dad's foul mood. He idled around a huge pinion tree on the edge of the draw just as four yearlings looked up and started to move away from the motorcycle.

A quick shot of acceleration in second gear, a shift to third while veering sharply to the left startled the cows and took Teddy into their escape route. They jumped, scared by the Honda's quickness, but this time they jumped towards the mesa and Teddy skidded the back of the bike around, squaring his shoulders the way his dad had taught him.

"Yah…let's go now!"

All four cows pretended it had been their idea to head toward the mesa and Teddy idled along behind as they joined the main herd. As Teddy cleared the trees he glanced to the right, looking for his dad. Tom was standing next to his 250, circling his arm over his head, then pointing past Teddy. The kid nodded and swerved in that direction to circle through the trees to double-check that all the yearlings were with the herd.

Three minutes later he was back onto the mesa and gave his dad a thumbs-up through the increasing snowfall. Tom kick-started his 250 and plunked along next to and slightly behind the herd, slowing or accelerating to discourage the cows from straying away from the group. Teddy matched his pace and style, pushing but not scaring the herd. Neither had to talk, neither had to have instruction and their herd ambled along, going with the pressure toward the hay that Brian Hill had brought to the next-door pasture. Tom knew the gate would be open and Brian would have the water full and the hay ready, and that once the lead cow smelled the hay the drama was over. Pressure fell off Tom's shoulders and he breathed his first relaxed breath of the morning. The smallest smile flickered across his face as he replayed their 'rush job' run up Skyline.

3

Herding cows can go from crazy to controlled in a split second, and vice versa. The crazy part can be panicked cows separated from the herd or scared into running mindlessly. The controlled part is when they realize they're among friends and the leader is leading. Tom slowly worked his way over to Teddy and the two Hills idled along almost touching handlebars, alert but relaxed now that the gang was moving smooth and steady.

Both Hills sat their bikes as if born on them, and that was almost true. Teddy mimicked his dad's actions on the bike but father and son were different-sized versions of the same person. Both were compact, wiry and moved with an economy of motion. Tom's athletic body carried not an ounce of fat and, while his twelve year-old son didn't have the musculature, anyone could see he was a spitting image of his dad from his short dirty-blond hair to his piercing blue eyes.

"I got it from here," Tom said.

"Okay. See you after school."

"Mom's at work, don't forget your lunch."

"Okay."

"Hey!" His dad's angry tone of voice snapped Teddy's head around. His dad's eyes flared. "Don't beat on that thing on the way to school, bikes have to last around here."

"I won't," Teddy managed to squeak out, his heart pounding with the upset tone of his dad's voice.

Tom nodded. "I'm not paying three bucks a gallon to have you wasting fuel riding flat-out everywhere."

Teddy's face burned bright red in his helmet as his dad's eyes burned into his. The kid nodded and slowed his bike to pass behind his dad and head down Skyline, back to the valley ranch house.

"Hey," Tom called out again.

Teddy stopped and looked back at his dad, his breath held, his heart in his throat. Tom Hill ran a tight ranch and was tough on his twelve-year old son, never mincing words or failing to correct.

"Good job this morning."

Teddy slipped the clutch out as his dad's praise hung in the air. He caught second gear, then third, fourth and he was onto Skyline as *Good job this morning* carried him down the trail and into the small ranch house and away to school.

Good job this morning.

4

Teddy's ride to school took him along Rye Road, a winding county-maintained dirt road, for about four miles, then onto a cut-through over the Jensen property that dumped him right at the school on the edge of Walsenburg. His dad had seen him hammering the little Honda along at full throttle on the Jensen cut-through yesterday, jumping and play-racing at the limits of his ability. His dad had been coming home in the Suburban pulling a trailer loaded with fuel drums and had said not a word until they'd moved the cows this morning.

The pace this morning was slower and easier on the machinery, Teddy Hill didn't need to be told anything twice. He knew that if his Honda blew up, seized, wore out…if anything happened to it, the strain of repair or replacement was a financial burden his parents couldn't handle immediately. He had seen the price of fuel rise over the last three years and knew it squeezed the ranch hard.

If I break this thing I don't get to ride for a while, Teddy realized as he listened closely to the 125 stroker beneath him. It sounded strong and sharp, despite being seven years old. Grandpa Carl had gone through it just after he brought it home from Pueblo, cleaning up the ports, de-carboning the piston and replacing the rings. And Carl had taught Teddy to maintain the oil and air filter religiously.

Keep a two-stroke's air and oil clean... the mantra Teddy had heard since birth.

⊜◦⟨◉⟩◦⊜

Teddy parked his Honda next to the school bus, on the west side of the teachers' parking lot, a place that often held two or three other dirt bikes. Not today: the little Honda was alone in the spot. Teddy hopped off and ran for the front door, realizing that he was late as the eight o'clock bell rang. He shrugged out of his backpack, heavy coat and overalls, hopping on one foot just outside his home-room door. Teddy wore the heaviest stuff Carhart made and it took effort to get in and out of, but it made great winter riding gear though it was about three sizes too big.

His teacher Mrs. Joss stopped mid-sentence as Teddy slipped in the door.

"Good morning Teddy."

"Morning."

Mrs. Joss smiled inwardly. Teddy Hill was her leading student but, man, was he quiet. The little Hill kid chose his words carefully, never said more when less would work.

Just like his dad and uncle, Mrs. Joss thought to herself.

"Snow slow you down this morning?"

Teddy had slid into his desk, two spots back in the third row from the window. "Yes ma'am. Moving cows."

"Did you ride your Honda?"

Teddy nodded.

Mrs. Joss nodded back. The eleven other students in the sixth-grade watched the discussion and nobody was surprised that Teddy Hill would ride his bike to school on a day that forecast at least eight inches of snow before school released at three PM. The Hills rode bikes, had always ridden bikes, that was all there was to it.

Mrs. Joss also knew that Tom and Judy Hill weren't about to drive their son into town just because of a little snow. Judy kept the books over at the Walsenburg Bank and Trust and her schedule didn't match Teddy's school schedule, but it wasn't just that. The Hills expected a lot of their son and getting himself to and from school was part of that expectation.

Mrs. Joss smiled at Teddy, noticing how the kid's boots didn't even touch the floor when he sat at his desk. He had to be the smallest kid in the sixth grade, certainly the shyest.

"Are you worried about riding home in the snow?"

Teddy glanced out the window, then back to his teacher.

"No," he answered quietly, "I like it."

5

The whole class snickered a bit and Mrs. Joss's smile broadened. She had grown up with Teddy's dad and uncle, the twins Tommy and Brian Hill, watching those 'country' kids through her 'town' kid eyes. They always seemed simple to her, but not in a bad way. They were simple in how they went about their lives. The ranch work drove everything, motorcycles a close second. Their father Carl had always appeared distant and uninterested in anything that didn't deal directly with the Hill ranch.

Mrs. Joss, then Shawnie Hendry, remembered the twins' sixteenth birthday party, held at the ranch. The small ranch house was immaculate, the surrounding acreage clean, neat and uncluttered. Tommy and Brian had shown their class-mates the barn and adjoining shop and each and every piece of equipment was spotless. But nothing was new, or near new, from the refrigerator in the kitchen to the dirt bikes in the shop.

That fact hit Shawnie Hendry hard and she felt sorry for the Hills until her father set her straight.

"Honey, don't feel sorry for Tommy and Brian Hill. Those boys are driven hard by Carl but he's fair with them. Fun and games and goofing around just aren't part of their lives. Are they good in school?"

Shawnie nodded.

"I'm not surprised. Carl was, too. He'd expect them to be at the top of the class. And I'll bet they're never late, never mouth off. Do they goof around at school?"

"Never...well, they do some crazy stuff on their bikes. That's the only time I've ever seen them laughing."

Her dad was nodding. "What are their bikes like?"

"Older than anyone else's, but cleaner too," Shawnie answered. "But even the high school boys on their new bikes can't ride like the Hills, especially Tommy."

Mr. Hendry shook his head with a rueful smile.

"Nobody could ride like Carl and I hear Tommy is twice as good."

Shawnie Hendry Joss flashed through this childhood conversation the instant after Teddy answered *I like it.* She had been away at college when Tommy broke himself up in California, but like most kids who grow up in a small town she had done her fair share of riding motorcycles. She knew how addictive it was and when she watched this kid's face light up as he answered she felt happy for someone with that much passion for anything.

"Alright class, let's get back to math."

6

The school year in rural southern Colorado finishes earlier than most districts because planting season happens in late April and early May. Planting 325 acres of hay takes all available hands and every Hill able to walk or crawl must work. From Tom's valley ranch house came Tom, Judy and Teddy, while Brian's mesa ranch house provided Brian, his wife Karen, their daughter Elsie and grandpa Carl.

Grandma Elsa had passed away seven years ago. The Hill clan missed her every day—the direct way she spoke, the love she gave, the liveliness she shared with Carl, her kids and grandkids. But she had left clear instructions that nobody would be sad or weepy about her passing, that the Hills were supposed to go on living, working the ranch, giving their best and staying strong as a family. Grandma Elsa loved the ranch and her family like a horse loves oats, and whenever a Hill thought of Elsa it was with a smile on their face.

Grandma Elsa's place on the seeder had been taken over by Teddy's cousin Elsie, the six-year old strapped onto the back of the rumbling machine, making sure the seed continued to flow from the main hopper to each seeding arm. Tom Hill drove the tractor that pulled the seeder and Teddy worked on the deck just in front of the seed hopper, continually feeding thirty-pound bags of seed into the hopper. The trio of Hills would trundle along in a maze of dust while Brian Hill followed in a second tractor to apply fertilizer and rake dirt over the seeds.

Ahead of these two tractors was Judy Hill, Tom's wife, dragging a harrow from a third tractor to break-up the land and give the seeds a chance to succeed. To say that the land in southeast Colorado was tough to plant in would be the understatement of the decade, but this three-tractor attack the Hills had developed could cajole the dirt into growing good enough hay to keep the herd fat throughout the winter.

Karen Hill, Brian's wife, pulled the trailer of diesel fuel behind the old Ford pickup, grabbed the bags that Teddy discarded and fed the entire clan snacks, drinks and meals out on the land. Grandpa Carl would rotate between all these stations, moving slowly these days but still wanting to be involved. As the herd-size increased, the number of acres of hay increased and getting 325 acres of hay going took a long and consistent effort from every Hill.

The hay plan was another reason the Hill ranch continued to prosper. Cows can be raised without growing your own hay but hay prices fluctuate with the weather and it's tough to budget when you don't know how much you might spend on feed that year. Carl realized this just about the time the twins Tommy and Brian were nine years old, about the time they could really help with chores. As the two kids grew stronger and worked harder, Carl found that his hay was sought-after among his neighbors. Any hay his herd didn't eat was sold to neighboring ranches.

Tom and Brian Hill continued to profit from the hay side of their ranching. It not only took care of the cows but fed Buck, Flytrap and Blossom, the three ranch horses kept at Brian's mesa house. The Hill ranch had recently saved enough money to buy a one-hundred acre parcel that attached to the east side of the Hill ranch. More acreage meant more cows and that meant more hay had to be planted.

Planting season involved more than limping across the land in a three-tractor parade, it also involved prepping the tractors, harrow

and seeder. Tom and Brian had learned early that machine maintenance should be a year-long habit because the best way to retain a
machine's worthiness is never to lose it in the first place.

Ranches, by nature, are remote and well-removed from the cities
most Americans inhabit and the Hill clan exemplified the American
ranching family. Tough. Self-sufficient. Independent...and proud of
all three. The extensive gardens at both the mesa and ranch house,
the small orchard at the mesa house, the chickens and cows...each
provided sustenance and profit in various amounts. The Hills lived
on the land and were of the land.

Carl Hill's mechanical abilities had passed directly to his son
Tom. The huge barn at the valley house held Tom's shop, an im-
maculately clean work space equipped with a small but complete set
of tools, a stick welder, desktop lathe, compressor with air tools...
nothing new, but everything working under Tom's hands to keep the
vehicles and mechanical necessities of the Hill ranch functioning.
As Tom trundled along in the tractor, checking his mirror to watch
his twelve-year old son and six-year old niece working the seeder, he
felt pressure and satisfaction in equal amounts.

The satisfaction came from the smooth operation of the three
tractors and the seeder. The pressure came from his knowledge
of mechanical limits, fatigued metals, stressed components. Tom's
mind clicked through the weakest spots as the trio turned a tight
180-degree right-hand turn to begin a westward run. The constant
monitoring of what would fail next, the miles and hours on each
component and the fluid changes needed kept Tom occupied, both
mentally and physically.

This May morning would be the final three hours on the seeder
before it had to be re-aligned and lubed. No problem there, easy
stuff. Brian's tractor had developed a slow leak in the left front tire
and Tom planned to plug it right after lunch. The wheel bearings
on the fuel trailer had to be looked at and repacked this month and

Tom had learned that trailer bearings fail when you most need them so that job had better get knocked out tomorrow, right after breakfast. As Tom automatically guided his tractor, naturally scanning the job he'd done since he was nine years old, he calculated the time and tools and parts and supplies necessary. Everything he needed was in the shop.

He looked out across the field and hoped it would be a wet year. His mind calculated the amount of seed needed to finish the day. The tractors rolled. The dust churned. The seeds found a home. The Hills worked.

7

Southern California

Preston Jupiter was still asleep 1100 miles west in California. The fourteen year old wouldn't wake until nine AM, then only to eat breakfast before meeting with his home-school instructor Patricia Castanos. They would study together until noon, break for lunch, then hit the books for two more hours, Monday through Friday except holidays and racing travel days.

Like most boys and some girls, Preston Jupiter loved motorcycles and his love of riding had been fostered and pushed by his dad Paul, a custom-home builder who had raced motocross at the pro-Am level in California before he married Lori and got serious about his construction business, Jupiter Homes.

Paul recognized Preston's riding skills when he saw his kid ride a bicycle at age three and then master a neighbor's minibike a year later. Preston's interest in bikes reignited Paul's passion and soon Preston had a minibike and dad his own playbike; soon after that, playing became play-racing. That led both Jupiter boys to enter a local fun race at the motocross track just outside their hometown, Redlands, an hour east of Los Angeles.

That was six years ago. Now Team Jupiter spent most weekends racing, dad in the Senior class and Preston steadily moving up through the ranks after becoming one of the fastest 125 Youth Intermediates anyone had ever seen. The Youth classes were for kids under sixteen and though Preston was only fourteen, his speed in the Intermediate class was impressive.

While Preston learned to master his 125-cc four-stroke Yamaha, Paul had sold his 250 Yamaha four-stroke race bike in favor of a YZ450F, the largest, fastest four-stroke motocross bike Yamaha sells. The guys winning the Senior class were all on open-class thumpers and the move to the big bike put Paul consistently at the front of the class. He was having a blast, not just racing for wins but spending weekends with his son.

Paul's thriving construction business had finally given him a chance to go racing 'right' rather than skimping along as he used to do in his late teens.

Those days were tough and Paul didn't miss them one bit. Back then his carpentry money all went to racing and it was never quite enough to get to the front. He raced out of the back of his pickup and was forced to run 'take-offs,' or tires that sponsored riders hadn't completely worn out. He ran premium fuel mixed with the two-stroke oil but the fast guys could afford high-dollar race fuel. He was busy swinging a hammer when the others were at Friday practice.

Not anymore.

Team Jupiter had a neatly-painted box van with built-in tool-boxes, workbenches, air-conditioning and stereo, plus room for four bikes. Above the work benches were racks for tires, cabinets for extra parts and a tall closet for riding gear, umbrellas and the pop-up canopy. Comfy folding chairs hung on the wall next to the small fridge/freezer; a generator and air compressor rode along under the workbenches. Between the mobile shop and the van's passenger compartment was just enough room for two fold-down bunks for Preston and Paul to spend the night in. Every piece had a trick Team Jupiter logo: a silver space ship blasting off with the team name on its flashy flank.

 Yep, thought Paul every time he saw the box van, *life is good.* There was nothing the Jupiter boys liked more than to ride all day, clean the bikes as the barbecue warmed, eat a meal with one or all of their racing neighbors and wake up to do it all again.

8

Living in southern California allowed the Jupiters to race almost every weekend as members of a half-dozen dirt bike clubs. On non-race weekends they liked practicing motocross at one of the local tracks on Saturday, then clean and prep the bikes all day Sunday at home.

Preston had a great racing role model in his dad Paul, though his dad liked to remind him how lucky the kid had it.

"I would have killed for a van like this when I was racing," Paul often said. "Aren't you the luckiest kid in the world?"

Preston always nodded, but Paul knew deep down that the kid might never realize how lucky he was to have a dad who rode motorcycles. Paul had to plead, beg and bribe his parents into a dirtbike and that didn't happen until he was fifteen. He had friends whose parents refused to even discuss bikes with their kids. Those kids were told they couldn't have a bike until they moved out of the house. So, yeah, Preston Jupiter was the luckiest kid in the world. He just didn't know it.

The best part was that Paul still loved riding.

"Let's get over to the Woodcrest track and work on those two double jumps," or, "How about going up to Lee's place and practice our starts?" Paul would say. These practice days would start with whatever Paul wanted to work on but would eventually become the two Jupiter boys racing against each other, whooping and yelling back and forth as they made laps.

In an all-out race, Preston's 125-cc four-stroke weighed less than Paul's 450-cc four-stroke, but that advantage couldn't overcome Paul's skills and his Yamaha's huge power. That didn't matter on practice days because Paul would let off and allow Preston to pass, only to wick it up again and run next to and then ahead of his son. These were the days Preston loved best and also the days he improved the most, trying to catch his flying dad on that big thumper.

The Jupiters were having fun, sure, but they also had a grand plan: the Fairground Circuit. All their practice and local racing would be put to the test as they attempted to accrue enough points to qualify for the all-Expert field.

The Fairground Circuit had been running since the late-1970s and was a traveling series of dirt-bike races that swung through America during the height of the State fair season, but only every-other year. Because the Fairground Circuit ran only on even years, it remained quite rare and elite. The 'Fairs,' as the racers called them, were expensive to enter compared with the club racing scene but the top finishers made good money, almost on par with true professionals. The increased purse often brought out the best of the best…and desperation to get to the front, like an Expert club race on steroids. Both Jupiters hoped to make the cut, then do two or three races in the western states: definitely the California State Fair, probably the Utah State Fair, then maybe the Colorado State Fair the weekend after Utah.

But first they had to qualify.

9

Qualifying for the Fairs meant earning enough points in local club events to become an Expert, then enough Expert points to make the cut. Only the points earned in even years counted, making those seasons even tougher in speed and consistency. Points were gained by finishing races: the better you finished the more points you earned. Preston's quickness in the Intermediate Youth class boded well for his Expert class pace, the class he would enter for the first time this Spring, but he would have to be quick, consistently, on the new 125.

Plenty of Experts across the country qualified for the Fairs, but most of them rarely traveled from their home states to compete due to the expense of travel and entry fees. The Fairs usually became a State-championship race, with an occasional racer visiting from a nearby state.

For many riders the Fairs were the first opportunity to ride in front of a large, often boisterous, crowd. Local races attracted almost no spectators beyond participating racers' families. But not the Fairs. The tradition of the Fairs, the added purse... plus the Expert status of all the racers drew huge audiences that expected and received fantastic racing through all age groups. And the Fairs in California were just a few steps short of a full-on National. Paul had tried to qualify for the Anaheim Supercross back when he was a hungry young racer and it hadn't gone well, so the upcoming Fairs were anticipated with a mixture of delight and trepidation.

Preston didn't know much about his dad's Anaheim race but he could feel the energy his dad had about the Fairs, about trying to become the fastest Senior Expert in three states…or at least California. Preston noticed his dad pushing harder in practice, doing extra sit-ups, tweaking his bike a little more frequently. The kid fed on that fever and knew he had to start running in the top five of the Expert club races he was entering. He wanted to race the Fairs with his dad.

10

The Hill Ranch, Colorado

Teddy Hill's twelfth birthday present was an AMA motocross DVD of the Unadilla race in New York, along with a used Sony DVD player out of the Pueblo classifieds. The young Hill's obsession with motocross racing gave him incentive to get his chores and homework done so he could sprawl on the living room carpet and watch his heroes. Every night. His mom and dad had practically memorized the announcer's words, they had heard them so often!

Professional motocross appeared as distant as Pluto to Teddy Hill. Nothing in his life remotely resembled the sights and sounds the Unadilla DVD brought to the ranch house. He watched with avid attention, soaking in everything on the small television, studying every move, catching every detail. His entire life on a motorcycle had been spent at the ranch, running chores, riding to school, moving cows. The racetrack in New York was a revelation to the kid in Colorado.

On the final day of planting, as Tom and Teddy pulled the steel overhead door down to close the shop, Teddy uncharacteristically spoke up.

"Dad?"

"Yeah." Tom stopped to look down at his son, surprised at the tension he heard in his voice.

"Could...um, can we build a racetrack?"

Tom, caught totally by surprise, scoffed, "A racetrack? No."

Tom turned to walk up to the house, but then stopped and turned back to his son. "You've got to quit watching that DVD, Teddy. Do you think we have the money to run bikes around in a circle, just for fun?"

Teddy couldn't look back at his dad. He heard the tone in his voice and knew the answer to his dad's question. Teddy took a deep breath. His body ached from the days of lifting grass seed, days when his body moved automatically and his brain spun with the argument he would make for a racetrack on the Hill ranch. He turned to face his dad.

"I want to use my chore money for the extra gas and stuff. The oil..." the kid's already-quiet voice faded away. He had planned to tell his dad that his chore money could go to whatever ranch expenses necessary, if they could build a little track. But he hadn't counted on his dad's expression. Tom Hill had his hands on his hips and he looked positively angry.

Teddy took a deep breath and tried again. "I've saved everything you've ever paid me and we can use that for anything on the...."

Tom huffed his breath out and cut off Teddy's voice.

"The last thing we need to do is waste money and time riding around in circles when we have cows to herd, school to attend and a ranch to run. You might as well learn right now that racing wastes time and money that can be used in a lot better places. Get home. Get cleaned-up for dinner. Quit talking foolish."

Teddy ran for the house, tears starting to stream down his cheeks. Tears at losing his dream of a little racetrack. Tears at being scoffed at by his dad. Tears for being so stupid.

11

Tom's walk to the house did nothing to reduce the frustration he felt with Teddy. Of all the dreams he wanted for his son, going racing was not among them and he once again questioned the intelligence of the birthday DVD of Unadilla.

As he stepped into the kitchen, his wife Judy looked up from stove.

"What's up with Teddy? He was bawling and wouldn't talk to me."

Tom resisted the urge to slam the door in frustration, instead turning away from Judy and slowly latching the door. He took a deep breath and turned back to his wife.

"Yeah, he wants to waste our money and his chore money on a bike track here at the ranch."

Judy nodded, looking from her husband back to the stew she was stirring. She nodded again, kept stirring. Moved the big pot a little, reached down and adjusted the flame. She felt the frustration boiling off Tom as he hung up his coat.

"Yeah," she finally said, "that would be crazy."

"I know it!" Tom blurted out as he turned, then stopped. His wife was smiling…almost laughing at him.

"Jeez, think of it," Judy said through her smile. "A twelve-year old kid wants a little racetrack on his 2200 acre ranch. Oh my, I don't think that's possible."

But Tom wasn't laughing and he wasn't thinking about laughing at his wife's sarcasm.

"So you think we're so rich we can waste money running circles on motorcycles?"

Tom's eyes burned into his wife's, his temper flaring and close to exploding.

Judy looked back at him, directly into his eyes. Her smile had faded but still played on her lips. She stopped stirring and walked over to her husband.

Judy Hill had grown up Judy Schellinger and her parents had moved to Walsenburg when she was sixteen. She and Tom had met in school and her scholastic and athletic abilities had been as attractive as her looks. She went on to graduate from the University of Colorado, Pueblo, with honors in agricultural chemistry and accounting. She was sharp, an equal to Tom Hill. When she walked up to him and looked him in the eye, he gave her his attention and respect even if he was seething with anger. This was one of those times.

"Tom, we have a great kid. He's ready to help with anything here on the ranch, his grades couldn't be much better...he even keeps his room clean. Don't look now but I just paid off the 4460 and we only owe another $1300 on the J80," Judy said, quietly, referring to the last two John Deere tractors the ranch had purchased.

"No, we're not rich," Judy continued, "but we've got a little wiggle room now. Take Teddy up on his offer to help pay for some track riding. Have him put some of his own money into it."

Judy stayed standing eye-to-eye with Tom, letting her words sink in, letting the tough rancher know that letting their son run a few laps on a racetrack would be okay.

Judy put her hand behind Tom's head and leaned her head into his. She whispered, "A little ranch racetrack isn't a Supercross in Anaheim, Tom."

Tom's eyes drilled into his wife's. Time stopped as his mind spun. Judy's whisper hung in the kitchen with the aroma of the stew.

Tom finally dropped his eyes to the well-worn kitchen floor and shook his head as if to shake water off his hair. Judy rarely had to snap him out of a funk with her quiet, well-thought-out reasoning, but this was certainly one of those times. He had heard the word *race* and lost his mind, remembering the pain and expense. Especially the expense. He pulled his wife into his arms and whispered, "Yeah…it might be okay…it might be okay. Thanks."

Tom turned from the embrace and climbed the stairs. He knocked gently on his son's bedroom door and pushed it open. Teddy was sitting at his desk and looked over his shoulder, wiping the tears off his face as his dad walked in.

"Dad," Teddy began, "I'm sorry…"

But that's as far as Teddy got because Tom held up his hand to quiet the boy.

"Teddy, I'm sorry I lost my temper at the barn. Your mother and I think it would be okay if we built you a little track, but you'll have to pay for the fuel you use."

A stunned pause froze the moment in Teddy's mind. His dad rarely spoke to him in this tone and the message took a moment to register. *He could have a track!*

12

Tom Hill and Uncle Brian reviewed Teddy's track sketch around the kitchen table early the next Saturday morning.

"How long do you think Unadilla is, Teddy?" Uncle Brian asked.

"Dunno, but the fastest guys were running laps in just under two minutes...the announcer said the fastest lap was a 1:57.3."

The two men exchanged glances.

Brian cleared his throat. "Well...you know we can't build a track that big, right? We can section-off that pasture area south of the barn for the track but we can't afford to use much more land than that, okay?"

Teddy didn't take his eyes off the track he had drawn. The twelve-year old couldn't believe his dad and uncle were going to cut him a track and he didn't dare say anything to spoil the plans.

"No, well...what? No...if it has some of these turns and stuff it would be great. I mean really great," Teddy stuttered.

⇒)(●)(⇐

Making the track took half a day of planning, walking, measuring and tractoring by the Hill men. Uncle Brian would cut the section with the Deere's blade and Teddy would try the corner or jump... he was in heaven and as Saturday ended the Hills had a reasonable facsimile of Unadilla in the south pasture, though on a smaller scale. Tom had refused to build the big jumps Teddy had drawn, telling his son, "We'll see…let's start with small ones."

Truth be told, Uncle Brian and Tom thoroughly enjoyed their track building. They each had a flashback to when they were Teddy's age, just beginning to race a little. They both caught themselves grinning like kids as they watched Teddy trying a new berm or jump; they forgot the hardships of Colorado ranching, at least for a few hours.

The little track sat dormant for the next week as the Hills concentrated on ranch business, but Saturday morning saw a trickle of Hills arrive at what Teddy called "Mini-Unadilla". First it was Teddy, then Judy walked over to watch. Then Brian rode down on his old 250 and started lapping. Next thing you knew, Judy had borrowed her son's bike to run a few circuits herself.

"I haven't ridden much lately but I like going around this track!" Judy exclaimed to her smiling son.

By then Brian's wife Karen and daughter Elsie had come down and Elsie was idling around the track on her little 80-cc Yamaha quad, laughing in delight. Tom had stuck his head out of the shop a few times, watching the growing glee with a surprised look. He finally set the wrenches down on the front fender of the smallest Deere and walked out to stand with Karen and Judy as Brian, Teddy and Elsie rode the track.

Teddy pulled up and handed his 125 to his mom for a few laps and took her place next to his dad.

"Dad," the kid started. "It's great, I mean the track is great. Thanks…."

Tom put his arm around Teddy's shoulders and pulled him against his hip. "Good, huh?"

Teddy looked up, nodding enthusiastically.

"Well then," Tom smiled. "I guess I better try it."

The Hills rode until the setting sun pulled them away to dinner.

Soon Teddy had a lap-time chart with everyone's name and best lap times, what bike they rode, weather conditions and any other notes, using Grandpa Carl's old wristwatch. Lap times averaged just about half a minute and it wasn't long before Saturday afternoons became 'track time,' a chance for all the Hills to let loose of the stress of budgets and cow counts.

Teddy continued to kick in his chore money for the extra gas and was happy to do it…and not just because he loved to ride. Every time Teddy fired up his 125 for a few laps, Tom seemed to find his way over on his Suzuki. Teddy would be lapping and in a rush of sound and fury his dad would sail past, then pull up and wait, let Teddy by…and fly past again. Tom knew Teddy would push harder to try to keep up. Tom would jet past and Teddy would get sucked into the next corner a bit faster than ever before, or attack one of the small jumps more aggressively.

It didn't always go well! Teddy's balance and throttle control were fantastic because he had been riding dirt bikes and quads on the ranch almost since birth, but his track skills were non-existent. The harder he pushed to keep his dad in sight, the more apparent the problems became. Adding speed to a problem usually created a crash and Teddy soon became frustrated.

13

Tom Hill used the quiet time after Teddy's tip-overs to coach his son, talking him through the problem, offering solutions and even showing him at a standstill what techniques were necessary. Tom's quiet voice calmed Teddy and brought him back from the edge of tears a few times. Not tears of pain, but tears of frustration.

Teddy had spent months watching the best motocross riders in the world on his Unadilla DVD, he had spent years going anywhere and everywhere on the ranch…and now he couldn't even get around his very own racetrack at a decent speed! His dad made it look so easy, made it sound so easy, but getting around Mini-Unadilla at speed was one of the toughest things Teddy had tried.

"I can't do it," Teddy finally said to his dad as he picked his 125 up out of the dirt late one Saturday afternoon. His uncle and dad had stopped to see if he was okay and the two men could sense Teddy's frustration.

"You're getting better," Brian offered. "Stick with it."

Tom was busy realigning Teddy's clutch perch and said nothing. He heard his son's frustration and he agreed with his brother: Teddy was getting better, a lot better, but going quickly on a motocrosser could be one of the toughest sports in the world. That's why so few people can do it.

"I don't feel like I am. I keep falling."

Tom's head snapped around at the new sound of his son's voice. He snapped down the Honda's sidestand and took a step toward his son.

"Hey, if you're going to whine, quit riding right now and we'll shut this track down forever. Crying never got anyone anywhere. I'm done for today."

Tom grabbed his 250, booted it to life and rode back to the barn.

14

Teddy stood in shocked, embarrassed silence. His heart was hammering but he couldn't catch his breath after his father's stunning words and look. Uncle Brian reached out and shook him by the shoulder.

"Teddy, that's your dad. Don't take it personal."

Teddy couldn't tear his eyes off the barn door, where his dad had disappeared on his 250. Finally Teddy came back to life and just dropped his head, his chin touching his chest.

"I'm sorry."

He didn't know exactly why he was apologizing. Maybe for his whining. Maybe for his lack of gratitude for the track or his dad's coaching. Maybe for ruining his dad's lapping session. For falling.

"You heard what your dad said, right?"

Teddy nodded.

"Your dad…well, his life doesn't include wishing, hoping, whining, excuse-making. Tom Hill, your dad, my brother…is one of the toughest men you'll ever meet and he's toughest on himself."

Brian was looking at the barn but seeing something in his memory. "And I'm glad he is. This ranch wouldn't be anything without him because he's got a gene in him called the 'work hard' gene; I've never met anyone who works harder at anything put in front of him."

Teddy stared at the barn and knew instinctively that his dad was special, outstanding, different in a good way. He'd known it all his life but until his uncle put it into words he hadn't realized it.

"But you guys are twins. You're the same."

Brian laughed and shook the kid again. "Yeah, we're the same in a lot of ways, but your dad has a drive like nobody you'll ever meet. His mind is always on *what's next*, that's what makes him such a good rider. Your dad's quiet because words don't replace work for him. He likes to dig in and work, not stand around and flap his lips. If he's talking, it's got to mean something."

Teddy nodded, hearing exactly what his uncle was saying. His dad didn't want to stand around and hear him whine, he wanted to offer riding advice, then get back on the bikes or quit riding and get back to work. Made sense, made perfect sense.

"So Teddybear," his uncle said, using his pet name from Teddy's childhood. "You're staying in the seat too long in the whoops section, you gotta get up on the pegs earlier through those bumps. Also, you're too late with the…"

And his uncle stopped mid-sentence.

"What?"

"Here's what we're going to do," Brian replied with a grin. "Fire that thing up and get going. I'm going to ride behind you and beside you and yell out a few things that will help you right at that moment. Coach you out loud!"

"How…"

Brian gave his nephew a little push toward his bike because, truth-be-told, none of the Hill men have ever liked to talk too much for too long.

"Jump on. Start riding. Let's go."

Brian didn't tell Teddy that this on-track coaching was something Tom had done for him back when they were stepping up the pace in their own racing. Back when they were fifteen and getting pretty quick, Tom would ride with Brian and shout out a few things now and then, timely reminders that helped Brian take that next step. Tom had always been a step quicker than his brother.

Well, more than a step, Brian laughed to himself as Teddy dropped the clutch.

Teddy's increased speed was just making him too late with almost everything. He covered the same distance but in much less time and he needed to be readier, earlier. So Brian rode close behind and sometimes beside the little 125 and reminded Teddy what was next.

Teddy got faster, immediately faster. His uncle's voice reminded him when to sit and stand, where to place the bike at different points on the track, what control to use and how much.

Tom finished cleaning his 250 and watched his son and brother from the shadow of the barn, remembering when he did the same thing for Brian twenty years earlier. He heard his brother's shouts and saw Teddy's improvement.

Great idea brother, I should have thought of that, Tom thought to himself.

The Hills didn't get back to the track until the next Saturday, but on that day Teddy began to have two coaches riding close. The speed came up and more problems came with that speed, but Teddy never whined again. He just listened and tried harder.

15

The Unadilla DVD had sparked Teddy's interest in motocross racing and Mini-Unadilla fed that flame. The Walsenburg library had four computers and Teddy signed in to learn more about AMA racing because he often wondered what it would be like to race. Not just turn fast laps on his Mini-Unadilla but really race. Teddy had thought about asking his dad about racing, if they could go to one, but his dad never seemed interested and Teddy could never muster the courage to ask about a frivolous trip away from the ranch.

Teddy's computer searches had started with AMA motocross and Supercross but then began to explore youth racing and he was shocked to see kids as young as four years old racing in sanctioned 'club' events. Southern California seemed to be the hotbed of motocross and then one Thursday afternoon he made a friend on-line: Preston Jupiter from Redlands, California. Fourteen years old and beginning his first year as a 125 Youth Expert.

The Jupiter kid had started a blog about his racing and each blog could be commented on. Teddy thought for a moment and then wrote, *What are the age groups and how do you start racing?*

When he checked in the next day, Preston Jupiter had written back. *Where are you from, Mars? :) You start raceing by geting a bike and going to the track and entering a novice race, thats where the new riders start because none of them have raced before its only for new guys. Each club puts you in a class depending on how old you are I race in youth expert because Im 14 and fast. I killed in intremediat.*

Jupiter's first sentence caught Teddy by surprise until he realized the smiley face Preston had included meant he was joking. As he reread the Californian's response, he imagined himself entering a novice motocross race. He hardly noticed the grammatical and spelling errors.

He wrote back, *No, I live in Colorado, by Walsenburg. We have a little track on our ranch. My dad and uncle ride, my mom and cousin too, on her quad. How long have you been racing?*

Preston was at his computer when Teddy answered and the two boys spent the next thirty minutes writing back and forth, Teddy with questions and Preston with information. Preston didn't seem to care about Teddy's ranch or track but he did care that Teddy knew how fast he was. *Im gonna kill in expert.*

Over the next few weeks Preston Jupiter opened a whole new world to Teddy Hill: youth motocross. Preston told him about the Fairs and said that Teddy should come up to Denver and watch the California kid beat up on all the Colorado riders because Preston and his dad were both going to race at the Colorado State Fair. Teddy Googled the Fairs and learned a little more about his new passion. *It sure would be fun to go to the Fairs in Denver, meet the Jupiters, watch them race,* Teddy thought as he signed off. But he couldn't imagine any way to get his dad to Denver to watch a motocross race.

16

Eleven AM California time. Preston had heard his alarm on his iPhone go off at nine but ignored it. He and his dad had gotten home late last night from a practice day at the Starwest track and he knew his dad would let him sleep in a little.

Just as he was about to drift off again, hoping to sleep until he saw a big twelve show on his digital clock, he was jarred out of bed by the loudest blaring noise he had ever heard!

He jumped up and ran to the window; as he stared into the drive way he could not believe his eyes. He froze for a moment and whispered, "No way..." then rushed off down the stairs.

To say the Jupiter house was big is an understatement; it was huge, enormous, gargantuan, but *big* just didn't quite cut it. Paul and his wife Lori had discussed their dream house for so many years, looked at so many model homes, talked to so many designers. The house they finally built mixed granite, hardwoods and real stone throughout. The paint was rich and deep in hues selected by their interior designer to accentuate the high ceilings and intricate woodwork. There was a library that would look right in the richest mansion in the country, a workout room modeled after the Gold's Gym in the neighborhood, an indoor/outdoor swimming pool with hot tub. The floors were heated by recirculating hot water. The garage was more like an airport hangar and included the

Jupiter race shop in the far corner. But Preston didn't notice any of his home's beauty this morning and, in fact, he took it for granted every other morning….he raced through the house still wearing his pajamas and burst out through the double doors leading onto the circular driveway. He slid to a stop and just stared: smack in the middle of the driveway sat a brand new-still-had-the-factory-sticker-on it Sportscoach motorhome.

His dad opened up the side door and shouted, "Surprise! Preston you gotta come see this!"

Preston raced up into the motorhome looking around in awe. Leather seating, flat screen TV, plush carpet, two couches with slide-outs, full kitchen, this thing had it all!

His dad, standing in the cockpit area next to the driver's chair, walked past Preston to the rear of the coach.

"You haven't even seen the best part yet."

At that he opened the door where there would traditionally be a bedroom, but that was not the case. Paul smiled to his son, "I had them put a full race shop in the back!"

Preston couldn't believe it; the back of the RV was amazing! It had stainless-steel work benches with built-in tool drawers, a tire rack on the side wall, a pneumatic lift gate, and stainless-steel-clad EVERYTHING. It was incredible. "Dad this is so awesome! Can I hook up my Playstation to the TV?"

"Sure kiddo! Get it wired in and we'll get this thing ready to rock for next weekend…and start to get you qualified for the Fairs!"

Preston was elated; the Jupiter box truck was fine but he had always wanted a motorhome to have at the track, just like he saw at the Supercross races he and his dad attended. Being able to come off the track and walk into an air-conditioned paradise would be great. He and his dad would show up with their new big rig, bikes riding right out of the back on the lift, just like the pros. Preston couldn't wait to show off.

17

The rest of the week dragged for Preston. Every day it was up early at nine and then working all day with Ms. Castanos on stuff he didn't care about. He was just going through the motions and his grades reflected his disinterest. Now the waiting was over, it was Saturday morning: Time to Ride!

Paul was loading the bikes when Preston woke up. He came downstairs just as Paul snapped the pin through the latch closing the lift gate.

"All set to go, Pres. Want me to make sandwiches before we leave?"

"Yeah, I didn't get any breakfast." The two of them walked through the massive stone and granite entryway with double staircases spiraling upwards. They bypassed the stairs and headed towards the long hallway to the rear of the mansion.

The kitchen was spotless with glimmering black-granite countertops and deep mahogany cupboards and woodwork. Paul walked over to the double-door fridge and pulled out some lunch meat. From the cupboard under the center granite island he produced a loaf of fresh bread and a cutting board and started to build sandwiches. Paul had spent plenty of time in that kitchen, making meals while Lori Jupiter traveled.

———⊙———

Preston's mother Lori spent a great deal of time attending fashion shows or flying to New York City, London or Paris. She worked for the largest fashion magazine in Los Angeles and headed the news division. Though Paul often reminded her that she didn't have to work anymore, she always said that it kept her busy and happy.

In many ways Lori's hectic schedule helped their marriage endure because the time they spent together was never boring: each had stories to tell and questions to ask. The two had met when Lori's parents hired Paul to refurbish their kitchen. Lori was in college and Paul had just completed the tests for his General Contractor license and was taking business classes at night. Paul had seen her studying at the dining-room table every afternoon and one question led to another—two kids with missions in life, driven by the desire to succeed. They still had that desire, Lori with a passion and eye for fashion, Paul with an innate skill in contracting, especially custom homes.

"We spend time apart and it makes our time together even better," Lori often said to her friends and coworkers. "Besides, when Paul isn't working he wants to be riding with Preston…and I love that."

———⊙———

After devouring their sandwiches Paul cleaned up their scraps, put away the meat and said, "You all packed?"

"Yeah, did you put my gear in the RV?"

"Sure did, let's roll."

The drive from the Jupiter Estate in Redlands to the track in Perris was a little over thirty miles. With light traffic it took a little under an hour to arrive at Starwest Motocross Park.

The weekend was a double-header weekend for the Jupiters. They had the Starwest Club race Saturday, then the CMC races on Sunday. Both days' results would count towards the points total to qualify for the Fairs.

First came the Starwest round. Preston would ride his brand-new YZ-F125 Yamaha in the 125 Youth Expert class for riders under sixteen. This would be the first time he would compete with the fastest 125 kids in the club. He had moved to the front of the Youth Intermediate class quickly, and three wins there had qualified him for Youth Expert status. Preston had glued himself to the fence during every 125 Youth Expert race over the winter and knew it would take huge effort to run at the front. But if he could get into the top five, consistently, he could qualify for the Fairs.

Paul had signed up for the Senior Expert class, which let older riders compete against one another without the younger crowd of usually over-exuberant up-and-comers slicing through the pack. Paul was thirty-five and loved this class because the racing was usually clean and moderated. Rarely did a Senior lose his head and put a nasty move on someone…it was more of a gentlemen's class than the usual Expert classes of other age groups but Paul expected an upbeat in the aggression due to the upcoming Fairs. *Whatever…I'm gonna rule the Seniors!*

They pulled into the track around one PM. One unique thing about the Starwest Motocross Park was its lights for night racing. Most of the outdoor motocross tracks only ran during the day but Preston liked the feel of night racing. It reminded him of watching his heroes racing Supercross in the big stadiums. Plus he got to stay up late to watch the pro race, and then they would usually camp in the bunk beds of the box van. Preston smiled to himself: this time they were sleeping like kings in the motorhome. Both couches pulled into beds and Preston's dad told him he could stay up late to watch the satellite TV.

As they drove through the pit area everyone stopped and stared at the shiny new forty-foot Sportscoach. Even in affluent southern California the Jupiter rig stood out. After they parked and dropped the automatic leveling jacks both Jupiters went to work unloading and setting up. The bikes came out first and were parked on race stands in front of the RV. Next came the pop-up tent, double the width of a normal EZ-Up, crested with a big Jupiter logo when opened.

With the pit area arranged the Jupiters headed to the registration booth. They both glanced back at their new rig and smiled. Paul's smile was in memory of the old Ford pickup truck he used to race out of; Preston's smile was pure happiness in how hot their pit looked. They joined the line of riders waiting to register.

The comments started—good-natured ribbing about the new motorhome and the new Yamahas parked under the huge Jupiter canopy. Paul and Preston were well-known and well-liked in the SoCal club racing community and they laughed along with the ridicule, answering a few of the questions about the motorhome's size, how long they had it and how fast it would go.

Club racers standing around in groups talk and jive and verbally abuse each other, just part of amateur-level racing. But occasionally things turn serious and a question silenced the group.

"So, Paul, you two gonna try and qualify for the Fairs this year?"

The group standing in line fell silent. Every club racer thinks of running the Fairs and it's always good to judge the competition. It's an expensive race to enter. Knowing who you have to beat will affect the money-spending decision.

Paul glanced at Preston.

"Yeah, we're both going to try to qualify. This is Pres's first Expert weekend so we'll see how it goes."

Everyone in line knew it would probably go pretty well because the Jupiter kid had been extremely fast as an Intermediate but a few veteran riders in line wondered if the rich kid had the drive needed to push his way to the front of the Expert field in southern California.

One muttered to his friend, "That motorhome won't make him any faster." His friend nodded, hearing what his buddy was and wasn't saying: riding a motocross bike at the limit takes a certain desperation and rich kids with everything handed to them don't often step up. Sometimes. But not often.

18

Preston's practice was up first and he began changing while his dad tended to the machines. Paul did most of the work on the bikes; it wasn't that Preston didn't know how to work on them, he just didn't really want to. He wanted to ride and Paul was fine with doing the work himself; that was how he had it back when he was racing.

Preston plugged his iPod into the stereo and dialed in a little HaleStorm, his all-time favorite band. He started thinking about the track, too, just like his dad had taught him. He saw the hairpin turns, saw himself driving out of them, getting on the gas, flying through the air and landing perfectly.

After a few laps in his mind he heard his dad yell, "Hey Preston! Hurry up or you'll miss your practice!" Preston threw on his chest protector, grabbed his goggles and was out the door.

The riders all filed into their practice lines, divided by metal gates that shuffled each rider into his or her designated practice session. Signs posted at the entrance to the staging area directed riders which line to slot into and Preston had entered the 125 gate.

Preston was near the front of the line for his practice group. Again he visualized the track, seeing himself turning perfect laps, corner after corner, flying. Riding faster and better in his mind than he ever had in real life. He was lost in his thoughts, daydreaming of perfect laps, when a huge roost of dirt smacked into his helmet and face.

He looked up and saw the flagman waving at him, "Go! Go! Go!" Then heard the bike behind him revving, "Get out of the way!" He knocked it into first gear, dropped the clutch and was off!

Straight from his mind's eye to reality, he was indeed flying, riding Starwest better than he ever had. Pushing the front into the turns, feeling the loamy dirt under his tires moving, but he and his bike moved with it. Cutting up out of the berm with incredible precision, he scrubbed over a jump, turning the bars sharply to keep the bike lower to the ground and maintain his speed, then landing smoothly, he grabbed a handful of throttle and wheelied past a rider in front of him. He entered one of Starwest's notable tight hairpin turns with a little too much speed, but just as it appeared he would run straight off the course, he backshifted and threw the bike into the embankment, the entire machine rotating like a swivel. He dropped the clutch and shot out of the turn.

In the five practice laps he rode, nobody passed him, but he was making passes left and right. The practice was a short twelve-minute session because a southern California motocross weekend is packed with riders and things moved quickly. But in that twelve minutes, Preston had ridden quickly right from the launch. He felt ready to race.

Paul stood under the canopy. His big grin said it all…he smacked Preston on the back and fired his 450 for practice. Preston watched his dad leave and thought, *Yep, I'm flying today!*

19

The racing started at 6:30. Paul's practice had gone well, he seemed to be the fastest in his session of Senior riders aged 35 to 45. The sun was getting low in the sky and Preston's main event was third on the schedule so the track would probably turn the lights on right around the time he went out.

The first two races of 80s and 250s ran and Preston watched the first but skipped the second because he had to get his gear on. As he dressed he went over the race in his head. How he wanted it to go, the good start he wanted to get, how he would lead the race. He heard the announcer call third and final call for 125 Youth Experts and his bike started on the first kick with an aggressive snarl. He pulled his goggles over his head and made his way to the track entrance.

He pulled up to the starting gate and when everyone was lined up the starter walked off with the thirty-second board. Engines screamed and Preston saw the board go sideways and about three seconds later the gate dropped. Now it was wide open, full power into turn one.

He made it into turn one just out of the top five and quickly counted his placing…seventh. He drove out of the turn just as well as he entered and headed for the first jump. Off the lip he flew, turning the bike in the air to stay lower and faster across it, slipping inside a Honda rider for sixth.

But it was a lonely sixth: the top five Experts had doubled the jump Preston had only singled. The kid was still pushing hard, wanting to widen his gap back to the Honda guy in seventh…but his brain screamed *Ya gotta double that next lap!* He knew his 125 could do it, he just had to commit. He finished lap one with a full second advantage back to the next rider but a good three seconds behind fifth.

In his mind he could hear his dad's voice from all those days of practice, "Stay smooth, keep those eyes moving, relax your hands and arms!" His dad loved to ride right next to Preston and coach him as they jumped, braked and accelerated. Preston heeded his dad's advice, but Preston also knew he had to sky that double.

Paul had been able to watch the first lap but then jogged back to the motorhome to prepare for his Senior main event, next on the card. He saw the top five guys double and Preston only single…and knew getting a top five would be tough for Preston. The kid's new 125 was really fast, so the run-up to the jumps was more hair-ball, the airtime and landing more difficult. During the winter Preston had struggled with the big jumps and Paul hoped he hadn't moved his son into the 125 Expert class too early. *He's only fourteen…but he's a big and tall fourteen.*

Paul hurried into his gear, gave his bike another check, jumped on and idled across the paddock toward the starting gates in order to watch the last lap of Preston's race. The leaders were on the far side of the track and Paul looked for his son's silver and red livery somewhere mid-pack. His eyes strained and then his heart leapt into his throat. No Preston. *He must be down…*

Paul's worried eyes looked for yellow flags, then searched the edges of the track, looking for his son. Paul had watched Preston crash a few time and always hated the sight, the worry. *I'd rather crash myself than have him crash, it's that bad…*is a comment commonly shared between fathers.

And that's when the lead pack of four bikes swept past to begin the last lap. Preston Jupiter was with them, hanging in fourth in his first 125 Expert race.

Paul couldn't believe it, couldn't believe Preston had come back from a distant seventh-place first lap to run this close to the top three Experts. And then he saw why as the blue Yamaha catapulted off the double. *I'll be ding-danged…he's doubling that thing.*

———◦《◉》◦———

Preston hung onto fourth in a daze. He thought about trying to pass into third, but that thought was discarded when he realized he had no idea where he could make a pass on this trio. He was on his limit, riding just a bit over his head, doing his everything just to match the pace of the leaders. He'd caught them because they started to block each other with some aggressive passing, but the last two laps were flat-out and Preston had nothing left. He was winded, his arms were pumped, his legs and stomach ached from the effort… but he never noticed the physical distractions because he was high on the adrenaline coursing through his veins. *I'm with the top three… I'm with the top three…don't screw up!*

And he didn't. Sure, he lost a little ground in that final crazy lap but he pulled off with a solid fourth in his first Expert race. His dad was there to greet him with a huge hug that just about peeled an exhausted Preston off his bike.

Paul gave him a big "Alright Preston! You got points towards the Fairs!" and ran to his bike, leaning against the front-straight fence. Paul was jacked up from watching Preston and the adrenaline that had fed Preston was now in full-race mode through the elder Jupiter's veins.

Preston didn't even bother going back to his pits. He pushed his 125 to the fence and climbed onto the front-straight bleachers to watch the Senior race. Preston sat with the confidence that a strong finish brings and knew he'd be beating those 125 Experts soon. *Real soon*, he thought to himself with a smile.

———⟫(◍)⟪———

When the gates dropped, his dad rocketed into the lead, leaning back getting his weight over the rear wheel for traction, dirt flying as they poured into the first turn. That was when Preston knew his dad would win that weekend, prove himself to be the fastest Senior Expert rider in soCal. Paul's consistency from lap to lap just wore down the other Seniors…a couple of them could run his pace for a lap or two but nobody at this level could stay with him over a full moto. And it really didn't matter how old Paul was or who showed up to race him at the Starwest or CMC motos that weekend. He was on fire, fueled by his son's strong showing, the thrill of racing a dirtbike and the expectation of winning the California State Fair race.

As the Sportscoach pulled back into the Jupiter estate that Sunday night, both Jupiter racers wore smiles of satisfaction and accomplishment. Paul had dominated the Senior events and Preston had taken a big step toward qualifying for the Fairs.

20

Eleven hundred miles away, the Hill family had just returned from the Pueblo County Fair and could only talk about one thing: motorcycle racing. An amazing event had occurred.

Most of the Hills had arrived in the Suburban, with Teddy and Tom riding up on Tom's old Suzuki 850G street bike. Immediately they grabbed corn dogs and sodas because "that's what you have to eat at the fair," Uncle Brian declared, and started the wandering and looking and enjoyment the Pueblo Fair always provided. Tom and Uncle Brian squared off in the basketball shoot, neither Hill winning anything, while Teddy and cousin Elsie each won a small stuffed rabbit in the coin toss. Nothing too big, until Judy won the fair's largest stuffed panda bear in the rifle shooting. They wandered some more, took turns carrying the panda, sipped Cokes, enjoyed the Saturday afternoon.

And then they heard motorcycles.

Motorcycles attract the Hills like water attracts frogs, and as one, the whole Hill clan moved toward the sound, Teddy in front. As they rounded the cotton-candy stand they gazed out on about two fenced-off acres. Within that two acres was a neat little dirt track laid out with hay bales. A thin haze of dust hung over the area and about ten lucky kids were riding Yamaha 80cc dirtbikes around the track.

"What...?" was about all Uncle Brian could say before a young woman in a blue Yamaha shirt shouted over to the Hill group.

"You guys want to take a demo ride on our bikes?"

"Hey, let's go take a look," Brian said, and then waved to the young lady and shouted back, "Well, we might."

The Hills walked toward the girl in the Yamaha shirt and noticed a line of kids and adults standing at the small booth decorated with Yamaha banners. In the small open tent next to the booth another ten kids were sitting and listening to two guys in Yamaha shirts, one sitting on a blue Yamaha dirt bike. It looked like the guys were actually teaching a class and as the Hills talked to the gal in the Yamaha shirt they learned what was going on.

"This is a chance for kids to get their first ride on a dirt bike, or for kids who already ride, a chance to experience our new 80. Everybody here in blue shirts is from the Yamaha dealerships in Colorado Springs or Canon City. If any of you want to ride, we're asking that you pay $5 just to cover the gasoline costs, sign our waiver and listen to our instructors for riding tips and the basic track rules. We have gear of all sizes in the back of the tent and we'll get you kids outfitted in helmets, gloves, boots and riding gear. Do any of you ride?"

"We do a bit of riding on our land," Brian answered.

Judy rolled her eyes and said, "Yeah, all they want to do is ride and I'll bet Teddy here would love to try your 80, huh Teddy?"

Teddy had been gazing intently at the track, watching the other kids circulating, but mostly watching the two instructors sliding the bikes around the neat little track. He turned his head toward his mom and he didn't need to say a word. She could see that he'd love to ride. Judy turned back to the girl in the Yamaha shirt. "Yep, sign him up."

As the group of ten kids on track parked the bikes, the second group of ten in the tent slipped into riding gear and each was assigned a bike. Teddy watched the process as he was ushered into the tent and was introduced to the instructors, Ken and Shane, who had just come off the track. Teddy found himself in a group of ten, seven boys and two girls, all older and bigger, but they soon found themselves laughing together as their two instructors did their best to reduce the nerves.

Teddy and four of the boys had some riding experience, while the five other kids were new to the sport. Ken took the five new kids over to the bike at the front of the tent and started to explain some of the basic operations, while Shane corralled Teddy and the four experienced riders to talk about track rules and advanced riding tips.

Shane began: "We have to make safe, polite passes, especially when you come up on a first-time rider. If you pass too closely and scare someone, we'll flag you in for a talk. If you do it twice, we'll ask you to leave. Makes sense, right? If you can't pass someone politely, you're pretty much out of control. Besides, we all want to be passed safely by other faster riders, right?"

The five boys nodded.

"We'll let you ride for fifteen minutes. Let's only enter the track there by the double-stacked hay bales, and exit the track over by the Yamaha banner. Don't stop on the track. If you fall down, we'll be right there to help you up. And don't worry about falling, it happens to all of us…that's why we wear all this cool gear.

"Ken and I will be out on our bikes, and we'll lead everyone around for the first two laps to help you learn the lines. We'd like to show you the proper body position, where and when to put your inside foot down, where we go to the brakes, how smoothly we accelerate. Let's look at our riding-techniques handout."

At that point, Shane handed each rider a single sheet of neatly-typed riding tips and they read through them together. Shane stressed smoothness, looking through the corners, using both front and rear brakes…Teddy couldn't help but think that Shane's advice sounded exactly like the things his dad and uncle had been preaching since he was four.

As his group moved toward the pile of riding clothes, Shane talked about which gears to use on different parts of the track and answered a few of the older boys' questions. Teddy caught every word, varying his attention from Shane to the riders on track. As usual, the Hill kid stayed quiet. The kids out riding showed varying levels of speed and skill, and Teddy saw a few tip-overs and stalled bikes. Everyone was having fun and the 80s looked quick and sharp. Teddy slipped into the gear Shane handed him, automatically saying a quiet "Thank you." Shane checked his helmet chinstrap and asked him if he was nervous.

"A little. I've never ridden a four-stroke."

"No problem, little guy," Shane replied. "This new 80 is so much lighter than the old four-strokes and you'll notice how much power it has all through the rev band. A lot of guys who've ridden two-strokes are switching now because of how good these four-strokes are. Don't worry, you'll love it."

With that, Shane gave Teddy's chest protector a light punch and turned to help another kid. Teddy said "Thanks" again and felt a lot more comfortable about trying the new bike…the first new bike he had ever seen.

21

The kids and instructors on track filed into the makeshift paddock area and Ken and Shane assigned each of Teddy's group a bike. The five new students and Teddy got the 'small-wheel' 80s, while the four older kids who had sat with Teddy got the 'big-wheel' versions.

Shane had told Teddy, "Let's put you on the shorter bike. You can try one of the big-wheel versions later. They're the same bike, but you'll be able to reach the ground easier on this one."

Teddy just nodded and said, "Thanks," not mentioning that his 125 at home was taller than either 80 version. He always wanted to try a four-stroke and as he kicked his bike to life, he couldn't believe how tight a new bike was and how great this 80 sounded. Shane led Teddy and his four classmates onto the track.

One of Shane's riding tips was to start slowly to learn the track and bike and that's what the group did, putting around in second gear for the first lap and increasing speed slightly for the next one. It reminded Teddy of what his dad did every Saturday, making a whole lap of Mini-Unadilla while standing on the pegs and just rolling around. Even at the back of the six-bike pack, Teddy focused on where Shane was placing his bike.

Because Teddy had watched the previous group, he felt comfortable with the layout by the second lap. When Shane pulled aside on the short front straight, Teddy accelerated with the rest of the group, trailing the four bigger boys into the first corner. Because of the higher speed into the corner, the first two boys ran wide and almost collected the hay bales on the outside of the turn, slowing drastically to stay on track. When they slowed, the two trailing boys had to slow as well, and Teddy simply slipped under all four of them to lead into the second turn.

Teddy wasn't comfortable with all the older boys behind him but his dad's advice of "just ride your bike, don't worry about me and Uncle Brian" rang through his head. Just like he'd done in the first turn, he used his brakes and body position to get his bike slowed and turned, accelerating out of the next eight turns to complete the first lap.

None of the older boys had passed him yet but he knew they would soon.

As his second free lap started, Teddy began to appreciate how smoothly the 80 accelerated, simply pulling out of the corner with a broad flow of power. He had become comfortable sliding his 125 around at home but the 80 made sliding even easier due to how it delivered the power. All those hours of practicing his throttle control on his peaky 125 two-stroke made riding this 80 relatively easy. He finished his second lap alone and was having the time of his life.

Three turns later, two other Yamahas came sliding past inside Teddy into turn four. "When Brian or I pass you, go to school on us. What are we doing better?" was Tom's advice to his son at home. Teddy remembered that advice, latching onto the back of the other riders like a piece of duct tape stuck to itself.

After sliding past him, the two faster riders had slowed slightly, one looked over his shoulder and gave Teddy a 'thumbs up.'

"Follow us!"

Teddy realized it was Ken and Shane on their 125s!

It took two more laps before Teddy started running with the two faster riders. They were simply carrying more entry speed into the corners, taking advantage of the four-stroke's engine braking to 'back' the bike into the corner. Teddy had seen this done on his birthday DVD but hadn't mastered it on his 125. But he was getting it now.

The two 125s and Teddy's 80 were tied together, Ken and Shane leading and Teddy taking advantage of their constant hand signals and shouted coaching. Ken would remind him to relax by shaking his left arm down the front straight, Shane would remind him to use the brakes with a 'slow down' motion entering the tightest corner.

"Eyes up! Eyes up! Squeeze on that throttle! All right man, all right!" Teddy was a sponge and the constant focus on riding skills made every lap quicker and he lost count of the number of other kids he and the instructors passed. Almost before he knew it the check-ered flag waved and his group idled back into the paddock.

As Teddy parked his bike next to the others he saw several of them look over as they pulled off their helmets. He hoped he hadn't passed anyone too closely, he didn't want to get kicked off the track. In fact, he wanted to ride all day! One of the older girls in his group walked over.

"You sure rode that bike fast. Do you race?"

"Um, just with my dad and uncle at home," Teddy stammered.

Just then Ken called out to the group, "Let's walk over and get our gear off," and then turned back to talk with Shane and an older gentleman, also in a Yamaha shirt.

"You've got to spend time with all the kids," Teddy heard the older man say in a slightly upset tone.

"Yeah dad, sorry," Shane said. "It was just that we were having such a great time with that kid. He's flying."

Teddy turned toward the tent, numb with the realization that Shane was talking about him. They had had fun with *him*. *He* was flying. As he set his helmet back on the gear table and shrugged out of his chest protector, Shane and Ken grabbed him roughly and shook him between them.

"Hey kid, you're really riding that thing, man, what a great time, you were running so good! What's your name, bud?" Teddy caught his balance and you couldn't have wiped the smile off his face with a roll of paper towels.

"Teddy. I…ah… I hope you didn't get in trouble for riding with me."

"Don't worry, that was just my dad," Shane said. "Our family owns the Yamaha shops in Canon and the Springs…and besides, we were having so much fun with you that it made getting in trouble worth it. It was fun to have a kid really running hard, someone we could have fun with. We both do a little racing and sometimes riding around with a bunch of new riders at the Fair gets a little old. My dad understands."

"Besides," Ken added, "we've already got you signed up in the group after this one because you didn't get a chance to ride the big-wheel version, right?"

Teddy nodded.

"Where have you been racing?" Ken asked.

Just then, the rest of the Hills arrived in the tent and heard Teddy say, "I've never really raced. My dad and uncle and I ride on our ranch and we built a little track. My mom and cousin ride too, Saturdays mostly." The words came out of Teddy's mouth in a rush and Judy stared at Tom in mock astonishment because that was about the most they'd ever heard Teddy say in one go.

"Well, pal," Shane said, "If you go racing you're going to do great. Why don't you stay in your gear and go out with our group, right after the group on the track right now?"

Shane then introduced himself to the rest of the Hill clan, telling them how well Teddy rode and that they'd scheduled him to run on the big-wheeled 80 in the next group.

"Who do I pay for the extra session?" Judy asked Shane.

"Don't even worry about it," Shane laughed. "My dad can afford it and besides, we had so much fun with your son that we'll pay the $5!"

With that, Shane and Ken gathered their new group of nine students plus Teddy and began their classroom session prior to their riding session. Before grabbing a seat, Teddy turned to his parents with bright eyes and they could tell that this year's County Fair was something special. As he turned to take his seat, Tom called his name.

Teddy turned.

Tom just tapped his finger against his head, their on-track hand sign to concentrate, concentrate, concentrate. Teddy nodded, turned and sat down in class.

22

K en took the new riders and Shane taught the riders with experience. Teddy noticed one of the other riders from his previous
session but he didn't really care who else was there or who they were.
He just sat and listened to Shane again, putting his advice to use on
different parts of the track, a track he now knew. As the other riders
picked their gear, Teddy focused on the group currently on track,
watching and imagining, concentrating like his dad had taught him.
He'd never felt so alive. He smelled the dust, heard the bikes, felt the
weight of his gear…but it seemed as if he were watching a movie, a
movie he was about to ride in.

Shane turned from buckling a kid's boots and shouted out,
"Teddy, my man! Let's get you on one of the big-wheels!"

Teddy jogged out behind Shane and climbed onto the bike
Shane indicated. "I want you in line first, right behind me for the
first two slow laps, okay?"

"Okay," Teddy chirped.

This second 80 felt a lot more like his 125 and Teddy noticed
that the front and rear suspension pieces were also oversized compared to the bike he'd first ridden. He kicked the bike to life, toed it
into gear and trailed Shane onto the track.

At the slow warm-up lap speeds, Teddy could accustom himself
to the taller bike, but also notice several places where Shane was

using the track better than he was. Teddy noticed how Shane held the bike wider, longer, before turning into the final corner leading onto the front straight. He hadn't seen that before but realized why he had been struggling to match the instructors' speed through the final corner. As Shane waved the group by Teddy didn't even think of the riders behind him; he just focused on the things he had just learned from watching Shane.

Teddy's world became the next corner, the next braking point, the next throttle application...a rhythm that depended on speed and controlling it. By the second lap on the big-wheeled 80, Teddy looked like he'd been riding the taller bike for years. Sure, he couldn't touch the ground with both feet at a standstill but that little fact didn't matter once he was rolling. And Teddy was rolling.

As the third flying lap started, Teddy heard and felt a bike closing on him and then he heard Shane's voice right behind him.

"Alright Teddy, looking great! You're too early on the brakes for turn five...get in there a bit better."

Teddy locked his mind onto Shane's advice and left the throttle open another five feet before closing the twist grip and going to both brakes, the bike arriving at the corner's entrance with enough speed to carry Teddy deep into the turn before he got it slowed, turned and began to fire it down the adjoining straight. Sure enough, that little extra entrance speed allowed him to get the bike deeper in the corner before standing it up and firing it out. Turn six came quickly and Teddy shifted his weight and backed the bike into the right hander as Shane yelled "Whhaaaooo, yeah baby!"

Just as before, Shane and Ken came sliding past half a lap later, battling with each other only two feet apart, giving and taking the way Teddy had seen the pros do on TV. Only this time, Teddy didn't need extra time to match their pace. He was right with them, his light weight allowing his smaller 80 to almost match the drives of the instructors' 125s.

The three quick riders would get separated slightly when catching and passing slower kids, but Ken and Shane would glance over their shoulders, slow down and wait until Teddy cleared the slower traffic and was back with them.

Then they let Teddy pass them both.

Shane and Ken moved to the far right side of the front straight and motioned Teddy by. The tiny twelve-year old slid under both instructors and as he accelerated off of turn one he guessed that Shane and Ken were going to lead other kids so they didn't get in trouble with their dad again. As turn two was dealt with, Teddy's mind went back to the challenge of riding a motorcycle well.

Imagine his surprise when Ken outbraked him into the final corner, then Shane slid by on the exit of turn one. As if on cue, both instructors slowed on the short chute before turn three and waved Teddy through again.

"Don't let us by next time!" shouted Shane as Teddy zipped past. "Here we come!" added Ken with a howl.

"It's on now!" he heard Shane shriek as the trio fired off turn five. Teddy responded by running his little 80 to the rev limiter in second gear and dropping the bike low into six to block any chance of an inside pass. That little move didn't fool Shane and the 125 appeared in Teddy's peripheral vision on the outside of the turn, both tires sliding and Shane yelling "Here I come for the national championship of the entire universe!" "Get him back Teddy," Ken's voiced urged and Teddy closed the door firmly but politely into seven, retaining the lead.

Next came Ken. This time the 125 appeared next to Teddy on the main straight into turn one. "Who's the bravest on the brakes?!" Shane narrated from behind Teddy at the top of his lungs.

"It's Teddy! No, Ken! Side-by-side…Teddy the boy wonder and Ken the almost-as-fast-as-his-brother-Shane!"

Teddy started laughing and bobbled his drive out of one, giving

Ken the lead.

The narration continued. "Ken finally leads a race! It's a miracle! But will it last? Teddy, show us it won't last!"

Teddy couldn't remember ever having more fun on a motorcycle. He was caught up in Shane's goofy narration and the more he listened, the more relaxed he rode. When Ken was slowed mid-corner by one of the other kids, Teddy's wide entrance allowed him to power by both Ken and the slower rider in one slick move.

And the narrator came with him.

"Oh my! Boy wonder in the lead! Again, Ken's eating dust! Boy wonder leading the entire national field!

"No, wait! Boy wonder's lead doesn't last because..."

As the trio entered turn six, the narration paused as Shane backed his bike into the corner under Teddy's sliding 80.

And then it continued as Shane deftly slid off the corner side-by-side with Teddy.

"...because the fastest guy in the universe has caught boy wonder in six and is about to outbrake him for turn seven and the lead of the national!"

Shane did just that, flicking his bike on its side later than Teddy ever thought would work, dragging the inside footpeg and what looked like the whole side of the engine as the sliding tires scrubbed off enough speed to slow and point the bike toward eight. Teddy ruined his turn seven entrance because he was so shocked by what Shane had done. Teddy's mind flashed to his dad's poster of Kenny Roberts dirt-tracking a Yamaha twin with the same amazing lean angles.

Ken's voice brought Teddy back to the matter at hand: catching Shane. "He always enters turn nine wide, let's stuff him!" And Ken cackled with laughter as he saw Teddy's right wrist go to the stop. He liked this kid.

Teddy caught Shane quickly because Shane was pretending to

wave to the crowd for his pass, and as the 80 pulled close to the 125, Teddy could hear Shane's voice saying, "Thank you very much. Thank you very much. I'm the greatest, thank you…WHAT?"

Shane's last squawk was a reaction to Teddy's 80 at full throttle, gaining on him rapidly. But the instructor was ready and waiting for the attack and pinned his throttle, leading Teddy out of turn eight by about four inches. Just as Ken had said, Shane veered right to open the entrance of the final corner and Teddy just ran his bike down inside, squeezing under Shane.

And as Teddy manipulated the throttle in an attempt to gain traction, he gasped as Ken slid by on his inside, missing the hay bales by about an inch. Ken's speed and trajectory carried him past both Teddy and Shane and that's when Ken's narration could be heard.

"But no! Boy wonder and Shane have been passed by the one, the only: Quick Ken. Numero uno. Who can match this incredible pace? Who? Who?"

"We can!" screamed Shane and Teddy together…and the next three laps were a blur of blue Yamahas ridden to the edge of traction and beyond, interspersed with a running commentary from Shane and Ken that had Teddy giggling as he struggled to match the instructors' incredible pace.

The checkered flag flew and both instructors gave Teddy high-fives as they pulled off the track. "Awesome Teddy, just awesome. Great riding."

—————— ((O)) ——————

That's when Teddy realized they'd been riding on the track all by themselves. Rather than fifteen minutes, they'd been out almost half an hour. The other kids had been flagged off and as Teddy came out of his racing fog he was shocked to see people ringing the racetrack three rows deep. Some were clapping, some whistling and most of them probably thought the race they'd just witnessed was part of the County Fair show, like the barrel-racing horses or fortune-telling gypsy.

The crowd started drifting away but more kids and parents got in line to ride after Teddy took off his helmet and they saw how little and young he was. The Yamaha people were capitalizing on the crowd, calling out to parents that each rider would receive instruction and protective riding gear. Every kid wants to ride a dirt bike, and the Yamaha folks soon had a line four times as long as when the Hills arrived.

Teddy barely got his helmet off before he was surrounded by total strangers wanting to tell him how much they enjoyed what they had just seen. He looked younger than his twelve years, adding to the whole scene. His face glowed as the attention embarrassed him. The Hill clan stood back slightly from the group surrounding Teddy and tried to digest the scene. Only Tom truly knew how well Teddy rode but now the cat was out of the bag. The kid was gifted. He'd just ridden at an extremely quick pace with few bobbles and mistakes. Shane and Ken had pushed him and Teddy had risen to the challenge. Just like at the ranch, but this time on a state-of-the-art four-stroke race bike, not a six-year-old 125 on hand-me-down tires.

Into this crowd burst the irrepressible brothers, Shane and Ken. Clearly they had devised a plan because they rushed in laughing and grabbed Teddy under the arms and in one quick move hoisted him high. Before he could protest, he found himself sitting on their shoulders and listening to Shane.

"Let's hear it for Teddy the Terminator!"

Of course, the crowd cheered and clapped for the tiny kid with the mean name.

Then Shane shouted out something that made Teddy's brain freeze, "Folks, stop back in for the next demo races tomorrow afternoon at two and five. The Terminator will be shredding!"

Teddy's head snapped to where his dad was standing. Tom was waiting and locked eyes with his son. Tom's eyes glinted and he nodded slightly.

Tom's arm was around Judy and she smiled and put her hand to her mouth and yelled over the noise, "Better sleep good tonight!"

Teddy's head reeled as Shane and Ken pranced him around awhile before finally setting him back on the ground. Teddy had never been around anyone like these two brothers, their infectious personalities and laugh-at-life attitudes that made him smile and giggle in his helmet. Ranch life in southeast Colorado had its fun moments but mostly revolved around work, family, cattle, weather and money. In less than an hour, Shane and Ken had earned a place in Teddy's heart, and the serious, quiet kid had affected the two brothers as well.

23

The 'demo-race' idea had been hatched by Shane and Ken's dad, Bill Pearson, the owner of the Yamaha shops. He'd kicked it around in his head, then laid the idea on Tom and Judy while the boys were on the track.

Teddy's parents listened politely to Bill's idea for a pair of demo races featuring Teddy and Bill's two sons, racing at two and five the next afternoon. Bill was a natural-born salesman and Tom and Judy couldn't help but smile as the shop owner put forth his idea. They both knew that Sunday on the ranch was just as busy as every other day and two days at the Fair was a luxury the Hills just couldn't afford. Figuratively and literally.

"That's a great offer," Tom began, "but we're about forty minutes out of town and can't..."

He was interrupted by Bill's hand on his shoulder.

"Mr. Hill, I grew up out by La Junta and my family ran a ranch, as I suspect you do, right?"

Bill had immediately noticed Tom and Judy's clean but worn clothing, sunburned features and work-hardened hands and carriage. Both Hills looked strong and Bill had correctly pegged them as people of the land. That initial judgment had been backed up when Bill felt the calluses on the Hill's hands upon introduction. Bill was good at reading people. He'd made a great living by making educated snap judgments, then giving those people what they wanted.

"Yes," Tom answered. "We've acreage down by Walsenburg. Tomorrow will be busy to make up for today."

Bill waited for Tom to say more, but it was clear that Tom was finished speaking and that Teddy was needed at home. But Bill Pearson rarely took no for an answer.

"I understand what you're saying," Bill said with a smile, "but what about this great idea? My whole family is staying here in Pueblo, over at the Wingate Inn. How about Shane runs down to your place tomorrow during the lunch break and picks Teddy up? Teddy can run in those two demo races we talked about and then Shane'll have him back right after we buy his dinner…how about that for a great idea?"

Bill's smile got even bigger and he winked at Judy. "You know we'll take good care of him."

The Hills were beguiled by the older man's attitude…and stubbornness. Tom looked down at Judy, then said to Bill, "Let us talk this over a bit."

They walked toward the fairgrounds to talk about Bill's outlandish offer, keeping an eye on the on-track action. Teddy had spent nights at friends' homes but nothing like Bill's idea had ever happened. Could they trust Shane? Could Teddy miss his chores and get his schoolwork ready for Monday? As they talked about these questions and more, they both knew deep-down that Bill's proposal was a dream come true for any twelve-year old boy, but especially for their son. The Hills couldn't provide a new bike and riding lessons, yet Teddy had shown today that he had a special talent and they had both seen him almost match the speed and style of the older Pearsons.

24

B ut it was too much. Letting Teddy go off to the fair, to play-race at the fair, with a group of people they had just met was simply beyond reach. They could probably do without his help and Teddy could probably get his schoolwork done by the time Shane arrived, but they returned to Bill Pearson to tell him "Thanks, but no thanks."

That's when Bill Pearson played his ace.

"Hey, Tommy Hill. I was the service manager at Yamaha of Colorado Springs from 1987 to 2001. I saw you struggle to become the fastest guy in Colorado. You used to show up in that ratty old van, missing most of the practice and just slaughter our guys. You were the best I'd ever seen. When you went to Anaheim our whole state was behind you and I always wondered what happened to Flyin' Tommy Hill after Anaheim went bad."

Tom and Judy just stood mute, dumbstruck with what Bill Pearson was saying. Bill saw that they were listening and plunged on.

"When your son was riding so well on our little track here I grabbed his sign-up sheet and saw "Hill." I asked Sarah to point out Teddy's parents and there was Tommy Hill and his pretty girl-friend," Bill nodded with a smile to Judy, "just like I remembered from back in the day. If I owned that Yamaha shop back then I would have helped you. I didn't...but I own it now. I want to help

Teddy get some of the breaks you never did. I've got money, I've got equipment. You've got a great kid. Let's put them together."

Tom was reeling with what Bill had said but Judy was nodding. She knew. She knew that if Tom hadn't had to miss Saturday practices or run worn-out hand-me-down tires or prep his own used bikes…if he had only caught a break, he would have been one of the fastest riders this country had ever seen. Living on a working ranch in southeastern Colorado wasn't conducive to factory-level motocross racing but Tom had always had a special God-given talent… but not enough support.

Judy patted Tom on the arm, stepped forward, stuck her hand out to Bill and said, "Mr. Pearson, I've thought those exact thoughts for over fifteen years. If you can promise you'll take good care of Teddy, Shane can come down tomorrow and get him."

Bill Pearson's million-dollar smile showed how happy he was. What he had said about watching Tom in the '90s was the truth. He couldn't help Tom then but he was sure going to offer whatever he could for Teddy. The dealership owner had never seen a twelve-year old ride like Teddy Hill.

"Mrs. Hill," Bill returned. "I promise to care for Teddy as if he were my own." He then found Judy not just shaking his hand but hugging him tightly. She whispered, "Thank you," in his ear. She stood back and watched as Tom and Bill shook hands, working out the details for tomorrow.

25

As Tom, Judy and Teddy walked into the kitchen, this amazing event was the only topic of conversation. Teddy simply couldn't believe Shane would pick him up tomorrow at lunchtime for a trip back to the Fair...and a chance to ride a brand-new 80 again, not once but twice, and with Shane and Ken on track with him...just him and them...and maybe a crowd would gather again. His imagination ran wild and his heart raced. When his mom told him to get up and get his bath, then come down and eat, he was up the stairs before her voice faded.

The ride back from the Fair on his dad's 850 had given him a chance to rerun every lap, his brain ingrained with the mental video of Ken and Shane's riding, especially Shane's riding when the older boy had slid into turn seven with the bike on its engine case. As the old Suzuki hummed along down Interstate 25, Teddy just relived the day, the most wonderful day of his life.

He was going back to the Pueblo County Fair

26

By the time Shane pulled into the ranch at 12:45 on Sunday afternoon, Teddy had been up for six hours. His chores were done, schoolwork finished and checked by his mom and Teddy had been sitting impatiently at the kitchen table trying to finish his tuna sandwich. His mom and dad, also just picking at their lunch, were almost as nervous and their anxiety peaked when Shane's Chevy pickup idled up the driveway.

"He's here!" exclaimed Teddy, almost as if he never truly believed this dream would happen.

As Shane stepped out of his truck, the Hills came down off the porch and walked toward the Chevy. They couldn't help but notice how beautiful the truck was, a brand new Silverado in blue and silver with black-painted rims. A large Colorado Springs Yamaha logo covered the back quarter of the bed and wrapped onto the tailgate. Shane was wearing clean khaki pants and a blue Yamaha shirt and looked as trustworthy as a military officer.

The Hills didn't know that Bill Pearson had repeatedly reminded Shane to act responsibly and sensibly with Teddy Hill. Bill knew what a huge step it was for a rural ranch family to let their only son drive into town with a young man they had only met the day before and Bill knew this because he had grown up in a similar situation. But Bill also knew that Shane wasn't an idiot or even a careless kid…

but he still delivered stern warnings before Shane left Pueblo.

Shane stepped toward the Hills, saying hello, smiling and extending his hand.

"You sure have a beautiful place here. I think I saw a bit of your track on the way in, right?"

"That's right," said Judy, "we built it into one of our hay pastures there."

"We call it Mini-Unadilla," offered Teddy.

"Well, we'll have to get a few laps on it sometime," Shane told Teddy, "I ran at the real Unadilla for the AMA Amateur Nationals two years ago and carded a fifth and a third, so it would be fun to see your layout."

Teddy just stared at Shane…this guy had really raced Unadilla… and had done well. Teddy was snapped out of his reverie when Shane said, "Well Teddy, we better get going, our first demo is at two. Any gear you need to bring?"

Teddy almost laughed out loud because the demo gear he had used yesterday was better than anything he had ever owned. He just shook his head.

"I think I'm ready."

"Jump in the truck then," Shane said.

Teddy turned, hugged his mom and said "Thanks" for about the hundredth time. He climbed into Shane's truck as Shane and his parents said goodbye. Both Tom and Judy were at ease with their decision, though each had thought many times about canceling today's plans.

"You take care of our boy," Judy said in a lighthearted way, but when Shane looked into her face he could see the true meaning behind the words.

"I promise you I will, and we'll be back just after the Fair ends."

Shane then reached into his breast pocket and pulled out a business card with his name on it. "Here's my card and I've written my cell number on it. See you tonight."

With that, Shane jumped into the Chevy and Tom and Judy watched as their son and a young man they just met circled the driveway and left the ranch.

27

All through that Sunday afternoon, Tom and Judy imagined what was happening at the Pueblo County Fair. Neither of them second-guessed their decision—it wasn't their way. Both parents knew that the Pearsons were good people. They could sense it. They also knew Teddy was getting an opportunity they just couldn't provide on a ranch in southeast Colorado. As they went about their Sunday routine, there was a lot of clock watching and watch checking…the evening couldn't come quickly enough.

The setting sun flashed off the polished sides of Shane's truck as it traversed the ranch driveway at five minutes to seven. Tom and Judy were relaxing on the porch, or trying to, waiting for not just the sight of Shane's truck but for a narrative of the day. They stood as the truck parked in the same spot it had occupied that morning, and the doors opened. All four doors.

Shane slid out of the driver's seat and Teddy out of the seat behind Shane but Bill Pearson himself stepped out of the passenger side with his son Ken exiting from the seat behind him. Everybody yelled hello at about the same time and Tom and Judy could feel the buoyant nature of the group.

"Man, you should have seen this kid!" Shane yelled up to the porch. "He was on fire today! We had to flatten both his tires so Ken and I could keep up!"

The Pearsons erupted in laughter while Teddy just hung his head and smiled shyly, shaking his head in disagreement, his face glowing red.

Bill Pearson had walked around the truck and gave Teddy a one-armed hug because he knew the kid was embarrassed.

"Well, we didn't make him ride on flat tires," Bill explained, "but after the two-o'clock show we had such a crowd of kids who wanted to ride that we shortened the sessions to ten minutes so more kids could ride. We put four times the number of riders out on the track today than yesterday! And you know why things were so popular today?"

Tom and Judy had stepped down off the porch. Both shook their heads, noting that Teddy hadn't lifted his eyes off the ground while Bill spoke.

"It's because we put your twelve-year old son on a 125 today and everyone saw this pint-sized kid having the time of his life on a blue Yamaha, that's why!"

Bill delivered this last with a big smile and both Ken and Shane grabbed Teddy and shook the shy kid between them.

Teddy lifted his eyes to his parents and they could see the joy radiate from him. "It was a lot of fun," Teddy said quietly.

At that understatement, both Ken and Shane hooted aloud. "A lot of fun? *A lot of fun?* That's all you can say about riding like a bunch of maniacs in front of the entire county of Pueblo?" The two bigger kids pummeled Teddy, laughing and hooting at the ranch boy's shyness.

"You were awesome, man," Ken said and Bill seconded it, telling Tom and Judy, "It was really something to see. My boys have always loved riding but getting these three together on the same track was like nothing anyone had ever seen. It looked like they choreographed every lap! People were yelling and screaming like they were at a Supercross or something. And I hope you don't mind that

Teddy rode the new 125 four-stroke...we watched him for about five minutes on that 80 he rode yesterday and upgraded him."

And then Bill Pearson dropped a bombshell. "He did so great on the 125 that I brought it down to the ranch."

28

Sure enough, the back of Shane's Silverado held a 125 Yamaha four-stroke dirtbike.

"Let's get it unloaded boys."

Tom swallowed and finally found his tongue. "Uh, Bill...we can't...we don't...we just can't afford that right now."

Halfway back to the truck, Bill turned around and smiled. "This bike isn't yours Tom. It belongs to my shop, the shop that wants to sponsor Teddy at the CMXA race in Denver next month. I want to leave it here so he can get a little practice before his first race."

Teddy stood riveted to the ground, eyes on his dad, heart thumping and jumping. The Pearsons had worked all this out during dinner in Pueblo and every time they had asked Teddy what he thought, Teddy had only been able to stammer out, "I don't know...it's up to my dad and mom."

On the ride home Teddy had gleaned that the Yamaha shop in Colorado Springs sponsored riders on almost all levels and in almost all categories. Bill Pearson knew the importance of getting his shop's name out there and sponsoring winning racers had proven to be an excellent way to reach the enthusiast motorcycle crowd. Bill had seen a remarkable talent in Teddy and the shop needed to invest in young up-and-coming kids. When he factored in Tom Hill's tough story, the sponsorship idea just made sense.

"Bill, we really need to talk about this," Judy put in, her lips tight with tension. "Come into the kitchen for a cup of coffee. Teddy, why don't you show Shane and Ken the shop." Judy's eyes flashed with anger as she spoke. She felt betrayed by Bill Pearson because suddenly a fun demo-ride at the county fair had turned into a racing sponsorship.

Back in 1995, Judy Schellinger was Tom Hill's steady girlfriend. Everybody knew the two were perfect for each other and that once Judy graduated they would marry. The Hills already loved Judy as a family member and Tom's Anaheim crash hit her just as hard as it hit his parents. Judy skipped two semesters at CSU Pueblo to work full-time at the Bureau of Land Management, giving every extra penny to the Hills to help offset Tom's medical and travel bills. It was Judy who took a night class to learn the physical rehabilitation techniques a young man needs to regain the use of his right leg. Despite not having a ring on her finger, she stepped up and helped her future family get through the toughest times the Hill ranch had ever seen. Riding motorcycles was fine, racing was not.

Teddy could hear the strain in his mom's voice and he felt guilty being the source of that strain. "Okay mom," Teddy whispered. "The shop's right over here," he said to Shane and Ken, pointing to the barn.

The boys walked toward the barn as the Hills and Bill Pearson headed into the kitchen. The Pearsons had all talked about the track the Hills had built and they even stopped the truck on the way up the driveway to check it out, but Teddy was so distracted by the day that he hadn't said much.

But Shane and Ken's exuberance on seeing the Hill's immaculate shop soon got Teddy talking a bit more, describing the Saturday morning races the Hills had on Mini-Unadilla, who in the family rides which bike and even how they herded the cows on bikes and horseback. The Pearson boys took in the posters on the walls, the small but pristine tool collection and the neatly kept dirt bikes, the 850G and Tom's 350 quad.

"I had an 80 Yamaha quad," Teddy admitted as the boys looked at his 125 Honda, "but we gave it to my little cousin Elsie for her birthday."

———◦《◦》◦———

The two features that the Pearson boys noticed, and would talk about later with their father, was how well-presented the Hill's shop was, but also how old the equipment was.

"There wasn't a bike or quad in there made within the last four or five years," Ken would tell Bill as they pulled away from the Hill ranch house. "Tom's got a 1980 850G, you know the shafty…super clean. And they're getting every last mile out of their tires. Tom's dirtbike tires looked slick, they were that worn out."

The Pearson kids then described the Hill's super-clean barn, the old but immaculate equipment…and commented on how quiet Teddy was.

"We got him talking a little," Shane laughed, "but all he was thinking about was what you guys were doing in the house. When you guys walked up to the shop pushing that 125, he almost passed out! How did it go in the kitchen?"

Bill Pearson, perhaps the best salesman the world will ever see, shook his head as the kitchen scene flooded back to him.

"I had barely stepped in the door when Judy spun around and accused me of tricking them. She was so upset, said I had no right to offer Teddy a race bike and a race entry." Judy's words had hit Pearson hard and he immediately regretted his plans. He tried to apologize but Judy didn't want to hear it.

"She told me that the difference between riding and racing was everything, that racing had almost destroyed the ranch, destroyed everything the Hills had built. She started to cry."

Shane and Ken felt their dad's anxiety in the retelling of the story.

Their smiles from the description of the barn and bikes were gone.

"But...how? How did it work out that Teddy's going to race in Denver?"

"Well...she stopped crying almost immediately and looked over at Tom, asking him what he thought. Up to that point, Tom hadn't said a word. Nothing. Tom poured coffee and we sat down at the kitchen table...he still hadn't said a word. Finally, he asked me a bunch of questions about the Denver race...I could tell he wanted to see what the deal was, how it would happen. Tom knows a local motocross track isn't a Supercross...I guess he wanted Judy to hear it from me. That's what I talked about...how the class structure is for kids, how Teddy will run in the Novice race against other Novices. Man, I about wore out my lips talking! But I wanted Judy to know that kids raced all the time, that we'd outfit Teddy from head to toe with gear, his bike would be looked after. Judy listened but I couldn't tell what she was thinking."

"Yikes...sounds a bit tense," Shane said quietly as he piloted the Chevy north on Interstate 25. "How did it finally get worked out?"

"Remember when I told you guys about Tommy Hill? In his day, he was just unbelievable. He'd show up on Sunday morning, practice in only one session to save gas and then just cream everybody in the main event. Luckily, Judy came to enough races to see how dominant he was. She was there when he won and I don't think I can remember a race he didn't win when his bike stayed together. The guy just never fell off. He stayed healthy when he raced in Colorado, it was only when he tried to run Supercross that he hurt himself. We talked about that, talked about local races versus national races. Judy knows how good Teddy rides and how a little help from our shop would be a huge advantage if Teddy wanted to race. And of course, after today, he does. She asked me if Teddy wanted to race our 125 in Denver and I had to admit that he did."

Bill paused while Shane and Ken nodded. They could imagine

their dad in that kitchen, pitching his ideas, making his points.

Bill went on. "But then Tom had problems with our bike."

"What?" Ken asked. "What's wrong with the bike?"

Bill laughed. "Nothing's physically wrong with the bike, it's the idea of sponsorship Tom was fighting with. Boys, with people like this, people who live from the land and don't have much…they value possessions, but they value their way of life even more. Tom worries about the debt they'd owe me for sponsoring Teddy. Except for necessary farm equipment, these people don't live on credit. If they can't afford it, they don't buy it. It's the way my parents were. I told them that all they will owe our shop is for Teddy to come to this first race and do his best. We're going to enter him in the 125 Novice race and all he has to do is ride. I'm telling you, it was a two-pronged battle in that kitchen, but we finally struck a deal, and I think we've got a great little racer on our hands. Do you agree?"

Shane and Ken stumbled over each other to answer their dad's question. "Dad, I couldn't believe what he did today on that 125," Shane exclaimed. "I know the crowd was blown away, but from where Ken and I sat the show was even better. Toward the end, when he led all those laps? We were trying everything to get a wheel on him and he was just ripping."

Ken added, "You know, he made mistakes but he didn't make them twice. Between the shows, we talked to him about how he was using the front brake, getting him to use it further into the corner… and you noticed how much he changed his body position for the last show? He just started relaxing more, moving more…Shane and I were both saying that we wished we could ride like that at twelve."

What went unsaid was how much the Pearson boys liked this kid. They had seen too many loud-mouthed fast kids in their shop and at the track, talking about themselves and their accomplishments. Bill had too, and thirty years in the dealership business had made him extremely strict with his own two fast sons.

"The fastest guys talk the least," was a common mantra around the Pearson house, especially when the boys started verbally beating up on each other.

The Colorado Springs shop had arranged to have an autograph session with Tommy Mason when the boys were nine and ten years old, and national motocross champion Mason told the group gathered at lunch that there was a big difference between being cocky and being confident.

"Confidence means you know you're fast, cocky means you're trying to talk someone else into believing it," Mason said. The crowd laughed and he added, "I just win, so I don't have to say a thing." The group roared and clapped at that.

The Pearson boys' conduct wasn't lost on Tom and Judy. They knew Teddy worshipped these two fast racers. More importantly, Tom and Judy saw that Shane and Ken were simply good kids. While in the kitchen, Bill had answered their questions about his boys, telling the Hills that both his sons worked at the dealership in the afternoons and attended Colorado State University in the mornings. Shane was a junior and Ken a freshman. They both raced at the Expert level, Ken in 250, Shane in Open. Each had expressed desire to continue the Yamaha shop and they were both taking business classes to that end.

"They're best friends and bitter practice rivals," Bill laughed.

Frankly, Tom and Judy couldn't imagine their young son hanging out with a better pair of role models. And it helped make their decision when Bill added, "Shane and Ken have taken a strong liking to Teddy. Not just the way he rides but how he conducts himself, quiet but not scared of anything. We get real spoiled kids in the shop sometimes, and Teddy is a breath of fresh air, I can tell you. You can bet my sons are going to treat Teddy like their favorite kid brother. Plus, they'd love to see this quiet kid put on a bike that matches his skills, even if it's only for one race."

Bill paused and added, "Think of it as a thank you for letting me borrow your son to promote my business."

Before unloading the 125, Bill, Tom and Judy had talked over next month's race in Denver and had agreed to let Shane come down to the ranch to change the 125's oil and filter and do anything else the four-stroke needed during the next month. Meanwhile, Teddy could get a handle on the new 125 by riding on the ranch and lapping Mini-Unadilla. Tom chuckled and said, "He'll ride that thing every waking moment. It might be worn out in two weeks."

"Then we'll get him another one," Bill replied.

29

The relief of being qualified for the Fairs had a remarkable effect on Preston Jupiter: he went even faster! Everybody at the soCal tracks noticed as the younger Jupiter became one of the quickest kids in the 125 Youth Expert class, running consistently in the top three or four and quickly amassing enough points to qualify for the Fairs. But the second weekend in July at the Hemet Speedway it became crystal clear to Preston Jupiter that he was a force to be reckoned with. He almost beat Davey Stevens.

Davey Stevens's racing resume was a long list of wins, podiums and prize winning. He had won everywhere, including the Motocross de Nations as a member of the winning Canadian team. Stevens was slightly past his prime and had to work hard to get into the top ten in the national events but won easily at the club level.

The buzz started at lunch on Saturday when the paddock heard that Stevens was coming out the next day to race in preparation for the upcoming Atlanta national. Preston had just finished two practices and had broken through to run his quickest laps of this track, and not just one or two. Every lap in his second practice had been just over two seconds quicker than he had ever gone and when his dad showed him his times all Preston said was, "Yeah, I'm riding real good!"

Then they heard about Stevens coming out on race day.

When Preston's friend Nathan blurted out the news, Paul

immediately looked at Preston for his reaction. Preston was staring at Nathan.

"Really? Davey Stevens is racing 125 tomorrow?"

Nathan nodded his head enthusiastically.

Oh man," Preston said with a smile, "I can't wait to take a shot at him!"

Interesting reaction, Paul thought to himself. *That kid's not scared at all.*

As lunch concluded and Preston's practice was announced, the kid was already in the zone, imagining Davey Stevens ahead of him. Imagining hanging onto the pro's roost for a lap, or even two laps. And it didn't take much imagination because two Davey Stevens posters were tacked above Preston's desk in his bedroom. He'd been watching Stevens race and win for years…and now he would see him in person.

As it turned out, nothing Preston imagined could have equaled Sunday's 125 final. The young Jupiter came to the starting line excited but extremely focused. All he wanted to do was see Davey's lines, where he placed his bike, what he did in the air on the first lap. It was the same way he rode with his dad, watching the faster rider and mimicking anything and everything he could for as long as he could. He just wanted to see Stevens ride.

For Davey Stevens, running this Sunday was a chance to break-in both his bikes, which he did in practice, slowly building speed until he ran a few quick laps on each bike. His tuner, the well-known KTM wrench Werner Milton, didn't bother to take lap times and actually didn't even watch Stevens practice because he was busy readying whichever bike Davey wasn't on. Winning the club race was simply taken for granted by this pro team.

But in fact neither Stevens nor Milton cared about winning… they were there to test parts and collect data in an effort to podium in Atlanta.

When the starting gate dropped, Stevens fired his KTM into the lead…as expected by everyone at the track, including Paul Jupiter. The elder Jupiter had stood trackside during the 125 practice and had watched his son and Stevens…their lines, their pace, their ability to get around the track. He could see the things Stevens could do that Preston just wasn't ready for, pro-level riding that often takes years to develop.

And the first person not to believe what was happening was Preston Jupiter. His start was good, but couldn't match Stevens's launch…but then the second-place Jupiter ran dead even with Stevens during the first lap.

"He's just getting into a groove," Preston thought…but the surprise came half a lap later when Preston's Yamaha arrived on the back tire of the KTM. And it was just those two, breaking away from the field as word raged through the Hemet pit via the loudspeakers.

"Jupiter is catching Stevens!"

Wrenches were dropped and the pits emptied as racers and families ran to the fence.

And there it was, the blue Yamaha glued to the orange KTM.

As Preston closed on Stevens, he never for a moment thought that he was faster than the pro, he just assumed Stevens was cruising. It was the race Preston hoped for, a chance to duck in behind a hero of his and study his lines, watch how he attacked the Hemet track. For the first four laps of the six-lap race, that's what the kid did.

By the fourth lap the realization hit Preston. *Davey's line in the final two corners isn't as good as the line I used in practice. I…I…I think I can pass him there!*

Stevens had been hurtling into the final two corners low, hitting the inside groove in second gear and wheelying out of both bends. In practice, Preston had been running a gear taller and hitting the outside berm…a longer path, but his entrance, mid-corner and exit speeds were higher. Preston knew his practice line was faster because he'd been grabbing more air off the finish-line jump in practice than he had been in the race following Stevens.

So on the next-to-last lap the kid made his move, railing into the final two turns high and fast, letting his momentum sweep him around the berms and fire him into the straights. He covered more ground but his exit speed made up the difference. And then some.

30

For Stevens, the race had been frustrating up to this point. Halfway through the first lap he'd lost his rear brake completely and his tuner Milton would later discover that both rear brake pads had fallen out of the caliper when the trick titanium slider pins snapped in two, victims of improper heat-treating at the factory. They were too brittle but Stevens was one of the first riders to get the new prototype pins. When his rear brake quit, Stevens wasn't even upset. He knew that he and Milton were at Hemet to uncover weaknesses just like this. *Better here than at Atlanta.*

Then Stevens heard the bike catching him. Tailing him. Stalking him. A quick look back showed him an immaculate new Yamaha.

"*Catching me is one thing,*" Stevens said to himself, "*but passing me is another.*"

Then the Yamaha sailed past over the finish-line jump to lead the last lap. Stevens heard the voice on the loudspeaker roar something and the crowd respond.

The loudspeaker and the crowd ignited Stevens, bringing to a boil that killer instinct the best racers have. That hatred of losing. That love of a fight. The thrill of a win. The drive to be the best. It might just be a warm-up club race in Southern California and he might have a damaged bike, but Davey Stevens loved a race. And he had one.

Orange now followed blue, but Stevens was probing, pushing and testing the quick kid ahead of him, the kid with *Jupiter* across his jersey next to a neat red rocket trailing a bright silver jet trail.

"Let's just see how tough this little rocket is," Stevens muttered in his helmet.

The wily pro had immediately known what the Yamaha rider had done to make his finish-line pass…he'd railed those last two turns, the ones Davey was taking low and tight. Running those last two turns high and wide would give the rider more straight-away speed…a lot more. But before Stevens could make that adjustment to his own line in the final turns, he had to have the lead. His mind focused sharply on where to put his bike ahead of the Yamaha, even without a rear brake.

As the final lap played out, Stevens knew his best chance for a pass was the super-bumpy mid-track straight. His factory KTM made more horsepower than the production Yamaha ahead of him but every time Stevens began to out-accelerate Jupiter, a corner would end his acceleration early because he simply couldn't control his speed into the corner with only one brake. Or could he? When he was leading the race and just waiting for the finish, waiting to get back to the pits so Milton could fix this silly problem, he hadn't really tried to push this particular situation. Now he decided to find out just how quick he could go with only one functioning brake.

As the flying pair approached the mid-track straight, Stevens had four more corners to practice his new strategy, a plan that was simple in theory but hard to execute. With no rear brake to slow and help slide the back of the KTM at corner entrances, Stevens decided to drop his bike down an extra gear, then control the additional engine braking with how quickly he released the clutch on the extra downshift. If he needed more rear brake, he'd let the clutch go earlier…less rear brake, he'd hold the clutch in longer. Not that easy, but actually not much of a problem for a rider with Stevens's skills.

One more step in his extra-downshift plan would require another relatively large adjustment, especially in left-hand corners: getting his left foot up to the shifter before he opened the throttle to begin the drive off the corner. If Stevens didn't make the upshift before he started his exit drive, his KTM would be in the rev-limiter and wouldn't accelerate further. In right-handers, no problem—his right foot was down in the corner and his left shifting foot was up on the peg, ready to work. But left handers presented the problem.

And the last two corners were both left handers.

Stevens laughed in his helmet as he played around with his new technique, having fun with the challenge, enjoying not just the physical difficulty of his extra-shift idea but the mental side of the planning as well. His theory worked. As Jupiter and Stevens entered the mid-straight whoops section, the KTM powered past the Yamaha in the bumps and the crowd heard the orange bike's engine scream with an extra downshift, and just as quickly they heard Stevens click the bike up again for the exit. The KTM led again.

31

When Stevens came past Preston in the fast bumpy section, the kid almost expected it. But rather than resign himself to second place Preston made a plan to duplicate his finish-line jump pass from the lap before, just rail those last two berms and beat the pro.

But hanging onto the back of Stevens during this last half-lap wasn't as easy as it had been. Preston pushed himself and his Yamaha harder than he ever had, harder than he thought possible, riding the ragged edge of control to keep close to Stevens, close enough to snake him in the last two corners.

Imagine the kid's surprise when Stevens ran his KTM high and wide into the 90-degree berm surrounding the next-to-last corner, on the same line Preston had used the lap before. But the pro's plan didn't quite work and the KTM hiccupped on the exit because Stevens had been late getting to the shifter and his 125 tagged the rev-limiter for a vital instant, an instant Preston used to fire his Yamaha up next to the now-accelerating KTM. The orange and blue bikes were locked together half-way down the short chute into the last corner, with the KTM's factory power vaulting Stevens ahead by a bike length entering the final turn.

"C'mon Davey," had been Stevens's only reaction to his late shift in the previous corner, the pro mildly upset with himself for his poor technique. He knew he could get the timing right with a bit more practice, but the time for practice had run out and he had to get his foot to the shifter a bit earlier in the last corner to beat this pesky Yamaha.

And he did. The crowd was screaming at the top of its lungs, none louder than Paul Jupiter, and they didn't hear Stevens's extra downshift, his lightning-quick upshift…all they saw was a perfect corner entrance and exit by the pro's KTM, and the orange bike sail over the finish line by four bike lengths. It was the best race anyone could remember at Hemet, not just because of the closeness of the competition, but because one of the club's rising stars had almost beaten a true legend of motocross.

32

Werner Milton stood under the awning next to Stevens' rig as Stevens pulled in. "No rear brake, huh?" were the first words Milton said. He didn't even think to congratulate Davey on winning a club race.

Stevens replied, "Yeah, something broke in turn six on the first lap. Did you hear me downshifting the thing to get it backed in?" Davey was smiling, thinking about sliding his bike into the corner with the clutch.

"Not until the last lap. But before that, just watching you roll into the corners, I knew something back there was off. I bet those new titanium pins got over-treated. How did everything else feel?"

As the two pros continued their conversation, an impromptu celebration was happening across the pits at the Jupiter rig. Preston's return to his dad's motor home had been slowed by high-fives and backslaps and hugs from anyone and everyone he passed. By the time he pulled under the packed Jupiter awning, Preston felt as if he'd just won the world championship.

Paul watched as the crowd practically lifted Preston off his bike, laughing and slapping him on the back. The kid was really enjoying it and Paul reached in and grabbed his shoulder, pulling Preston into a big bear hug.

"Great ride. I'm sure proud of you, kid."

"I almost had him! I almost beat Davey Stevens!" Preston's elated expression and excited words had the whole awning buzzing. The Jupiter kid had run neck-and-neck with Davey Stevens, factory KTM rider.

33

Kel Cranther of *Cycle News* magazine stood outside the Jupiter awning, smiling at the scene, wondering if he was witnessing history, the blooming of another wonder-kid out of California. Cranther's byline had appeared in *Cycle News* for over two decades and he covered everything from Supercross to club racing, with a few dirt-bike tests thrown in for good measure. He was there to file a race report on this Hemet club meeting and his job had suddenly become more interesting with the appearance of Stevens and the race from Jupiter. He turned to walk across the paddock and interview Stevens first, then return and talk with the kid.

"Hello, Kel," Davey Stevens sang out from his lawn chair sitting in the shade of his awning. "Need a water?"

"Hiya Davey, hello Werner," Cranther replied, shaking both men's hands, "and I'd love a water."

Werner snapped the cooler open and tossed Cranther a bottle of water, pulling over an extra chair to let the writer sit next to the racer. Werner went back to his work on the KTM.

"Are you covering this weekend?" Davey asked Kel.

"I am, and I must admit it looked like a boring weekend until you arrived. What are you guys doing at Hemet?"

Davey gestured to the KTM and replied, "Werner dragged me out here to R&D a few things in the heat of battle. We're off to

Atlanta tomorrow and he thought we needed a few racing laps."

Stevens paused as Werner interjected, "Yeah, I'm a slave driver."

"Well," Cranther laughed, "we all sure enjoyed that last race. Did you have a gearbox problem?"

Werner came over to listen to Davey's answer. Davey looked at Cranther and said, "Off the record?"

"Yeah," Cranther said, "What's up?"

Davey looked up at Werner and the mechanic turned and opened a drawer of his toolbox, reached in for the broken retaining pin and handed the two pieces to Cranther. Stevens and Milton liked Cranther because he was a quick racer in his day and knew his way around a dirtbike and a computer keyboard.

"Feels like titanium," the journalist said, weighing the pieces in his hand. "Just snapped, huh?"

"Yep," said Milton. "It's part of the lightweight kit Brakeco is developing and we're the first guys to race with it. We practiced with it last week on Davey's track and all morning here. I think those extra heat cycles started to crack it and it gave up after about five turns. Tricky stuff."

"So you rode around without a rear brake? Why didn't you just pull in?" Cranther asked Davey.

"Because Werner would have pulled a fit! Plus, we had a few other things to test and I wanted to get to Atlanta with everything ready to go. I actually like the Brakeco lightweight calipers, so we'll run those in Atlanta, but with the steel pin, right Werner?"

"No doubt," agreed the mechanic.

"Okay, so how much of this can I print?" Cranther asked, getting back to business.

Davey looked at Werner and the mechanic answered, "How about none of it? You know Max Capri over at Brakeco, right? His team worked overtime to get us this first kit and I think it's going to help us quite a bit in Atlanta. I'm planning on just running a steel pin, but Max will have these titanium pins figured out in no time. If you write something, everybody's going to shy away from his new kit."

And then Werner added with a smile, "Plus, you should write about what a great ride that kid on the Yamaha put in. Don't mention the brake deal, okay?"

Cranther agreed. Having a pro scrap with a local kid makes for a fun story, and any mention of Stevens's brake problem would not just hurt the racer's relationship with Brakeco, it would also make the *Cycle News* story a lot less entertaining. Cranther had been around long enough to appreciate the trust that Davey and Werner put in him when they showed him the pin, and he also knew that research and development of motorcycle parts isn't without setbacks. He finished up with the KTM team and returned to the Jupiter motorhome.

34

The buzz of Preston's near win over Stevens had settled and Cranther found Paul Jupiter in his riding gear getting ready to pull his 450 off the stand. The journalist introduced himself.

"Sure was a great ride that Preston put in against Stevens."

Paul nodded and said, "Yeah, it was. I think another lap or two and Preston would have had him. Stevens blocked him in those last two corners, right where Preston had passed him before. That KTM is so fast…if my kid had that kind of horsepower, he would have won that race."

Cranther almost disagreed and mentioned the rear brake issue, but checked himself.

"Is Preston around? I'd like to talk with him for my story."

Paul heaved his bike off the stand and swung his leg over. "Yep, he's right inside and will be coming out in a sec to watch my race. Knock on the door there, I've got to go."

Just as Paul kicked-started his bike, Preston stepped out of the palatial motorhome still wearing his racing jersey, but over shorts and sneakers. He looked like any other 14-year old kid and as he jumped down from the last step he yelled, "Go get-em dad, make me proud!"

Paul gunned his 450 and spun the rear tire, shooting his fist in the air as he headed toward pre-grid. As the sound of the big Yamaha faded Cranther stepped toward Preston and stuck out his hand.

"Preston, I'm Kel Cranther with *Cycle News*. How are you?"

Preston gave Cranther's hand a shake. "Nice to meet you. I was hoping you guys would be here. Did you see me almost beat Davey Stevens?"

Cranther laughed at the kid's enthusiasm and nodded, saying, "Oh yeah, I was lining the fence with everyone else. Was that the best race you've ever had?"

Preston glanced nervously toward the track and Cranther added, "Let's go watch your dad race. I'd like to ask you some questions."

Preston said, "Great, let's go sit in the front-straight stands, I like to watch that last jump, those last two turns where I passed Stevens."

The Seniors were getting set at the starting gate and Cranther jogged over to the stands behind Preston but before they could sit at least five people congratulated Preston on his great race against Stevens.

Cranther repeated his question as he sat next to Preston.

"Yeah, I've always gone good and been fast but today was the best I've ridden. I mean, I almost beat a pro and nobody else in our class was even close to me and Davey. My dad thinks I would have had him in another lap or two and I agree."

Cranther was scribbling in his ever-present notebook. He had spent plenty of time around racers of all types, some who liked to talk, some who never talked, some with too much confidence and some with none. He baited the kid by asking, "Was the KTM fast?"

Preston laughed. "Are you kidding me? That's factory horsepower and my dad said that if I was on similar equipment I would have been first. My dad thinks he can talk to the guys at Yamaha and see about a race-kit top end, now I've proven to be so fast. He thinks the guys at Yamaha will really take notice."

The whole time Preston talked, he was watching the riders file into the starting box. Preston stood as the Senior class brought the rpm up prior to the gate dropping.

"Go Jupiter!"

When the gate dropped the field surged forward as one, but a blue streak came out of the mix to lead the race into the first turn.

"That's him! That's my dad!" Preston shouted exuberantly. Paul Jupiter was truly the class of the field and kept stretching his lead, despite a slight bobble in the whoops section on the first lap.

"C'mon old man! Get your weight back. Pin the throttle!" Preston shouted as his dad recovered and got the big Yamaha rolling again. Despite the bobble, the second place rider was still twenty bike lengths back.

"Do you and your dad ride together a lot?" Cranther asked.

"Yeah," Preston answered. "We try to ride once a week at least. My dad was a pro-am rider, but we both think I can be a pro because my speed is so good and I'm so young. I guess we can just ask Davey Stevens if I'm fast enough, huh?"

Preston laughed and continued, "I'm qualified for the Fairs and we'll probably run here in California and maybe one other state, show people who I am. My dad's qualified too and we're going to make sure everyone knows the Jupiters are rockets!"

Cranther hid his smile and pretended to jot down Preston's comments, and then said, "Thanks for your time and great job today. I'll see you at the Fairs if I don't see you before that, okay?"

Preston had turned most of his attention back to his dad's race and absently waved to Cranther, but then he thought of something and whipped his head back toward the journalist.

"Hey, have you been to the Fairs?"

Cranther said he had, not bothering to mention the three podium finishes in his home state of Arizona.

"Okay," said Preston, "so I was wondering if there is anyone there as fast as me and Davey Stevens?"

Cranther swallowed the laugh that almost burst out of him when the kid mentioned himself with Stevens.

"Well, uh…not usually, no. Occasionally you'll get a hot local who has the track wired and is on good equipment but there's usually nobody at the Fairs who could run with Stevens."

"Good, good," Preston mused. "'Cause I plan to win the California Fair and any other Fair I enter. If I can almost beat Stevens, I'll slaughter guys at the Fairs. Slaughter 'em."

"Best of luck," Cranther said as he turned to leave. Tempting as it was to pass judgment on Preston Jupiter, Cranther had often seen such confidence. Racing motorcycles took confidence and an unflinching belief in oneself.

Usually the confidence Cranther witnessed was hollow bravado, simple words strung together to convince someone, anyone, that you were good enough. But occasionally the speaker had the goods to back it up. So Cranther gave a wave and made a mental note to keep an eye on Preston Jupiter. The kid was good…good enough to keep up with Davey Stevens sans rear brake.

35

Teddy hadn't quite worn out the Yamaha 125 that Bill Pearson left at the ranch, but he sure tried. His mom and dad saw the extra spark in their son and as he became more and more focused on his riding, his schoolwork and chores improved too. Teddy naturally understood that racing was a bonus based on how he handled himself at school and at home. As he thought about where on Mini-Unadilla he could shave some time, he also began treating the rest of his life like a lap time. How could he do better? How could he be better?

His only problem was time. Teddy wanted to ride before school and after dinner, on weekends and holidays. As the summer days lengthened, Teddy lapped and lapped. He began to run the track forward and backward and then hit upon a great idea.

"Hey mom, could you park the car and truck by the track and turn on the lights tonight"?

He had to shorten the track to run within the headlights' beams but on Mondays, Wednesdays and Fridays Teddy would ride from dinner until nine PM.

And Tom joined him almost every-other night. Uncle Brian would ride when he could and soon Teddy could catch and pass his uncle on any of the track layouts the Hills ran. But catching his dad was a whole different deal.

"You almost caught me tonight," Tom would occasionally say as the Hills wiped down their bikes. But the word "almost" was always included—Tom was still magical on a motocross bike.

Shane came down twice, both times armed with extra tires and a manual tire changer plus the promised oil and filters. He brought his bike too, and the Hills and Shane would just tear the track up, with the older two riders pushing and prodding at the kid.

On Shane's first visit he brought all the tools needed to help Teddy tune the advanced suspension on the YZ-F and expected to use the day to help Teddy set up the 125 for his size, weight and speed, but the tools never came out of the truck. As Shane watched Teddy lap, he couldn't spot a problem in what the bike was doing. When he mentioned it to Tom, the elder Hill quietly replied, "Yeah, we messed with it a little last week." The bike looked perfect under the kid.

Shane and Tom never really squared off and raced but Teddy secretly thought his dad had Shane covered. Those two days ended with discussions of the upcoming race weekend in Denver. As usual, Teddy said little, hanging on Shane's every word.

36

"Well, is the kid ready?" Bill Pearson sat forward on the living room couch when Shane walked in the door from his visit to the ranch. The race was three days away.

"Dad, Teddy is haulin' butt and just rides so relaxed. If he's nervous, I can't tell."

"Hmm," Bill stared out the window into the inky night as he thought back to the days when Tom Hill was young and healthy. "You know, that was how Tommy Hill looked on a bike. Sounds like Tom has really worked with Teddy."

"Yeah, but they don't talk much. It's not like Tom is coaching him or preaching to him or anything. Tom shows him stuff more than tells him stuff. They just get out and make laps, talking a bit after Teddy makes a mistake, then go again. And dad, you should see Tom on his old RM. That thing's got no knobbies left on the tires but he's got it flyin'. I'm not kidding, I don't think I could catch him if we really started to go. His style has just rubbed off on Teddy. "

Bill watched his son, nodding in agreement. Tom Hill seemed to almost ignore his past racing success…as if it were a part of his life he'd rather forget. He certainly wasn't being the pushy 'little-league' dad Bill had seen so often in youth motocross.

"Does Teddy have any riding weaknesses that you saw?"

"The only two things I messed with him on were his starts and him getting passed. The Hills are on such a shoe-string budget that Teddy doesn't want to wear out the clutch plates practicing his starts...I forced him to do five starts and he got pretty good, though they don't have a starting gate like he'll see in Denver. When his dad or uncle come up next to him, Teddy's in the habit of just letting them have the line, not fighting for it. We talked about it and he got a little tougher about defending it. Other than that, he's riding really well."

"Son, if he's another Tom Hill, the Denver Novices aren't going to see which way he went," Bill said as he clapped his son's shoulder. "I'm off to bed, thanks again for heading down there."

"See you in the morning,"

Shane didn't add that his two visits to the Hill ranch this past month had been a labor of love and a terrific getaway from the shop and the university. That ranch had a simplicity and pureness to it... the little track, the incredible beauty of the land...even the cooking tasted better in the Hill kitchen. Shane's life was the hectic world of a factory-supported motocross rider and college student with a part-time job. Sitting in the twilight outside the Hill barn, wiping down his YZ-F and listening to country music with the Hills was an alien world. And he liked it.

37

Teddy and Tom Hill drove to Colorado Springs early Sunday morning with the 125 on a home-made bumper mount bolted to the Suburban. Shane met the Hills at the dealership and the three transferred into the shop truck for the run to the Denver track, tying the spotless little Yamaha into the bed.

"I sure wish you could have cleaned the bike first," Shane dead-panned to Teddy.

"But," Teddy blurted out, shocked…he had spent all of Saturday afternoon cleaning the bike.

"I'm messin' with ya!" Shane shouted as he grabbed the kid and spun him around. "That thing looks brand new!"

Teddy laughed out loud and gave Shane a punch. A smidgeon of the worry he had about the race weekend in Denver dissolved.

———◦((◦))◦———

But now the butterflies had returned. Teddy sat next to his bike with his dad and watched in amazement as the hustle and bustle of the paddock blurred around him. The Yamaha of Colorado Springs pit area took up two spots and was one of the busiest at the Denver track because it housed Ken and Shane Pearson; the Pearsons were well-liked and their pit was simply the best place to spend the weekend. And tucked in the far right corner of the canopies was Teddy Hill's little 125, with '312' on the number plate.

The Pearsons had taken care of his entry and he would run in the 125 Youth Novice race and possibly the 125 Youth Intermediate race, depending upon his novice-race finish. The club would allow the top-three finishing Novices to enter the Intermediate race and Bill Pearson had made it clear that it would be up to the Hills to make that decision. The Expert class could only be entered by riders with three or more Intermediate podium finishes.

As the announcer called for the first practice, Shane and Ken grabbed the Hills. "C'mon Teddy, let's get you up to speed on this track."

The Pearson boys led the Hills across the paddock toward the track and it seemed to Teddy that Ken and Shane knew everyone. As the track came into view, Shane and Ken scampered atop the largest motorhome Teddy had ever seen, calling to the Hills to follow them up the ladder.

"Ah…who's is this?" Teddy stammered.

Ken looked down from the top of the palace and laughed. "It's our buddy George Grass's…I'm gonna beat him in 250 but he still lets us up here! C'mon!."

Teddy started the long climb up the aluminum ladder and couldn't help but smile at the Pearsons, who they knew, what they did and how they did it. Tom followed his son and from up there the view of the track was breathtaking, the first real motocross track Teddy had seen in person.

"Wow," Teddy breathed.

"Wow? Wow?" Ken chortled. "You look at Denver Raceway and all you can say is "wow"? How about HOLY MACKAROON?" This last bit shouted at the top of his lungs. People turned and stared up at the motorhome until they realized it was Ken Pearson acting like his usual fun-loving self.

And then Shane pitched in, "HOLY MACKAROON AND JUMPIN' JUHOSIFATS!"

"WOWIE POOZOWIE!" Ken screamed.

"MAMMA MIA!" Shane returned.

The sound of bikes starting and accelerating onto the track ended the exclamations and just like that, the Pearsons got serious.

"Look at how deep the sand is just off the start, Teddy." Shane began. "Make sure you rev out each gear or you'll bog. And those first two turns open up, so don't feel scared about going around the highside on everyone—there's plenty of room."

"Yeah," Ken added, "I pass Shane there all the time."

Shane ignored his brother and kept up a dialogue in Teddy's ear. "Don't double that first jump. Single it, and then double the next two, it's faster. We always try to really attack the first whoop in that whoop section—you don't want to get into those first two bumps because there's always knee-deep sand in there. Look, see that kid eat it? He didn't clear that second bump."

Ken had knelt next to the enthralled young Hill. Teddy's eyes were glued to the two riders leading the 80-cc practice.

"The next two sweepers have two lines through them; try to rail the outside line if it's open. If you're forced to go low, make sure you get it stopped and turned before you pin it, or you'll jump the rut and lose the drive. That will goof you up for the next bump section.

"Don't try to be a hero over those next four jumps because it's easy to over-jump and land on the flat. I don't think your 125 has enough steam to double them, so just get it up and back down on the ground to keep it driving."

"There's a blind uphill after that fourth jump." Shane resumed. "The smoothest line is up the far right side and the track goes left after the crest, so be ready to turn it in the air if you're going good. You're going to love the last section because it's got three big, bermed turns that you can just fly into, almost pinned. Actually, probably pinned on a 125. Plan on doubling the finish line jump, but don't over-jump it because you'll want to get a good drive off the last one and through the sand section."

As the 80-cc practice ended, Teddy came out of his fog and looked around to see only Ken standing next to him.

"Shane's up next so let's watch him from here. You're up after him. Your dad's checking your bike."

Teddy nodded and returned his focus to the track as Shane's bright blue jersey rocketed to the front of the Open-class practice. Ken knelt next to Teddy and narrated, Teddy glued his eyes to Shane; his anticipation to ride was palpable.

38

On Shane's final practice lap Teddy climbed down and met his dad at the Colorado Springs Yamaha pit. Just like at home, Teddy's helmet and chest protector were hanging from the handlebar and the kid shrugged into them while his dad warmed the engine.

"Teddy," his dad said, catching his son's attention. "Let everyone go and then start your laps." Teddy nodded as the announcer made last call for 125 Novice Youth practice.

Teddy idled over to the track entrance, standing easily on the pegs as the bike putted along. His last-night's nerves were gone, replaced with a burning desire to ride, to lap a real motocross track just like he'd seen on TV. One minute later, Teddy accelerated away from the starting gate, the last 125 on track, and clicked into race mode.

For Shane and Ken, Teddy's first lap of Denver Raceway was surprisingly, amazingly quick. He caught and passed three other yellow-plated novices, though he had let everyone clear the first three turns before gassing it.

"Huh," joked Ken, "I guess he was listening."

But as the Pearsons watched Teddy's second lap they saw the kid's discomfort with the four big jumps. Shane caught Ken's eye and knew his brother saw the hesitancy. Teddy was okay on the smaller jumps and singling the jumps the others were doubling but even by the fifth lap, Teddy hadn't even tried the big tabletop.

Tom stood next to Ken and had been watching his son practice. He had asked Teddy to go out last to avoid being landed on over the big jumps. Tom knew that Mini-Unadilla didn't have anything close to the jumps here in Denver and that Teddy would be a bit over his head when it came time to race a bunch of kids who had been sailing over these jumps all season. But Tom didn't count on Ken and Shane Pearson.

Practice happens in an eyeblink at a club race and before Teddy knew it the checkered flag was out and the 125s were done. He coasted back under the blue canopies and his dad was waiting to take the bike and hand him a cold water.

"That looked like a lot of fun," Tom Hill said to his grinning son.

"I really liked it," Teddy returned, but his sparkling eyes and mile-wide smile said much more. A quick shadow passed over his expression.

"The jumps are scary."

Bill Pearson shouted across the pit, "How'd it go, young man?"

Teddy looked away from his dad and answered, "I really liked it."

"Yeah, it looked like you did," the older Pearson laughed. "I only saw a couple of yellow plates ahead of you at the end of the fifth lap." Bill had seen Teddy's hesitance over the jumps but his speed on the rest of the track put him right in the heat of the battle with the rest of the Novices.

"Hey," Shane shouted as he ran into the pit area, "I hate to interrupt this sweet moment, but let's get our butts over to the motorhome and watch Ken, he's up right now!"

"C'mon dad," said Teddy as he parked his helmet on the handlebar.

39

Back up on Grass's motorhome, Shane knelt next to Teddy.
"Okay, Ken'll come out behind Dale Keefer, the Honda of Denver rider, and show you some passing lines around here. Ken and Dale are the class of this field so it should be a pretty good show. Dale doesn't know he's being used as a demo, so it's our secret!" Shane laughed with unbridled glee.

"Look, there's Ken and he's sitting right behind Dale in line. This outta be good! Oh, and by the way, you looked good out there, just a few things to clean up."

The 250 practice started with Ken behind Keefer's Honda, but not for long. Shane narrated as Ken passed Keefer high, let him by, then passed him low. He passed him on the left and right, each time slowing enough to let Keefer ease past again. On the last lap, Ken looked directly at the motorhome and gave the Hills and Shane a big thumbs up as he crested the finish-line jump.

Teddy returned the gesture and then looked up at Shane.

"Thanks, that helped a lot. Your practice is up next, can I stay up here?"

"No, young man, you cannot!" Shane said with mock seriousness. "Follow me."

Shane was already clambering down the ladder.

Ken pulled into the Yamaha pit as Shane and Teddy walked up

and didn't bother pulling off his helmet.

"Learn anything?" he asked Teddy.

Teddy nodded in the affirmative.

"Grab your gear and your bike then," Ken replied.

He then yelled over to Tom Hill, "Tom, follow us."

Shane had slipped back into his riding gear and was kicking his 450 to life as Teddy rolled over on his 125 with Tom right behind him on foot.

"We're going to the mini track," Ken said in answer to Teddy's confused look.

"What about Shane's practice?" Teddy asked.

"Got something more important," Shane replied. "Follow us."

Ken and Shane exited the pit and spun a quick left turn around the end of the canopy, accelerating toward a small track Teddy hadn't noticed. The track had a few riders, all small kids, circulating in a light haze of dust almost as if it was a babysitting device for kids who weren't racing. And in fact, that's about what it was.

But not for Shane and Ken Pearson.

The two racers had been recognized by the kids riding around and that brought the whole scene to a standstill. But not for long. The Pearsons rode to the exact middle of the little track and Teddy followed them. When they shut off their engines, so did he. Tom walked up, his curiosity piqued by the three racers sitting in the middle of the kid's track.

Shane and Ken were talking quietly, looking at a pair of berm turns. "Let me try it," Ken said.

He fired his 250 and ran it to the far corner of the little track, spun around and accelerated right into one of the berm turns the brothers had been looking at, but he ran directly into it at a right angle. His Yamaha flew up the berm and into the air, landing neatly fifty feet later on the downside of the second berm.

Tom shook his head and a quick smile creased his usually-serious face as he realized the brothers wanted to get Teddy jumping the bigger jumps and planned to do it right now.

"Teddy, you're going good but need to double in two spots and also clear those two big tabletops," Shane began. "See that jump Ken just made? If you can get that jump, you'll do good on the real track too."

Teddy had been watching intently but he finally found his voice when he realized that he would soon be trying to clear a fifty-foot jump.

"I...ah...I don't know, I think..." Teddy began to stammer but was cut-off by Ken shouting to him from the takeoff berm.

"Teddy, ride your bike over here."

As Shane narrated, Ken went off the makeshift jump twice more. Ken made the jump in third gear, so Shane thought Teddy's bike should hit it in fourth. Shane focused Teddy's attention on Ken's body position and throttle usage, showing Teddy how his brother accelerated all the way up the ramp and 'popped' off the lip.

Then Teddy tried it...sort of. The first try was terrible, not quite a disaster but close, as the 125 nosed-over in the air and landed well short of the second berm on the front tire. Everyone held their breath and expelled it in a huge gasp of relief as Teddy brought the bike back under control.

He returned to the brothers and his ashen-faced dad. He had just jumped his biggest jump and it was almost a big crash.

"I don't..." Teddy began in a quavering voice.

But Shane cut in with his usual exuberance. "Not bad, not bad for a first try, huh Ken?"

"Not bad at all!" Ken exclaimed. "You just didn't stay in the throttle long enough and by the time you got in the air, the front was already coming down. Watch."

Ken kicked his 250 to life and roosted away to the far side of the berm, spun his bike back around and soared effortlessly off the berm.

Teddy watched, still a bit uncertain but buoyed by the Pearson's attitude.

Ken came back and shouted "Watch again!" as he idled past.

"Listen to how he drives the bike up the jump, right to the lip," Shane said as he knelt next to Teddy.

Ken accelerated and Teddy watched and listened as the blue 250 railed up the jump and sprung into the air. He heard the 250 *ww-wrrraaaapppp* up the jump, then go silent. He was nodding his head, thinking about what he saw.

Ken coasted up, engine off.

"See what we mean?"

Teddy nodded, still looking at the berm.

Ken caught Shane's eye and wondered if they were asking a twelve-year old kid who had never raced to bite off more than he could chew. As one, both Pearsons turned to look at Tom Hill.

Tom stood silently, about five feet from his son's bike. He turned his head from looking at the berm and saw the Pearson boys staring at him. Time stopped as Shane and Ken looked at this lean, tough rancher and wondered what he thought of their attempts to get Teddy used to big jumps before his race.

Teddy noticed the silence and looked at the Pearsons, then followed their eyes to his dad. Tom caught his son's look and the two Hills held each other's eyes.

"You gotta jump big to win," Tom said to his son in a quiet voice. "I know you can do it."

His dad's words removed the doubt in Teddy's mind like a gale wind blows the seeds from a dandelion. He had seen Ken, heard the 250. He could almost feel his 125 hit the jump and soar through the air because he had imagined it so many times while lying on the living room floor watching his Unadilla DVD. Not only had Ken Pearson given him a close-up example but he'd watched the best motocrossers in the world get big air. He could feel it.

Ken and Shane laughed aloud as the kid snapped out his kick-starter and fired the 125. As the bike started, Tom stepped forward and leaned down to Teddy's helmet.

"Fourth gear. Drive it up the face."

Teddy nodded, slipped his bike into gear and rode to the far side of the berm. He spun his 125 around to face the jump and hesitated for a moment, as if to take a breath…in fact, exactly like taking a breath. The kid looked at the massive jump, saw his dad and the Pearsons watching, noted a few kids on their minibikes watching after they'd seen Ken Pearson fly through the air.

For those who have never lined a dirtbike up for the run to a big jump, it's a mental step that requires faith and confidence in one's skills. Try it sometime. Everyone should get a chance to stare down their demons of insecurity and doubt, relying on skills and equipment and technique and a bit of luck.

Teddy swallowed and snapped out the clutch.

As Shane Pearson watched Teddy pause for a moment, he wondered again about the wisdom of his decision to bring Teddy out here. Most kids who race begin with little jumps and sneak up on the big stuff over the course of months and even years. *What drove me to get Teddy to clear the bigger jumps?* Shane asked himself as the 125's engine revved.

The little 125 scrabbled for traction, hooked up and Teddy caught second, third and then fourth. The smallest kid in the 125 class stayed in the throttle and drove his Yamaha up the lip just like he had been told. His bike vaulted into the air and to Teddy it seemed like it would never come down. The enjoyment of jumping the little stuff at Mini-Unadilla was replaced with a mixture of excitement…and unadulterated fear.

Like everyone else who jumps big for the first time, Teddy froze in place as his bike soared into the air. He forgot to close the throttle and the 125 went into the rev-limiter as it skied past the Pearsons and Tom Hill. They followed the bike silently, all three of them knowing the feelings Teddy was experiencing…the thrill, the fear.

Then the joy as the 125 came to earth on the far side of the second berm…not beautifully and gracefully back to earth, but back to earth on the tires and with the rider still in the saddle.

The Pearsons cheered, the onlookers cheered, Teddy cheered and even the stoic rancher clapped his hands. Twice, in fact. Teddy got a good shaking by the Pearsons when he rode back to the group and they quickly gave him a few more pointers about throttle control and body position. Teddy went again and it was better, cleaner. The third attempt better yet. More talk and the fourth try finally started to look easy and smooth. The fifth and sixth attempts actually looked relaxed and Shane finally answered his own question. *I brought him over here because if Teddy can jump a bit better he'll win his first race. And almost nobody gets to win a first race.*

40

Shane Pearson was right. Teddy Hill launched his motocross career by winning the 125 Novice race in a runaway. He bobbled the starting gate when it kicked him up and almost off the seat, but regrouped and got into the first turn in tenth, ahead of nine other Novices. But tenth only lasted one corner…Teddy passed the other Novices like a shark through a school of tuna. He led the end of the first lap and Bill Pearson was right: The Novices never saw which way he went.

The kid's return to the Colorado Springs Yamaha pit area was a rollicking party, as if he'd just won the world championship, walked on the moon and solved world hunger. It was Shane and Ken leading the partiers but the whole paddock seemed to join in the screaming, jumping, cheering and whistling. Everyone who had met Teddy Hill liked the quiet, shy kid and enjoyed watching him turn every shade of red as the celebration for the Novice win swirled around him.

Tom Hill snuck the 125 away from the partiers and popped it up on the stand, gave it a quick double-check, then waded back into the crowd to give Teddy a gigantic bear hug. Tom remembered what it was like to win and his joy for his son mixed with pride and relief.

The dad had watched the morning practices and the Novice race from two viewpoints, one as a father and one as a racer, and both views had been wonderful. He crouched next to the 125 and wiped the bike down, checking the spokes and oil level, thinking about the

Intermediate race.

When Teddy finally made it to the bike, Tom asked, "You want to run the Intermediate race?"

"Should I?"

Tom looked across the paddock and then back to his son.

"Seems a shame to come all the way up here for just one race."

Teddy was studying his dad's face and saw the smile in his eyes. He smiled along with his dad.

"Yeah, it does."

Both Hills nodded, agreeing that Teddy should exercise the option of entering the Intermediate race.

"How's the bike?"

"Good, no problems," Tom answered. "I'll check the fuel...I took a pound of air out of the rear tire after talking with Denny Smith at the Dunlop tent."

"Sounds good," Teddy replied, caught by surprise that his dad would know the name of the tire guy. But Teddy's mind was somewhere else. He looked at his dad pointedly.

"What can I do better?"

Tom was waiting for the question, one his son asked all the time after lapping Mini-Unadilla.

"Two things the quicker 125 Experts were doing in practice: scrubbing the second and third jumps toward the end of the lap, not flying high off them. Scrub them. Get the bike back on the ground to drive it. Second, you're not looking into those two big berm turns early enough and that's killing your speed."

Teddy nodded, "Thanks, dad."

He was staring at the ground, envisioning the two sections his dad was talking about. "Thanks," he said again absently.

Tom smiled as he checked the bike's controls, getting a kick out of this kid lost in his world. He looked across the paddock and realized how great it felt to be back in the racing community.

41

The track announcer made it a point to let the crowd know that Tom Hill was here with his son Teddy and plenty of people stopped by the Colorado Springs Yamaha pit to say hello to Tom. They had watched Tom rule back in the day and several were still racing in the Senior classes.

You could tell they were a bit worried when they asked, "Do you plan to do some racing?"

The relief was evident when Tom answered in the negative.

"I just ride with Teddy," was all he'd ever say. The elder Hill appeared fit, due partly to his ranching job, but also because he rode just about every day. He looked like a racer in training.

Tom was more than happy just to be there with Teddy. He could see his son's nervousness and the only advice he'd given Teddy before practice and before the Novice race was calming words.

"Just go out and ride smooth, just like with me and Uncle Brian."

Tom had realized long ago that good riding is the simplest way to win. The ranch boy never wasted time on trash talking or mind games, he'd just line up and ride his best. That was usually good enough for the big trophy. If he got beat he'd be back at the ranch working on his weaknesses, not making excuses.

This focus on riding was what he liked most about the Pearson boys. At no point had they mentioned rivaling riders, put down other brands or spoken out of turn. Ken and Shane appeared freewheeling and fun but Tom saw that their approach to racing was still nuts-and-bolts basics. *And that's why they win,* Tom thought to himself. *Their dad has it figured out.*

From his spot in the corner, he'd watched Bill Pearson deal with his sons, the fans and his son's sponsors. Pearson made time for anyone and everyone, his enthusiasm for this sport apparent to all. But between the outgoing friendliness and big smile was a mind that took care of the details and watched over the assets. Despite the showy pit area, money hadn't been wasted. Pearson relied on well-prepared bikes and fast riders for success, not hoping that show and bluster would convince sponsors to help...or sell bikes. The Colorado Springs Yamaha shop won races, and the way Bill Pearson had spotted and groomed Teddy showed his genius. Tom had already seen over a dozen kids looking at Teddy's 125 after his Novice win, so Pearson's investment was paying off.

As Tom added fuel for Teddy's Intermediate race, he caught himself in a moment of sadness. *I wish I had known Bill Pearson in the '90s.*

Then he silently cursed himself for the weakness of that thought, remembering what the Hill men always said: "Wish in one hand and spit in the other and see what you've got."

As he screwed on the gas cap he made a mental note to quit feeling sorry for himself. He knew Bill Pearson now, and that was great for his son.

42

Teddy's start in the Novice race had been only average but he had quickly charged to the front against the weaker riders. Ken and Shane had taken him down to the starting line to watch a few other classes, talking to him about the timing of the gate drop, body position and lane preparation. It helped. In the Intermediate race the smallest kid in the class jumped into sixth in turn one. Everyone knew it because his was the only bright yellow number plate that close to the front. The announcer made sure that the crowd knew this was Tommy Hill's twelve-year old son.

The Intermediate class at a large club race makes for serious racing and Teddy found himself with his hands full. At the end of the first lap he'd been pushed back to eighth as he settled into the fight. Riders passing and riding close didn't faze Teddy much. It was like riding with his dad and uncle and Shane. It wasn't the proximity of the other riders that made his first lap slow: Teddy was just too nervous!

The butterflies had started banging against his ribcage as the Intermediate class was announced. As he lined his yellow-plated bike up against the white-plated Intermediates, he could sense their dismissal of him and that put an aggressive edge on his nerves, an edge that had him over-ride the first lap, trying too hard in the wrong places. His dad's voice rang through his helmet.

"Ride smooth, just like with me and Uncle Brian."

As the second of six laps began, the number 312 Yamaha got back into sixth. The top five guys were running a close battle, about twenty bike lengths ahead of Teddy, urging him forward. On the third lap, the yellow number plate was alone, clear of the seventh-place rider and about half-way toward the top-five battle, but unable to make much headway on the top Intermediate group. In many ways the Intermediate class shows the most desperation because these racers want to win and move on to the Expert class. The pace is high, only a click off the lap times most Experts can run.

But with two laps to go, one of the top five guys fell on the second big berm turn, momentarily bunching up the group and giving Teddy a five-bike-length jump. Half a lap later the yellow-plate bike was tailing the top four machines. His dad's advice had quickened his pace by almost two seconds a lap and those two seconds put him right up with the fastest Intermediates.

Teddy got stronger as the race went on. No other kid in that group had his own track a few hundred yards from his house. No other kid rode as much or as often and no other kid had Tom Hill to moto against. The four Intermediates who had battled all race were now firmly in the cross-hairs of Teddy Hill.

With a lap and a half to run, Teddy snuck into fourth and momentarily had a wheel into third before the rider turned down and slammed the door on that passing opportunity. Teddy regrouped and got a run through the whoop section but the same rider changed lines drastically and practically punted the smaller Hill off the course. Teddy fumbled and almost fell, but pulled the bike back in line, now relegated to fifth.

As the last lap started, Teddy outjumped the fourth place rider and again found himself on the heels of third, the same rider who had put him off the track. Teddy ran the low line into the second corner and seemingly had made the pass but the third-place rider stormed out of the corner and kept turning, slamming into Teddy's front wheel, snapping the bars to full lock before Teddy recovered.

Teddy saw red and a mist of righteous anger settled over the youngster.

As the lead group entered the final two berm turns, Teddy simply ran straight into the first corner and didn't even bother to try to turn, instead ramming into the third-place rider and using him as the berm. Teddy's front tire contacted the other bike's swingarm and the third-place rider was pushed out and over the berm as Teddy turned and accelerated for the final turn and finish line in third.

43

If you thought the party for winning the Novice race was fun, the party for finishing third in the Intermediate class was unbelievable. Until Tom Hill asked Teddy and the Pearsons to step inside the team trailer.

The Pearsons lifted Teddy into the trailer with a laugh, but abruptly froze as they saw the look on Tom Hill's face.

"I don't know what you're celebrating out there," Tom Hill said tensely. "All I saw was dirty riding."

The elder Hill continued in a voice as cold as ice, "I know that boy was riding dirty but two wrongs will never make a right with me and my family."

Ken, Shane and Teddy stood mute. Bill Pearson cleared his throat and said to Tom, "I was here at the pit during the race. What happened?"

Shane jumped in "Buddy Cleary, you know the kid from Longmont? He turned down on Teddy real hard, and then in the whoops, he just changed lanes and slammed into him!" Shane was still worked up about what Cleary pulled out there and his eyes blazed as he remembered the moves. "So in that big berm corner, Teddy ran it in and bumped Cleary wide, getting third place."

Bill nodded quietly, eyes on his son. He then looked over to Tom.

"How did you see it, Tom?"

Tom's eyes were on his son. Teddy looked like a deer in the head-lights of an oncoming eighteen-wheeler as he saw his dream of rac-ing ending right here in this trailer.

"Come here, son."

Teddy walked to his father and Tom knelt down, putting a hand on his son's shoulder pad. The Pearsons had to lean forward to hear the elder Hill.

"Teddy…I saw what Cleary did and I got hoppin'-mad too. You rose to the challenge with a desire to fight and battle and we can't teach you that, it's a quality that comes from inside. And you've got it.

"But you let that fight get ahold of you, rather than you have ahold of it. I've seen guys ride like that for years and nobody wants to be around them, sponsor them or even practice with them."

Tom looked over at the Pearsons.

"Bill, you remember Davis Spade? Out of Castle Rock?"

Bill Pearson nodded.

"How fast was that guy?"

Bill answered, "When he wasn't hurt, he was awful quick."

"But did you ever want anything to do with him?"

Bill shook his head, "Nope."

"And boys," Tom continued as he looked at Ken and Shane, then back to Teddy, "That's my point. Guys who lose their heads and ride dirty, even when provoked, get nowhere. Your dad certainly didn't want to be associated with someone like Spade and the reason he was hurt all the time is this…are you listening?"

Teddy nodded, as did Ken and Shane. The Pearson boys had never heard Tom Hill say more than twenty words in a row, but they were hearing him now.

"When you ride dirty, you paint a target on your back and every-one takes a shot at you. I've seen it happen. Teddy, I'd rather go back and just ride on the ranch than see you get that reputation. You need to funnel that desire to battle into clean passes. Am I clear?"

Teddy had tucked his forehead against his dad's shoulder, listening with a pounding heart. He stepped back and looked his father directly in the eye.

"Dad, I'm so sorry. I understand what you're saying."

Teddy didn't know what he feared the most: disappointing his father or never being able to race again.

Just then, a sharp rap against the trailer door broke the moment. It was Craig Peris, the racing club's vice-president.

"Bill, boys," Peris nodded to the Pearsons as he stepped into the trailer.

Peris reached out his hand to Tom and introduced himself. "Tom…used to admire your racing."

Peris then looked down at Teddy and said, "Teddy, we'll need to see you in the starter's stand in five minutes. Tom and Bill, we'll need you there too."

44

Buddy Cleary and his dad TJ were already there when the Colorado Springs Yamaha group arrived at the starter's stand. Teddy could hardly walk due to nervousness and the feeling of dread. He couldn't believe his racing career was starting and ending on the same day and he moved as if in a nightmare that had spun out of his control.

Craig Peris and two other club officials were there and nobody looked happy. Peris started, "Boys, we had some riding today that could get both of you thrown out of this club right now. Buddy, what happened out there?"

Buddy looked up at Peris and said, "I didn't do nothin' wrong, we just got together a few times and then he," gesturing at Teddy, "slammed into me when I had third place."

Buddy's dad added, "Yeah, some little Novice gets lucky and then loses control in the middle of the Intermediate group. Buddy's third-place would have put him into the Expert race. I don't know why you guys let the yellow plates out there."

You could almost hear the blood boil in the veins of Bill Pearson and Tom Hill. Teddy stood stock-still, staring at the ground, wishing it would swallow him up and stop this bad dream.

Peris returned Mr. Cleary's challenging stare and answered, "TJ, you let us take care of who enters what. I asked Buddy what happened." Peris continued to stare at TJ Cleary, waiting for another outburst. None came.

"Alright." Peris turned to Teddy and asked the same question. "Teddy, what happened out there."

Teddy looked up at Peris, but then back down at the ground. "Buddy's right, we did get together…"

Peris interrupted the boy. "Teddy, we can't hear you."

"Buddy's right," Teddy responded in a louder voice, "we did get together…twice just as the last lap started." He paused, kicked the dirt with his boot. Swallowed.

"Then I got mad. Lost my head…I ran into him on purpose."

TJ Cleary erupted. "See? It was his fault!"

Bill and Tom's blood pressures rose ten more points.

"Easy, TJ," Peris said, stepping toward Cleary to let him know he wouldn't tolerate any more outbursts.

"Mr. Peris?" Teddy said, looking up at the official as all eyes pivoted toward him. "My dad and Mr. Pearson were talking to me about the race, about how I should have put my efforts on passing Buddy, not hitting him. I'm very sorry for what I did."

At that point, Teddy reached into a paper bag he had clutched in his right hand…and pulled out the third-place trophy. He stepped over to Buddy and extended the trophy to the Cleary boy.

"Buddy, I'm sorry for hitting you. You were riding great and deserve third place." The glittering trophy hung in the Colorado air held by Teddy Hill's left hand. Buddy was dumbfounded. He reached out in slow motion and took the trophy from the much-smaller boy.

"Thanks," was all he could muster.

The entire group stood frozen in place. Teddy and Buddy looked at each other, Buddy standing six inches taller than the Hill boy but seeing Teddy as a much larger person. Time stood still. Then Buddy smiled.

"You're cool. Sorry we got together out there."

Peris was the first to break the spell. "Okay…any other problems?"

The men shook their heads. Teddy turned to Peris and said, "I'm sorry Mr. Peris."

Buddy stepped up behind Teddy and added, "Me too. Sorry."

45

Bill Pearson and the Hills walked from the starter's stand to the Yamaha tent in silence. Teddy entered the tent and sat down in the corner by his bike, looking at the first-place Novice trophy he had won. Bill and Tom knelt down in front of the kid.

Bill said, "Well, that was a cool move. How did you think of that?"

Teddy looked at the older man and said, "When I slammed into Buddy, I knew it was wrong. I didn't deserve that trophy. When I looked at it I felt ashamed, especially after what dad said in the trailer."

Teddy then looked at his father. "Dad, remember last year when the brand inspector missed those thirty-five head in that hidden arroyo on the other side of the mesa?"

Tom nodded.

"Well, you told the brand inspector about them, though it cost you more in registration fees."

"Yes, I did."

"And you told me that if you hadn't told the inspector about them, you'd feel like a cheat every time you saw those cows." Teddy started to cry. "That's what I thought about when I looked at that trophy. That's how I felt."

Teddy swiped at his eyes with the back of his hand. "Dad, Mr. Pearson. Please let me race again. Please."

Tom and Bill looked at each other and they knew the lesson was learned. "Son," Bill Pearson said as he squeezed the kid's knee, "You can race on my squad anytime."

"We're good,"Tom said quietly as he hugged his son. "We're good."

46

Rider confidence is an intangible, immeasurable quality, and Preston Jupiter's race against Davey Stevens gave the California kid a huge dose of this necessary ingredient. Preston had always been quick and controlled but after running with Stevens he had taken another step in his riding, especially at the corner entrance. Paul Jupiter was the first to notice the improvement during a practice day but at the next CMXA round at Saddleback everybody noticed Preston Jupiter's speed …and his cocky swagger.

Paul didn't know what to do about the swagger and the newly-displayed confidence…or was it overconfidence? The elder Jupiter wasn't sure and had been on the verge of talking to Preston about it several times during the week but couldn't find the right opening. At Saddleback, Paul was loath to get into an argument with Preston during a race weekend but he made a promise to himself that he would speak about it after the races.

Kel Cranther attended Saddleback too. He had seen the Jupiter kid's speed, watching Preston gap the 125 Expert class during practice, then recover from a bad start to head the field in the first heat race. Preston looked to have the field covered for the main event but perhaps a bit of overconfidence saw the young Jupiter get an even worse start, finding himself almost last off the starting gates into turn one.

"This should be interesting," Cranther murmured to himself as he spied the silver-helmeted Jupiter well back in the pack on the first lap. Cranther knew that a couple of the 125 Experts were awfully quick, especially George McQuiston, who had handily won the second heat. McQuiston might not be as mercurial as Jupiter but Cranther wasn't sure Jupiter could catch the quick kid from the San Fernando Valley in just eight laps.

By half way, Preston had pulled himself into third, directly on the heels of Paul Turpin but more than the length of the front straight behind leader McQuiston. Preston had been enjoying the race to this point, knowing that he could catch and pass anyone in the field, but when he saw how far ahead McQuiston had pulled, his confidence took a hit. Preston hadn't bothered to watch the second heat race so he had no idea McQuiston was that quick…but there he was, way out ahead.

"Go, go, go!" Preston shouted to himself, mimicking his dad's words.

And Jupiter went. Preston put Turpin behind him and set sail for McQuiston, inexorably closing the gap until pulling to within striking distance as the last lap started. There had been a few on-the-edge moments for Preston, a few instances where the boy and bike had almost fallen, but he had saved every slide and arrived on the rear fender of the Valley racer.

Then it happened: a desperate move that Preston couldn't save and in fact, Bob Hannah probably couldn't have saved. In the extremely fast sixth turn at Saddleback, Preston altered his usual line in an attempt to go around the outside of the sliding McQuiston. Preston had misjudged George's entry line and Preston's front tire tagged McQuiston's rear, snapping the bars out of Preston's hands and flinging him to the ground at over 45 mph. It happened so quickly that Preston couldn't even get his hands out to brace his fall, landing squarely on his chest, stomach and chin. The crowd gasped and those close to turn six winced as Jupiter's body tumbled through the dirt. A red flag stopped the action and the corner workers and emergency crew rushed toward the motionless kid, Paul Jupiter in the lead.

Cranther turned away from the scene as another spectator asked, "Why did he try to pass there?"

Because when you're overconfident, you do stupid things, the veteran reporter thought as he walked back into the pits.

47

Hospitals are no fun but Preston's family had made his room about as great as a hospital room can get, complete with motocross posters, his riding gear hanging in the corner and his helmet on the table by the window. Preston's riding gear had saved catastrophic injuries, especially the chest and shoulder protector but he had suffered two broken ribs, a bruised sternum, bad cuts to his chin and a broken nose. His helmet's chin bar had taken a huge hit and the doctor determined that the force of the impact had bent the chin bar enough to allow Preston's nose and chin to hit the ground. Preston wasn't a pretty sight, with wrapped ribs and a bandaged face, but his usually upbeat spirits had taken the biggest hit.

"It looks like Preston can head home tomorrow," Dr. Klein told the Jupiters, "but he'll have to take it easy on those ribs and that nose. I know you guys want to ride but Preston should give it two weeks before getting on a bike." Preston didn't argue much because it even hurt to take a shallow breath and his nose was too sore to touch. He just nodded at Dr. Klein.

"No problem, Doc," Paul answered, "it will give us time to get the bikes ready for the next few races. Preston was going to run the Fairs here in California but they're two weeks away so he'll miss those."

Paul turned to his son, "But guess what, Pres? We'll head up to Colorado for the Fairs in Denver next month. What do you think of that?"

"I hope I'm ready," Preston replied slowly in a low voice. He'd never been hurt before and as he sat in his hospital bed he couldn't imagine riding a bike again. He hurt all over and was more than a little spooked from the crash. The hit had knocked him unconscious and coming back to consciousness in a speeding ambulance surrounded by strangers is tough on a fourteen-year-old.

"Man," Preston groaned, "I wish McQuiston hadn't taken me out."

Paul held his son's shoulder and replied, "You had him covered, kid."

But Paul didn't voice his opinion about an obviously desperate pass in an impossible location. He figured they'd talk it over when Preston was feeling better.

48

Paul kissed Preston goodbye, promising to visit again that evening with a bucket of Kentucky Fried's best, but the older Jupiter's jovial demeanor vanished as he walked toward the hospital's elevator. Paul wasn't worried about Preston's injured body, he was worried about the kid's injured mind, his bent confidence and dented enthusiasm. He had seen bad crashes, heck, he'd even experienced a few first hand…he knew how tough they could be.

Lost in thought, alone in the elevator, the elder Jupiter rubbed his face with his hands. He couldn't stop thinking about the comment most veteran riders made when a fast kid showed up at the track: "Let's see how fast he is after his first big one."

The vets knew that painful crashes can detune some riders, especially crashes that involve hospital stays, time alone in a room to think about why you were there, flat on your back.

"Lord," whispered Paul, "Please help Preston come back strong from this." As he finished his quick prayer he felt a wave of guilt because another voice in his head was telling him that his son had gotten more than a little cocky and even uncomfortable to be around. As Preston's speed built, his attitude had moved from *desiring to improve* to *I know it all.* As the elevator sank to the lobby Paul knew that karma had a way of handling those types of attitudes, sooner or later, in business or sports.

As the doors opened and Paul stepped out, he didn't notice the beautiful southern California day and hardly thanked the man who held the door for him. Imagine his surprise when a voice yelled out to him, "Hey, handsome!"

Lori had just parked her car and was walking toward the hospital entrance.

"How's our little racer doing?" she asked, then stopped in her tracks, the smile draining from her face. "Paul, what's wrong? Is he okay?"

Paul had stopped by his truck and was leaning against the fender, looking at Lori with an expression of pain and sadness. Lori ran up to him and took his face in her hands. She looked into his eyes and the frightened look on her face made Paul laugh just a little.

"Sweetie, sorry…I didn't mean to scare you. Preston's doin great, really great…it's just that, well…"

"What is it, Paul?"

He laughed again, an embarrassed chuckle, and looked sheepishly at Lori.

"I'm just being a little baby, feeling sorry for myself. The important thing is that Preston is doing well."

Lori punched him on the arm and smiled: "Yeah, I heard you about Preston…now what's your problem?"

Paul took a deep breath and looked into his wife's caring eyes.

"I'm a selfish idiot. I'm worried that if this crash makes Preston want to quit riding, I'll lose my riding buddy and we'll never get out and play and race and be together. In the elevator I realized how much I love going riding with that kid. If he's done riding…" Paul's voice trailed off and he looked at Lori with an embarrassed grin.

"I sound like a selfish idiot, don't I?"

"Oh honey…" She pulled Paul into a hug. "Yes, you're an idiot, but you're a cute idiot. There's no way Preston will quit riding, he lives for it."

"I know, I know…but I've seen guys get hurt and then quit, sell their bike, their gear, everything. Remember John Page? I was thinking about him in the elevator…he crashed at Saddleback, broke his wrist and was spooked to ride again. Sold everything, just quit. I mean…Preston doesn't have to ride or race or anything…it's his choice…I was just imagining what it would be like if he wanted to quit…" Paul's words came out in a rush.

Lori hugged him again, then stood back and looked her husband in the eye. "Don't worry. Give him time. Let's not pressure him either way. But if you're not sure I want you to know that I think your riding bikes together is the best thing that could happen, to you and Preston. He's a better young man because of it, and you…I just love this fit body of yours!" She laughed and playfully squeezed Paul's biceps. She stood on tiptoe and pecked Paul on the cheek.

Then she stepped back with a sudden inspiration and asked, "Hey! Are you still running the California Fairs?"

Paul nodded.

"Then have Preston come along as your tuner, your wrench. Have him take lap times and keep an eye on your competition. You guys can still spend time together, even if he's not riding. And you talked about running the Colorado Fairs in Denver…do it. You guys drive the coach and go racing, let Preston hang around…he'll get the fever again. "

Paul hugged her even tighter. She was right about not pressuring Preston, and he loved the idea of Preston tuning for him at the California Fairs. *Who knows,* thought Paul, *by the time the Colorado Fairs roll around, Preston might be racing again.*

"I love you…great idea," he whispered to his wife. "I'm heading to the office to check in and then I'll be back with the biggest bucket of chicken you've ever seen."

49

Preston had agreed reluctantly to wrench for his dad at the California State Fair Championship, but then warmed to the task by helping organize the Jupiter pit area, doing everything necessary to get his dad ready to race. The younger Jupiter's nose and chin were swollen and he had two black eyes, but it was the healing ribs that bothered him the most.

"I can't lift too much stuff," he told his dad, "but I can help you win the Fairs! Heck, I'm probably a better crew chief than a rider!"

Paul bit his lip, remembering his plan to not push Preston to ride. "Glad you're here to help me, Pres," he said with a smile.

Paul Jupiter arrived at the California State Fair Championship as hands-down favorite in Senior A, the class for expert riders aged 35 to 45 but his status as favorite disappeared the moment everyone heard that Charlie Mann had also entered. Mann had been asked by the local KTM dealership to campaign the company's new 450—everyone knew that a Fair winner always became a big seller, especially in Southern California.

And everyone knew Charlie Mann, the ex-factory rider who seemed to have lost none of his touch over the years… a tough guy to beat fifteen years ago had only gotten better.

"Dad," Preston called as he jogged painfully to the Jupiter motorhome, "did you hear Charlie Mann's in your class?"

"Yep," Paul answered, "I heard…on a KTM, right?"

Preston nodded.

"Well, let's do our best to get this little Yamaha going good to-day, huh?"

Preston did a quick double-take at his dad, who didn't seem scared or even nervous. "Have you ever raced Mann?"

"Once," Paul answered. "But it was a long time ago and I didn't have you crewing for me. I think we've got Mann covered now."

Preston's breath caught in his throat…until he realized his dad was kidding.

"Mann's a pro, son." And Paul looked out across the Orange County Fairgrounds as if he was looking back in time. "Then again," he added in a quiet but firm voice, "there's a reason we go racing, rather than just hand out the trophies to whoever *might* be fastest."

50

It's tough to get lap times when Expert motocross riders are on track because each lap is an experiment in finding the quickest line and they often go easy in a few sections to concentrate on other sections. They will roll over a jump one lap, double it the next.

But one thing was clear as the final Senior A practice ended: Charlie Mann was one fast dude.

Preston had spent both Senior A practices perched in the announcer's booth armed with a pair of stopwatches and binoculars. Even with two black eyes, he saw right through his dad's easygoing attitude…his dad wanted to challenge Mann. Preston vowed to help him do it.

Preston got back to the motorhome as Paul shrugged out of his chest protector and asked, "Howdit look?"

"You're haulin'…" Preston hesitated.

"Yeah…but what?"

Preston couldn't believe he was about to coach his dad but the older Jupiter was pulling two chairs together and sitting down, motioning Preston over. Preston grabbed the track map from his back pocket and plopped down next to his dad.

"Okay," the kid began. "I watched from above the front straight and could see everything you and Mann were doing. Here's the deal…" The two Jupiters spent the next forty minutes bent over the track map, discussing what Mann was doing, what Paul was doing...and what the amateur on the Yamaha could do to catch the pro on the KTM. Preston's face showed signs of his crash and his ribs were sore but his mind and riding knowledge were intact. And helpful.

51

Charlie Mann never knew what hit him at the California State Fair. He found himself in second place in the first turn…and his placing never got better. He couldn't believe it…he couldn't believe he wasn't catching the blue Yamaha with the overly-cute rocket logos…and nobody else could believe it either. Except for Preston and Paul Jupiter…and Kel Cranther.

The *Cycle News* journo had not only watched practice but he'd seen Preston and Paul huddled over the track map after the second practice, while Mann was signing autographs. The Jupiters continued talking about the race while final-prepping Paul's 450, and Cranther already knew how quick Paul Jupiter was. Cranther felt something big coming after watching the Jupiters prepare, the look in Paul's eyes, the desire he showed in practice. For Mann it was another Fair but for Jupiter it was the Championship of the Universe. And he was ready for it. Cranther made some notes, then walked into the celebration under the Jupiter awning.

"Paul! Paul!" Cranther shouted toward Jupiter. Paul's win had been popular because every amateur Expert at every Fair in history has dreamed of doing what Paul Jupiter had just done: hand it to the pros. The pit was packed with fans and racers who had seen a rare event.

Paul heard Cranther and waved while walking to the veteran journalist. Cranther started with a handshake—he wanted to personally congratulate Jupiter; he knew how tough it was to beat Mann. Paul thanked him and realized the sincerity of the writer's words.

"I walked past before the race and saw you and Preston with a track map," Cranther began. "What was up?"

"You know Preston qualified for the Fairs but crashed hard at Saddleback, right?"

"Yep, saw it. Pretty ugly."

"Yeah, knocked him out, broke his nose and a few ribs...so, I asked him to coach me here and that's what we were doing...my kid was coaching me," Paul laughed.

"Did it help?"

"Yeah...he sat up in the announcer's booth and watched me and Mann practice...I'm telling you, he saw a lot of good stuff. That's what we were discussing when you walked by. The biggest thing was how Mann was getting into the whoops between the sweeper and the table-top on the back side...Mann would mini-hop the first one, then start to double them off the second one...I was coming in and hitting the first one." Cranther was jotting notes, enjoying Paul's excitement and energy, a mood that winning the Fairs creates.

"That got me behind in the rhythm and put me in the air over the last one, rather than on the back. Mann would land on the back of the last one and grab an extra gear before the tabletop." Cranther nodded. He'd seen the same thing in practice. He'd also seen Jupiter make the adjustment for the race.

"Good to have him in your corner, huh?" Cranther asked, scribbling his shorthand version of Paul's quotes.

"Well, he helped me into the whoops and he helped me by listening to Mann's shift points...he was grabbing fourth just before the doubles, while I was stretching third into the over-rev...Preston said Mann's bike was driving up the face while my power was going flat and that's why Mann was way down the landing ramp and I was barely making it. I made that change too...sure made the doubles easier."

Cranther scribbled for another ten seconds, then looked up: "Awesome, congrats Paul. So, the big question: how's Preston?"

Paul knew exactly what Cranther meant. He looked away, took a big breath.

"Not so good. Everybody around here saw his crash or heard about it and he's had plenty of guys asking why he tried to pass McQuiston there. They don't mean to but their questions and comments have detuned the kid. Preston's still hurting physically but it's the mental side I'm worried about."

"Me too," replied Cranther quietly. "You can guess how many kids I've seen get scared away by a big crash…add all the attention and Preston's got to be a little spooked. What will you do about it?"

"I'm doing it right now," Paul responded. "It was Lori's idea that I ask him to crew chief for me here and at the Colorado Fairs in three weeks. I'm hoping he gets psyched about it here and decides to race up in Denver."

"Is it working?"

Paul paused, knowing inside that Preston might truly never ride again, he was that spooked. But he didn't want to say so.

"I can't tell yet, but I gotta admit that his help today was how I beat Mann."

"Does Preston know about you and Mann?"

52

Paul squinted at Cranther as if he didn't understand, then looked away. "Nope. Never told him."

"Well," Cranther replied. "He should. Hey Preston! Preston! Come over here."

The younger Jupiter detached himself from the crowd and came over to shake hands with Cranther. The writer didn't waste any time.

"So, do you know the history of your dad and Charlie Mann?"

"What do you mean, history? Today?"

"No, not today. Today was another chapter. I mean the first chapter of their history, Anaheim Supercross 1995. Ever heard that story?"

Preston's head snapped from Cranther to his dad and back. "Anaheim? No…whadya mean? "

Cranther knelt, unslung his camera bag and looked up at Preston. "Well, I don't want to be rude to your dad, but back in 1995 he was a pretty good amateur rider, but nowhere near the professionals." Cranther stopped and looked over at Paul. "Fair to say, Paul?"

"Almost too kind," Paul answered, laughing.

"All right," Cranther continued. "So Paul makes it through qualifying for the Anaheim Supercross and gets gridded in the fourth heat. Back then, there were seven or eight heats, each with about thirty riders…over two-hundred riders trying for forty spots in the 250 main. It was crazy, Preston, guys going all-out just to make the main, much less try to win it.

"So your dad lines up with his two-year old Honda and starts the heat. Brian Myerscoff and Johnny O'mara were also in the fourth heat…do you know their names, Preston?"

Preston nodded, "I've got all their posters."

"Okay, so you know there's serious talent here…including Charlie Mann, also in the fourth heat. So Myerscoff and O'mara have a battle royale with Paul Thede third …who was fourth Paul?"

"Bell," Paul answered immediately.

Cranther grinned up at him. "Mike Bell…right. Still remember, huh?"

"Like it was yesterday."

"I'll bet. Okay," Cranther turned back to Preston. "So your dad launches his Honda and basically gets taken out in the first-turn pileup that happens when thirty desperate riders try to win the race from mid-pack in turn one. We're all watching the lead group and your dad's trying to start his bike. He gets it going and is probably half a lap down."

"At least," added Paul.

"Back then the heats were eight laps and your dad gets lapped by Myerscoff and O'mara, then Thede and Bell. He's riding around in about twenty-fourth, well out of the transfer slots. Here comes Mann and basically body-slams your dad while lapping him, knocking him into the hay bales and…why didn't you restart Paul?"

"The clutch and shift lever were broken and the shift lever punched into the engine case," Paul answered quietly.

Cranther nodded. "Mann wasn't being pushed for fifth and he had a transfer to the main, no problem. It could have been a simple racing incident but back then I was trying to give extra ink to the amateurs who entered their local Supercross and I remember how tough it was for your dad."

Cranther looked from Preston to Paul.

"Yep. That crash broke the end of my little finger and it took two months of saving at my framer's job to have the cases welded." Paul shook his head. "I can't believe you remembered that, Kel."

Cranther shrugged. "It hit me today when I walked past Mann's pit. It's been a long time coming but this win must have felt good."

It was Paul's turn to nod, eyes closed contentedly. Cranther looked again at Preston and added, "Winning the Fairs is incredible but your dad beating Mann is a piece of history. Thought you might want to know it."

"Dad?"

Paul looked down at his bruised but smiling son.

"You rule!"

53

Kel Cranther wrote the article of Paul's win in *Cycle News*, complete with Preston's coaching and advice. But few readers knew the significance of the only mention Cranther added in reference to Anaheim 1995…two words at the end of the caption below Paul in the Fair winner's circle: *Sweet Revenge*.

Paul, Preston and Lori Jupiter reveled in those two words the morning *Cycle News* was delivered. Lori had watched the Anaheim action from the stands and remembered her shock as Paul was deliberately knocked off the track. All these years later she looked across the table at the man who had come from a lapper at Anaheim to the Mann-beating Fairs winner.

"Pretty good old man, pretty good," she said quietly, hoisting her coffee cup in mock salute. Paul just grinned.

Preston looked up from the paper, saw his dad's grin and smiled himself. "I think we're a good team, dad. With you riding and me crewing, we should destroy Colorado." The two male Jupiters high-fived and Lori had to join right in, slapping her open hand against her son's and husband's.

"So Pres, are you racing in Colorado?" Lori asked as innocently as possible. The subject of Preston riding, much less racing, had not come up yet.

Preston shrugged. "I…probably not. I think I'll crew for dad and get my ribs to heal, they're still sore." Preston looked at both his parents and before the pause became awkward Paul jumped up and said, "I can sure use your help. Let's get the coach cleaned, bikes loaded, throw yours in just in case. We'll start for Denver next Sunday."

54

Teddy Hill's riding talent had changed his life and the life of the entire Hill clan. The kid with the big skills had become the talk of Colorado's front range, for several reasons, the first being his honey-smooth speed. The help from the Pearson group didn't hurt either. Then you added in who Teddy's dad was…well, the kid had become quite a phenomenon.

Few could remember another young racer appearing on the scene quite like Teddy Hill, though old timers recalled Tommy Hill fifteen years earlier. Sure, fast-riding kids were coming on all the time but they slowly evolved from a good Pee-Wee to a fast Novice to a quick Expert…and everyone in the paddock watched the evolution. There was no evolution with Teddy Hill. He just appeared at age twelve and went to the front. Bang. A Hill kid off the ranch and onto the podium with almost no time in between. It had happened in the early '90s and it was happening again.

The second reason Teddy Hill had become a local phenomenon was because he didn't race everywhere, all the time, as most kids did in summer. He was busy with the herd and the harvest because the Hill ranch work remained the priority. Teddy wasn't hanging around the pits. Nobody really knew him. As summer wound down, Teddy had run three more Intermediate races with three clear victories, and his first Expert race had resulted in a hard-fought second place. He raced clean and quick and added handsome trophies to the Colorado Springs pit area. Not many, but all top finishes.

◦ «()» ◦

Bill Pearson saw Teddy Hill's raw talent at the Pueblo County Fair and got him aboard a Yamaha, but that wasn't the elder Pearson's best move. His best move was taking the show to the Hill ranch rather than trying to pull Teddy north to Colorado Springs. Bill Pearson's plan began with the vital step of gaining Tom and Judy Hill's blessing.

Pearson had approached the location problem straightforwardly.

"Well, you can guess I would like Teddy running 125s for me… so can I adopt him?" The Hills froze for a moment before laughing along with Pearson. "But really," Bill continued, "we have the problem of us up there and you down here…and Teddy's too young to drive."

"And he's in school and has daily chores here," Judy reminded the older man.

"Yes, I hear you," Bill nodded thoughtfully. "But I have an idea…"

"Oh boy, here we go," Tom joked, pulling his wife closer for support. Tom got a kick out of Pearson and respected the dealership owner. He smiled encouragingly at the older man.

"Alright…look around, what do you see?"

"Our ranch."

"Right. What else?"

Tom and Judy looked at each other and shrugged. "You tell us."

"Mini-Unadilla! And lots of land around it. Here's what we do: I bring my gang down and we build a full-on track. You've got the room. I've got the tractors. Then my boys come down to train with Teddy and you, Tom, with your brother riding and even you, Judy. Am I brilliant or what?"

The Hills looked at each other again and Judy laughed, "He's doing it again, Tom." They looked back at Pearson's expectant face and Tom said, "Let's hear the details."

Pearson grabbed the notebook out of his truck and the Hills shouldn't have been surprised when he flipped it open to reveal twelve pages of plans, notes, drawings and schedules. "Ah…the boys and I have been thinking about this a little…"

An hour later Pearson had laid out a detailed plan not for just the racetrack but which tractors would come and when, where the water truck would be parked, who would maintain the track. He talked about the starting gate they would install, how Mini-Unadilla would be preserved and available for those who wanted an easier track, when his boys would come down…and who would cover all the costs: Bill Pearson.

"Why are you doing this?" the Hills blurted out simultaneously.

Pearson looked them straight in the eye. "A few reasons. First, Teddy can't travel so we're bringing the show to him. Second, my boys have raced and practiced everywhere in the west but we've never had our own land to build the ideal track. Third, your winters are so much milder down here…you get snow but it's gone in two days. You'll see highs in the 40s and 50s, we won't get above freezing on those days…my racers could practice all winter and finally get on par with the racers in the warm states."

Pearson hesitated, cleared his throat nervously and looked away before continuing. "And finally? Your family reminds me of why I got into this sport…the love of riding motorcycles. I started riding again last month and I would love cow-trailing around your ranch, if you'd let me. You won't see me on the track but some of the trail riding Teddy talks about sounds perfect for an old guy like me."

The Hills sat open-mouthed.

"So, I guess I'm being selfish, huh? You can't say no to an old guy like me, can you? All I'm asking is to ride around a little!"

The sparkle in Pearson's eye could be seen from the International Space Station.

Silence from the Hills, their minds spinning. *Would it really work?*

"Are you sure you can do this?" Tom asked, his mind reeling in the face of Bill Pearson's big-thinking world.

"Positive."

55

Pearson's crew arrived at seven AM Friday and by seven PM Monday the track was completed. When the diesel tractors and bulldozers finally pulled back onto the driveway, a national-level motocross track adorned the Hill ranch. Mini-Unadilla remained the core but sections stretching north and west added every component the Pearsons and Hills could think of. Each big jump included a 'roll-around' feature to let lesser riders skip the jump, and the truly huge leaps were tabletop jumps that didn't punish a rider badly if he or she came up short. The track had been built with maintenance in mind so the water truck and tractors could reach every section quickly and easily. Halfway through Saturday Bill Pearson had realized that Tom and his brother Brian were better tractor drivers than the guys he'd hired, so in true Bill Pearson fashion he made a deal to leave the biggest tractor with the Hills and to pay Uncle Brian to do maintenance.

Heaven? That's where Teddy Hill thought he was. The track itself boggled his mind but it was the Pearsons' energy that swept him away. As the track was being knocked out by the big machines, Shane or Ken would fire up their YZ-F, wave the tractor out of the way, and give that particular section a try.

"Build that berm a bit taller...take something off that third whoop...lengthen that run-up another twenty feet," they would yell up to the operator.

As the big machines finally shut down, Teddy heard Shane yell his name. The kid turned toward the barn and there were Shane and Ken in their motocross gear, holding their bikes…and right beside them sat Teddy's bike and all his gear.

"What are you waiting for…an engraved invitation?" yelled Ken. "You get the first lap!"

They rode until dark shut them down.

56

Teddy had held onto the humility the Hill family instilled and the lesson he'd learned during his on-track run-in with Buddy Cleary. Colorado Springs Yamaha had sponsored Teddy and his stellar results could have made his head swell and his attitude turn, but his head stayed normal and his attitude never wavered. Because Teddy had grown up around Tom Hill.

In fact, Teddy's attitude toward school, work and his parents improved…because he had been to the races. He had watched the fast guys, racers like the Pearsons and other Experts…and none of them rode as well as his dad. It keeps a kid humble when his dad can leave him in the dust anytime, anywhere, even on an old two-stroke Suzuki with a bald rear tire. Teddy couldn't count the number of people who recognized his dad at the races and paid their respects with kind words. Tom always thanked them but never seemed to accept their compliments, as if he wasn't really as good as they remembered.

Teddy wondered about that. His dad was so quiet about his riding yet he'd obviously impressed people enough to be remembered fifteen years later.

"Dad," Teddy finally said, "it's neat that those people remember your racing, huh?"

Tom looked at his son, then down at the ground. "It's nice of them to say so…but I was just a local guy, never really got out of Colorado."

"Did you like racing?"

"Loved it…more than anything."

"Would you race again?"

Tom hesitated, sighed. "No son, I took my shot. I just want to ride with you and run the ranch."

Bill Pearson had been about to step out of the transporter but stopped when he heard Teddy's questions. His mind spun at Tom's answer. He stumbled back and leaned against the trailer wall, deep in thought, stunned. *Could I get Tom Hill to race again?* His first reaction was not how much business Tom Hill's racing might bring to his shop but a memory of watching Hill struggle to find enough money to make the step to the nationals back in the day. When the men first met at the Pueblo County Fair, Pearson told Hill that he wished he could have helped him back then…and he meant it. Leaning against the trailer wall, the salesman's mind began to hatch a plan…and the first step was to get his two sons and Teddy and Judy Hill in on it.

57

The weekend before the Colorado State Fair races the Hill track was a busy place. Shane and Ken had qualified for the Fairs and were past podium-finishers there but each arrived at the Hill ranch with five or six new combinations of suspension and engine tuning to test. Ken's testing regimen on the 250 just involved chassis and ignition tweaks but Shane planned to try not just a new shock and fork but a completely revised cylinder head. The Pearson boys arrived with the team's trailer and their chief mechanic, Sam Biganski, ready to work through their combinations in preparation for their run at the Fairs.

But things went wrong for Shane off the double jump at the far end of the track, on just his third lap. He disappeared from view on the landing and there was a sudden silence and no YZ-F450 reappeared. The entire group of Pearsons, Hills and Biganski scrambled and found Shane lying under his bike, groaning and holding his right knee. His testing day was finished because he could hardly walk; Biganski got him back to the trailer and sat him down with an ice pack.

"How'd that combo feel?" asked the tuner as everyone milled around Shane.

"Weak in the middle," Shane replied with a groan. "I ran up that double and there was just no pop off the lip, the thing just nosed over. Even off the slow corners it ran out of steam. No way that thing's gonna win the Fairs the way it sits."

Silence settled over the group. Biganski said, "Then you gotta get out there and try this new head, or at least let me tweak the ECU."

Shane flexed his knee and immediately cried in pain. He looked up at Biganski. "No way I'm riding today."

Biganski appeared lost in thought, then turned to Ken. "We got to get you on that 450 to test these setups or Shane's in big trouble for the Fairs. There's not enough practice time there to get this thing right."

Ken backed away and said, "No way Bignasty...I've got too many things to try on my 250, plus...I don't ride that 450 worth beans."

Silence reigned in the trailer. Everyone looked at Ken and understood. The step from a YZ-F250 to the 450 was mammoth and nobody could blame the younger Pearson.

Biganski snapped his fingers, spun to Tom Hill and said, "Tom... you could test these combos...just ride the bike and tell me 'better' or 'worse'."

Hill, caught by surprise, laughed out loud. "Sorry Sam, I've never ridden a four-stroke racebike...I'd be no help."

Shane straightened and blurted, "No, wait! Sam, that's a great idea...Tom, you could do it. You could get that thing figured out...I may not be able to practice much at the Fairs if this knee is sore but if you and Bignasty could get this thing right I could jump on it just for the race."

Tom looked straight at Shane and replied slowly and clearly. "I hear you...but I have no experience on a bike like this. I'd be no help."

Bill Pearson stepped in: "Boys, you better figure this out. I have a business to run, selling Yamahas. If Honda wins the Fairs in my state, Honda sells a lot of bikes in my state. Tom, Shane's bike can't win a drag race against a Pinewood Derby car right now. You could really help us out. How about if you just run some acceleration tests for Sam?"

Tom looked around the group, saw Teddy nodding as he mouthed "Do it."

Judy looked up from attending to Ken's icepack and found her husband's eyes focused on her. Judy hesitated…she had seen the ugly aftermath of Anaheim…but had also seen Tom rule at the club level in Colorado. She knew how quick he rode. Judy swallowed and said "You could really help this team Tom."

Tom ran his hand through his hair and expelled a big breath. "All right Sam, I'll run a few passes up and down the driveway. Let me grab my gear."

Everyone in the trailer watched as Tom entered the barn to get his gear. As the elder Hill's back disappeared through the doorway, the trailer erupted in a spontaneous but hushed cheer of victory. Bill Pearson's plan was working! Shane got up and walked unassisted across the trailer to shake his dad's hand.

"You are a genius, sir," Shane said with a smile and mock bow of his head.

"And you…all of you, actually," Bill replied, looking at Sam, Judy, Ken and Teddy, "are worthy of an Oscar! I've never seen such good acting!"

Bill reached for Judy's hand, taking it gently, giving it a squeeze. "Judy…thanks for supporting this. I know you weren't crazy about the plan but we both know how much Tom's gonna love a new bike like this. Let's just offer him the chance…'cause it's a chance he never had."

Judy squeezed his hand in thanks. Thanks for giving her husband and son an opportunity few dirt bike riders ever get.

Teddy looked at Mr. Pearson and giggled out loud. He'd never seen anyone like this man and his sons. In this week's sixth-grade vocabulary lesson, one of the words was *audacious* and Teddy looked at the living definition right here in the race trailer.

"You're audacious," Teddy said in his quiet voice. The trailer erupted in laughter.

58

Tom had listened to Teddy's wondrous comments about the new four-stroke motocrossers and his first blast down the driveway on Shane's 450 brought his son's comments into focused clarity.

"Holy Moley," he muttered as he squeezed on the brakes to make a u-turn. He picked up the throttle half-way through the turn and the engine's linearity let him drift through the rest of the swing with precision not always available on his pipey two-stroke 250.

Everybody there was watching, while pretending not to watch or even care…they all saw the 450 drift off the turn and snap up into a second- and third-gear wheelie as Tom headed back to the trailer to confer with Sam. Next trip down, following a quick timing change by Sam, Tom swerved into the depression next to the driveway, then snapped the bike left and bunny-hopped all the way across the driveway. He stood on the pegs and drifted the rear end through fourth and into fifth gear before shutting it down and whipping a donut to head back to Sam.

Sam and the Pearsons wanted to ask Tom, "How do you like it?" but refrained from showing their burning curiosity. Sam stayed busy by lining up the next tests, while Bill and Ken worked on changing the shock on Ken's bike. Shane sat in his chair, his perfectly-good knee freezing, pretending to confer with Sam, while Judy peaked out the kitchen window with Teddy by her side.

"Whadya think, kid?" she asked.

"He looks comfortable…bet he loves it."

"Yep," she answered quietly. "And this is the first time he's ridden a bike less than six years old."

Teddy nodded. He'd already imagined how fast his dad would be on a current bike.

The next few changes Sam had Tom test were quick changes but then the new cylinder head was unboxed and Sam told Tom it would take him forty minutes to install it. Tom sat down next to Shane and asked about his knee, then said, "Man, that bike really accelerates. Do you let it run to the top of each gear or shift it early?"

As Sam worked on the bike, Shane and Tom discussed riding an open-class motocrosser. Before they knew it, Biganski was calling Tom for another run up the driveway.

"You guys were discussing revs? This head should make a difference but I don't want to tell you what to feel, I want you to tell me. It's ready."

Tom took three runs up and down the driveway before returning to the trailer, nodding.

"Okay," he began. "There's a lot more over-rev at the top, it doesn't quit making power like other head, it just starts to get a bit soft but at higher rpm. That lets me upshift with more revs and now it's topped out just before the bridge. What I noticed most was how much quicker it revved off the bottom, like you changed the flywheel. This setup is the best so far."

The entire trailer had stopped working as Tom Hill completed the longest run of words anyone had ever heard from him. He looked around and realized he was the center of attention and felt a bit sheepish at his open show of enthusiasm. Sam jumped in to cover the silence.

"Great! I was hoping this combo would do that…this head has sodium-filled titanium valves and I ported it from specs Tony

Halverson at US Yamaha gave me. It's got a touch more compression too…did it detonate?"

Tom shook his head.

"Great," Sam said again. "Well, that's it for engine testing, so thanks for standing in for Shane. The rest of the chassis stuff we'll try to get sorted next week at the Fairs."

Bill Pearson cleared his throat and tried to sound casual. "Unless you want to run some laps to, you know…give Sam some feedback."

Everybody held their breath.

Tom looked at Bill, at Sam and back at the bike. A shadow of a smile creased his lips as he looked Bill Pearson in the eye.

"You know…I *would* like to run a few laps on that thing."

59

Tom's desire to lap Shane's 450 didn't surprise Bill Pearson. He knew the hours the Hills had spent looking at magazines and talking about the new bikes, while maintaining their second-hand stuff and making the most of what they had. He'd watched Tom study Ken and Shane lapping, watched as Tom examined every detail of the four-strokers. Tom might have been initially hesitant to ride Shane's bike but now that the bug had bit the elder Hill just had to try it around the track.

The hidden interest from everyone on the ranch became outright interest as Tom idled onto the track for the first lap. Judy and Teddy stood alongside Bill and Ken while Sam helped the 'injured' Shane into a trackside chair and Uncle Brian came out of the garage where he'd been pretending to change oil on the quad.

True to form, Tom spent the first lap cruising while standing on the pegs and rup-rupping around the course but warm-up ended quickly and positively as the 450 arced into the air to begin the second lap. Tom seemed to hang in the air like a hovering hawk, the ranch silent as the quickest rider Colorado had ever seen squeezed on a little rear brake to lower the nose for landing.

In that moment, Bill Pearson flashed back 20 years to the first time he'd seen this guy ride. It was Tom's ability to catapult off jumps at insane speeds, then make any and every adjustment necessary to line-up the landing that other riders couldn't imitate. Where other riders rolled off as they left the jump's lip, Hill would be hard in the throttle and somehow soak up the impact and seemingly float. It reminded Pearson of a cat jumping, the quick explosion of muscles, then the float to the landing.

Hill was floating now, adjusting and making the incremental movements to soften the landing and get the 450's power down the moment the rear tire touched. It was motorized ballet, a dance done only by those few who could remain smooth and unruffled while setting lap records. Safe to say, Ken and Shane had never vaulted off this first jump as Tom did on only his second lap. A collective outlet of "Wow" emerged from the watching group.

"Hello, Tom Hill," Bill Pearson said aloud. For the next ten laps Tom Hill got up close and personal with Yamaha's YZ-F450.

Teddy hadn't gotten his lap charts going yet for the new track but no-one doubted that Tom's first ten laps on the 450 were the quickest on the new track. When he pulled in, everybody present reverted to the disinterested routine but couldn't miss Tom's smile and strong words of praise for the bike. The elder Hill and Biganski worked through two different chassis setups that the team wanted to try, and by the end of the afternoon Shane's bike was ready for the Fairs.

But Bill Pearson's plan wasn't yet complete.

60

As the Pearsons finished loading their trailer for the trip back to Colorado Springs, Biganski rolled out a brand-new 450 and popped it up on a race stand. The price tag and information card still hung from the handlebar and Biganski returned with an owner's manual and a box with oil, oil filter and an air filter. The tuner leaned a new front and rear tire against the bike and continued getting the hauler ready for the pull north.

Tom had returned to the barn to shrug out of his riding gear and when he came out just before twilight Bill Pearson motioned him over to the team trailer.

"Tom, with Shane's knee like this, we've got another problem. He was going to break-in this YZ as his backup bike for the Fairs but we've got to rest his knee all week. I need you to get some miles on this thing, change the oil, lever on those new tires and bring it up to the Fairs next weekend. I know you and Teddy are coming to watch the boys so I hope you can get this bike ready and bring it with you."

Tom hadn't caught on to Shane's fake injury or Bill's plan but now a whiff of something off kilter caught his notice. He took a long look at Bill and could see the gleam in his eye and the smile just playing on the older man's lips.

"You sneaky old dog," Tom laughed. "You don't need to leave me a bike to ride, I've got my 250 and I'm fine with it."

Pearson's smile broke out full and wide. He knew that Tom still didn't realize what lay at the heart of his plan. He clapped the younger man on the shoulder.

"Let's just say it's a thank-you for helping Shane and Bignasty. Plus, you only get it for a week and we *do* need it as a backup bike. Double-plus, you'll have to do some work…new oil, new tires, maybe an air filter. Hey, I enjoyed watching you ride a modern bike and I know you'll have a fun week."

Tom looked at the 450, the price tag, the owner's manual and he couldn't contain the giddy feeling of having a brand-new 450 all to himself, even if only for a week. He had spent time around new bikes in showrooms and raced against them on the track but he had never owned one. This unscuffed, shiney-clean blue Yamaha was a life-long dream.

"You are a salesman, Mr. Bill Pearson. We'll deliver it to the Fairs first thing Saturday. And thanks."

61

As the Jupiters were prepping, loading and driving north from California, Tom and Teddy Hill were having the time of their lives on Bill Pearson's Yamahas. It was pure fun, just as a meal purchased for you is extra delicious. For the first time in Hill ranch history, new bikes sat in the old red barn. The ranch work carried on, Teddy attended school…but the focus of those five days before the Fairs was enjoying and exploring the tremendous capabilities of these new Yamahas. The most amazing thing to Tom about the new 450 was its ability to absolutely swallow the bumps, ruts and whoops. He found himself attacking in places he'd be rolling off on his 250, accelerating where he'd hold steady throttle and smiling more often while circulating at lap times his old 250 could not touch.

Teddy lost count of the times his dad said, "Things have come a long way, Teddy." The younger Hill wanted to hug Bill Pearson for giving his dad such a joyous week but never once did Teddy reveal Pearson's grand plan: getting his dad to race the Fairs in Denver.

The Hills planned to leave at 4:00 Saturday morning for the four-hour drive to the Denver track, so Friday afternoon's riding was cut short and father and son went to work on the 450 as Tom had promised. Country music filled the Hill workshop as Tom pulled the wheels and Teddy handled the oil change, each Hill occasionally talking about the bikes, the upcoming Fairs, the Pearsons, the new track. Little talk, much work.

More than once Tom marveled at how nice it was to work on a new bike, a machine without stripped fasteners, years of corrosion, broken spokes or worn-out chain and sprockets. Over the years, the Hill clan had seen it all…except a new bike. Tom tried to remain thankful for the week's riding but one side of his brain was sad to see it go. He would occasionally glance at his 250 and the comparison between the two bikes was a contrast too stark to ignore.

And Tom's feelings weren't lost on Teddy. As they finished up the maintenance, Teddy snapped off the stereo and said, "If the stock sale goes well this year, you need a new 450 dad."

Tom spun around from the doorway of the barn and grabbed Teddy, lifting the kid off his feet in a bear hug. "Need a new bike? Me?" he thundered in a make-believe monster voice. He spun in a big circle with Teddy and shouted, "But I'm untouchable on my 250! I rule this ranch! Me and my 250 rule this ranch! We need nothing!!" The two Hills wrestled a bit and the run was on to the house, both riders laughing and pushing at each other to be first in the door.

"That was funny dad," Teddy said. "You reminded me of Ken and Shane."

Not such a bad thing, Tom thought. The Pearson family had brought a new light to the Hill ranch.

62

Sixty miles west of Denver snowflakes began sprinkling down on the California motorhome. The white stuff surprised the Jupiters but the radio made it clear that snow in September wasn't uncommon when you're a mile high in the Rocky Mountains…but this much snow was.

They reached the Colorado State Fairgrounds in a blizzard and lined up with hundreds of other racers to gain access to the pits. The Jupiter motorhome idled along with the stream of traffic, standing out from the crowd of vans and smaller rigs but victim of the same blinding snowstorm.

"No, we haven't seen it this bad for a long time," answered the girl signing the racers in at the gate. "Have fun!"

"Ever raced in the snow, dad?"

"Not me!" Paul exclaimed in a sing-song voice. "I'm a SoCal boy…I'm not even good in the mud! I want hard-pack, cement bumps, rock faces on the jumps…"

Preston laughed. Then Paul's face got a bit more serious.

"I'm not that worried about the weather, actually. Everybody's got to race on the same track so it evens things out. I'll get a handle on it." He paused. "What I should worry about is how quick some of the Colorado boys are…"

Preston laughed again, thinking his dad was joking…but stopped when he saw his dad's serious look. "Really?"

"You watch. It's different than California. You won't see as many fast guys in each class…but you'll see two or three, maybe four… guys who can really go quick. California has deeper fields, but the competition at the front here is tough, tough. Colorado has produced quite a few quick guys…Andrew Short, for instance."

"He's from here?"

"Yep. Won the Fairs two years ago and now look at him. The other thing about Colorado is how much money and effort these guys put into their bikes. I think it's because they have all winter to fiddle with them, while we SoCal guys just ride them into the dirt." He laughed. "But actually it's the altitude. These guys build their engines to get back the power the altitude robs."

As the rig's generator idled in the blinding snowstorm, Paul explained the power-robbing effects of altitude. They watched a movie and bedded down for the evening, looking forward to sign-up in the morning.

63

Tom and Teddy left for Denver punctually Saturday morning, the 450 strapped to the Suburban's bumper. As they cleared Pueblo and approached Colorado Springs, an hour south of Denver, snow flurries hazed the windshield. As the Suburban climbed out of the Springs, the flurries turned serious and snow began pelting down in huge white flakes.

"I guess this is why Bill wanted to build a practice track at the ranch," Tom said to his son. "It's still nice there." Teddy nodded, wondering if the fast guys at the Fairs raced in the snow.

Motocross races at State Fairs do run in the snow but not in the amount Denver received that Friday and Saturday. The Colorado Fairs organizers had contingency plans in case of bad weather, ways to change the track if it flooded, moving the paddock, even handling spectator parking. The final contingency plan, never used in the seventeen-year history of the Fairs races, was to postpone the racing one week. As Saturday morning dawned, it became clear that no motorsports would happen anywhere in northern Colorado. In fact, the entire State Fair was closed and scheduled to re-open six days later, on the following Friday.

Twelve miles from the track, Tom had to slip the Suburban into four-wheel high to push through the two feet of snow accumulated on the highway up to the track. The Colorado Springs Yamaha hauler wasn't hard to find and the Suburban crunched to a stop just as Bill, Shane and Ken Pearson emerged, Shane still pretending to hobble on a painful knee. The Hills and Pearsons greeted each other and before they could talk about anything substantial, the loudspeaker announced a rider's meeting in the lounge under the starter's tower.

"Let's go see what's happening," Bill Pearson said.

"Wait!" It was Ken's urgent voice and everyone turned to look.

"I gotta get my snowshoes!"

In an instant the tension of the weather dissolved and the group of men and boys was laughing. Bill Pearson was shaking his head and in the next moment Shane and Ken had grabbed Teddy and lifted him high onto their shoulders, just as they had done at the Pueblo County Fair.

"He's too little to walk in this snow, he'll disappear!" Laughing and stumbling through the snow, the Hills and Pearsons joined the riders filing into the lounge. Teddy was finally set down in the warm room and could look around at the fastest motocross riders in Colorado.

64

The big room was filled with over one hundred riders and it appeared to Teddy that just about everyone was looking at Ken and Shane Pearson, standing with him. Greetings were exchanged and it took a few minutes before Teddy noticed that his dad was getting more than a few nods and hellos.

An older gentleman asked, "Tom, are you racing the Fairs?"

You could almost feel the Pearsons and Teddy holding their breath as Tom turned to the questioner.

"Me? No, no. Here to watch the Pearsons. I don't race, I'm not qualified."

The man nodded and chuckled, "Well, the Seniors will be happy to hear that! But you know, any rider who has qualified for an AMA national is exempt from Fair qualifying. Your run at Anaheim means you could enter any Fair. Charlie Mann does it for KTM all the time."

Bill Pearson glanced at his sons. He counted on this qualifying loophole in his plan to get Tom Hill to the starting line. The older Pearson shrugged and raised his eyebrows at Ken and Shane. *Oh well*, he seemed to say, *at least now he knows about being qualified.* None of this was lost on young Teddy.

Tom didn't even bat an eyelash. "Well, I wouldn't have much for those fast guys anyway."

"That's funny," the man replied as he stuck out his hand. "Good to see you again Tom."

He turned and walked back to a group of racers across the room and shook his head *no* as he approached them, answering the question many Seniors were wondering. Most of the Seniors qualified for the Colorado State Fair had been in the sport a long time...they couldn't beat Tom Hill twenty years ago so few thought they could now, especially when Hill looked so fit.

At that moment the PA crackled to life and all eyes moved to the front of the room where three men stood on the small stage. In the center stood a tall grey-haired man who raised the microphone.

"Can you hear me?"

The entire room responded *yes* and the tall man continued. "Okay, good. First practice starts in thirty minutes."

The room erupted in laughter and that's just what Carry Mathers wanted. He knew the tension in pre-race rider meetings and the weather wasn't helping much.

"All right," Mathers continued as the laughter died. "I'm Carry Mathers, this is Lance Black and Jay Holst. For those who don't know us, we run the Colorado Motocross division for the AMA and the Colorado State Fair race. Lance here is personally in charge of the weather."

Boos chorused, and more laughter. Black laughed along with Mathers and took a mock bow.

Mathers continued. "This is the first time in our seventeen-year history that we've had to reschedule the races to next weekend." The crowd was silent. "Next week's schedule will mirror the original schedule in your entry booklet, no changes. We will have a rider's meeting seven days from now, right here. Any questions?"

"What if we can't make it next week?" a rider in the middle of the room asked.

"We'll refund your entry fee, or carry your entry fee into the next

Fairs, your choice. Ah, Dave…why can't you make next week?"

The man replied: "Our new baby is due next Friday."

"So what's the problem?" Mathers deadpanned. The room burst into laughter again.

"Any other questions?"

"What's the forecast?" this question from the back of the room.

Black handed Mathers a sheet of paper.

"Okay, forecast: Snow stops this afternoon, freezing temps through Monday night…but next week will be warm and getting warmer. Should be low- to mid-sixties by the weekend."

Mathers scanned the room and added: "The entire Colorado State Fair is being postponed, so you can expect big crowds next weekend, just like the last five years. Crews will start working first-thing tomorrow to get the track and paddock ready for next week. More questions?"

Seeing that there were no more questions, Mathers closed the meeting and the group filed out into the snow.

65

"Is that Tommy Hill?" a man's voice called out as the Hills and Pearsons shuffled toward the exit. The group turned as one to spot the questioner and saw a man roughly Tom's age wave to them from across the room. Next to the man was a tall teenage boy, clearly his son to judge from the eyes and hair, but with two bruised eyes and a bandage on his nose. Both man and son wore a silver ball cap with a small rocket on the front.

"I'm Tom Hill."

"Hang on," Paul Jupiter replied, "I want to say hello." Paul then turned to his son and said, "C'mon Preston, I want you to meet someone."

The Jupiters eased across the room and Paul introduced himself and Preston. Teddy hung back but had recognized Preston's name from his youth-racing blog. The kid was going to say hello but Preston moved behind his dad, looking down at the floor, then around the room, everywhere but at the group. Teddy saw his injuries and realized that he hadn't seen blogs from Preston Jupiter since school started. Now he knew why. The kid looked whipped.

"We came up from SoCal to race your Fairs and this is the weather we get?" Paul asked with a smile.

Bill Pearson liked this pair immediately and replied for the group, "Well, we usually race in hurricanes and tornadoes but a little snow mixes things up a bit." Everybody chuckled but all eyes were on Paul.

"If you're from Cali, how do you know Tom?" Ken asked in his usual outgoing manner. It was the question everybody was wondering.

"Well," Paul smiled. "First of all, he looks the same as he did fifteen years ago, how does that happen?"

Tom shrugged, obviously embarrassed as all eyes turned to him.

"But seriously," Paul continued, "Tom and I both entered the Anaheim Supercross in '95, both of us privateers. I remember his van had Colorado plates and was the only vehicle in the paddock that looked worse than my old pickup. If you remember, Tom, the organizers put us in the last row, back against the fence."

"Yep, I remember," Tom replied with a slow smile. "You had that brown Ford F150 with the ladder rack on it, right?"

"That was me."

"Yeah…we didn't exactly fit in with that crowd, huh?"

"That's an understatement," Paul laughed. "I pretty much did what everybody expects of a privateer…crashed in the first turn of my heat race and finished way back, no chance of making the main event. I'm not sure I was quick enough to make the main even if I hadn't crashed."

Paul shook his head, almost as if shaking off the memory.

"But I remember Tommy Hill…in fact, Preston here knows your story too." Preston nodded, glancing at the group. "You not only qualified for the main but ran up front. You were into sixth, weren't you?"

Tom answered quietly: "I might have run sixth or seventh."

"Man, you should have heard us yelling for you…all of us who were there on our own nickel to take on the big boys…we were screaming our lungs out. We waited for you after the race but you were in the hospital, right?"

Tom looked down, then back up to Paul. "Yep, I tore up my knee and a few other things."

"Well, we threw your bike into your van before they kicked us out of the paddock but all the privateers wanted to slap you on the back. Hell of a race, Tom."

"It didn't end well," Tom replied in a quiet monotone.

66

The Pearsons, Hills and Jupiters were the last riders in the meeting room and Tom's terse comment silenced the group. Clearly the Anaheim crash had ended Tom's racing career but nobody knew the details. Not only had the injuries taken months to heal but the cost of the medical services, bike repairs and travel had devastated the Hills. If you don't finish, you don't earn prize money. Tom finished in the hospital—always expensive.

Tom's dad Carl and mom Elsa never mentioned the expense of their son's crash. Tom's twin brother Brian had to fly into Los Angeles to collect Tom from the LA County hospital, pick up his van and then drive the seventeen hours home to the ranch. The cost of the airline ticket, the cost of the taxi to the hospital and then to the Anaheim track were nothing compared to the hospital and ambulance-service bills. Those unexpected costs had to be covered with savings.

But the Hill savings weren't enough.

By the time the twins arrived back at the ranch Carl and Elsa had arranged a short-term loan through Walsenburg Credit to buoy up the depleted funds and get them through the winter. That spring Carl sold seventy-five percent of the ranch's cattle, about double the number of cows usually moved through auction. By the time summer rolled around, Carl and Elsa had repaid Walsenburg Credit and were again debt-free thanks to forced frugality that pinched hard.

As Tom crutched around the ranch, then limped through rehab on his beat-up knee, he promised himself to forget about racing and put all his energies into rebuilding his dad's ranch. *I had my shot at the big-time and screwed up,* Tom told himself again and again as he watched his family struggle to get back on its feet. It was the spring after Anaheim that Tom proposed to Judy and redirected his passion towards his family and ranch.

Paul looked over at Tom in the silent meeting room and could feel the tension of the elder Hill's words. Paul laughed to break the moment.

"Yeah, but you're here now, racing the Fairs!"

All heads swiveled from Paul to Tom. If anything, the tension ratcheted up a notch and Paul and Preston couldn't understand their new friends' solemnity. Tom shook his head and dropped his eyes.

"Nope. I quit racing after Anaheim."

Paul didn't understand and blurted out, "But Tom…I know the crash sucked, but everybody has mechanical failures! It happens!"

Tom's head snapped up and his eyes shot sparks at Paul. "Mechanical? Do you call casing the doubles a mechanical failure? I don't. I cross-rutted and then spent the winter on crutches with my family working sixteen hours a day to make up for my mistake. My parents almost lost that ranch because of my crash. I don't kid myself about crashes and if you do, well…"

Tom glared at Paul and his words hung in the room. Bill stepped forward and put his hand on Tom's arm.

"Easy Tom, we hear ya." Pearson could feel the iron tension in Hill's arm.

Paul took a step back and his hands came up in an act of self-defense. "Wait, wait…Tom…"

Preston had stood mute behind his father the whole time, but he looked quickly up at his dad.

"Dad…the video…we've got it here."

Paul met his son's eyes and then clapped him on the shoulder. "You're a genius."

He then readdressed Tom. "You need to come to my motorhome."

67

The Pearsons and Hills slogged through the snow behind the Jupiters, arriving at the largest motorhome the Coloradoans had ever seen.

"Yeah, this will do, let's just live here," Ken joked in an attempt to lighten the mood. It failed. The men and boys loaded into the palatial motorhome in silence. Nobody knew how tough Tom's crash had been but they were beginning to understand. Bill Pearson knew Tom's Anaheim tumble had ended his racing but he hadn't tried to keep tabs on Hill in those days. He had no idea how close the Hills had come to bankruptcy. All because of a racing crash.

Preston went to the cabinet over the driver's area and slid open a door to reveal a flat-screen TV while Paul offered the group drinks. Nobody accepted. Preston then began rummaging around a second cabinet, searching for the video of the 1995 Anaheim Supercross that Paul's friend David Henkle had shot. Meanwhile, Teddy Hill stood gawking in the center of the motorhome, partly aware of his father's uneasiness and partly blown away by the grandeur of the Jupiter setup.

Paul saw the kid's amazement and smiled.

"Teddy, let me show you the best part while Pres loads that video." The elder Jupiter led the youngster through the galley, past the bathroom to the door leading to the garage. "Ready?"

Teddy nodded, then couldn't restrain a "Wow!" when Paul revealed the motocross bikes snuggled into the rear garage. Just then Preston announced, "Got it!"

68

The fifteen-year-old video started with Henkle's voice announcing the location followed by jittery images of the drive into the Anaheim paddock area.

"My buddy Dave raced a little, but not at this level...he came out to wrench for me but really I think he just wanted to be in the pits at a Supercross," Paul explained as the videographer jumped down, then panned to reveal Paul's old Ford truck and, further away, the factory big rigs.

"Preston, we can fast-forward through this stuff."

"No!" the three Pearson's blurted out simultaneously. "This is too cool," Shane said. "Let's watch it all."

The video continued in stops and starts. Henkle had turned on the camera when something interesting caught his eye and he'd narrate while he was shooting. He went from Paul's parking area to a shot of the Honda rig to Johnny O'mara walking out of the riders' meeting to a slow pan of the Honda factory area.

"This is heaven right here, the Honda pits. Looks like two wrenches per bike," Henkle intoned as he focused on two mechanics hovering over the '12' bike on a work stand, minus its wheels.

"These guys asked me to ride this weekend but I have to tune for Paul...so...they got Bailey instead." Henkle laughed at his own comedy but the watchers in the motorhome hardly cracked a smile because the discomfort steaming off Tom Hill was palpable.

Henkle wandered away from the Honda pit, panned across the paddock to see Bob Hannah duck under the banners into the Yamaha pit. Henkle called out, "Hannah!" and the Yamaha star just gave a backhand wave without even looking. Henkle laughed into the video camera's microphone, "That, my friends, is the fastest boy on earth."

Next time the camera clicked on was to watch Jeff Ward sign autographs next to David Bailey, Bailey's dad in the background. The Pearsons and Hills were entranced with this time-capsule video the Jupiters had in their collection and the mood relaxed slightly, for everyone except Tom. He hadn't the time to walk around the pits at Anaheim and as he watched Henkle's footage he remembered how hard he'd worked to prep for this Supercross.

69

For Hill, it wasn't simply a matter of jumping on his bike and running in the first practice. Yes, his bike was prepped and clean, but had arrived in California with Colorado jetting and tires designed to work on the clay of his home state. Hill had unloaded his bike, strapped on his helmet and run up and down the practice area to determine what mixture changes to make in the carburetor. The first guess gets close but richer and leaner jetting must be tried to make sure of the right choices of main and pilot, plus needle position. While Henkle roamed the paddock, Hill's fingers dripped gasoline.

Hill had stood in the Dunlop tire tent for a few dazed minutes, watching the gigantic operation before him. His local club support brought a tire machine and about two hundred tires to the races in Colorado but this Anaheim Supercross effort seemed ten times larger. Tire machines were everywhere, the sound of compressed air hissed, beads popped and techs in yellow bustled back and forth.

"What do you need?" a tall Dunlop tech finally asked Tom.

"I'm Tommy Hill, entered in the 250 class. What do you recommend for this weekend?"

The tech checked Hill's pass.

"You're out of Colorado, aren't you?"

"Yep"

"I'm Denny Smith," the Dunlop man said, giving Hill's hand a shake. "You guys probably run the A302 mostly...or the B?"

"I've been on the A a few times."

Hill didn't mention that he ran whatever hand-me-down-tires, or take-offs, were available from local track tire suppliers. They were rarely Dunlops but he liked Dunlops best.

"Yeah, well, that thing's gonna be too hard down here. We're putting guys on this new B430." Smith leaned behind the desk and brought out a new knobby.

"The knobs are taller and we've spaced them out. You'd tear this thing up in half a moto where you're from but it's perfect for down here. Plan on one set for practice and qualifying, a new rear for the heat and new set for the main. That's what I'm recommending for the 250s."

Hill took the tire from Smith and it did indeed feel softer, more pliable.

"Alright. But I'm here on a budget. One set will have to stretch the whole weekend."

Smith's eyes narrowed and he noted Tommy Hill's matter-of-fact tone, his straightforward manner and the fact that he was looking Smith directly in the eye, without shame. Smith had a quick flashback to his own racing career, arriving at Daytona with a dream and $173 in his pocket. He had clawed his way through the main and arrived back in Tennessee with the purse from a ninth place finish, about twenty-times the amount of money he'd left with. That had bought a new bike and launched a terrific career.

"Well," Smith said slowly. "That's gonna be tough but I've seen it done. Have you got Dunlop stickers on your bike?"

"I don't."

"Alright," Smith paused in thought. "Do this: Dunlop stickers on the forks and swingarm. You buy the first set of tires for $142 and if you tear them up, I'll slide you some take-offs from the big boys.

You bring us your wheels and we'll swap out the tires. Good?"

Hill and Smith shook hands and Tom left the tent with his first set of new tires, four stickers and a new friend. Smith's effort to help Hill was vindicated when the Colorado kid breezed through practice and qualified easily for the main by running a tight fifth in his heat. The only new components on Hill's Yamaha were the Dunlop stickers and the fresh tires Smith gifted Hill with before the main.

"You've earned these. Bring over your extra wheels and let's get you set up."

"Don't have extras, I'll pull these and be right over."

70

Tom's attention snapped back to the video as Henkle announced the first heat and shot video from just behind the mechanic's area, a location that could only catch the bikes over one jump and on the pit straight. Henkle was focusing on the first heat because Hannah and Bailey were in it, plus Jeff Emig and Brock Glover. Henkle was clearly a Hannah fan as he excitedly announced the proceedings that the men in the motorhome could only see for a short burst. Bailey just edged Hannah and Henkle claimed that Hannah couldn't care less about a heat race and was saving himself for the main. Henkle jogged back to Jupiter's pit with the camera on.

"Let's get Paul ready." And the camera clicked off.

The camera started again with a view of the starting line and Henkle announcing that Paul Jupiter, lined up with Charlie Mann, Paul Thede, Mike Bell, Brian Myerscoff and the O-Show O'mara, was in the silver helmet about six bikes in from the left. Henkle had made his way up to the second level of the finish-line tower and the camera panned down the thirty riders but then zoomed in on Jupiter as the gate fell. Jupiter's start wasn't bad but the young privateer was cannon-balled over and lay in a heap with six other bikes in the first turn.

"The highlight of my Supercross career," Paul Jupiter muttered in the silent motorhome.

"Hey, you were there, trying," Bill Pearson offered.

"Yeah, but it gets worse."

Henkle had remained focused on Jupiter and the Californian got his bike refired and took off at the back of the pack. Henkle followed him for the next two laps of the eight-lap heat, then began focusing on the leaders for the next five laps. Henkle found Jupiter again…and a rush of air escaped from the lungs of the men in the motorhome when Charlie Mann punted Jupiter over the berm.

"That sucked! He was lapping you!" Ken blurted.

"Yeah, I was something like twenty-fourth."

Preston reached out and froze the video with the remote and then looked from his dad to the group standing in the motorhome, then back to his dad.

The young Jupiter then turned to the rest of the group, animation lighting his face for the first time all morning.

"And guess what?" he asked the Hills and Pearsons.

All heads turned to look at Preston, who up to that point had said almost nothing.

"Mann entered the California Fairs two weeks ago and my dad hole-shotted him and beat him!"

A mini cheer erupted, with Ken clapping enthusiastically.

"Bet that felt good!"

Paul was smiling and nodding his head. "Especially after seeing this video again. Don't let 'em kid you, revenge is sweet!!"

71

The air had gone out of Henkle's sails and the next time the camera clicked on was to categorize the damages to Jupiter's machine, damages that would take months to fix on a carpenter's salary.

Jupiter tried to put on a brave face for the camera but his bandaged finger said it all. Paul finally said: "Dave, turn that thing off. Let's go get a beer and watch the main."

The camera clicked on as the Anaheim Supercross main event started, with both Henkle and Jupiter narrating. Jupiter had recovered his good humor and Henkle made him laugh by narrating as if Jupiter was leading the factory boys into the first turn. Henkle and Jupiter had ensconced themselves in the start-finish tower again and the footage was surprisingly clear, especially through the final portion of the track.

Two laps into the main, Jupiter started cheering for Tommy Hill. "Go Privateers!" Jupiter would yell every time Hill cleared the start-finish jump.

"Where is he now, Dave?"

"Ninth, maybe tenth. He's killing 'em in those three bowl turns but gives it back in the whoops. But I can't stop shooting Hannah, Ward, and Bailey. Here comes Wardy with McGrath and now Emig on his rear tire!!"

The race for the podium at Anaheim was epic. Fans still talk about that race…it involved all the factories and kept the crowd on its feet the entire twenty-six laps. Hill had never seen the race and watched with rapt attention as the fastest riders in the world battled for supremacy.

Hill was mentioned again on lap ten.

"Don't look now Paul but your Colorado boy is clear in seventh."

"Go Privateers!" screamed Paul. "Shoot him this lap."

The camera showed riders streaming past and then focused on a yellow Yamaha firing out of the final bowl and into the straight before the final jump.

"Dad! That's you? Is that you?" Teddy asked in barely-controlled excitement.

"It is," admitted Tom. "Your grandpa bought me that Yamaha jersey as an eighteenth birthday present."

Hill attacked the final jump and soared into the air, correcting minutely to put the bike on the ground with the throttle pinned.

The motorhome erupted again in spontaneous applause. The shot was impressive.

"Awesome," Ken said. "Just awesome."

Henkle focused on the leaders for the next two laps but Jupiter kept up with Tom's progress and chimed in verbally occasionally. Hill had caught Myerscoff for sixth and it was as epic as the fight for first.

"Man, I'm getting worn-out just watching!" Jupiter said on the video. "Dave, shoot Hill and Myerscoff for a few laps."

Henkle shot the leaders going by, then panned back to the final corner to catch Myerscoff and Hill. The camera recorded the pair as they launched; as they reached the zenith of their flight, the video froze. Paul Jupiter held the remote.

"See anything?" Jupiter asked.

The group studied the flat screen looking for whatever Paul saw. There was a general shaking of heads.

"Okay, let's fast-forward." Paul zipped the camera ahead and hit play just as Hill led Myerscoff out of the final corner on lap eighteen. Again, Jupiter froze the action mid-jump.

"Now?"

Everyone in the motorhome's main room took a step closer to the screen.

"Is...is his rear wheel coming apart?" Bill Pearson asked.

"Let's go another lap." Fast forward, again the action frozen mid-jump, this time with Hill in a solid sixth place about twelve bike lengths ahead of Myerscoff.

"I'll be damned..." Bill Pearson muttered under his breath. "Tom..."

"That thing's missing about six spokes right now," Shane announced as he studied the screen from about two feet away.

"Let's go another lap."

The next lap showed Myerscoff next to Hill as the pair hit the face of the jump. Jupiter froze the tape and Hill's bike was slewed to the side, the rear hub clearly collapsing.

The Play button was touched. Myerscoff's Honda hammered into the face and soared aloft. Hill's bike hit the face at speed but couldn't accelerate due to a collapsed rear wheel. The bike arced ungracefully through the air, Hill already sensing the oncoming crash and stepping forward with his right leg as if to walk off his bike that was nose-diving into the front of the next jump, a jump that Hill and the rest of the racers used as a landing ramp. But they used the back of the jump and Hill's bike impacted the front and drove the Coloradoan into the California dirt.

But Hill's Yamaha wasn't done. The fork bent, then rebounded the bike up in the air again. It cartwheeled over the lip of the jump and hammered itself to pieces half-way down the adjoining straight. It was a big, big crash and Henkle and Jupiter's on-camera shrieks helped illustrate the drama that the camera recorded.

Riders streamed past Hill's motionless body as Henkle zoomed in on the hurt rider. The camera recorded the corner workers rushing to Hill and moments later turning to signal wildly for the ambulance. As the paramedics arrived, Henkle's video work ended and the motorhome's screen went blank.

"The battery in his camera died," Paul said in explanation.

"Show it again." It was Bill Pearson's strained voice.

Paul rewound the tape and the silent group watched the almost-unwatchable crash again.

When the TV again went black, Tom Hill spoke in a near whisper. "My rear wheel came apart."

"You didn't know that, dad?"

Tom looked over at his son as if he had just waked from a daze.

"No...no. I thought I'd cross-rutted into the face and looped it. I thought the crash had torn up the rear wheel. They told me the bike cartwheeled and the forks were bent, the tank was torn off...and I thought the wheel broke then, too."

"Were you knocked out?" This question from Ken.

"Yeah. You can see where the handlebar got me. They told me I was out for about three minutes."

"Did you remember the crash?" Ken again.

"No. It wasn't on TV because the action up front was so good. The corner worker told me I cross-rutted and then I went to Anaheim Memorial to get stitched up."

Silence. Then Tom continued.

"When my brother Brian showed up he asked me how it happened and I couldn't tell him exactly. But I told him, and I've always believed..." Tom hesitated and put his hand on the back of his neck, rubbing it without knowing what he was doing..."I've always thought that I choked under the pressure of running sixth in a Supercross, at the pressure from Brian Myerscoff."

Without thinking, Bill Pearson reached out and gripped Tom's shoulder.

Every eye was on Tom Hill. Paul Jupiter broke the silence.

"So all these years you thought you screwed up?"

"Yep."

Paul looked down at the carpet and shook his head, exclaiming under his breath.

"And you never raced again? Because of Anaheim?"

"Yep."

"Tom," Paul finally answered. "I wish I'd known you fifteen years ago because Henkle and I...and most of our friends...knew your wheel came apart before you hit that jump. We loaded your bike and packed all your stuff when you went to the hospital but never thought you didn't know the wheel failed. We've watched this video a few times over the years...I mean, even Preston has seen it. We just didn't know...we didn't know...I'm so sorry."

A shocked silence filled the motorhome. Nobody spoke. They hardly breathed. Everybody's mind was spinning in an effort to grasp what had transpired in the last five minutes, and the last fifteen years. Tom stared at the black screen, his mind back at Anaheim. He looked from the screen to Paul Jupiter, his new friend and old privateer partner.

Tom looked down at Teddy and reached out to pull his son close. He looked back at Paul and exhaled...he'd been holding his breath. In some ways he'd been holding his breath for fifteen years.

"Well...I..." he cleared his throat. "I...Paul, don't apologize, you couldn't have known. This...the video just shocked me, I still can't believe it...the wheel exploded."

Tom again looked down at his son, a boy who only knew his dad had raced but knew nothing of this horrendous crash, a crash that ended a phenom's racing career but created a successful rancher and terrific dad.

"You didn't cross-rut," Teddy said, almost as if he knew his dad had to hear it from him. Teddy then squeezed his dad's hand and broke into a huge grin. "Dad…you never cross-rut!"

Teddy's outburst broke the funereal silence and the Pearsons and Jupiters exploded with laughter at the young Hill's teasing of his dad. As the laughter died, Tom looked around at his friends.

"You guys…you… you don't know how much that video means to me. Don't get me wrong, I thank God every day for my family, the ranch, my health…" Tom looked around at the faces turned to him, holding Teddy tight against his side.

"…but I always wondered what could have happened if I had finished Anaheim sixth, or even the top ten."

Heads nodded. Everyone there, including Preston and Teddy, knew the impact a privateer would have with a top-ten AMA Supercross finish. They all looked at the lean, tough rancher and could see a lean, tough racer standing in his place, work boots traded for race boots, Carhart winter jacket for AlpineStars riding gear. Shane knew, more than anyone—he had ridden with Tom Hill— that Tom's life would have been significantly different if his wheel had stayed together. The man was insanely fast.

Tom smiled a quick smile.

"But living in the past, wishing about things that didn't happen isn't something I've ever done and I'm not starting now. Let's just say I'm relieved to know I didn't crumble under the pressure from Myerscoff!"

With that, Tom scooped up Teddy and gave him a hug while the Pearsons and Jupiters laughed…in relief, along with Tom. But the motorhome fell silent when Tom turned to Shane.

"Shane?"

Shane saw the lightheartedness in Hill's eyes disappear. He stopped mid-laugh.

"Yeah?"

"Can I race your backup 450 in the Fairs next weekend?"

72

Paul and Preston Jupiter served up grilled burgers and treated the Hills and Pearsons to a memorable dinner in their motorhome while the snowstorm piled on the white.

"Hey, Bill," Tom said to the older Pearson. "Shane here just told me you left that 450 at my ranch because you planned to trick me into racing it...you knew I could enter because I qualified for Anaheim..." There was a twinkle in Tom Hill's eyes. "Is that true?"

The elder Pearson caught the mischievous look not only in Tom's eyes, but everyone in the motorhome. He couldn't withhold a chuckle. Paul Jupiter's video revelation and Tom's desire to race the Fairs had an effect on Bill Pearson he was still struggling to understand. Back in the day, he'd wondered why Tommy Hill had quit racing. He discretely looked into it and found that the quick Hill kid had gotten married and taken on serious ranching obligations. Pearson's upbringing on a ranch allowed him to understand the importance of family in the daily operation of ranches and the importance of passing the land and business to the next generation of family. In fact, it was only due to Bill Pearson's two older brothers staying on at the Pearson spread that allowed him to escape to Colorado Springs and his love of motorcycles and sales.

Pearson's chuckle was contagious. Soon the entire motorhome was a chorus of laughter, deep belly laughs that don't stop, the kind of laughter that produces tears and sore stomachs. Through the giggles and guffaws, Teddy managed to stammer: "Dad! We were all in on his plan, even mom!"

Shane added: "I faked that crash on the back side and man was that ice on my knee miserable!"

This produced another round of roaring and Tom managed to shout out, "You're all dogs! No good dogs! Paul, Preston…you're in bad company, get away as quickly as you can."

Nothing could have pried the Jupiters from these five Colorado motorcyclists. Preston looked over at his dad and gave him a thumbs up through his tears of laughter. Both Jupiters could picture Bill Pearson's plan to get Tom Hill racing. But their video had led to this magical and hilarious moment in the middle of the worst blizzard in Colorado State Fair history.

73

Ken and Shane ganged up on the dishes while Teddy and Preston cleared the table and toured the motorhome, especially the garage. That left Paul, Bill and Tom sitting in the lounge. Paul and Tom talked a bit about racing and clearly Paul had come a long way since the privateer they'd seen on Henkle's video tape.

"I never tried to qualify for a national again," Paul explained. "But as my business took off I had a chance to get a better bike and when Preston was old enough we started riding together all the time. He started racing as a pee-wee and that got me racing again."

"You've done well...not just this motorhome but winning the California Fairs against Mann," Bill commented, looking around at the lounge.

"Yep, that was probably the highlight...it felt good."

Paul glanced quickly over his shoulder to check on Preston...his son was still in the garage with Teddy. He leaned forward and said in a low voice, "But just before the Fairs, Preston put a desperate move on a kid at Saddleback and tossed it...broke his nose, ribs... knocked him out. Really scared him bad. First really big crash...it was in top gear."

Pearson and Hill were both nodding...they'd been there.

"Now he's spooked?" Bill spoke quietly.

"Yeah...just wants to crew for me. Hasn't even ridden his

scooter…says he doesn't care if he races again or even rides…says he enjoys helping me."

A quick smile lit Paul's face. "Darn thing is, without his insight I wouldn't have beaten Mann."

"Is he good?"

"Oh yeah, yeah. Started winning the Expert class and that's going good in California." Paul looked over his shoulder again. "But he was getting so cocky and I know that's why he tried that move on McQuiston. But now…he's gone from overconfident to all done."

Bill Pearson was listening to Preston's story but his mind was six steps ahead of the Californian's narrative. Preston's fear of riding again was another piece in the puzzle Pearson was working on. And Pearson loved puzzles…how to own two successful motorcycle dealerships…how to get both his boys to succeed in this sport…how to get a gifted little ranch kid to ride a few demo races at a county fair…how to get a private motocross track built down at the Hill ranch…how to get Tom Hill racing again. He loved puzzles like that. He was good at them…and his latest plan was almost formed.

74

Pearson's plans relied on proper timing. It wasn't until an hour later that an opening presented itself. Paul Jupiter had grabbed his GPS and asked Bill about the best local KOA Kampground.

"Hmm…Paul, I'm not sure there's anything close. Are you guys just going to camp out during the week?"

Paul looked over at Preston, then back at Bill.

"I guess so. Preston is home-schooled so he can do a few things over the internet. We already decided to stick around for a week when the radio said the Fair was postponed. Heck, we drove all the way up here and we must defend California's honor!"

Everybody laughed.

"Well, this is certainly a nice place to spend the week," Bill said amiably. "You could practically park anywhere and have all the luxuries of home, it looks like."

"We sure like it, huh Preston?"

Preston nodded in agreement, his eyes glued to the flat screen that showed last-year's Supercross highlights. He and Teddy were sprawled across the floor, heads on pillows, eyes on the racing. Teddy's natural quietness agreed with Preston because the Californian felt even more ashamed of his injuries in front of these Colorado racers.

"Plus, you get to pull your garage along with you. How great is that, Preston?" Shane asked. Shane and Ken had heard the story of

Preston's crash and subsequent reluctance to ride. They could sense his total loss of confidence.

Preston turned from the screen and answered Shane, "Yeah, we're like factory riders, huh dad?"

Everybody laughed again, and Paul answered, "Yes...yes we are...all we need is the talent!" The room broke up again.

"And umbrella girls!" from Ken.

"And rich sponsors!" from Shane.

"And trick suspension!"...Ken.

"And big horsepower!"...Shane added, over the building laughter of the rest of the guys.

"But most importantly...!" shouted Ken. The lounge quieted for Ken's observation, but burst into laughter again when Ken screamed, "Umbrella girls!!"

As the laughter died, Paul was shaking his head ruefully. "Yep, we're like factory riders...except for all those things you mentioned."

Tom Hill had been chuckling along with everyone else. As the mirth subsided he cleared his throat. "Paul?"

All eyes turned to Tom but only Bill Pearson suspected what was coming. Bill had been biting his tongue but when he looked at Tom he knew the beginning of his plan was about to fall into place.

"None of us are factory riders but we have one thing that most factory guys have...our own private motocross track."

The Pearsons all murmured in agreement.

"Bill built it on my ranch about four hours south. You can park your rig by the barn...there's electric and water right there. We can ride all week...it's gonna be cold tomorrow and Monday, but we didn't get this snow."

Paul looked at Preston, then back at Tom.

Tom saw the hesitation and added, "Preston can go to school with Teddy if he wants, even help Teddy with the chores, do schoolwork together, groom horses, whatever."

Bill jumped in. "Great idea Tom. Our team can be down there on Wednesday, ride Thursday and Friday and be ready for the Fairs. Now that you're racing Ken's backup bike, you and Paul can beat on each other a bit and get this Colorado/California debate started! Paul…whadya think?"

"Preston?" Paul looked to his son.

Preston shrugged, "Sure." He looked over at Teddy and the kid smiled and nodded.

Paul turned to Tom. "If you ride like you rode at Anaheim, this state battle is already over!" Everybody laughed and Tom hung his head, smiling.

"Nah, I'm old now."

"Right," Paul answered sarcastically. "But coming down to your place would be so much better than sitting here in the snow. Thanks for the offer…should we roll in Wednesday?"

"Yep."

"I've got an uncle in Aurora and we'll visit him. This rig needs maintenance. I'd planned to take it to the dealership near my uncle's house before heading back to California but I'll take it in Monday, pick it up Tuesday, then head down."

Directions were given, phone numbers swapped and the Pearsons and Hills jumped out into the snow. "See you guys Wednesday!"

75

Monday and Tuesday were regular ranch days but Uncle Brian spent Tuesday afternoon prepping the track with the equipment Bill Pearson had left behind for that purpose, while Tom designated a spot for the Jupiters' motorhome and ran into Walsenburg for supplies.

Tom had shared the story of Preston's crash with his family and the Hills had determined not to push Preston to ride but to include him in everything. Just before this gang had said goodbye up in Denver, Bill Pearson had pulled Teddy close.

"Can you keep a secret?"

Teddy caught Mr. Pearson's seriousness and nodded.

"Preston crashed hard a little while back and hasn't ridden since. He's spooked."

Teddy was looking into the older man's eyes and nodded again. He had sensed that Preston had lost enthusiasm for racing, that he wasn't going to run the Colorado Fairs, but the California kid never talked about it.

"Maybe on Wednesday, after school, get Preston out with you to check cows. Tell him you need help and try to get him on the four-wheeler. See how it goes, okay?"

"Okay."

"You can tell your parents the plan but nobody else, okay?

"Okay."

"See you Wednesday."

76

The Jupiter's chariot rolled in just past one in the afternoon, about an hour after the Pearson team arrived. Paul and Preston were greeted warmly...and amazed at the immensity of the ranch and the perfectly-groomed track.

"This all started with a little track we built for the family to ride on, mostly Teddy," Tom explained a bit sheepishly.

"Mini-Unadilla, we called it," Teddy added. He had begged his parents to pull him out of school at lunch and they complied because his afternoon classes were gym and study hall. "We race every Saturday, take lap times...me, dad, mom, Uncle Brian...even my cousin rides laps." Teddy looked at Preston as he explained, hoping to make the young Jupiter boy feel at home.

Judy took over the story. "So then we met the Pearsons at the Pueblo County Fair. They had a Yamaha demo deal setup and Teddy rode with Ken and Shane...next thing you know, Teddy's racing a 125, Bill comes down and builds this track..." Judy's voice faded as if she still couldn't believe what she was saying. The news of Tom's collapsed rear wheel had completely changed her mind about racing, especially if her son and husband were on new, well-prepped bikes. The Jupiter's video vindicated her long-held belief in Tom's phenomenal talent.

Paul and Preston were looking at the track as Judy talked. Bill

Pearson took up the narrative.

"Well, that's just the tip of the iceberg, right boys?" Ken and Shane nodded.

"Paul," Bill continued, "you know how quick Tom was back in the day, right?"

Paul had turned to the elder Pearson. "Oh yeah."

"Well, I was around back then, when Tom was pasting everybody in Colorado on an old Suzuki. Used tires. No help. I couldn't help him back then, either. Now I can. When I saw Teddy's talent and then learned who his daddy was...well...let's just say I'm making up for lost time."

Bill chuckled, shaking his head in disbelief. "We came up with this crazy plan to get Tom to run the Fairs..."

Bill was interrupted by his son Ken. "Ah...excuse me? *We?* I think *you* concocted this crazy plan..."

"Yeah, yeah I did. And I got everybody in on it, we got Tom onto a 450...but at that point, we didn't know about the hardship Tom's Anaheim crash caused the Hills. He liked the 450 but I doubt he would have agreed to race the Fairs if not for your video. Am I right Tom?"

"Yep."

"Hey!" It was Ken again. "Are we gonna stand around and talk all day or are we gonna ride?" Typical Ken, and everybody screamed at once, "Let's ride!!"

As the shout subsided, Tom turned to Teddy.

"Teddy, before you go out you need to move the gang off that mesa, through to the water. You know what I'm talking about?"

Teddy nodded. His dad and he had worked out this little skit in advance.

"Are you coming?"

"No, I can't," and then Tom turned to the rest of the guys and explained, "You guys can get unloaded and onto the track, but Teddy's got to move some cattle and I've got a phone meeting with the brand manager in five minutes."

As the group started to disperse, Teddy grabbed Preston's arm.

"Preston, can you help me?"

Preston looked at his dad with a question in his eyes.

"Go ahead Pres, I can get my bike ready. See you kids when you get back."

Preston looked back at Teddy a bit nervously.

"Um, I don't know what to do."

"C'mon, I'll show you. It's easy."

77

Teddy led Preston to the barn and showed him around. As Preston checked out the older bikes next to the brand new 125 and 450 Pearson had loaned the Hills, Teddy was getting his helmet and gloves on.

"Are you riding?"

"Yeah, it's a pretty good pull up to the mesa. Would you mind riding the quad, so we can take a rope and fence tools?"

Preston blanched, not knowing what to say. Admit to his new friend that he'd crashed his brains out and wasn't sure about riding again? Stand around and watch while Teddy headed off to move cows and his dad got ready to moto? And was riding a quad the same as riding a bike?

"Glad you're going, it's impossible to move the gang without help."

That did it.

"Let me get my helmet."

The boys idled past the Jupiter's motorhome and the Pearson's rig; Preston was getting used to the thumb throttle on the quad and didn't notice Bill Pearson's huge grin or his dad's expression of amazement. He also didn't notice Teddy's parents watching from the window. As the boys disappeared Tom walked out and, together with Bill, explained their little plan to Paul Jupiter.

"Stick around...I'm sure Bill here has more tricks up his sleeve. Now: let's ride!"

As Ken, Shane, Paul and Tom got their gear on, Teddy led Preston slowly up the main draw towards the mesa. Teddy had glanced over his shoulder a few times. The third time he looked, Preston had pulled the quad right up behind Teddy's old Honda and yelled out, "This is fun!" with the first smile Teddy had seen on the California kid.

Teddy smiled and hammered the throttle, listening as the quad accelerated behind him. The two boys zipped up the main canyon trail for another half mile before Teddy raised his hand and stopped.

"They're just up over this next ridge and they'll stampede if we pop over too fast. See that round juniper over there?" Teddy pointed to his left and Preston nodded, looking at the tree.

"Go left of that juniper. You'll see a trail up the cliff...I'll go straight, you go left, and we'll start the cows moving, okay?"

Preston nodded. "So...ah...will they, you know...are the cows dangerous?"

Teddy couldn't help himself and laughed, but quickly remembered that Preston was a city kid.

"No...they're scared of us. Too scared sometimes and they'll stampede if we spook 'em. We need to kinda sneak up on 'em, but let 'em see us. They'll move away, even the bulls."

"Alright."

Preston refired the quad and circled the tree as Teddy putted forward. The two boys climbed the final ridge in tandem and Teddy could hear Preston gun the quad and spin the tires. He was having fun...so was Teddy. The young Hill loved ranch work and having Preston along was pretty great. *Are the cows dangerous?* Teddy laughed aloud again as he topped the ridge.

Preston popped over the ridge and looked across at Teddy. The kid on the Honda had stopped so Preston stopped too. The cows were spread out before them on the mesa and a few of the close ones had already started to move away. Preston had never been this close to a cow and he watched as they rambled away in a loose-jointed way, marveling at the colors of their coats.

Preston glanced at Teddy and saw the Honda idling forward, so he eased his quad forward. Sure enough, the cows kept moving away. *I'm herding cows!* Preston exclaimed to himself. *And I like this quad.* Teddy had put Preston on his dad's big Yamaha and Teddy knew he'd like it. The thing was a torquey devil and Preston was tall enough to handle it, no problem…Teddy knew he wouldn't be bored because the quad was fun.

As the boys moved forward slowly the cows retreated toward the gated fence that led to the pasture with the water tank Tom had designated.

Teddy stopped and yelled to Preston, "Hold right there, I'll run over and get the gate open."

Preston watched as Teddy idled along the edge of the mesa, parked his bike and ran along the fence to swing open both sides of a huge pipe gate. Teddy ran back to his bike, jumped on and headed back towards Preston. The boys started to push the cows again and Preston saw that the cows knew the drill. They began to file through the gate; ten minutes later they were all through.

Teddy rode up to Preston and killed his Honda's engine, so Preston killed the quad.

"Great, thanks. You did good…it's easy to move too fast and then create a bunch more work. You like that quad?"

"It's fast!" Preston replied. "I've ridden a quad in California but it was just a 100. This thing went up that ridge like nothin'." Preston was smiling, looking down at the quad. "Your dad doesn't mind me riding it?"

"Nope, he knows you can ride." Teddy swallowed and asked the question Bill Pearson had told him to ask.

"On the way back, we've got to circle around and make sure there aren't any strays. Do you want to ride my Honda?"

Preston had been looking at the quad but his head snapped up toward Teddy. "Um, no thanks," he replied, a bit too quickly. "I've got hurt ribs. I'll just stay on this quad."

"Did you crash back home?"

"Yeah. My ribs aren't healed quite yet. Crashed in a big sweeper and tumbled a bit. Have you crashed much?"

Teddy laughed. "Oh yeah. When I started, of course…but also when I get pushing trying to keep up with my dad."

Preston was nodding but not smiling. "Have you ever hurt yourself?"

"Yeah," Teddy said as he held out his left hand. "Three years ago I caught my little finger on a root when I lost the front, broke it and had to wear a cast for two months."

Preston's head swiveled. "Hear that?"

Teddy had heard it too, the sound of motocross bikes echoing up from the track. "Sounds like the fun has started," said Teddy, smiling. "I'll cruise over the next rise and see if we've missed any cows. Will you stay here and help me push 'em to the gate when we come down?"

"Sure."

"If you see that I've got some, ride over to open the gate, then circle back here so they don't go down towards the house."

"You got it."

With that, Teddy fired his Honda and wheelied off across the mesa towards the hill he'd indicated. Preston watched him jet off and then looked around in wonder at the stark beauty of southeast Colorado. The California kid couldn't believe he was at a ranch, riding quads with a kid who seemed more grown up than most grownups. The snow in Denver had seemed to put a damper on his dad's enthusiasm for the Fairs but once they met the Hills and Pearsons this trip had turned into a whole new adventure.

Preston heard the little Honda and looked up to see three brown, black and white cows coming out of the bushes at a trot. He fired the quad and spun the tires through first, second and third gears as he carved a big arc toward the gate. After sliding to a stop and opening the gate, he roared back to his starting spot to help herd the cows through.

When the boys met at the gate, Preston closed it again.

"Does it always go that smoothly?"

Teddy laughed. "No...they get freaky in the weather or if they get separated too much or if we ride too crazy. We use our horses to move them too but my grandpa Carl discovered how good bikes were on a ranch. My dad and Uncle Brian kept using bikes and I started riding when I was about three. My mom rides and so does my cousin Elsie—she's got my old quad. My grandma Elsa rode, my grandpa rode..."

"That's cool. Me and my dad just get to ride at tracks, mostly. My mom's okay with us riding but she doesn't ride." Preston paused, still looking around the land. "Thing is...we have to load our bikes and drive to a track...it's awesome you get to ride on your own land."

Teddy had never known any different but Preston's words made him pause. "Yeah, yeah it is. Especially since we built Mini-Unadilla...and when Mr. Pearson built the track...and we can just ride right out of our barn."

"Yeah, and all these great trails."

Teddy was nodding. "Ever since Grandpa Carl started riding here we've had a 'trail only' policy...we try to stay on existing trails so the whole place isn't torn up. The cows like walking on trails and we ride those, plus we've built a few of our own. Hey, let's go back down to the track and see what's happening."

78

What was happening was a full-on moto. Paul Jupiter got up to speed quickly, especially with Ken and Shane showing him around. It took a few laps to adjust to the lower horsepower due to the altitude but Paul had changed the fuel-injection's settings before loading his bike in California, based on information on the Yamaha website. The elder Jupiter was going well.

Paul had pulled to the side occasionally to watch Ken, Shane and Tom negotiate that section. Once, all four riders had stopped together and Paul was quick to say how great the track was…and how fast the Coloradans were riding.

"Well, thanks," Ken replied to the compliment. "Building this track gave us a chance to design exactly what we wanted. Teddy and Tom, and Tom's brother Brian, had built Mini-Unadilla based on what Teddy saw on TV, so we built this big track based on sections of tracks we like best."

"Yeah," Shane chimed in. "That whole back section is like Hangtown and we tried to make that middle section, with the whoops and two doubles, like Saddleback."

Paul nodded. "That's funny, because I've raced at Saddleback and that middle section was the easiest part of this track for me to learn."

"See how incredibly smart we are?!" exclaimed Ken.

The men talked a bit more about the track, then restarted their bikes. Tom hadn't said much…it was his first time on the track since the revelation of the Henkle video and he was still swimming in relief. And a wave of confidence…confidence he had always raced with as a kid. The confidence was back, matching his remarkable skills.

As Teddy and Preston rolled up they saw the older riders start their bikes and jump back onto the track. Tom was first on track and popped off the first jump and smoothly, steadily rode away from Ken, Shane and Paul. These three were having a fantastic little race but Tom rode in a class of his own. He wasn't racing these guys, he was simply enjoying a new 450, a terrific track and a brand-new attitude. In two laps, he was seven seconds ahead and disappearing fast.

"Your dad hauls."

"Yeah, your dad's goin' good too," Teddy replied, but he was only watching Tom Hill. There was a brightness to his dad in the last three days, a spark that had always been covered, rarely shown. But that cover had been moved aside by the Henkle video and Teddy watched as his dad railed past, riding with a controlled abandon that was borderline impossible.

"Hey Preston, let's put these away," Teddy finally managed to say. The boys tore their eyes off the older riders and idled their machines back into the Hill shop. "Want to grab a hot chocolate?"

"Yeah!"

Out of the corner of his eye Teddy saw Sam Biganski standing with Bill Pearson over by the team transporter and saw that Mr. Pearson was watching them.

Half-way through their cups of hot chocolate, Bill Pearson walked into the kitchen.

"Oh, that smells good!"

"Can I make you some?" Teddy asked.

"Yes, please!" Bill answered with his usual enthusiasm. His tone turned serious: "And then we've got more work to do."

Both boys turned to the older man.

"Teddy, your uncle called and eight head of cattle have decided they don't want to leave that boggy area over by his place. Know the area he's talking about?"

"Yeah, there's a spring there that they love hanging around."

"That's the place. Brian says he's tried to move them but they keep circling around. He's had to run Elsie into town for her soccer game and asked if we could ride over and move those cows up to the east-side water tank."

"Uh…well…do you mean…I mean, are *you* going to ride?" Teddy managed to stammer. This man had more surprises than anyone could imagine. *Is this part of his plan?* Teddy wondered.

Bill Pearson laughed at the expression on the boys' faces.

"Yeah I'm going to ride! I grew up on a ranch out by La Junta and trail riding is what got me hooked on riding. I'm not sure I ever told you about that."

Teddy shook his head.

"Yep, I got hooked on bikes, just like you guys. My brothers knew I'd rather ride than ranch, so they encouraged me to open a little repair shop for the neighbors' bikes, lawn mowers, tractors…stuff like that. When I got older, I left the ranch to my brothers and went to work for bike shops in the Springs. That's when I first started seeing your dad ride.

"Sometimes you start working so hard in this business that you forget why you got in this business," Bill smiled. "Last time I was down here I putted around on Shane's backup 250. I realized that I still love to ride and I brought down a little 230 for this week. Let's go move those cows and do some trail riding, OK?"

Teddy nodded enthusiastically. He'd do anything for this man, especially after watching his dad ride that 450. If not for Bill Pearson his dad would have never met Paul Jupiter…and would never have seen that video. Teddy turned to Preston.

"Come with us and ride the quad."

"I'm in. That thing's fun!"

79

As Bill Pearson followed the boys back toward the shop he looked over at Biganski, still standing by the hauler, watching the on-track action with his usual array of stopwatches. Biganski looked back and smiled, giving Bill a slight nod. Bill smiled back… he loved it when a plan came together.

The boys paused to watch the track action, then stepped into the shop to grab their gear. Bill said: "I'll get my 230 ready."

"Okay, we'll be over to your trailer in about two minutes," Teddy answered.

As Bill started walking away, he heard "Oh no, we've got a problem."

Bill turned around and stuck his head in the shop, "What?"

Preston was standing by the quad. "Tire's flat. Is your dad going to be mad that I flattened his tire?"

Teddy had walked over to look at the tire. "No, it happens out here. You didn't do anything wrong, don't worry. We'll patch it later today."

"Do you have any other quads for Preston to ride?" Bill asked.

"No, my little one is up at Uncle Brian's. It's too small, anyway."

"Well, shoot," Bill exclaimed. "We've got a problem then. Those guys out there are getting ready for the Fairs so we should let them practice." The older man chewed on his thumb for a moment, lost in thought. Then he snapped his fingers. "Hey Preston, I know your ribs are too sore to motocross but we can't move eight cows all that way without your help. Do you think you could ride your bike if we just cruise real easy?"

Teddy almost laughed aloud but managed to control himself. He looked at Mr. Pearson, then at the mysterious flat tire and finally to Preston.

"Yeah, we need your help, just like you did on the quad. We can't do it with just two bikes."

Preston had unknowingly put his right hand on his ribcage. He looked at Bill, then at Teddy, unsure of his desire to ride again. He thought of those days in the hospital after the crash. The pain. The embarrassment of everyone at school asking what had happened. The hassle of everyone at the track asking how he felt when he was coaching his dad at the Fairs. Looking in the mirror at his black eyes. His ribs hurting when he coughed or sneezed.

Preston looked at the quad again. *It was pretty fun riding the quad,* he thought to himself. *My ribs didn't hurt hardly at all.*

"I don't think I'd be much help."

"Hey, you saw the cows this morning, right?" Bill asked. Preston nodded.

"Well, a small group is harder to move than a big group, but all we've got to do is show them which direction *not* to move in. Three guys can surround them and take away all the options but one, the option we want them to take. So even if you ride at two miles per hour, you'll be a lot of help."

Teddy was nodding along with Mr. Pearson's words.

Preston looked back and forth between Teddy and Bill Pearson. He expelled his breath as if he'd been underwater for two minutes. "All right, I'll give it a shot."

80

Teddy was still marveling at Bill Pearson's audacity when he pulled his Honda up to the Jupiter motorhome. Preston had started his 125 and was buckling his helmet. Just as he swung his leg over the saddle, Paul Jupiter pulled up…and just about fell off his bike when he saw Preston all suited up.

"You going out, kid?"

"Not on the track, dad. My ribs are too sore. But Teddy's uncle called and we've got to move some cows, and the quad's tire is flat. I'll putt along and help Teddy and Mr. Pearson."

Paul raised his eyebrows. "Oh…so Mr. Pearson is riding along?"

"Yep. He brought down a 230 for trail riding."

"I see. Okay, have fun."

And Paul Jupiter did see…another of Bill Pearson's schemes. As the two boys rode over to the Yamaha hauler, Paul shook his head in disbelief. While he had been tip-toeing around with his son, Bill Pearson had jumped in and done something. As Paul mulled this over Bill backed his bike out of the hauler and looked over to see Paul watching him, smiling. The men exchanged a small nod and both knew that they knew. Preston Jupiter cruised off behind Teddy and in front of Bill, standing on the pegs of his Yamaha. Sore ribs and all.

"Did I just see Preston riding?" It was Ken.

"You did. They're going to move cows…with your dad."

Ken laughed out loud. "Say no more! Is he the sneakiest guy you've ever met?"

"Yeah, I was just standing here thinking about that. I've racked my brain on how to get Preston going again. His ribs are almost one-hundred percent. It's his brain that's spooked. I've been stewing about it for weeks and here's your dad getting him on a bike right away."

"Yep, that's dad. He has a certain picture of how the world should be and spends every waking moment making it happen. Don't be surprised if Preston's racing the Fairs this weekend. My dad thinks it should happen."

"Then it probably will."

"Now you've got it figured out! Don't fight it, enjoy it. We do!" With that, Ken slapped Paul on the shoulder. "Good riding out there."

81

It would be tough to identify which of the three riders who idled away from the team hauler was having the most fun. Bill Pearson's smile came from another plan of his coming together as he trailed Teddy and Preston along the dirt driveway that led over toward Brian Hill's mesa house; but as he shifted into fourth gear and settled onto the seat, he realized with a shock that his joy came from being on a bike again.

He laughed aloud and felt embarrassed...here's a grown man giggling like a kid, riding a dirtbike around with a twelve- and fourteen-year old. *What's next? Gym class and Junior High School dances? I'm riding a dirtbike and laughing out loud.* He shook his head and took a huge breath of ranch air...*My life is good.*

And it was. Bill Pearson had married Janey Sato and together they'd built the two Yamaha dealerships in central Colorado, raised a pair of great sons and achieved more than either could have imagined when they used to hold hands walking in downtown Colorado Springs near their apartment. Janey brought a business degree to the marriage; her ability to manage budgets meshed perfectly with Bill's natural inclination in sales. Janey created the proposal Bill gave the owner of the first shop he bought, the shop where he had worked his way up to sales manager.

"I knew you could sell bikes but I didn't know you were this well-versed in the business side, Bill," Bob Boedecker told him as he studied the purchase proposal. Two weeks later the men shook hands and the dealership belonged to the Pearsons...and everything accelerated from there.

In fact, things accelerated so quickly that Bill found less and less time to enjoy motorcycle riding. Soon he was driving his truck to work every day rather than his trusty XS1100, simply because he had so much paperwork to lug around. But he always remembered what his favorite writer, Paul Egan, liked to say, "Once a rider, always a rider. You might not own a bike at the moment but you're always a rider."

Now he was! He saw Teddy and Preston stand up on the pegs so he stood and gave the 230 a squirt of throttle. The tire spun and it just felt so right, just as it did all those years ago when he fell in love with this sport. *Is there anything this good?* Nothing Bill Pearson knew of.

But his distracted thinking was suddenly challenged because Teddy had quit the main trail and his little red Honda was hurtling up a short side-hill, before leaving the ground for just an instant and landing on its rear tire. Right behind him came Preston, and Bill third. Preston didn't jump like Teddy had, neither did Bill, but the little Honda was now leading them along a much smaller, single-track trail that disappeared around a thick juniper. The trio took a quick right onto a downhill trail and Teddy threw his hand up and slid to a stop at the bottom of the dip.

"Okay...this is the boggy area my uncle was talking about. They like the bog...it's tough to get them out...we ah...we gotta kinda burst around this thicket here...surprise 'em into moving... push 'em up that way," Teddy pointed to his left, "same place we put the others."

Teddy stammered a bit in front of Mr. Pearson, completely un-used to giving orders, making plans. He usually did ranch work with his dad and uncle and they rarely even talked, all instinctively knowing the plan of action.

Preston was nodding, still overwhelmed with his first ride in Colorado.

"Okay," Bill said, "got it. You give the order." He was smiling at Teddy's discomfort.

Teddy swallowed. "Okay...let's go."

Bill went right, Teddy went left, and Preston went nowhere for about ten seconds. As he eased out his clutch and snuck around the cedar thicket, he saw Teddy and Bill riding behind the small herd of cattle, moving them toward the watering area. The cows had broken out of the bog together...Preston didn't know that Brian Hill had selected the eight cows for this part of Bill's plan because they would move happily together. Preston brought his bike up next to Bill and Teddy and the three riders idled along in first gear behind the cows.

Teddy put his hand out and the trio of riders stopped...the cows kept walking because by now they realized they were headed to water and their friends. "I'm going to ride ahead, get the gate...keep pushing them, okay?"

Teddy snuck around the left edge of the ambling herd and eased ahead toward the gate.

"Having fun?" Bill asked Preston.

"Yeah, I've never been to Colorado...never herded cows, that's for sure."

"How are the ribs?"

"Oh...um...pretty sore."

"Well, just cruise along...let's follow these guys—or girls, I guess—though they seem to know where they're going."

Teddy had shut off his bike and opened the gate, watching quietly as the cows approached and walked through as if they'd practiced it. *Mr. Pearson probably did have the cows practice,* Teddy thought. As Preston and Bill idled up, Teddy closed and latched the gate.

"Ready to ride home?"

Bill and Preston nodded but they were both admiring the fantastic scenery. Their attention was grabbed by Teddy when the kid spun a 180.

"Let's go!"

Preston put his right foot on the footpeg, leaned his Yamaha left and snapped out the clutch, spinning a 180 as neatly as Teddy's almost before he could think about his actions. Teddy had jumped up on the footpegs and so did Preston, right behind him. Bill hadn't tried the 180, but he smiled as he saw the two kids accelerate away. He caught the two kids zipping along in fourth gear, sitting on the seats, letting the air flow over them. Teddy led them along a cow trail that dipped and turned and the pace was brisk and lively but not crazy. Preston was right with Teddy and Bill tailed them both.

Teddy's hand came out and the three slowed...Preston was caught by surprise as Teddy veered sharp left between two huge juniper trees onto a downhill trail hidden by the greenery. Again, before he could think, Preston matched the arc of Teddy's Honda... Bill followed the boys between the trees.

This has got to be the most perfect trail in the world, was his first thought.

Bill heard Teddy's Honda accelerate, matched with Preston's Yamaha and he thought, *Here we go!* And go they did, three blurs hurtling along the path, eyes glued to Teddy, mimicking his lines and his body. When the kid stood, Preston and Bill stood because they knew a bump was coming...when Teddy accelerated, he pulled the three-car train along...when he braked, the train slowed. It was back and forth through the junipers, constantly decreasing in elevation, but smooth and fast...the perfect trail, almost as if groomed.

Teddy finally threw his hand up and slid to a stop in a good-sized clearing that looked down toward the ranch house and racetrack.

"Whew, what a great trail!" gasped Bill Pearson, slightly breathless.

"Yeah, we call it Skyline," Teddy replied. "It's the greatest way to get up to the high land... my aunt, uncle and cousin ride here. It's their favorite. Uncle Brian grooms it every month."

Teddy didn't add that his dad's outlook on 'fun riding' had never included a blast up Skyline just for the heck of it...until the track was built. Once the entire family started to re-enjoy bikes on Mini-Unadilla, Skyline became a usual after-lapping fun ride for Tom and Teddy.

Bill turned to Preston. "How does it feel to be back on a bike?"

Preston had been in his own world since they'd secured the cows. He wasn't sure about his decision to ride as the trio left the hauler but with each passing minute his natural ability overcame his trepidation. By the time Teddy swerved onto Skyline trail, Preston was starting to find his groove.

As he sat and stood, his ribs reminded him of their tender condition but on the smooth trail things were good. Really good.

"Really good."

Teddy nodded, knowing just what Preston was saying. Teddy usually rode with his dad or uncle so it was extra fun to have someone his own age...and to be able to show Bill Pearson a good time.

"Skyline runs along here for quite a while," Teddy said, pointing to the west. "But," and he turned to Preston and Bill, "...uh...I like to arroyo race on some parts of Skyline."

Preston asked, "What's arroyo race?"

"Well...it's this thing where I drop off the trail and then jump up the next side of the arroyo..." Teddy's voice faded away. He felt like he was bragging, but then Bill said, "Show us what you mean."

82

Teddy idled away from Bill and Preston, then *rupp*, he bunny-hopped over the edge of the trail and landed on the downside of the arroyo with the throttle pinned. He disappeared, then re-appeared seconds later, firing the Honda up the far side of the arroyo and soaring in the air in a delicate spin-twist.

Preston couldn't help himself. "Cool!"

Teddy arroyo raced through three more jumps, then reversed and arroyo-raced back to where Preston and Bill sat, impressed and smiling.

"Wow, where did you learn to do that?" Preston asked, visibly inspired by Teddy's riding.

Teddy blushed.

"We have a DVD with Carmichael, Stewart, Reed…they sometimes flick the bike at the top of the jump to change direction mid-air.… I saw them and…well, I just try to do what they do."

"So you learned to do that from a DVD?" Bill asked in an amazed voice.

"Yeah, I guess so. Wanna try it?"

"No, no," Bill laughed. "I'm going to stick to Skyline here and leave you boys to it, I'm sure Preston will give it a shot, huh Preston?"

With that, Bill started his 230 and shouted to the boys, "I'm going down here to watch."

Preston rolled his bike over to Teddy and asked, "Okay, so how are you doing it?"

The boys talked for about three minutes and Preston rolled into the arroyo for his first try. It didn't go so well and he came back shaking his head, "I barely got in the air!"

"Yeah, you went up good but you have to stay in it at the top a bit longer. Be ready to flick the bars to send it sideways. Watch."

Teddy hopped in and pulled two beautiful jumps, then swung around and waved to Preston. "Come on!"

The Californian had forgotten all about his sore ribs, the Fairs, his dad...when Teddy yelled *Come On* he fired his 125 and hopped into the arroyo. The first attempt was better, the second jump pretty good...then Teddy spun his bike around and jumped into the arroyo ahead of Preston. The two boys rocketed from side to side, the wail of Teddy's two-stroke Honda cutting through the growl of Preston's four-stroker. As they approached Bill's viewing spot, the older rider could see that Preston was figuring it out.

Arroyo racing Bill said to himself, shaking his head. *No wonder Tom's kid is so good.*

By the time the trio reunited in the meadow at the bottom of Skyline, Preston was grinning and hooting with the thrill of arroyo racing.

"That's the most fun ever! Let's do it again!"

Fine with Teddy...he spun his Honda around and then remembered Bill Pearson.

"Oh, uh...Mr. Pearson, are you good with us runnin' the arroyo a little more?"

"Absolutely Teddy, you guys have fun. I'm going to trail around and just enjoy this little 230."

Bill remembered something.

"Hey Teddy, why aren't you riding your new Yamaha?"

83

Teddy looked like he'd been caught with his hand in the cookie jar.

"Uh…well Mr. Pearson, my parents said that the Yamaha is your bike…that I should ride my own Honda unless I was practicing for a race…or racing."

Bill laughed aloud again, shaking his head at the kid's nervousness.

"I see. Do you like the new Yamaha?"

Teddy nodded.

"Alright…I'll make a point to tell your mom and dad that you should ride the Yamaha anytime you want, okay?"

"That would be great, thanks!"

"Okay, you boys have fun." With that, Bill dropped the clutch and spun the tire in farewell.

"I know what you want to do," said Preston as Pearson's engine note faded.

"What?"

"Go get your Yamaha…"

"You're right, I do."

"Let's arroyo race a little more and then head back, okay?"

84

As the two new friends catapulted themselves through the air, Preston held back from his usual riding abandon. He stayed close to Teddy but he could see the smaller boy looking back and waiting for him, not using a lot of throttle on the lips and limiting the speed. When Preston pushed harder he found his ribs were fine but his confidence wasn't there. His body knew what to do, knew how to pick up the pace and push but his mind wouldn't let him.

As the boys rolled up to the barn, Preston couldn't match Teddy's smile of delight in the arroyo racing…and Teddy saw it.

"Hey, let's walk out and watch from the double over there," Teddy said.

Ken and Shane were circulating, Shane's 450 booming and Ken's 250 snarling, and the younger boys saw Paul and Tom standing at the double.

As the boys walked out in their riding boots, Teddy asked, "How are the ribs?"

Preston reflexively put his hand on his ribcage and pushed a bit.

"Not bad, really. Not bad." Preston's voice trailed off.

"Good," replied Teddy, looking up at the taller boy.

Preston like this quiet kid. He was so different than most of the kids he knew in the southern California bike world. Teddy had just schooled him in the arroyos and Preston admired how quickly smooth the kid was, even on his old Honda. This kid seemed to just enjoy riding and his enjoyment didn't spill over into bragging or even much talking.

"You sure ride that two-stroke good."

Teddy dropped his head at the compliment, looking at his boots scuffing through the dirt. "Thanks, it's a rocket."

If he rides that old stroker that fast, he must be awesome on a new YZ-F, Preston thought to himself.

"Have you been on your YZ-F much?"

"It belongs to Mr. Pearson's shop but I've been riding it for three months. He's let me race it four times."

"How did you do?"

"Okay."

Preston waited for more, but Teddy was done answering. In fact, Teddy had won three of the four races he'd entered...if Preston's California friends had won like that, they would be announcing it to anyone and everyone. Preston didn't know how Teddy had finished, but he could see how good the kid was, even playing on the trails.

"Can you run the Fairs?"

"No...don't have enough points, I've only run one Expert race, but I'm going up there to watch. Now my dad's racing, I can't wait!"

"Uh...have you crashed on the track much?" asked Preston in a quiet voice. He had stopped walking, though the two boys were still thirty feet from their dads.

Teddy stopped too and saw the anxiety on Preston's face. He thought briefly before answering.

"My dad always says one crash is too much," Teddy answered with a smile. But his smile disappeared instantly because he could see Preston wasn't taking the matter lightly.

Teddy took a breath, looked over at their dads, glanced at Ken's bike in mid-air on the back side of the start-finish line and took a step closer to Preston.

"I've had quite a few tip-overs and two big, big crashes."

"Were you hurt?"

"Yeah. I told you about my finger...the other one didn't break anything but it bruised my right side really bad," Teddy ran his hand from his hip up to his shoulder, "knocked the wind out of me, broke my helmet and shoulder protector."

"I..." began Preston.

Teddy looked into his eyes and could see the doubt. Preston began again, "I was winning in California and hadn't crashed much... but..." Preston looked around and Teddy could see the big kid's eyes fill with tears.

"Let's walk back to the barn for a sec," Teddy said, "I want to get my hat."

Preston turned and fell into step. "So what happened?" Teddy asked.

Preston sniffed and wiped his eyes real quick.

"I was running second to McQuiston at Saddleback. I got a bad start, passed a bunch of kids...I thought I could pass McQuiston real easy but as the race went on he was going a lot faster than I thought. I couldn't find a way past, then decided to go around him in the sweeper. I just couldn't stand losing to him because I'd beaten him before. I'd already told everyone I was going to win. But there's no room in that sweeper and I just tried to force it past and man, I crashed so hard."

Teddy just nodded and kept walking toward the barn.

"I haven't been riding until today."

"Really? Man, you looked good!"

Preston glanced over at Teddy. "I feel okay on the bike but I don't trust myself. I'm scared a little bit."

Teddy's compliment stuck with Preston as the kid ran into the barn and emerged with a pair of brand-new Yamaha hats that Bill Pearson had given him. "Here, wear this because the sun is really strong up here."

"Thanks."

"It took me awhile to get going again after my crash, get a feel for stuff again…really push again," Teddy said, looking Preston in the eye, remembering his feelings. "Is your dad pressuring you?"

"No, not at all. He's hardly mentioned it…he asked me to help him at the Fairs…California and here."

"Help him how?"

For the first time since the boys met, Preston's face lit up and Teddy saw a glimpse of Preston's usual enthusiasm. The Californian told Teddy what had happened at the California State Fair, how his dad had beaten Charlie Mann.

"That's so cool." Teddy loved the story and saw Preston's true nature emerge in telling it. Preston had been withdrawn and seemed troubled when they first met but the reservations were gone…at least for those minutes of storytelling. Preston's head swiveled to where their dads were standing, now talking with Ken and Shane; Teddy saw the reservations reappear in Preston's eyes.

"I'll bet your dad is glad you're here to help him again."

Preston smiled but his eyes never left the motocross track and the men talking by the doubles. The two kids started walking back toward their fathers just as Ken and Shane refired their bikes to idle to the transporter, Paul and Tom following on foot. The dads met their sons halfway.

"Hey, how was the trail ride?" Paul asked his son.

"Really great," Preston answered with genuine enthusiasm. He turned to Teddy, "What were we doing?"

"Arroyo racing."

"Yeah, arroyo racing. It's like jumping off a cliff, then g-ing out in the bottom of the gulley, then climbing up a cliff and jumping, but turning in mid-air to come down on the cliff again. Like the Winter X-Games guys in the half-pipe."

"Sounds exciting," Paul laughed, equally pleased with the light returning in Preston's eyes.

85

The four riders had arrived at the transporter on foot, where Biganski was pulling Ken's 250 apart. Shane's 450 sat next to it and the elder Pearson was changing the rear tire.

Shane said, "Paul, any final thoughts on gearing?"

Paul and Tom had been watching the Pearson boys circulate and had heard the power nose over twice per lap, both times in fourth gear on the longest whoop sections. They had mentioned it to Shane when they were talking by the doubles. Shane hadn't realized he was that near the top of the gear because a rider is busy in the whoops and he couldn't feel the power loss.

"Two teeth at least. That should help in the far hairpin too—you can go down an extra gear rather than bog out."

"Two, got it."

Biganski's talented hands were flying and Ken's 250 had shed its bodywork in record time, and the pipe was coming off next.

"We're going to try one more combo on this thing," Biganski explained. "Can you guys watch it again?" This question directed at Paul and Tom.

"Sure."

"I'm going to test-fit the extra bodywork, just in case…plug on this pipe and then run two more motos with it. The second moto will come after a mapping change. Ken, five minutes!"

"I'm ready," Ken replied, walking to the bike, helmet in hand. He looked at Preston and Teddy.

"Where'd you guys go, and what did you do with my dad?"

Preston explained arroyo racing again, and Teddy added, "Mr. Pearson went up Skyline."

Everybody chuckled at the picture of Bill Pearson tooling around the ranch on his 230.

"Shane, did you know dad wanted to ride?" Ken asked his brother.

"No idea…we were so busy riding we never thought of him. Cracks me up, dad out cruising around."

Shane had replaced the rear sprocket and was slipping the wheel back in.

"Bignasty, get that 250 ready so I can school my bro a little more!"

Ken rose to the bait and heckled his brother right back. Biganski worked silently, smiling at the Pearsons' wisecracks. He knew how tight their friendship was and soon the trash talk between Ken and Shane had everyone laughing.

As Biganski replaced the seat and give Ken the thumbs up, Teddy turned to Preston.

"Let's grab our bikes and watch from a few places."

Preston nodded and as the boys turned to walk to the barn Paul gave Teddy a thumb's up.

"Hey Teddy!" It was Ken, and both Teddy and Preston spun around halfway to the barn.

"Ya?"

"I'll be the one in front!"

More laughter and Preston joined in, further releasing his nervousness…he turned and jogged along with Teddy to get their bikes.

"Those guys crack me up," he said as Teddy started to roll out his new Yamaha.

"Yeah…" Teddy paused, looking at the transporter and the Pearsons getting ready to moto. "I really like 'em."

"Who's faster?"

"Shane."

"Huh. And who's faster out of them and your dad?"

Teddy laughed, thinking Preston was kidding, but then realized he wasn't.

"My dad."

86

Preston and Teddy joined Paul and Tom and the four idled to the far side of the track, stopping next to a whoop section where Shane's 450 had been over-revving.

"Are you guys going to ride too?" Preston asked his dad.

"We rode a lot when you guys went trail riding…I'll probably take one more moto…what about you, Tom?"

Tom was already listening to the Pearsons' bikes starting their first lap.

"I'm good for today and we've got chores." He looked at Teddy and his son nodded. "But we're planning on moto-ing tomorrow after Teddy gets out of school and I get back from Walsenburg."

"What are you doing there?" Paul asked.

"Two meetings, one with the brand inspector on this year's cattle sale, the other with the water guy…we have three water shares on the ranch that I register every year."

Paul nodded. "Can we help you with anything?"

At that moment, Shane's bike burst off the near berm and vaulted into the whoops, accelerating through second and third gears, into fourth. Ken's 250 close behind. To the boys the bikes went past in a blur of speed and sound but Paul and Tom caught the nuances of Shane's gearing change and Ken's new pipe.

"Shane's is better, but I didn't like Ken's," Paul offered, looking at Tom.

"The 250 sounded flat. Let's listen at the hairpin."

The four bikes kicked to life and carried the riders to another viewing spot. As silence settled again, the sound of the two Yamahas on track could be heard. Half a minute later, Shane's bike flicked into the hairpin and wheelied off into the first of three table-tops.

"Oh, yeah, he's got to like that!" Paul exclaimed.

Ken had fallen further behind and clearly his bike wasn't right.

"I can hear it now," Teddy said to Paul. "It sounds weak… everywhere."

"I agree," said Paul. "How many laps are they running?"

"They've been riding at least ten," but as Tom spoke they lost the sound of Ken's 250. "I think Ken's in. Teddy, run over and see what's up, we're going to watch Shane."

"Okay. Preston, want to go?"

Preston nodded and fired his bike, easing out the clutch as Teddy moved away. The boys sat casually on their bikes and shifted into third gear as Teddy led the way around the outer perimeter of the track, riding on the flat land outside the boundary.

But Teddy couldn't resist the urge to hit the little tabletop that delineated the far corner of the track…he snapped a downshift and leapt to the pegs, spinning the rear tire to help point the Yamaha onto the track, grabbed third and blasted into the ramp of the jump and off the lip in glorious flight. The beautiful blue Yamaha soared into the Colorado air and Teddy's spirit soared with it.

Teddy's quick move to the left caught Preston by surprise, but only for an instant. Preston saw Teddy's plan and his mind jumped to speed…but his body didn't follow. The Californian stayed seated and didn't follow Teddy's Yamaha, he just kept putting around the edge of the track and watched Teddy's flight and landing. The two Yamahas rejoined and resumed their trajectory toward the pits.

Teddy's flight and Preston's lack of flight were witnessed by the dads.

"Ahh…not good," Paul said, sighing.

"Nope."

"Looked like he might follow Teddy for a minute."

"I thought so, too…don't sweat it, Paul…let him trail-ride with Teddy and Bill. Sounded like he enjoyed Skyline."

Tom could see the pain in his new friend's eyes. Paul was staring at the receding boys. He finally turned to Tom. His smile was full of doubt and pain.

"Yeah, it did. He never trail rides much, he just runs laps…maybe we should all go for a blast up Skyline?"

Tom grinned back. "Sure. But we've got trails a whole lot more fun than Skyline…"

Now Paul's smile was full and genuine. "That would be great… think Ken and Shane would want to go?"

"Oh yeah…and let's grab Biganski and Bill too!"

87

Teddy and Preston had just pulled off their helmets and walked over to where Biganski and Ken were working on the 250 when their dads slid to a stop.

"Hey, everybody!" shouted Paul. "We're all going trailriding! Biganski, you too. We're going to go find Bill and then ride the best trails in Colorado!"

Teddy's eyes had lit up at Paul's words and he glanced at his dad, smiling hugely. Teddy knew Preston hadn't followed him onto the track yet he had seen how well the bigger kid rode on Skyline. He could see this trail-riding plan was a great way to keep Preston riding, rather than watching others circulate the track.

"Dragonback?" Teddy asked his dad.

Tom nodded with a huge grin, "You got it."

Tom then hopped off his 450 and walked it over and leaned it against Pearson's trailer.

"Big, ride this thing, I'll get my two-fiddy."

"I'm going to grab Shane," Ken announced. "He won't want to miss Dragonback, whatever that is!" He fired his 250 and swung around to head off his brother, about three turns away.

"I guess you heard it running lean?" Paul asked Biganski.

Biganski nodded. "Yeah, heard it right away. I just took a little timing out of it, should be fine for trail riding…I'll grab my gear."

Preston had been staring at Teddy since the kid had asked his dad about Dragonback. "Better than Skyline?"

"Tons! Best trail in the world!"

Preston and Paul laughed aloud at the quiet kid's reply.

Tom stuck his head out of the barn: "Hey. Better fill up."

"Yeah, Dragonback runs off our land onto the Friedman spread north," Teddy added, pointing to his left. He leaned his bike against the trailer and went for the team's gas can.

Tom rolled his 250 over as the Yamaha gang finished topping off, and five seconds later Bill rolled up on his 230. Shane filled him in on the plan, filled his tank and handed him a bottle of water as the rest of the posse donned their helmets.

"I like this service, I feel like a factory rider," Bill joked. He looked at Tom and asked, in a serious tone, "Think I can keep up."

Tom hesitated. "Ah…actually, probably not with this group… but we'll wait for ya."

"Don't worry Bill, I'll ride with you," Biganski added.

Shane and Ken could feel their dad's hesitation.

"C'mon dad, let's go!" they both exclaimed at once.

Bill looked at them, in turn, fired his 230 and gave it a big rev and a war whoop.

The ride was on.

88

The talent that wheelied away from the hauler was impressive to watch. Tom led and everybody waved Teddy into second, the rest of the gang falling in line and mirroring every move of the Hills. Bill accelerated away gamely but his bike and experience put him in the back right away. Not a problem. He was having the time of his life and Biganski was running right with him.

The pace started fast and the stylish moves began immediately with Tom and Teddy bunny-hopping along the ravine that Teddy, Preston and Bill had taken earlier. Again, they swerved onto Skyline's meandering, smooth dirt, the occasional arroyo jump thrown in for good measure.

Air time provided enough silence to hear the shouting of Ken and Shane and each time Teddy hung in the air, engine at idle above the lip of the arroyo, he would laugh at the crazy Pearson boys behind him.

"Launch it baby!"

"Air Teddy cleared for landing!"

"Say hello to the man on the moon!"

On they went, dishing out the humor at the top of their lungs, no group member immune to their screamed narration. Little did the Pearson boys know that Tom, in the lead, was enjoying this run up Skyline more than any other.

This gang ran close, close together. The trust was there, the talent obvious...and the closer they ran, the less time the dust had to rise and obscure their views. So nose-to-tail the six flew up Skyline, sliding, jumping, wheelying and styling. If you had a video of it, you would be a rich person. The country added red dirt and amazingly green trees in the middle of richly tanned rocks and shear bluffs, highlighting the multi-colored bikes and riding gear; nature's beauty and man's talent on display in southern Colorado.

The combination hit Paul Jupiter the hardest. *This sure ain't California* crossed his mind just before he launched off the lip of the arroyo behind Shane.

At the top of Skyline Tom raised his hand and slid to a stop almost exactly where Teddy had paused earlier. As the other five slid in, there were whoops and laughter.

"Was that Dragonback?" asked Paul.

"No, dad," Preston answered, "that was Skyline and we were arroyo racing!"

The group hesitated, noticing the total enjoyment expressed by Preston's words and look. He radiated happiness...and why not? He'd just flown up Skyline with some pretty amazing riders.

Into the almost-awkward silence came the drone of Bill's 230 and Biganski on the 450.

"Oh man! I forgot about dad and Big!" Shane exclaimed with a laugh.

Bill pulled up and let out a whoop. "Wow! I love Skyline!"

His outburst created another round of laughter and they all agreed: Skyline was one of those perfect trails, groomed enough to really let things go but still edgy when you threw in a few arroyo jumps.

"Did you arroyo race, dad?" Shane asked.

"Ha! Are you kidding? I'm just trying to hang onto your dust. I was flat out just trying to keep you guys in sight. Uh...is Dragonback tougher?"

All eyes went to Tom.

"Yeah…yeah it is. It's got some gnarly sections." Teddy nodded in agreement.

"All right…I'm gonna stay here. I've been riding for three hours now, so I'll run up and down Skyline awhile, then head back to keep Judy company."

"I'm with Bill, you guys are too crazy for me," Biganski admitted with a laugh. "This is the best trail I've ever seen, so I'm gonna run it with Bill, then head down and prep the hauler."

The racers put up an argument but Bill and Biganski were adamant.

"You guys go and enjoy."

They would go. And they would enjoy.

89

Tom had been checking over his shoulder all the way up Skyline, getting a feel for the riders behind him and especially watching Preston. Twice he'd seen the California kid stutter a bit, rolling off when others were rolling on. Tom had caught Ken's wave to bring the pace down a bit and he did, keeping the group together, yet at a pace that was pure fun.

He and Teddy had discussed this particular pace during their track laps. They figured it was about ninety percent of a try-as-hard-as-you-can race pace. Leaving that ten percent as a safety margin let them smooth out and place the bike where they wanted, whether trail riding or lapping the track.

As Teddy developed, the ninety-percent pace accelerated. As he got faster, his ten-percent-off speed increased until he was flying around without pushing himself to the edge. Father and son naturally clicked into this pace most of the time. Of course, Saturday morning races were another story and the time and place at which both Hills pushed to one hundred percent and beyond.

Tom knew that if Preston enjoyed himself, relaxed more, gained confidence…the pace would build throughout the trail ride. Paul caught his eye and gave him a wink.

"Dragonback?"

"Let's go!" the Pearsons yelled together and everybody fired their bikes.

Dragonback starts on the high mesa and everybody was standing on the pegs, cruising in top gear behind Tom and Teddy...at a surprisingly slow pace. The Hills rolled up a moderately-steep incline, then disappeared over the top. Suddenly the Pearsons and Jupiters understood why Tom Hill was leading everyone so slowly: They had just crested a gigantic fall-away jump. Sure enough, Tom leaned right and began a big loop. Obviously the Dragonback ride would start with serious air time.

Tom circled around and this time he led the group up the lip a bit faster and the six riders soared through the air. The best part of a fall-away jump is the landing—no matter how far you jump, you always land on a down slope...perfect. The Pearsons and the Jupiters had immediately recognized that it was probably the best fall-away they'd ever seen. *Epic* would be the word.

The third time off the fall-away would have frightened most riders but the speed and subsequent air time only fueled the smiles and whoops...by the time the six riders fired off the lip for the fifth time, it looked more like Navy fighters catapulting off the deck of the USS *Ronald Reagan*.

The fifth time off the lip was faster and farther than Teddy or Preston had ever jumped and when they glanced at each other they realized they were a bit over their young heads.

"Let's watch?" Teddy suggested and Preston nodded in relief. Both kids had been pushing all the way up Skyline, hammering to keep pace with the bigger bikes...they parked at the top of the jump and the real show began.

The jump turned into a high-speed game of Simon Says...whoever led the group off the circle into the acceleration zone called the shots. When Shane led with a gigantic cross-up he was mirrored by Tom, Paul and Ken. Then Paul wheelied all the way into fifth gear before setting the front tire back on the ground only ten feet before soaring into the air.

Leave it to Ken to up the game.

"Together!" he shouted as the four riders circled around to line up for another flight. The acceleration zone was a flurry of spinning tires, flying rocks and horsepower as the four friends raced toward the lip. Moments later it was silence from the engines as the four bikes left the lip simultaneously...the only sound was the Pearson boys' screaming. Teddy and Preston watched wide-eyed.

Tom Hill was pushing his comfort limits and enjoying it. The Pearson boys were young, brave...and talented. Paul Jupiter had been racing at a high level for years and was comfortable with big air, though not this big. Racetrack jumps, even triples, were tiny compared to this fall-away on the Hill ranch. A few times the two older riders smiled and shook their heads ruefully at each other, as if to say, "Are we going crazy?" And it was a little crazy. Paul estimated that the bikes were flying over three-hundred feet before touching down. When he and Tom pulled over beside Teddy and Preston, both were out of breath and almost trembling.

"Yeow...now *that's* a jump!" Paul exclaimed to Tom.

"Yeah...especially following those two," Tom replied with the same wide-eyed smile, nodding toward the Pearsons who were circling around for another run.

"We've got to be in the air for three-hundred feet, huh?"

Tom studied the jump and the landing area and nodded. "At least. Seems like we're up there forever. How'd it look, Teddy?"

"Amazing."

Teddy and Preston had been listening to their dads but their eyes were on the Pearson boys—it was just fun watching these two play on motorcycles. They never just *rode* their bikes, they were always doing something goofy...sliding on the throttle or brakes...wheelying...kneeling on the seat...riding sidesaddle...grabbing each other's arms, legs, bike. They rode with joy and now they were lining up for another run off the jump. The gang on the lip saw the two brothers confer quickly, both nod and then it was on.

Shane and Ken parted, then both looped around for a run at the jump, each coming from a different side of the acceleration zone. They were about eighty feet apart, both full-throttle, standing on the pegs and shifting through the gears. Just before the lip, Ken swerved toward Shane and Shane toward Ken. Shane hit the lip a split second before Ken and the Pearsons criss-crossed in air, both crossed-up to the point that the bikes looked flat, the sides of the gas tanks parallel with the ground. To the four watching, the bikes seemed to miss by inches, defying gravity as they floated down the hill like Winter Olympics ski jumpers. As Ken's bike, fully sideways, cleared Shane's Yamaha, he looked back at the Jupiters and Hills. It was a look of pure joy, life at the limit...a look that few activities can provide.

The Pearson's x-jump was nothing less than astonishing and the young riders watching imagined themselves doing just that someday, while the older riders watching could only marvel at the Pearson boys' skill and guts. As the two Yamaha riders circled around to stop at the top of the jump, a round of applause and whistles greeted them.

As the comments and compliments subsided, Ken said "That's the farthest I've ever jumped, huh Shane?"

"Oh yeah! I've never even seen a jump this good...that landing area...perfect. I'd like to re-gear and see how far we could go...I was tapped in fifth on a few of those!" Everyone could see that the Pearson boys were amped on adrenaline, turned on by a challenge that was doable but super-edgy. The two brothers were both still looking at the jump, obviously torn between more flight time and the knowledge that Dragonback was waiting, along with their friends.

Ken snapped out of it first, turning to Tom and saying, "I can't remember the last time we got to ride just for fun...to hit a jump a bunch of times just for the thrill of it."

Shane was nodding. "That's just what I was thinking about as we left Skyline, and then when Tom circled around for the second run here? I was smiling with my whole body!"

Everyone laughed as his enthusiasm bubbled over and covered the group.

"We're always worried about lap times, practicing blocking lines, passing lines...getting through whoops...split times, regearing, Biganski's tuning changes..." Shane's voice faded away as he looked around the Hill ranch. "It's nothing like this."

Teddy's eyes had stayed glued to the Pearson boys. He knew his dad was faster around a racetrack than these young men, but it was the flair with which these two rode that made his mind race with possibilities. For the Hills, motorcycles were primarily tools supporting a southern Colorado ranch. Teddy was amazed to hear that Shane and Ken were enjoying this trail ride as much as he was.

Teddy looked over at his dad and his dad looked right back. They nodded to each other, both Hills hearing Shane's voice, both Hills realizing how lucky they were to have this ranch...and both happy to be paying the Pearson family back with great trail riding.

"Hey...listen!" Tom suddenly shouted. "Hear that?"

The group froze and strained to listen for whatever Tom had heard.

But Tom's foot was already perched on his kickstarter and as the group froze he yelled out, "It's the sound of me gone!" His 250 crackled to life and he dropped the clutch and fired the old Suzuki down the landing ramp toward Dragonback.

The group responded but was hampered in their actions by laughter and amazement at the usually-quiet Tom Hill. They started their bikes and began to chase the quickly-disappearing 250. Teddy and Preston were away last...Preston because he didn't want to get in anyone's way, Teddy because he was laughing so hard his foot kept slipping off his kickstarter. *My dad's getting crazy…and I like it!* If whooping and hollering could make a motorcycle faster, this group was the fastest on earth.

90

Dragonback challenged each of them and the scenery awed them to a standstill more than once. At times the Jupiters and Pearsons didn't know whether to ride or drink in the surroundings. Tom and Teddy had been cajoled into an infrequent trail ride by Uncle Brian over the years but riding Dragonback with their new friends let the Coloradans see their land through others' eyes.

This Dragonback ride was different for Tom and Teddy for another reason. The Anaheim video Paul had shown that snowy day in the motorhome suddenly and immediately erased the bad taste of racing that Tom had known for fifteen years. The secret moments of joy the elder Hill had felt during the occasional jumps and wheelies during the 'rush jobs', the moments he had berated himself for, were now okay. Teddy felt the difference in his dad during the past few days and this run up Dragonback was the first time in Teddy's life that riding a motorcycle at full speed along the Hill ranch trails felt truly okay. Actually, it felt wonderful.

⟫⟪◉⟫⟪

The group finally idled up to the barn and trailer as the sun set. The fuel tanks were low and the riders worn out, as if they'd run five full motos back-to-back.

As the Hills parked their bikes in the barn and the Jupiters went to their motorhome, Ken and Shane met Biganski at the team trailer. The two Pearsons were spent and Biganki could see their exhaustion.

"Good ride?"

"Amazing…super-fast in sections, rocky and technical in others…then we're on a fourth-gear downhill in shale, then traversing along the side of a cliff…and the whole time we're just haulin', chasing Tom on that 250," Shane replied with a mile-wide smile. "Total gas."

Ken slumped down in a chair. "Yeah, haulin' everywhere. You know Shane, that's awesome training…not just physically but how quick you have to see things, how far you're looking ahead. We gotta do this more…and we'll drag dad along too."

Shane was nodding. "Yeah, where is dad?"

Biganski just pointed. Both kids turned and a second later they burst out laughing. There was Bill Pearson, spatula in hand, barbecuing on the Hill porch. Smoke billowed around him and just then he turned and spotted his sons. He gave a big wave, adjusted his cook's hat.

"Steaks in five minutes! Five minutes! Steaks!"

"Looks like someone's made himself at home," Paul Jupiter called over.

"Yeah, that's dad. He's not shy."

Ken paused and, not seeing Preston, called back to Paul, "How was Pres's ride?" Teddy and Preston had ridden together the whole time, slightly behind the older riders, not quite able to match their pace, but close.

Paul just smiled and gave the Pearsons and Biganski a big thumbs up.

They nodded. Tom and Teddy Hill had parked their bikes and changed out of their gear…they came out of the barn with Teddy perched on Tom's shoulder, both Hills laughing when they saw Bill Pearson on the porch.

"Steaks! Three minutes! Steaks!"

"Your dad had me stop by Whole Foods last night...*Get ten filets, corn, artichokes* he told me," Biganski explained as the Hills walked up to the trailer. "We're gonna eat good tonight."

"Your dad know what he's doing?" Tom asked with a smile.

"Just you wait...the man can barbecue," Biganski answered for the Pearsons.

"Didja like Dragonback?" Teddy asked.

"Loved it!" Shane responded, really meaning it. He and his brother had been away from trail riding, fun riding, group riding for so long...racing had been their main goal for too many years. This day...up Skyline, then Dragonback...chasing each other along the cow trails, through the washout arroyos...they had talked about it during the infrequent stops as everyone caught their breath and took in the ever-evolving scenery.

Paul walked up with Preston, both Jupiters had washed up and looked tired but clean. "Hey...you guys look too clean!" Ken shouted, springing up. "C'mon brother, let's clean up and go talk to those steaks!"

The Pearsons scrambled out of their gear as the Jupiters and Hills walked to the ranch house in the fading light. Bill Pearson and Judy greeted the riders as they filed in through the front door to a dining-room table prepared for the most delicious dinner these tired, hungry riders had ever smelled.

"Let's get cleaned up, kid," Tom said as he swung Teddy down. As they headed off to wash the dirt down, Paul and Preston jumped to help Judy bring dishes out of the kitchen.

"Good ride?" Judy asked Paul.

"The best...really, the best...huh, Pres?"

Preston's eyes were glowing with happiness and matched his

bright smile.

"Awesome. We had so much fun…"

Judy knew about Preston's crash and his hesitancy to ride again. She'd seen enough racing to know all about career-ending crashes…her husband's, for instance. She had also witnessed the vitality return to Tom's motorcycling after he found the truth on Henkle's video of Anaheim. She suspected Preston was getting revitalized here on the ranch.

"How'd you boys keep up with those 450s?" she asked with a smile.

"Hah!" Preston snorted involuntarily. "Up some of the hills…I couldn't even see those guys! Me and Teddy would just be buried, WFO…just really stretching it and dad would just wheelie away…"

Preston's love of riding had returned and his dad and Judy smiled at each other as the California Expert continued. "But we'd be close…well closer…on the downhills and through the tight stuff, like that boulder section we hit just after we went onto the Friedman property next door…remember that, dad?"

"Yeah, our bikes barely fit in a few spots and I could hear you and Teddy right there," Paul answered.

Preston was interrupted by Bill Pearson coming through the door with filets piled high and right behind him came Shane with the corn and Ken with the artichoke halves, all done on the old-school Hill barbecue, a fifty-five gallon barrel cut in half. The smell brought Teddy and Tom running and two minutes later the family and friends were sliding their chairs under the dining room table.

91

"How about a blessing?" Bill Pearson suggested, after the food platters had been passed around.

"Please," Judy answered.

Bill held his hand out to Teddy on his right and Shane on his left. Everyone saw Bill's action and followed suit. Bill bowed his head and there was silence as the entire table held hands to pray.

"Lord, we bow our heads to thank you for this food, this day, our health and wonderful friends."

Bill paused for a moment and his words sank into the group.

"And Dragonback." Everyone snickered but contained themselves. It was a prayer, after all.

"Please lead us and guide us in all we do."

"Help us find the winner's box at the Fairs."

More snickering. Teddy snuck a glance at the elder Pearson as his hand was squeezed. He caught the barest hint of a smile in Bill's face, before it became serious again.

"Hear our words of thanks for all you do for us. And for internal combustion. Amen!"

The prayer ended with outright giggling, especially from Preston and Teddy.

"So, what was the best part of your ride today?" Biganski asked the smiling Teddy. He really liked this kid, a kid so different from what he had seen at most racetracks.

"Ah…" Teddy thought for a second and then in a quiet voice, a bit bashful at being the center of attention, he continued, "Shane and Ken off the fall-away, just before the start of Dragonback."

The Jupiters and Tom Hill each murmured their agreement.

"And those stoppie things we were doing…um, trying to do."

Biganksi looked around at Ken. Ken had just taken a mouthful of corn and looked back at Biganski and shrugged, pretending not to know what Teddy was talking about.

"Shane?" asked Biganski.

Shane had seen Ken shrug and shrugged too, Mr. Innocent. The Pearsons both looked back at Teddy…they wanted him to talk more—they got a kick out of the shy kid.

Teddy became the center of attention again.

"They," indicating Ken and Shane, "found this little kicker that stepped up onto the mesa…just a first-gear lip, almost straight up. They'd go up the lip, blip it, then come down and land on the front tire, balance on the front tire for…thirty seconds…more. We all tried…I couldn't do it."

Ken and Shane grinned, listening to Teddy utter sentences of more than a few words. They had gotten a kick out of him trying their trick…they'd both commented on how close Teddy was to completing the 'stoppie stop.' Tom and Paul had just watched: Preston had tried it twice with little enthusiasm but Teddy would have tried it all night.

The trick was tough, a combination of popping off the lip, rotating the bike over the nose, landing almost vertically…but not beyond vertical…and holding the bike on the front tire with the brake and body position. Sure, it was a slow, first-gear trick, but scary nonetheless. Going too far and endo-ing could be painful—the bike would definitely land on you.

"Um…I think you balanced pretty good on a couple," Ken said, then continued with a glint in his eye and laugh in his voice, "for about point-zero-one seconds!"

The table broke up at Ken's teasing of the kid. Teddy laughed along and shook his head at this crazy motorcycle racer. Bill grabbed his shoulder and gave him a friendly shake, knowing the kid was having the time of his life.

As dinner wound down Bill cleared his throat.

"Guys, we better talk about Denver. I plan to bring two rigs from the dealerships, so let's get up there Friday night and stake out three spots right next to the front straight, on the right of the concession area. Paul, we've got room under the canopies if you'd like to pit with us…might ask you to wear a Springs Yamaha shirt though," he finished, smiling.

Paul looked at Preston, then over at Bill.

"Yep, that would be great…we'll sneak our rig in there with you guys and we can all use it to hang out, or cook or whatever."

Preston was nodding enthusiastically and added, "Yeah, we've got all the Supercross races and there's a barbecue that slides out just in front of the rear tires."

"Perfect," Bill replied, "that will handle lots of things and I'll make sure we pick up some groceries, okay?"

Everyone was nodding, waiting for whatever Bill came up with next.

"Tom, we need to get you entered first thing Saturday, right?"

Tom nodded, "Okay."

"Great. And everybody else is pre-registered…right Paul?"

Preston answered for his dad, "Yeah, we got our entries in a month ago."

You could have heard a feather drop but Preston didn't notice. He was busy finishing his artichoke.

"You feel good enough to race the Fairs, Pres?" his dad finally managed to ask.

"Oh...yeah," Preston nodded, looking up at his dad. "My ribs didn't hurt today on Dragonback...I'd like to ride the track tomorrow morning, get some practice."

The whole table smiled...and Bill filled the silence with the words everyone was thinking.

"This is gonna be one heck of a State Fair Championship."

92

The Fair entrants, Ken, Shane, Tom, Paul and Preston got in various amounts of practice during the next day and a half. Preston rode the most, Tom the least…mainly because the elder Hill had the meetings he'd mentioned earlier and a ranch to run and the younger Jupiter was getting back to the joy of riding, the joy that Skyline and Dragonback had sparked.

Teddy hooked up with Preston after school and was impressed with the Californian's speed. "You're going good. Do you like the track?" Teddy asked Preston when they pulled over to the trailer.

"Thanks. Love it…better than anything our club races on."

"Really?"

"Yeah…most of the tracks we run don't get groomed and they rut up bad. Your uncle went over the bad spots at noon and I just love the track."

"Cool."

Paul Jupiter and Tom Hill spent a lot of time talking…about their past, about Colorado, about their families. Both racers had come from nothing and though Tom Hill didn't have Paul Jupiter's income he had the ranch and cattle. Different riches, but riches just the same. Paul asked a lot of questions about Tom's ranch and found himself fascinated with the life of a rancher. Their common tie of Anaheim rapidly grew into a strong friendship.

Paul Jupiter had accepted that he would not win the Colorado State Fairs—not this year, anyway. He said nothing to anyone but it was clear to him after watching Tom Hill ride. Hill's lapping had economy of motion, an ability to keep the bike driving forward, hooked up and accelerating. Both Senior Experts did much the same thing at the same time but Tom's 450 was always turned a bit better, pointed better, accelerating earlier and harder. When Paul tried to match Tom's pace, he had to ride over his head and a mistake or two popped up, running him wide or sliding sideways on an exit.

I'm good, I know I'm good, Paul told himself more than once, *but Tom Hill is just one of those special riders.*

An elite motocross rider's special skills are hard to quantify. Beyond great eyesight, perfect balance, cat-quick reflexes, there's the inborn desire to triumph, the warrior's spirit, the I-won't-lose outlook...plus an ability to remain calm at the limit and beyond. Tom Hill had these tangibles and intangibles within him. And he'd been riding almost since birth, almost every day of his life. Anyone around bikes knew Tom Hill was special the moment they saw him on a racetrack, flashing past with a pureness of energy that translates into lap records. Paul Jupiter won the California Fairs, beat Charlie Mann. But Tom Hill possessed something special and was riding exceptionally in part due to the video Paul had shown him four days ago, riding with an energy that comes from confidence...and Paul Jupiter found himself feeling enormously happy for his new friend.

"Anyone ride like you around here?" Paul asked Tom.

Tom looked back at him for a long moment, wondering how to answer, thinking about what the question really meant. He thought about playing the humility card, thought about pretending he didn't know what Paul was asking...but finally Hill just shook his head.

"No."

"Man," Jupiter replied, grinning. "I hope not! I'd just like to be on the podium!"

Tom Hill's answer wasn't something he just came up with. During Teddy's race weekends, Tom had watched the Open Expert class and the Senior Expert class, seeing that there wasn't anyone there who could put together enough good laps to beat him. Back before the Henkle video that information meant almost nothing. Now that he had committed to running the Fairs, he knew that the only person who could beat him was himself.

During the two days of practice with the Jupiters and the Pearsons, Tom spent every moment of every lap focused on reducing and eliminating his mistakes. When he jumped a rut and ran wide on a berm, he would immediately circle back and hit the corner again with whatever adjustment he needed to get it right. The other riders noticed…they realized that Tom had little desire to practice-race with them—he was in his own world. And they saw that he was getting even faster with an intensity seemingly stored up for years.

"You ready?" Ken asked Tom as the second day wound down.

Tom nodded, he knew what Ken meant. "You?"

"We are more ready for this Fairs than ever before," Ken stated as Shane nodded in agreement. "And it's because this track, huh Shane?"

"Oh yeah. We've never had a chance to spend the days before the Fairs training like this…and getting pushed like this. But you know what else helped me? It's gonna sound goofy…"

Everyone had stopped and was looking at Shane.

"That fall-away jump we kept running off. It was so gigantic and we went off it so many times…I'm just completely relaxed in the air now, no matter how I leave the lip. I feel like I can gather it all up, I know what's going on…"

Shane was looking at his brother. Ken was nodding.

"You're right…I didn't even think of that but I feel the same way. Let's hope they put a gi-normous triple into the Fairs course!"

93

The second riders meeting for the Colorado Fairs sounded and looked the same, with two major differences. First…the weather was perfect: mid-fifties at eight AM, forecast to be mid-seventies by noon, more of the same Sunday. The second difference was the air of expectation surrounding the Pearson-Jupiter-Hill gang standing near the front of the room, to the left of the podium where Mathers was running through the weekend's details.

A week ago these same riders were present but the days they had spent together at the Hill ranch practicing on the track, riding the trails, helping the Hills with the ranch chores, eating in the Hill house had not only added to their riding skills but had given each of them a feeling of happiness, friendship, comfort.

Happiness, friendship, comfort…where do these three items fit into the makeup of a successful racer? Bill Pearson mused as he listened to Mathers. The dealership owner had been around a long time and had more than his share of success in bike sales and racing. He remembered Tommy Mason during the champion's visit to his dealership, how Mason touched on the importance of *team makeup*. The mx champ had discussed so many aspects of bike riding and racing but Bill could sense the importance of team makeup, judging from how the factory racer talked. He had told the group about his struggle to surround himself with the right people.

Mason had told them: "My dad and I had our little team and we did well, always finishing top privateer at almost every level. Finally I got an offer from Honda and we thought things were going to really take off, that I'd start winning right away. But it took six months to finally start winning on that bike…because it took that long to get the right people around me…get rid of the politics, the half-way workers, the negative thinkers…to get guys who were on my side, first and foremost.

"I guess I'm saying that it's more important *who's* around you than *what* you're on," Mason had said, looking around the group for emphasis. "If you're hanging with what I call *stinkin' thinkers*," the group laughed as Mason smiled, "their negative thinking will infect you. Get away from those people, surround yourself with positive, goal-oriented people who'll work as hard as you to win championships. It wasn't until my team was right that I could mount a serious challenge for the title. I rewarded those guys and gals, kept them together my whole career."

Mason had paused, wondering if he was talking over the heads of the mostly-young racers in the room. Perhaps he was, but Bill Pearson had been taking mental notes. He was already reviewing his dealership team, making mental personnel changes, realizing that he had a couple of winning-minded people who needed to be moved up as he moved others out.

Pearson was hands-on at his dealerships, walking the sales floor, working the paperwork with his sales guys, discussing parts and service challenges whenever they cropped up. This approach let him anticipate and intercept most problems, though a few still boiled down to what Mason called stinkin' thinkin'.

I'll hire on personality and attitude from now on…I can teach procedures and get guys factory trained, but I can't teach attitude.

Shane and Ken had sat in the audience during Mason's talks, but the two racers were more interested in learning a knack-knack than in team-personnel choices...but their dad was listening.

Mason's insight was the main reason Sam Biganski had moved from Southern California to Colorado...Biganski had that can-do attitude, a seriously strong work ethic and enough experience not only to handle the kids' racing careers but allow him to make good money as a flat-rate service mechanic. Biganski had been a strong privateer roadracer but realized his ability to build race-winning bikes exceeded his ability to ride them. He began building two- and four-stroke roadracers, doing everything from porting to chassis setup but when he tried his hand at four-stroke motocross engines the first 250 he built grabbed the holeshot of the second heat of the San Diego Supercross, bringing him an endless line of privateer engines to be built for local racers. Pearson had heard of him...and made him an offer he couldn't refuse. Biganski had packed his truck and never looked back, arriving in Colorado with knowledge, desire and ability. The Pearson boys started to become the racers to beat.

These last few days at the Hill ranch couldn't have gone much better, Pearson reflected as the meeting wound down. Mathers invited questions and a few riders asked about scheduling, warm-up areas and the like. Pearson was only half listening; his mind was reviewing the day, his people...

"Is that it for questions? Okay...one last thing, on a personal note: we had a late entry this morning from Tom Hill...some of you might be too young to remember him but it's great to see him racing again," Mathers said.

Spontaneous applause broke out.

"All right, that's it. Good luck out there, first practice starts in forty-five minutes."

As the riders filed out into the sunshine, many took a moment to greet Tom or just wave across the room. The attention embarrassed Tom, yet it was like a warm hug from a grandmother you hadn't seen for years. Tom felt at home and couldn't wait to race...the years seemed to have melted away and he found himself jacked up to line up. *Let's go!*

94

The Fairs schedule is basically the same from state to state…the smaller bikes get two practices on Saturday and race that same afternoon, while the bigger bikes get one practice on Saturday, one on Sunday and race Sunday afternoon. Kids on 50s, 100s and 125s find the schedule a relief—they are so nervous that they don't want to have to try to sleep Saturday after a day of practice.

To say Preston Jupiter was ready to race wasn't quite true. Physically he was flying and picked up the Denver track quickly and easily. He was one of three or four 125s doubling the center-straight jump and it looked like getting on the podium in his first Fairs appearance was do-able. As his dad had said a week ago, seriously fast Colorado kids were on track…but Preston was among the handful of possible race winners.

But mentally the kid wasn't up to speed and his lack of confidence came out as he encountered traffic during practice. His pace brought him up to a few riders during practice and Preston could pass the significantly slower riders. But he never passed anyone who was remotely as quick as he, though he caught them easily. Preston would arrive on their rear fender and then put his hand up and roll over a jump or idle through the whoops to gain himself some room. Once he even pulled off and re-ran a section.

He's not passing, Paul Jupiter thought to himself as he watched

Preston's practice with Tom and Teddy Hill. Teddy didn't notice Preston's unwillingness to pass faster riders but Tom picked up on it and silently raised his eyebrows toward Paul. Teddy could see how fast his new friend was, how only four or five 125 guys could run the Californian's pace.

"If you'd qualified for the Fairs, these are the guys you'd race," Tom said quietly to his son.

Teddy nodded, watching the action with rapt attention. The kid was overwhelmed with the scene swirling around him, the number of bikes, the large crowd just for practice. His eyes were glued to Preston and a few other 125 kids hauling the mail. He watched the Californian's every move.

"Preston and those two Honda guys are the only ones to double there," Teddy said.

"Yeah…that kid on the Kawasaki tried it twice so far…" Paul answered.

"I'd have Preston try a little taller gear…" Tom offered in his quiet way.

"What are you seeing?" Paul asked.

"He has to shift too early coming off the left-hander onto the back straight…has to get his foot up and by the time he does, he's past the power peak."

"Good…two teeth?"

"Yeah."

"What else?"

Tom had been focusing on Preston, watching the kid who had been one of the quickest 125 Experts in Southern California. He watched him for a couple of reasons: he knew that Preston's speed would be Teddy's target to reach someday if he kept racing. And he watched Preston because California had produced some of the most breathtakingly fast motocross racers in history, guys Tom had read about and raced against. He wondered if Preston Jupiter would someday take his place in motocross and Supercross history. *He's good…really good. But something's wrong.*

"I think he just needs some more laps…"Tom added.

Paul nodded, hearing what Tom wasn't saying. Riding a dirt-bike at the limit has a certain recklessness to it, a barely-controlled fury that combines balletic grace and poise with a UFC fighter's aggressiveness quickness. Preston's first practice at the Colorado Fairs had grace and beauty, but the explosiveness was absent. As practice continued, Paul felt that Preston was probably the fourth quickest 125…maybe the fifth, if the kid on the Kawasaki committed to doubling the front-straight jump. Another handful of 125 riders were only slightly slower than Preston. These were the best 125 Experts in Colorado and the surrounding states.

Preston's crash had been big, a painful experience that lingered as his injuries healed. *He's afraid of crashing again,* Paul thought to himself. *But at least he's out there.*

———————

As the first practice wound down, Teddy ran across the paddock area to meet Preston as he rolled in. The kid had Preston's stand ready and took his helmet as Preston levered his Yamaha onto its perch.

"Yow! That was fun…I started doubling that front-straight jump but it was scary!" Preston exclaimed as he turned to Teddy.

"Yeah, we sat right there. You looked real good…only a few other guys are doubling there. Do you like the track?"

Preston looked across at the front straight for a second. "Ah… yeah. I guess so. Not too hard to learn, really. Have you ridden here?"

Teddy shook his head.

"Oh…" Preston laughed. "I keep forgetting that you just started racing, huh? I swear you could run with me or anyone else here."

Preston had been blown-away by the kid's speed at the ranch. Although Preston's laps were quicker, he felt as though Teddy was never pushing, never out of shape. He rode like his dad...controlled and relentlessly driving the bike forward. Not flashy, showy...just extremely efficient with his movements.

Preston's comment stunned Teddy. He studied his new friend's face for a sign of sarcasm or derision. Preston was pulling off his chest protector, unaware that his comment was anything more than an apparent fact. Teddy blushed at the compliment and looked away but his mind reeled from Preston's words. It's always hard to tell how quick you were riding. For one of the quickest experts in California to pay him that compliment was heady.

Paul and Tom arrived at the tent as Preston and Teddy sat down in a pair of lawn chairs. "Hey bud, looked good...how did you feel?"

"Good...ribs are no problem. Bike felt good."

"Great...I think we'll make a gearing change for the second practice...what else?"

Preston nodded. He trusted his dad with whatever the bike might need. Biganski had given them the best fueling combination for the mile-high altitude but even with the right fuel mixture Preston could feel the loss of horsepower.

"It ran better at the ranch," Preston said looking at the bike.

"It's about 1500 feet lower there," Tom offered.

"I thought it sounded strong...hey Big?" Paul called out to Sam. Biganski stuck his head out of the trailer.

"Did you get a chance to watch Preston's practice?"

"Yeah, went out to the big sweeper."

"Whadya think?"

Biganski smiled. "Boys, welcome to Colorado. Pres...that's as good as it'll get. I can throw a different injection map at it but I've tried all sorts of things on the dyno and the combo you have is the best we can get with that cam and ECU." Biganski smiled again...

"and I'm afraid you're going to be up against a few guys with full-kit motors."

Biganski returned to his work but a moment later popped his head out the door again. "Ah...I'd go up two teeth on the gearing."

Paul smiled at Tom and nodded but Biganski's kit-motor comment had silenced the group.

"Kit motors..." Teddy repeated. All eyes turned to the kid. Teddy looked at his dad, then at Preston. He smiled: "Then it will be that much more fun to beat them!"

If you wondered when Preston Jupiter fully recovered from his crash...the moment at which the Colorado Fairs became joyous... when he quit *riding a motorcycle* and started *racing a motorcycle,* it was the instant Teddy Hill uttered that challenge. Preston's head came up, his eyes fired with the spark of the hungry, the oppressed, the underdog.

"I just gotta outride them." Preston said, almost to himself.

Preston looked at his dad and locked eyes. Paul Jupiter stood with his back to his quarter-million-dollar motorhome. He was dressed in AlpineStars casual wear with sneakers that cost more than most dress shoes. Paul's perfectly-prepped YZ-F450 sat gleaming atop the best carbon-fiber race stand made, his AStars riding gear sitting on the chair beside it...a chair that reclined, had a leather headrest and cup holders. In the cup holder sat an aluminum drink bottle filled with a custom mix of electrolytes and vitamin water that Paul's nutritionist had prepped just for him.

Paul's mind was processing the same things his son was reviewing. He nodded slowly and said what was on both their minds. "We're the underdogs around here."

Paul Jupiter's overdog status in California was well-earned. He bought the best for himself and his family because he had struggled for so long with second-hand stuff, used gear, old tires. Preston never knew those struggles: he rode new bikes, swapped out tires whenever they showed wear and was now comfortable showing up to a club race in a factory-level motorhome. Yes, he stepped up and rode hard...a new bike and fresh tires don't guarantee a win. Lap times don't reflect bed-sheet thread-count. Preston Jupiter practiced hard and had raced well...but always as the overdog, the favorite, the guy who had the best equipment and was supposed to win.

And in that moment of clarity, Paul had a flash of insight. *My kid crashed because...because I gave him too much. That pass he tried, that impossibly stupid move...that's the move of someone with false confidence, believing that everything is easy and possible.*

Tom Hill knew the problem inherently but as he watched the Jupiters it became clear to him too. He'd seen it when he raced... the abundance of money and equipment in his competitors' camps led them to a false belief that every decision they made was golden. Another thought had been at the back of Tom's mind ever since he met the Jupiters last Saturday. *I've rarely seen a rich kid get to the top of this sport.* This line of reasoning had set-off Tom's alarm bells when Bill Pearson tried to do too much for him and Teddy. Tom believed in work...hard work, making do with what you have, earning your place, paying your dues. Too much help can make someone helpless and he had been watching his son for signs of overindulgence.

Paul's eyes were still locked on his son's. *I don't want to smother his confidence but my kid needs this dose of realism.* "Hey Big..." Paul called out again. "How many horses are we down."

Biganski's voice echoed from the trailer, "Five-ish...maybe seven, compared to the two State Sport Hondas and that one Kawi."

"Is that a lot?" Preston asked his dad.

Biganski heard the question and laughed out loud. "Oh yeah! I'm surprised you guys didn't build that engine before coming out here. You're going to have to ride your butt off."

Silence. The threat of losing often brings it. The last nine months had seen a happy, cocky Preston Jupiter cruising around the pits before a race, chatting with friends and enjoying himself, knowing he would at least get a podium. Now, a mile high and seven horsepower down...that Preston was gone. His crash had knocked his self-belief like a right hand from Muhammad Ali; now Biganski's news brought a moment of bleakness...but it was just a moment.

Probably a good thing he doesn't know how much seven horsepower really is, Paul thought to himself.

95

The single 250 and 450 practices of Saturday ran just after lunch. Biganski rolled out a pair of rocketships for the Pearson boys and they made the most of them.

"What do you need?" Biganski asked them both after practice.

"Nothin'. Let's race it."

Shane and Ken were ready, ready, ready. They were brimming with well-earned confidence and that is a wonderful and magic feeling. Practiced, fit and well-armed. They were the class of their classes and everybody knew it. Bill Pearson looked on with pride, and an eye that measured confidence against cockiness.

"You boys have targets on your backs this weekend. Are you ready?"

Both Pearsons turned towards their father with a flippant comment on their lips…but Bill's intense glare silenced them. They had listened to too many lectures about spoiled kids, seen too many prima donnas, had taken to heart Mason's comments…and they saw their father's intensity when he asked, "Are you ready?"

At a Fairs race, being ready means being able to fight race long with Experts intent on winning at almost any cost. Desperate moves. Riding over their heads. Leaving the throttle open longer than they should. Poorly-planned passes in the first corner of the first lap… and every lap after that. For many amateur-level Experts, this is the biggest race of their careers and win-or-crash-trying wasn't just a saying, it was a theme.

That flashed through both boys' minds as their father stared them down. Bill Pearson had seen it all. First-corner pile-ups. Guys trying to double an impossible jump. Kamikaze blitzes into corners that have little or no chance of working. Riders losing in the last corner of the last lap to an unknown who just wanted it more. "Are you ready?" encompassed so much.

"I think so," Ken answered for them. "We'll watch Tom's practice and talk things over."

His dad nodded.

Preston Jupiter's second and final practice started with a little desperation, three quick mistakes in a row, the final one leading to an easy crash as the front washed out in the flat sweeper. The bike died and as Preston picked it up and rolled it to the side of the track to restart Teddy ran over to the fence.

"Preston! Pres!"

The Californian paused with his foot on the kickstarter, looking at Teddy.

Teddy clapped his hands together. "You can do it! Remember what we talked about!"

Tom, Paul, Teddy, Shane and Ken had been in the grandstands to watch Preston's final practice and couldn't believe Teddy had run to the fence to yell to Preston. "What did you say?" Ken asked Teddy when the kid returned to the grandstands.

"Um…nothing really. Just to remember what we talked about."

"What did you guys talk about?"

Teddy focused on the track, on Preston, as he answered. "In the trailer, when Biganski was changing the gearing…I just told him how my dad rides his old 250 against you guys on your newer bikes…and he does good."

"Ah yeah…you could say that!" Ken laughed. He and his brother had marveled at Tom's speed on the older bike…on used tires.

Tom pretended to not hear the conversation; he was just watching the practice.

"What else did you guys talk about?" Ken asked.

"That you can make up for horsepower with mid-corner speed... my dad does. But you've got to get the bike pointed...you can't just run off into the corner with no brakes and toss it in."

The Pearsons had seen Teddy mimic using the front brake, Preston nodding as he restarted the bike.

The older riders in the grandstand smiled as the kid told his story, as Preston Jupiter got going.

Of the thirty-five riders entered in the 125 class of the Colorado Fairs, the second and final practice showed that only four were professionally quick: the two kids riding for State Sport Honda, a racer for the Kawasaki dealer in Colorado Springs and Preston Jupiter out of California. The Honda riders were talented and tested, having run the Fairs two years earlier with a one-two finish, and the Kawi rider looked fast but inconsistent. The two Hondas were bullets. Any time the throttles came open, these Mark-Medley-built CRFs showed their mettle with astounding acceleration and a scream that only a high-compression motor spinning to 12,000 rpm could provide. Preston made up for his horsepower deficit with mid-corner efficiency and Paul started to see a little of the old recklessness creep back into his son's riding. *A little craziness is good,* Paul thought. *Too much or too little just doesn't work.*

Preston returned to the pits with an intensity Paul had never seen in his kid. Preston knew he was up against it, that winning the Colorado Fairs wasn't a guarantee, not with those three built bikes in the mix. As he rolled up to the tent where his gang waited, he suddenly realized how badly he wanted to win his first Fairs. *My dad won in California...beat Charlie Mann. Shane and Ken are probably going to win. Tom Hill's here...*

Tom Hill had been a revelation to every racer at the Colorado

Fairs…the pits emptied when he rolled onto the track for the only Saturday Senior practice, the racers and racer-families lining the track to watch the elder Hill. His first two laps were nothing…literally the slowest laps of any Senior rider. His wheels barely left the ground, the bike never revved over 4000 rpm…if you had a radar gun, his speed probably never exceeded twenty-five mph. Viewers with no clue wondered if what they'd heard about Tom Hill, the racer who flashed in and out of stardom fifteen years ago, was just a time-worn rumor. But watchers who knew the sport saw something different, how Tom's body worked during those first two laps…they saw greatness.

The third lap Hill ran was the quickest lap the officials in the tower had timed all day. Hill ran two more blazing laps and pulled off as the crowd reeled with what they'd seen.

Tom pulled over to watch Paul Jupiter through the final, toughest, fastest section. He heard Paul running third gear, then watched him for another lap…third gear again. On the next lap, Paul threw his hand up and rolled to a stop next to Tom. Both riders wore a smile.

"Just like the old days, huh?" Paul asked.

"Better. Better…this bike…" Tom was at a loss for words about how he felt, how the bike felt, the joy of running flat-out in front of a packed grandstand. It wasn't a national Supercross but it was the next best thing. This time he was in with a chance to win on a bike made within the last six months. The racers packing the edge of the track…that phenomenon was not lost on Tom or Paul. Racers are usually the worst fans: they can't stand to watch, they want to ride, work on their bikes, ride some more. But they had come to the fence to watch Hill…and *that Californian.*

"How are you going?"

"Not bad, I feel good," Tom replied in his understated way. "You?"

Paul laughed… "Yeah, I bet you're *not bad.* I saw you studying this morning's practices."

Tom smiled ruefully. Paul was right…Tom had walked to every grandstand, looked at the track from every angle, talked things over with Teddy…where the big exits were, the fastest lines, the toughest trouble spots. Tom's focus was entirely on the track because his riding was so ingrained that he trusted his eyes, mind and body to do the right thing at the right time. His YZ-F450 was brand-new and had Biganski's blessing, so the bike was not an issue. Bill Pearson had insisted on having Biganski crew for Tom, so tires, chain tension, clutch adjustment…all handled.

"I'm struggling with a couple sections," Paul said, leaning in toward Tom to talk over the sound of the Senior practice. "I'm used to a little more pop off the jumps, especially at high rpm…the elevation, huh?"

Tom nodded. He had never ridden a 450 at sea level but he knew all about the power loss because he had loved his 250 at Anaheim all those years ago. It felt supercharged down there.

"I watched you for two laps…I'm shifting earlier than you everywhere in this section…running fourth through here," Tom nodded at the sweeper.

"Ah…torqueing it more, huh?"

Tom nodded.

"What else?"

Tom had been studying the other riders. He saw more than a little craziness.

He locked eyes with Paul. "Can you feel the target on your back, California boy?"

Paul looked away. He scanned the fences packed with faces that were studying them. He had seen the attention he and Preston had received, the only two Californians at the Fairs. He returned his attention to his friend, sitting silently on his 450. "Yeah…Californians aren't too popular out here."

"You've got that right."

Just then two Seniors flashed into view, sweeping into the corner side-by-side on a pair of Suzukis. They touched mid-corner and the inside rider stood his bike up and drove off the corner, pushing the second Suzuki almost off the track.

Tom and Paul saw the move up close. "And this is just practice," Tom said. They sat for a moment, pondering the craziness they had just seen. Tom snapped his fingers. "Hey…how many clutches did Biganski bring?"

"Not sure but I've got two extras…both stock."

"Good…I'm gonna need them."

"Whadya mean?"

Tom looked at his new friend and reached out to grab him by the shoulder. "I'm done running laps…I'm going to practice starts—we have to get out ahead of this group. We gotta get gone."

Paul nodded. He was amazed that Tom was done practicing after five laps but he saw the clarity of his words. "I'm going three more…work on shifting it earlier, run fourth through here…then I'll see you at the start gate."

For the final fifteen minutes of Saturday's Senior practice, Tom Hill practiced starts. The first one he held the clutch too long and the bike didn't drive hard. The second one he dumped it too abruptly and his 450 snapped into a wheelie. He took a moment to think and the third attempt was almost perfect…but the next six were an eye-opening display of motor-vehicle propulsion. In an instant Tom Hill went from relaxed and ready to full-on attack mode as the Yamaha charged forward in a seamless rush, clicking through the gears in the starting area as if the bike had an automatic transmission. Paul joined him for the last five minutes and managed two starts but though Paul had launched his 450 dozens of times in races, he couldn't match Tom's efforts.

From the fence, the action was too quick to catch. If the fans could have watched in slow motion they would have seen the hundreds of small adjustments Tom Hill made to body position, throttle, clutch and even the rear brake on each start. He didn't waste time worrying about where he lined up, worrying about the dirt at the starting gate, about what any other riders were doing. He focused on his starts... and they were blindingly quick.

96

As the two Seniors peeled off their chest protectors under the Yamaha tent, Tom slowly came out of his haze and noticed the attention they were garnering. He acknowledged a few nods, but his years on the ranch had made him comfortable only when alone or with a few people in town...the crowd gathered around the Springs Yamaha tent reminded him of how he felt at Anaheim fifteen years ago, the sole out-of-town privateer to make the 250 main event. The one-week delay for the Colorado State Fair plus the beautiful weather promised a massive turnout and many fairgoers took the time to visit the motocross races. The pit area that Bill Pearson put together looked like a factory setup. Add the five pristine race bikes and Paul Jupiter's motorhome, it was no surprise that the crowd gravitated there.

But within that crowd of weekend fair attendees were plenty of racers who wanted to check out the two Californians, the two Pearson brothers and Tom Hill. Especially Tom Hill. Many of the youth racers had never heard of him, but anyone who had been around Colorado motocross in the early '90s remembered the name and the speed. The announcing crew had mentioned Tom's lap time on his third lap... nobody else was within two seconds, even the Open Experts.

The main announcer, Bill Spencer, had worked the Colorado Fairs for 12 years and had seen Andrew Short and other fliers run this track. He made it clear that the track changed every year…before mentioning that Hill's fifth lap was within one second of Andrew Short's best racing lap four years earlier.

"Now folks," Spencer drawled in his deep baritone, "that was four years ago and we all know how much dirt changes week-to-week, or even between practices…and young Andrew was on that early version of Honda's four-stroke…but I guess I'm just lettin' ya know that magic is happening here today."

Tom heard none of this. He was busy perfecting his starts…but his son heard it all and saw his dad in a different light. As Teddy listened he caught Bill Pearson looking at him, smiling, nodding, pointing to the speaker on the pole above their pit.

"Didn't know that about your dad, did ya?"

Teddy shook his head.

Bill just nodded, smiling, thinking, reviewing, planning. He felt niggling pressure on one side of his consciousness, the pressure crew members feel when their riders are contending for the win. *That bike's gotta be perfect*, Bill thought. *If it breaks, runs out of gas, burns up the clutch*…Bill Pearson had seen it all.

"Hey Big?" he called out.

Biganski looked up from Ken's 250. "Yo."

"How we doin'?"

Biganski held Pearson's steady gaze. Teddy watched and listened. All three looked up as Tom Hill pushed his 450 back from practice, talking with Paul. Biganski looked back at Pearson.

"Talk to me, Mr. P."

Bill took three steps toward Biganski and said in a low, firm voice, quiet enough so Tom wouldn't hear. He tilted his head toward Tom's 450. "That thing's gotta finish."

Biganski glanced at Tom's 450, then back at Bill, nodding, hearing what Bill was saying in those few words. Biganski knew all about the wheel coming apart at Anaheim, had seen the video. He had seen perfect bikes drop a valve, lose an ignition, spin the tire on the rim and rip the valve stem out, and a hundred other dramas.

But what Biganski had *seen* was different than what he had *done*. This wrench had an amazing finish percentage, a knack for getting stuff to the end of the race, giving his riders a chance to win. Bill Pearson hired him for that talent. Now Bill was asking him to focus on Tom's 450.

"It's coming apart tonight in the trailer. The boys are happy with their stuff and I'm just buttoning up Ken's clutch…Shane's getting a new chain and that's it…then I'm on it. It'll be perf tomorrow."

That's all Bill Pearson needed to hear. He'd seen Biganski pull all-nighters…two years ago when Shane cartwheeled his bike through the whoops and the throttle stuck as the bike lay on its side at the edge of the track, starving for oil, Biganski had not only repaired the crash damage, he had gone through the engine and replaced two valves, the cam-chain tensioner and the lower piston ring. A battered and bruised Shane climbed on the next day and grabbed valuable points toward his eventual Open Expert championship. Biganski hadn't slept that night. And his bike hadn't broken on race day.

— ◦«◦»◦ —

For Biganski, having Tom Hill on one of his bikes was like carving a baseball bat for Hank Aaron. The better the bat, the better the batter. At the ranch, Biganski got his hands on every part of Tom's 450…as Tom attended his water-commission meeting in town, his 450 had been carefully, intelligently massaged. As good as it was off the showroom floor, Biganski knew how to make it better. By the time Tom arrived at the Fairs his 450 wore a combination of Yamaha Racing kit parts and Biganski labor.

Tom felt Biganski's extra attention and was initially uncomfortable until Biganski explained: "I've had all winter to get these two bikes right," motioning to Shane and Ken's race bikes. "Let me mess with yours a bit."

Tom hadn't seen all the work that went into his bike but Teddy hadn't missed much. Biganski slipped in titanium valves…handing them to Teddy so the kid could feel the weight. "They're filled with sodium…keeps 'em cooler, made of titanium so they're lighter."

The clutch had come out and Biganski restacked the fiber and metal plates, changing the order "to get a better initial bite," he told Teddy. He used his air-powered die grinder to lighten the basket "so it'll spin up quicker." Biganski changed the sprockets, messed with the ECU mapping, added wave Braking rotors, changed out the pads, put on wider footpegs, fitted a titanium Graves Performance pipe with a carbon-fiber silencer. Teddy had been employed to cut open parts boxes that Biganski had brought down, turn on the trailer's air compressor, hold a light while Biganski examined the piston rings. For a Colorado kid raised on a cow ranch, this guy's machine-gun-like work style was a revelation. The tuner's hands never stopped moving, his brain never stopped clicking. A lot of things got done in a very short time.

"I'm not sending Tom Hill to a gun fight without a serious gun," Biganski said more than once. He had snuck out to the fence to watch Tom's last lap and his practice starts. *That gun's workin' good… and I've got the right shooter.*

———— ◦《◉》◦ ————

As Biganski snugged the bolts on Ken's clutch cover, he recalled his last two years in California…two years that held promise but no rewards. His privateer stuff was hauling the mail, running at the front at club races, even getting quicker Experts strong finishes at the state level. But the big break Sam Biganski had been working toward ended in disaster...when Bill Pearson called from Colorado, Biganski jumped at the chance to leave California.

The disaster was Biganski's fault, beyond doubt...but he felt justified in what he had done and knew in his heart that it was an innocent mistake. The bottom line: he broke the rules, cheated...and was caught and eventually crucified in the media. As he slipped on Ken's rear brake pedal his brow furrowed with the memory.

His motocross stuff was becoming popular and a two-rider team approached him to build a pair of Kawasaki 450s for Honda-dominated Supermoto competition. Biganksi built the engines to the motocross specs he knew but testing showed that Supermoto pavement sections ran the engines at higher rpm longer than any motocross track. Biganski changed the porting to get the power to last longer, modified the ECU to raise the rev limit and tested again. Great results but still down from the dominant Hondas, so Biganski tried two more changes...he raised the compression ratio with a light milling of the head and added a little cam to brighten the top end.

The engines came alive with these final mods and the team's testing put them in the thick of the hunt...until the second test day when the team's lead rider Scott Gray was knocked unconscious in a fourth-gear highside when the engine locked solid. Not the best day at the track.

Back at the shop, Biganski found that the right-side crank journal had cracked, letting the crank slew sideways with the resulting seizure. He studied the problem, talking to the boys down at Kawasaki US, called a few tuners he respected. *Why did this thing crack?*

Rob Muzzy had the answer, he'd gone down the same road with a Kawasaki Superbike engine for Scott Russell. Russell had suffered a few engine breakages until Muzzy figured it all out.

"Kawi likes to keep that journal thin and light," Muzzy told Big. "Our mods add stress right there...so I learned to run three beads of weld up from the floor of the cases, stopping just under the bearing surface. Know what I mean?"

Biganski was holding the phone in one hand, shining a light on the area Muzzy was describing. "Yeah…I've got Andy Tachibana's engine apart right here…he wasn't running as many laps as Gray but I can see his journal starting to crack."

"Sam," Muzzy said. "They all come apart unless you weld them."

"Perfect, easy stuff Rob," Sam replied as he eyed his welding cart on the other side of the shop. "Any tips?"

Muzzy and Biganski talked about the job, how to keep the cases from warping, how to protect the bearing surfaces. When Biganski hung up, he knew he had the answer that would put his Kawis on par with the Hondas. Weld the cases.

That weekend Gray ran a tight second to Honda's Gene Haney… and all three podium bikes were torn down in the tech area after the race. The officials saw Big's welds and the fireworks started because the AMA Supermoto rules clearly stated: *Engine cases must remain stock, as supplied from the manufacturer.* Biganski was shocked and dismayed, angry with himself for assuming that welding the cases in Supermoto would be okay, as it is in roadracing.

Gray's finish was disallowed. The team turned on Biganski, accusing him in the media and separating themselves completely from the tuner. It hurt Biganski, it hurt his business. But he'd done what he thought was right, done it innocently, and suffered the consequences with stoic silence.

Biganski's career hadn't ended because of the cheating fiasco but it was severely dented. His best customers stuck with him but new work dropped off due to the publicity. Biganski kept his nose to the grindstone and a late-night phone call from Scott Gray just after the news broke helped Sam stand firm in his reasoning. Gray had called to thank him for all he'd done, let him know he appreciated all the work and understood the sacrifice Biganski had made to keep him safe on the Kawasaki.

Biganski kept working but the call from Bill Pearson sounded like a call from heaven: Get out of California. Build Yamahas in Colorado. Make real money.

Now he was in Colorado with a chance to win three Fair championships, one by Tom Hill. Vindication…and this time the bikes would be within the letter of the rulebook, guaranteed.

97

Ken and Shane's bikes were tight and right, gleaming on their stands. Tom's bike had been wheeled onto the work bench in the trailer and the oil was draining, the clutch out. The bikes sat alone because Preston Jupiter's 125 main event was set to begin.

The Springs Yamaha crew sat in the front-straight stands surrounded by people enjoying the spectacle, but Teddy wasn't there. He'd spent most of the afternoon watching Preston ride, then watching other practices with Preston. They'd both watched their dads ride and practice their starts, inspiring Preston to run two extra practice starts himself.

Preston had asked Teddy to come down to the starting gates with him. Paul walked beside the two boys, pushing Preston's 125. They found Preston's gate position and eased the stock Yamaha between the two Medley Hondas they'd seen in practice. Paul's alarm bells went off immediately. *They're sticking the California kid between the two local favorites!*

His anger had risen in an instant but he bit his tongue and forced his anger back. *If you say something you look like a cry-baby... and Preston doesn't need the drama right now.*

Paul's son had enough to worry about...his gate position wasn't anything more than the luck of the draw in his mind and he hadn't seen that these were two of the fastest 125s at the Fairs. All day, he and Teddy had talked about how to try to beat faster bikes.

They had realized quickly that every time they lapped with their dads they were trying to beat faster bikes.

"So....it's like riding with our dads!" Preston had exclaimed when they realized the challenge.

"You're right...right." Teddy said, lost in thought. "All we ever do is chase a faster bike around, huh?"

"Yep...so how do we beat our dads?"

Teddy's head snapped around to see Preston staring at him. They both had the answer at the same time: *We don't!*

But that answer never emerged out loud. They both looked away quickly, trying to ignore the answer, trying to think of a time...any time...they'd beaten their dads.

"Sometimes..." Preston began, "...sometimes I can catch my dad sleeping, kinda cruisin'."

Teddy flashed back to the first time he'd met the Pearson boys, at the Pueblo County Fair. When Shane had passed him, then pretended to wave to the crowd, pretended that Teddy wasn't gaining. The kid was nodding, looking at his taller friend.

"Especially lately," Preston went on. "As I've gotten faster...I can surprise him sometimes."

"Where, exactly?" Teddy asked, staring at Preston. "Where are you strong?"

Preston looked away, thinking about the tracks he and his dad rode on, how they were laid out, where he was closest to his dad's speed.

"Combo corners...you know, like a left-right-left kinda thing. At StarWest I can gain on him there, in the back section." Preston had forgotten that Teddy had never been outside of Colorado but Teddy was nodding just the same.

"How tight? What gear?"

"Second and third."

As one, both boys swiveled their eyes to the Fair track, zeroing in on the mid-track section that bent back and forth. "Right there," Teddy said. "Right-left-right…and they look tight."

Now Preston was nodding. "They are…and I felt good there this morning."

Teddy agreed. Nobody in the 125 class had been railing through there like Preston Jupiter.

The two kids had walked around the entire track, always keeping in mind the tight center section. They walked and talked and watched practices. They made a plan…a plan to beat the factory-kitted 125s at the Colorado State Fair.

98

Paul Jupiter's outward calm made him appear like just another dad holding his kid's bike in the starting gate but his eyes told a different story. He was jacked up. Sticking his son's bike between the two favorites didn't sit right with him but he held his tongue as Preston and Teddy walked down the starting area, looking at the dirt. Preston pushed it around with his boot. Both boys looked to Paul, then to the first turn, talking, planning. Paul couldn't hear them but felt the focus in Preston. *That little kid's good for him…good for his riding. He looks serious about this, not scared.*

As the two boys walked back to get Preston ready, they were in an earnest conversation.

"…and you can't run too close early," was all Paul heard as Teddy finished his sentence.

"Ready, bud?" Paul asked his son.

"Ready to roost!" Preston answered, his habitual answer at the starting gate.

"Nervous?"

Preston started to say no, but caught his dad's eye. "Yeah…but we've got a plan, huh Teddy?"

Teddy looked at Paul, nodded. "I think he can beat those kitted bikes."

Teddy hadn't said that to Preston. He wasn't even sure if it was true. But he could feel a more important truth: Preston was a tick away from being unbelievably quick here in Colorado. Teddy knew the crash had derailed him mentally but the days on the ranch had brought him back, almost.

"You looked better than them in that last practice."

Preston searched Teddy's eyes for humor and found only truth. He nodded slowly. He trusted his new friend. If Teddy thought he looked better, then he did.

"All you've got to do is offset their horsepower...is that what your plan's about?" Paul asked.

Both kids nodded, then the two-minute horn sounded, telling the racers to get their helmets on and fire their bikes. Preston scrambled a bit, bobbling his helmet and goggles until Teddy put his hand on Preston's arm to calm him. Preston took a deep breath and settled onto his Yamaha, blipping the throttle evenly to warm the engine, his exhaust noise completely swallowed up by the barking of the trick Hondas on either side. As the thirty-second board came up, Paul gave his son's shoulders a squeeze.

"You can do it! Run your plan!" Preston nodded as the thirty-second board went sideways. And then he was gone.

Teddy and Preston knew Preston couldn't holeshot the race, not with this competition. Even so, their plan dictated that he must not lead. In fact, the plan was not to lead until half-way through the twelfth and final lap.

Sure enough, Medley's Hondas jetted into the lead with Preston mired in sixth. The Californian had shared his fear of passing with Teddy during their walk that afternoon and much of their discussion had revolved around where to pass. By the second lap Preston had moved into a strong fourth and could see the two leading Hondas and a bright green Kawasaki glued to their tail, the KXF125 built by another standout Colorado tuner Dan Anderson.

But then it was only two Hondas and Preston was third.

The Colorado tuners build things to the limit and sometimes that knife edge gives way. In this case, the kid on the Anderson-built KX125F back-shifted in mid-air over the start-finish line, shifting the wrong way by mistake in the heat of battle. When the bike landed the rear tire hooked up and stuffed the piston into the valves as the bike went beyond redline mechanically. Anderson heard it from the pit: the sound of losing, junk parts and more hours at the work bench.

For the Springs Yamaha crowd, it was "one down, two to go!" They didn't exactly cheer the Kawasaki's misfortune but they might all have smiled just a little bit more. Teddy and Paul were watching from the pit and Paul clapped his hands: "Third. That would be great!"

Teddy nodded but said nothing. To all eyes it looked as if the blue Yamaha wasn't quite holding onto the Hondas. Each lap, the two Medley bikes would gap the stock YZ-F just a bit. As the eighth lap started, Preston was in a solid third, eight seconds down from first, six down from second. The race looked settled, done, over. Just got to grind out the last four laps.

But Medley's second-place rider had something to prove and he had been pushing to and beyond the limit just about every lap in an effort to catch his senior teammate. That two-second gap was a tantalizing carrot dangling in front of second place. Unfortunately for Preston, it kept both Honda riders pushing late into the race.

Then came Preston's break. The second-place Honda went down…hard. It happened on the second table-top jump when the hot-rod Honda over-jumped the landing, rebounded and put the second-place rider over the bars and out of the race. As the eighth lap ended the kid from California was running a distant eight seconds behind first place. The leading Honda rider, PJ Horwitz, got the pit board that let him know first place was in the bag. Lap nine saw the gap stay at eight seconds…or was it slightly less now?

As the tenth lap began Teddy stepped out boldly from the signaling area and held up two hands as Preston flashed down the straight.

"Lap ten," was the sign—three laps to go. "Start the plan," was the message.

The plan revolved around giving the Honda guys a big lead well into the race, then gambling everything with three berserker laps to catch them napping, worn-out or unaware. The boys knew that Preston had to pass Horwitz in the tight, technical, mid-track section where he was strongest. Preston saw Teddy's sign and clicked into the style that had gained him so much attention in California.

As the tenth lap ended Preston had made up four seconds on Horwitz and Medley hadn't gotten the message to him in time. Half-way through the eleventh lap, Preston put an inspired effort into driving his Yamaha forward with no wasted motion, setting sail for the leader. But now Medley had Horwitz's pit board out: *trouble—Preston—was coming.* The crowd was on its feet and the last lap began with Preston only one second back.

The last lap couldn't have been more fascinating. The bright-red Honda jetted off the corners, flew over the bumps, soared through the air, while the blue Yamaha hung doggedly to its rear fender with last-second braking and astounding mid-corner speed. The two riders entered the tight mid-track section and Preston made his move, cutting his 125 inside Horwitz on a line that required him to drift both ends in and out of the corner. He did...and took the lead.

The blue 125 railed the next right hander and a two-bike-length gap appeared as the kids fired their bikes into the last half lap. The all-Colorado audience screamed as Bill Spencer affirmed what their eyes couldn't believe: *The Yamaha from California was leading.*

But it wasn't enough. A seven horsepower deficit can rarely be offset. Horwitz trailed Preston out of the slower corners of the mid-track section and then pulled the trigger of his Medley motor, jetting past with his seven-horsepower edge. Preston got second by three bike lengths.

Although the little Yamaha didn't win, second at the Colorado

State Fairs was reason to celebrate, considering that Preston had arrived in Colorado intending never to race again. The Jupiter kid had stared at the hospital ceiling, breathing through a broken nose, cringing with damaged ribs, promising himself he'd never race dirt-bikes again. Bill Pearson and the Hill ranch had changed that…and Preston and Teddy's plan almost netted a win.

99

As Preston pulled off, thrilled but drained, he saw something that made his heart catch in his throat: his mom was standing beside his dad and the gang and everybody was cheering, whistling and laughing. For the fourteen year-old racer the sight was shocking: his mom standing in the pit of the Colorado Fairs racetrack. He shook his head quickly...*Am I dreaming?* Moments later he was pulled off his bike and one of the biggest hugs he got was from Lori Jupiter.

"Your dad called me after you guys went on some crazy ride... Dragonbreath?"

"Dragon*back*," Preston answered as they walked back to the motorhome, family and friends in tow.

"Dragonback...and he said you were riding again...then he called that night, after your barbecue and told me you planned to race. I called Southwest right away and got tickets to Colorado Springs and Judy Hill stopped to get me on her way up. We got here thirty minutes before your race...you, dad and Teddy were walking down to the starting line so we figured we'd leave you alone.

"But Preston..." his mom cleared her throat and tears welled in her eyes. "I'm so proud of you, how you raced...the last three laps."

She put her arm around her son as they walked, pulling him toward her.

"I'm proud of how you fought hard...but most importantly I'm proud of how you accepted your finish."

Lori wiped her eyes quickly, remembering when her son had not been gracious or gallant or respectful of getting beaten. She had seen thrown helmets, kicked gas cans…pouty excuses that had, frankly, embarrassed her. Over the past few months Preston's increasing cockiness had made her miss almost all his races because his attitude was so hard to take. Her arm was still tight around her beloved boy.

"You raced like a real man today, a man I'm proud of."

Preston had put his arm around his mom, hearing her words and feeling her emotions. He remembered his tantrums and his mother's reaction. She had spoken harshly to him but then he had thought she just didn't understand. But walking through the dirt of the Colorado paddock, he realized that his mother was a major over-achiever in her world, a woman who moved mountains in the fashion world. A winner. And this mom he loved so much was proud of him.

100

Preston had seen Judy, Teddy's Uncle Brian and Grandpa Carl too. All had given him big congratulations and told him how much they enjoyed the race. As Preston shrugged out of his riding gear his eyes glowed with the sense of accomplishment, of a job well-done, a plan that got him to the front and the exhausted sensation of having given everything he had.

"Hey, we're the first stock bike across the line," Paul said often that night. Horwitz, Medley and their crew had come over to the Yamaha tent to celebrate and Medley told Preston that he would have won if his bike had more juice. That meant a lot to the Californian.

"The plan almost worked," he told Teddy as the two walked back from the scoring tower with Preston's trophy. They'd spent the whole day talking about how to beat their dads, how to overcome a horse-power deficit, how to set up the Honda guys for a last-lap move.

"Too bad those three tight corners weren't at the end of the lap," Teddy offered.

"Yeah...too bad I didn't give my bike to Biganski last week," Preston grinned back.

The two young friends sat next to Preston's dusty bike. Teddy nodded, smiling at the thought of Preston on a Biganski bike. Then he giggled.

"What's so funny?"

Teddy was staring through the door of the team trailer at his dad's 450. "My dad's got a Biganski bike…" It hit him in that moment, the unreal happiness he felt for his dad.

Preston had turned and was looking at Tom Hill's 450, bathed in light on the workbench in the trailer. Biganski was just refitting the exhaust system. The bike had been torn down to the frame and rebuilt after Hill's practice and Big was about twenty minutes from having it ready to race.

Paul, Tom, Shane and Ken sat with Biganski, watching him work, talking about the day, scheming about tomorrow. Shane and Ken knew they could win if they put in their best ride. Paul felt good about a top-four finish, possibly a second if he could get out with Tom early. But Tom Hill had no thoughts of winning, only the excitement of getting on a Biganski bike and running it to the best of his abilities. His confidence couldn't be quantified because it couldn't be measured in any normal way. He didn't think about the competition, the start, the corners or the jumps. He thought about speed, the flow of a motocross machine ridden at the limit and beyond, each part of man and machine working at the edge of grip and gravity, of courage and determination.

Tom Hill watched Biganski with an appreciation few would understand. This tuner worked on a bike the same way Hill rode a bike: no wasted effort. The hands moved precisely. The brain led the hands. Tom had watched this rhythm undress and dress his 450. He'd watched the clutch come out, the torque wrench work, the cam get timed. *All for me,* echoed through Tom Hill's mind. *Tomorrow I will fly…I will repay Big by riding his creation to the best of my abilities.*

Biganski's creation wasn't a single item that onlookers could point to, such as the billet handlebar clamps or his titanium valves. Think of the creations of the best chefs, meals that simply melt in the mouth, though no one ingredient stands out. That was Biganski's effort with Tom Hill's 450…everything touched, nothing ignored, all blended into a motocrosser that made more power all across the rev range, turned, stopped, jumped and landed better...even Biganski probably couldn't tell anyone exactly what went into a bike like this. How to explain the perfect radius on a connecting rod, the deburring of a clutch hub, the lighter-weight grease on wheel bearings?

"Why is Big doing all that to your dad's bike?" Preston asked Teddy as the boys stared into the trailer. Teddy had asked Biganski the same question when he started pulling the bike apart at the ranch last week. Teddy didn't take his eyes off the lighted workbench when he answered.

"He told me that every tweak will help my dad go faster. He said most guys are overwhelmed by a stock 450, but my dad can "up his game if the bike is better."

Preston was nodding, remembering Tom Hill's pace at the ranch. "My dad told me your dad was the fastest guy he's ever seen."

Both kids were swiveled around in their chairs, looking into the trailer. Preston's second-place trophy sat on the seat of his YZ-F125. Their dads were in the trailer with the Pearsons. The light was fading, that time of day when the colors are muting and the track-side barbecues are lit. Both kids just sat and watched Biganski work and felt an air of preparation, expectation, exhilaration as thick as the smoke pouring off the hamburgers and bratwursts Bill Pearson was cooking up on the grill of the Jupiter motorhome.

"Come and get it!" Bill cried.

Biganski looked out the trailer door and saw the two kids watching him, saw the expectant looks on their faces and his heart fluttered. Biganski liked the pressure of race-day prep, enjoyed putting his work to the ultimate test. He knew they were watching him prep Tom Hill's bike, talking about the bike, him and Hill. He nodded to them and both kids smiled. Biganski felt the magic in the air, the purity of competition, the coldness of the stop watch and finality of finishing positions. The Californian knew he had put his best efforts into this bike, doing in five days things that had taken decades to learn and perfect. The tuner turned back to the bike and stared at it for a second before laying down his tools and looking over at Tom, Paul and the Pearson boys.

"Let's eat and then I'll button this thing up."

As the racers filed out of the trailer, Lori Jupiter and Judy Hill returned from their walk, still deep in conversation. The two women had met at the airport earlier that same day but their common bond of loving a long-time motocross racer started the friendship and the talks moved into careers, family and lives. Bill Pearson and Grandpa Carl had kicked them out of the motorhome kitchen, telling them to take a hike and leave the cooking to the men. Uncle Brian pitched in and by the time the women returned dinner was hot and ready.

"Hey, we could get used to this!" Lori laughed to Bill Pearson.

"Well, I hope you do."

In those five words, Bill Pearson said a book-full. He'd been having the time of his life, prepping dinner with Carl and Brian Hill, two men who reminded him of his own ranching family. He had watched an astounding race, had seen his kids and his new friends Tom Hill and Paul Jupiter ride amazingly well. And when Lori Jupiter and Judy Hill arrived...*Does it get better than this?*

Lori held the older man's eye and his thoughts traveled across to her. She felt it too, the rightness of being here...with these people...at this moment. Lori's life had its share of beautiful moments but her career was fraught with politics, double-speak, favoritism and back-biting—the nature of big-time fashion. Too often it was about who you knew and how they felt about you. But here at the Colorado State Fair her career was a distant memory. Here she was the wife and mother of fast racers, friends with the state's best riders, part of a group that worked hard and expected great results from that work. She felt the cohesion of this group, the push of everyone in the same direction, Sam Biganski's energy, the calming Bill

Pearson contributed...the almost holy confidence of Tom Hill...
and the quiet knowledge of his son Teddy.

—)《◎》—

Preston's tremendous second-place effort dominated the talk
during dinner and the question on everyone's mind was finally posed
by Paul Jupiter.

"So, Teddy...Preston...tell us about the plan you guys cooked up."

The two kids looked at each other, hesitant to answer in front of
the entire gang. Preston finally broke the silence.

"We both ride with you two," Preston nodded toward his dad
and Tom Hill, "and we're always trying to beat you. We realized that
me chasing those Hondas was like us chasing you guys. We just keep
riding, keep trying, pushing hard in the tight stuff...sometimes you
let up a little and we get next to you, even pass you."

"Did you plan to let the Hondas get that far out on you?" That
was a question from Tom Hill.

"No...not that far," Preston laughed. "But those guys were pushing each other and I didn't know how close I should be...I was just
waiting for Teddy's signal of three laps to go."

As the tale unwound in the Jupiter motorhome on that beautiful
Colorado night, the new-found friends laughed and wondered over
the two kids' plan to win the Fairs, a plan that had almost worked.
But through dinner, into the ice-cream dessert, nobody could shake
the sense of something big coming tomorrow, something that had
stewed for fifteen years in the spirit of Tom Hill.

101

The freight train that was the Colorado Springs Yamaha racing effort had developed a head of serious locomotion by the time practice ended Sunday. Ken started the party on his 250, spinning laps that would have put him in the top five of the big-bike class. Shane took it from there. Both Yamaha riders were among the two or three fastest racers in their classes. The two Pearson brothers had benefited from how Paul and Tom saw the track, the veteran-riders' views helping to focus their talent and abilities.

On Saturday night, the four riders spent time in the trailer watching Biganski work on Tom's bike. They also sat together after dinner and talked about the track, the upcoming day and everything else an in-for-the-win rider might discuss the night before the Fairs. The young Pearsons were simply over-riding two spots on the track, trying too hard and putting themselves in a position to be forced to forfeit speed. Paul and Tom had seen them both make the mistakes, lap after lap...typical in young, aggressive riders. Sometimes the discipline to slow the pace *here* isn't available to adrenaline-addled racers trying to go fast *everywhere*.

Neither Paul nor Tom knew the Pearson boys well enough to know how to approach the two problem spots, but both were determined to at least try to offer advice. Tough situation—they weren't being asked...at least not at dinner. That changed after the meal, when all four racers sidled outside to sit in lawn chairs.

The talk turned to the rhythm of the track compared to the rhythm at Hill ranch.

"The ranch track just flows better. There's no stop-and-go stuff, nothing that breaks up the lap," Shane said. The other three racers nodded.

Paul asked, "Where are you struggling here?"

Shane described the places where Tom and Paul had seen him over-riding. Ken agreed: "Yeah…those two spots are killing me, too. They just don't flow."

Tom and Paul couldn't disagree…the track was awkward, a combination of the corner radius, the dirt used, the ruts and bumps. But both older riders knew that the challenge was to figure out the difficult parts of a track.

"I've got something for you to try there tomorrow," Tom began, throwing out this small suggestion in his quiet way, checking to see if the Pearson boys were interested.

They were. Their eyes locked on Tom's face and he could see their intensity. He mentally kicked himself for doubting that they'd be interested in his opinion. Paul saw the same reaction in the Pearsons and waited for Tom's next words.

"That right-left combination…early in the lap?"

Ken and Shane nodded…neither liked that section.

"Try getting into that right-hander low, down by the tough-block…use your brakes longer, a lot longer. Get in there and park it, go down to second even, don't run third…let the thing turn right longer, then snap it up and you can run straight and pinned through the left."

The Pearsons were imagining what Tom was describing.

"In practice you guys were railing the right-hander, putting you late and slow through the left…slow all the way down that straight," Paul added.

Ken and Shane were nodding…Ken looked at Paul and then at Tom. He smiled.

"Now you tell us!! How long were you going to wait, huh? What else, what else?"

Tom and Paul laughed along with the Pearsons, all worries about coaching forgotten. They spent the next twenty minutes discussing the second weak spot. Right behind them, sitting on the step of the motorhome, Preston and Teddy missed not a word.

Ken and Shane used the advice to good advantage, both dropping their practice times by just over a second. Paul spent his practice laps getting used to his 450's diminished power and trying a slightly different setup on his rear damper.

Tom Hill spent his practice flying. Literally. He ran six laps, and on the sixth he tripled on the back-straight. Everyone at the track was taking the back-straight jumps in a double, single combination but by the fourth lap on Saturday, Tom Hill could see that his pace off the previous corner positioned him to jump all three. He'd thought about it all night. On the sixth lap of Sunday's only practice he did it.

Two riders in the history of the Colorado State Fairs had tripled on the back straight, Bill Spencer explained: Andrew Short on his works Honda and Travis Pastrana when he came west for a guest appearance on his factory 450 Suzuki. Spencer reminded everyone that tracks change and bikes are now better, but the point was made: Tom Hill rides in rare company.

Tom finished his practice with two perfect starts, handing the bike back to Biganski with a smile and a quiet, "Thanks Big, great bike."

Biganski and the entire Colorado Springs Yamaha gang witnessed Tom Hill's backstraight flight from the front-straight bleachers. From that angle it looked like a jet airplane taking off. Hill hit the jump going incredibly fast and soared aloft as if gravity had taken a vacation. He only did it once but the image was burned into the retinas of the whole Springs gang.

Shane was the first to grab Tom. He gushed, "That was amazing Tom, really amazing!"

Tom had to laugh at the kid's comment. "Yeah…well…it just felt right."

By that time the rest of the group had gathered around, generating a feeling of nervous hilarity—a surreal environment that would have been hard to explain to anyone not there. It revolved around the explosion of riding talent emanating from this quiet, humble rancher. One might expect Shane to throw a triple there, but a thirty-five year-old rancher from southeast Colorado? The move was shocking, outlandish…the height of the bike, the distance it traveled.

As the scene played out and Tom retired to the motorhome for lunch, Shane stood mute by his 450. He finally snapped out of his reverie.

"Hey Big."

"Yeah?"

"Are our bikes the same, mine and Tom's"

"Yours is a little lighter…we only had one set of Poggipolini titanium bolts so all your engine and chassis bolts are ti…but the motors are the same."

Shane nodded, staring at his bike…turning to stare at Tom's bike. Shane loved to jump. He had told all his friends about the fall-away on Dragonback—the greatest jump he'd ever seen, but it had an easy, long run-up…the three backstraight jumps were sandwiched between two berms.

"How'd he do that?" Shane mumbled to himself. "How?"

Biganski hadn't walked away and heard Shane's question.

"Shane…go ask him. That move will win you the Fairs."

102

Shane found Tom sitting on the couch with Judy and Lori, talking about life on a ranch in southeast Colorado. Teddy and Preston were lying on the floor watching last year's Vegas Supercross finals on the flat screen.

"Tom...I've got a question for ya," Shane began, when Tom looked up.

Tom saw there was more meaning than the words implied. He excused himself, stood up from the couch and motioned Shane to walk out into the sunshine.

"What's up?"

"That triple you pulled off on the last lap...nobody's doing it but you. If I can pull it off, I've got Hansen covered."

Tom knew who Shane was talking about: Brady Hansen, the 20-year old factory-support rider who rode a Honda built by the same guy who built the 125 that beat Preston, Mark Medley. Tom had seen Hanson's skills at the four rounds Teddy had contended, had seen him fight against Shane's Yamaha and even beat him once. Hansen was the kind of rider who probably couldn't beat Shane week-in and week-out because he was prone to riding over his head...but when he stayed on the track, he was brutally, recklessly fast.

"I wouldn't have tried that triple on a stock bike," Tom admitted. "Has Biganski...ah...is your bike like mine?"

Shane knew what the older rider was saying, had seen the effort Biganski had put into Tom Hill's 450…Shane knew that Tom had given Sam Biganski a spark of inspiration, a chance to be part of history, the return of Tom Hill.

"Yeah…Big told me I had the same motor, but my bike's got the ti bolt kit, so it's lighter."

"Okay…so what are you doing off that last corner, the one before the jumps?"

"I'm off there in third, catching fourth…doubling and singling."

"Squaring it off?"

Tom's question about Shane's line in the berm seemed weird to Shane. Berm lines were berm lines—run it in, slide it sideways, fire it out. The left-hander onto the back straight was no different.

"Ah…yeah."

"In third?"

"Yeah."

"Let's sit down."

Settled in lawn chairs under the canopy, Tom leaned forward, elbows on his knees. The buzz of race-day at the Fairs swirled around them but their minds were locked on getting Shane to triple the back-straight jumps. They could have been alone at the summit of Pikes Peak.

"Walk out to that turn and you'll see my tire tracks all the way on the right…leading into the very beginning of the berm, where the tractor started working the dirt up…probably about eight feet right of the line everyone's running."

Shane was nodding, imagining.

"Do whatever it takes to get into that berm early…and in fourth gear."

Shane snapped his head toward the older rider at this last bit of information.

"Fourth?!" he exclaimed.

"Fourth."

Shane's belief system went on high alert. "You're kidding…"

"Fourth."

Shane got up and walked over to where Biganski was slipping a new front tire onto Ken's 250.

"Big…is our gearing the same…me and Tom's?"

"Yep…14, 42," Big said over his shoulder.

Shane returned to his chair. "Alright…fourth."

"You'll get in there a little slower than the usual line but getting in the berm early lets you pick up the throttle and start to rail the whole thing. Do it in third, you'll spin the tire at the exit…and you'll have to grab a gear. The spin and the extra shift will kill your speed…"

Shane was thinking hard.

"The last part is the clutch work, so you don't spin the tire in the middle of the berm, where the dirt changes as you come onto the regular line…ya gotta be in the clutch a little there."

Shane was lost in thought, his mind playing the scene Tom described.

"How did you figure that out?"

Tom shrugged…*Good question,* he thought. He left his answer at the shrug but seeing something like this just came to him. He had tried the early entrance in third, then fourth…then added the clutch work on the final attempt during the sixth lap of practice. The earlier attempts had to be aborted as his 450 hammered into the face of the jump—he instinctively knew the speed wasn't high enough. *How did I know? I just did.*

"Tom…how tough is it…this move?"

Tom looked away, his eyes seeing the crowd gathered around their pit area but his mind reviewing the question. A false answer was possible when talking about it around the dinner table to friends and family but the answer before the finals of the Colorado State Fair to one of the fastest Experts in the state carried more weight.

"It's a....a little crazy."

Shane nodded. "Whadya think? Can I pull it off?"

Tom snapped his fingers, realizing the second answer to the question Shane originally asked.

"I forgot something...something I did on the first two tries, the ones I checked up on. You gotta be ready to use the brakes on the lip of the jump if you don't get the exit perfect...if you spin or over-clutch or make a mistake and run third. If you don't go to the brakes, you'll overjump the doubles but not even come close to tripling."

Shane stared at the older rider. *Use the brakes on the jump face, of course...gives me a chance to experiment and not pay a big price.* A smile broke out on the young racer's face.

"That's...that's great. I can play with it early in the race and see...see if I can do it."

"You can...but don't let it fly unless the exit is perfect and you can stay pinned all the way off the berm..."

Tom paused, mid-thought.

"What? What else?"

Tom leaned closer to Shane. "Take a page from Preston and Teddy's plan...even if you could triple on the second lap, save it... save it for the last two because Hansen is good enough...crazy enough...to try to triple there too. Don't show him anything early."

Shane couldn't hold back a laugh. He'd listened in wonder as Teddy and Preston described their plan last night at dinner. Now he knew where Teddy's inventiveness came from!

"You're a sneaky devil," he commented, smiling.

Tom feigned innocence. In truth he had seen the possibility of tripling on the backstraight during yesterday's practice but held the move in check until his final practice lap today. He knew it was the buzz of the paddock and all the top big-bike guys were considering it, trying to figure it out, muster the guts to throw the bike into the air. But the main events were next, practice was over and anyone who wanted to try to triple had to learn the move on the fly. Shane Pearson had Tom's secrets but even he faced the unknown.

Motocross racers who jump short often land on the top or even the up-slope of a jump. It's called 'casing it'...it's painful on small jumps, bone-breaking on big ones. Literally. Few big-bike racers in the paddock would try to triple where Tom had tripled but the Fairs often bring out the most heroic or perhaps the most desperate racing anyone has ever seen: the desperation of an amateur trying to make a mark, move up the ladder with a Fair win, place his name in the record books and reach for that elusive professional factory ride.

Shane's eyes caught Tom's and they both knew the score. If Shane's move failed it could hurt him badly. If it succeeded but Hansen duplicated it he would lose his edge. Shane could probably win without the triple...he had beaten Hansen six out of nine races this year...but those weren't the Fairs. Racing Brady Hansen was like fighting off an angry Grizzly while holding a pot of warm honey.

103

Shane's desperation was checked by the options he had begun to work on for his future. His college career was opening his eyes to the business side of motorcycling and he had already collaborated with his dad and younger brother to fine-tune the sponsorship program and create a cleaner, simpler paperwork procedure on all sales.

But the biggest change Shane brought to the two dealerships was something he learned while running at the Supercross in Las Vegas the previous year. He had stopped in the Wynn resort to visit the Ferrari dealership he had seen advertised…a car dealership built right into the resort—one of the world's top Ferrari dealerships. He had gone down to the service department and watched through the huge windows as the techs bustled about the gigantic, spotless work area. Shane was impressed…blown-away.

Shane wore a Colorado Springs Yamaha race shirt and it caught the eye of the service manager who introduced himself as Tony Ferracci.

"You in town for the Supercross?"

"I am, but I wanted to see this shop. My family owns two Yamaha dealerships in Colorado," Shane replied. "Man, this place is spotless."

Tony smiled. "Thanks. Come on in, look around."

Tony pointed Shane through a doorway and hustled off in the other direction. Shane found himself at the edge of the mechanics' bays, finding it hard to believe the scene. Compared to their shops in Colorado, this Ferrari dealership was mind-blowing. The sounds matched the view as a pair of 430s started up to get backed off their respective lifts. Shane had never heard one V-8 Ferrari, much less two running together. He soaked it in, but from a shop-owner's point-of-view.

A tap on his arm signaled Tony's return. Tony motioned with his head and Shane followed him into a clean but busy office.

"I started in a bike shop," Tony said. "Not much dirt stuff but we did custom bikes, track bikes...back when Ducati was getting rolling in America. Remember Jimmy Adamo? The roadracer?"

Shane shook his head.

"Yeah, well...we built stuff for him. Richard Chambers...fast guys like that."

Shane was nodding. He had found a connection with racers before and liked Tony right away.

"How's your biz?" Shane asked.

"We're killin' it...super busy...taking a lot of work from California. People who own these cars need to be treated right... and we do that."

Shane was nodding, clearly seeing Tony's personality clicking with customers. He was busy but organized, nice but not a babysitter.

Shane looked out the window facing the detail booth...an older four-door Ferrari sedan he didn't recognize was getting waxed.

"What's the secret?"

Tony laughed at the kid's question. The kid's *right* question. He sensed that this kid wasn't in love with the cars, he was in love with the shop, the business. Plenty of tourists wandered into the Wynn to look at these cars and gape open-mouthed at the exclusive shapes wrapped in perfect paint. But this Pearson kid had been looking at the overhead air lines, the in-wall grease guns, the tool rack placements, his eyes hardly pausing on the cars, even the Italia that had just come in.

"It's customer service, you know…same as you guys do." Tony answered, waiting for the kid's reaction.

Shane heard Tony but his eyes were on the second desk in Tony's office, the one covered with three computers and trays holding four digital cameras, each one labeled.

"Yeah…but we're on a completely different scale," Shane replied, then added, "What's with the computers and cameras?"

Tony checked his watch and grabbed the radio by his desk. "Paulie-boy, how's that muffler comin'?"

The radio crackled back, "Torquin' bolts now."

Tony replaced the radio, turned to grab a camera and said over his shoulder as he headed out into the shop, "C'mon, I'll show ya."

Shane trotted to keep up as Tony crossed the shop to the furthest space. A yellow 318 balanced high on the lift and a mechanic, presumably Paulie, was indeed tightening the clamps on shiny-new stainless mufflers. Tony asked Paulie to step aside and snapped two quick photos, and just as quickly was headed back to his office, Shane close behind.

Tony swiveled his chair around to the computer-laden desk as Shane closed the office door. A second later Tony had the camera plugged into the computer.

"So this guy wants to make his 318 run better, sound better… comes to us and buys a set of $4200 mufflers, you with me?"

"Okay…that's a lot of money for mufflers."

"You got that right. So rather than take his money, take his car and then leave him sitting at home wondering, we take two photos as his car comes in the shop and e-mail them to him. Two more as the old mufflers come off. Two more as the new ones get tightened. When Paulie fires it up I'm out there with a video camera and I e-mail the guy the sound as it drives out of the shop. It's like he's here watching…he's involved."

Tony tapped the 'send' button and swiveled around to face Shane.

"That's the secret. I'm the service manager but you might as well call me the camera manager too."

Shane had been nodding, watching Tony e-mail the two photos, listening and thinking about replicating the Ferrari shop's habit in Colorado. He could see how it would keep the customer connected, show him what work was being done, how it was going. Shane knew there were customers who distrusted shops and Tony's pictures and constant contact would go a long way to proving to the customer that good work was being done. He was thinking about Biganski, the quality of his work and how it would come across in photos, even video, all sent in a moment across the internet.

"Hey Tony...mind if we copy what you're doing here?"

"No, you should. Customer service is the name of this game. Just promise to send me down your best customers so we can sell 'em a Ferrari..."

<hr />

When Shane returned to Colorado the first thing he did was grab his dad and Biganski, laying out the Ferrari dealership's methods to the two men. Bill acted immediately, buying a pair of digital cameras that could shoot stills and video, and the service department began asking for e-mail addresses and cellphone numbers. Tony's plans took less than a week to migrate to Colorado and the results were instantly positive. A positive result for a motorcycle dealer means happier customers, which always leads to more customers.

Some of the youthful desperation began to leave Shane's riding as the business side of him evolved along with the dealerships. The more his dealership efforts paid off, the more his mind focused on expanding that part of his motorcycling love.

Shane's passion for racing began to cool.

Then he met Teddy Hill at the Pueblo State Fair. The kid's pure enjoyment of a world Shane had known all his life helped re-ignite the older racer's passion. Shane watched Teddy react to a world that had become commonplace, and the kid's reaction helped Shane look around with new, more appreciative eyes. Tom Hill sprayed gasoline on that spark because his approach to racing combined technique and intuition. Tom didn't need bravado to get charged up for a race, didn't spend energy worrying, whining, talking, bragging... yet Shane could see Tom's mind was full with the puzzle of lapping a track as fast as a bike can go. That's who Shane wanted to be: the guy who *thought* his way to a lap record.

The timing couldn't have been more perfect. Shane faced Brady Hansen, a rider who counted on bravado and emotion to push himself beyond the limit. That style usually doesn't last long but Hansen had serious skills and the ability to save crazy situations. Hansen never gave up, he just kept charging.

Tom sensed Shane's calmness, mixed with the usual nervousness of a big race and the additional emotion of trying a new triple. As fun as this kid was to be around, Tom knew his mind was as business-smart as his father's, his exuberance backstopped by The Big Picture: *Sell Yamahas.*

Tom stood and shook Shane's shoulder.

"Your main event is twelve laps. Put in ten hard ones, work on that backside berm like we talked about. If you get it and feel good, pull the trigger on the last two laps. There's a good chance Hansen won't even be around by then—he's always on the ragged edge."

Shane nodded, his eyes narrowed in thought. An old needle of excitement focused him, the needle he used to feel at every race, a needle he hadn't felt in at least a year: the thrill of the race, the challenge of a new move learned on the fly while racing against the fastest riders in the state. He smiled and shook his head. *No...I'm being coached by the fastest rider in the state.* These last few months had revitalized Shane Pearson's riding and he felt himself rise to the challenge of beating Hansen and becoming only the fourth rider to triple at the Colorado State Fairs.

104

Ken Pearson needed no needle of excitement. The boy was more than ready and couldn't remember anticipating a race more than this Fair main event. His time at the ranch running against the 450s of Tom, Paul and his brother had forced him to push his 250 harder than he ever had. The 250 main event was first up and Ken felt like an eager racehorse straining at the bit, the excitement of the start building to a feverish pitch.

Shane and Tom accompanied Ken and Biganski to the start gate, little to say, little being said. Most of the 250 Experts were like Ken: young, precocious, borderline reckless and entirely too confident. Tom could sense the adrenaline, almost smell it. Riders were snapping open the throttles, sending their revs to the moon in a screaming crescendo. Others riders were hitting themselves in the chest protector, psyching themselves up…jumping up and down to warm-up, swinging their arms and legs—a mass of barely-controlled hysteria, Ken right in the middle of it.

Shane lined up Ken's 250 and Tom held his gloves as Ken buckled his helmet. Ken's eyes were wide, almost bulging, his breathing heavy and intense. He was in the moment, filled with the aggression you need to run a 250 at the front. Tom soaked it in, thinking that he would need that intensity when he lined up here in just a few short hours.

Running perfect starts by yourself is one thing…I'll have to be ready in this crazy zoo, Tom thought.

Ken reached out for his gloves but Tom held them until Ken looked into his eyes. "Ken…remember those two spots, the two places you've got to sacrifice…okay?"

Ken's breath caught as Tom's words sunk in and his gaze focused for the first time since he arrived at the starting gates. He nodded, hopping up and down to loosen his legs. He slipped his gloves on, still nodding, still hopping, as if to a rhythm in his head. Shane just held the bike, watching his brother, watching the riders around them. Ken looked at Shane and Shane nodded. Ken swung his leg over the seat and kicked the Biganski motor to life. It sounded sharp and sweet. Ken revved it with the joy of living.

Shane remained behind Ken's bike with Biganski until the riders next to Ken climbed aboard. Shane stepped back a few feet and looked at the relative directions of the bikes neighboring Ken's, seeing that the KTM on the left was angled toward Ken's Yamaha. Shane stepped forward and grabbed Ken's rear knobby and slid it a few inches to the left, to direct the Yamaha away from the KTM. A good start has the front wheel in the air for the first few gears and steering is tough…the Pearson boys had learned this last-minute redirect the hard way.

Shane had raced 250s and knew that the smaller, slower bikes rewarded a high degree of recklessness…crazy entry speed, big throttle movements, headlong jump approaches. Those techniques could really hurt a 450 rider but the 250 wasn't the hurtful beast that the big bike was. Sure, you could overdo it and crash your brains out, but Shane wasn't about to calm Ken down. As the one-minute board went up Shane grabbed Ken's shoulders and leaned into his brother's right ear.

"Win this thing, brother!"

Ken nodded, fully fueled on pure adrenaline. At the thirty-second board he bent his arms, got his chest forward, took the clutch to the friction point with the throttle pinned. Tom and Shane had stepped back around the barriers with Biganski but they felt the wildness of the scene as the gate dropped and Ken Pearson launched himself into the record books. He led the first lap. He led the last lap. He put his Biganski bike on the top step of the Colorado State Fair.

And he fed the hunger of Tom Hill.

105

The track went quiet for grooming and then came time for the Shane Pearson/Brady Hansen showdown. Bill Spencer's voice boomed over the PA and he almost forgot to mention the other racers in the event. His focus was on the rivalry between Pearson's Biganski Yamaha and Hansen's Medley Honda. Spencer loved to build suspense…and he was good at it.

Spencer's suspense-building relied heavily on his knowledge of motocross racing history and he liked to throw around the names he'd watched from the announcing booth. As the 450 Experts walked down to the starting gate, pushing their bikes in the silence before the storm, Spencer regaled the crowd with the names of local legends who had won Fairs in this class and moved to the AMA national and FIM world series. The Fairs had been a stepping stone for most American professional motocross riders and Spencer's gift of gab added drama to a tense situation.

"Find a seat but don't sit down! You don't want to miss this Turn One action, folks. These are the big guns, the fastest of the fast, the open-class Pros. There isn't a rider here who hasn't won something, somewhere in Colorado this year. But let's get specific. When the gate drops we're going to see a thirty-bike drag race, and most are betting on either Shane Pearson or Brady Hansen to win that sprint. Pearson's on that Sam Biganski Yamaha out of Colorado Springs

Yamaha, Hansen on the Mark Medley Honda out of State Sports Honda. If I know Biganski and Medley, and I do, those bikes are built to within an inch of their lives."

Spencer's patter rolled across the listeners like a wave of suspense; the more he talked, the more people came in from the fairgrounds to see the action. Ken and Tom had walked with Shane and Biganski to the starting gate and listened to Spencer as the starter assigned the gate positions.

"Man, he sure likes to talk!" Ken said, laughing. Neither Tom nor Shane returned even a smile, Shane because he was studying the gate layout, Tom because he knew his race was next. Ken knew the feeling but he was on a high that comes from winning the Fairs. *I can't stop smiling,* he giggled to himself.

The brothers reversed roles, Ken behind the bike, Shane straddling it. Ken stepped back and liked what he saw. Hansen had been gridded next to Shane but Mark Medley had pointed Hansen's bike slightly away from Shane, as you'd expect from a pro.

Medley saw Ken eyeing the situation and smiled to himself. *These Pearsons have it going on,* he thought. Medley had spent fifteen years at the highest level of Supercross with Honda and knew he was in a fight anytime a Biganski bike came to the grid. And then Medley chuckled under his breath. *I'm glad I don't have a bike in the Open Senior class...Hill's gonna humiliate them.*

Medley had joined Honda the year Tommy Hill ran sixth as a nobody out of Colorado on a pile of junk. Team Honda had noticed the quick kid but he had crashed and disappeared. *But boy is he back.* Medley had given Tom a quick handshake after Preston's second-place and said, "Good to see you back." He meant it. *Someone with those skills should never stop riding.*

Shane had his helmet and gloves on and as the two-minute board went up he reached out to Tom for his goggles. Tom was standing right next to the handlebars and had something to say. The older man leaned in and spoke loud enough so only Shane could hear.

"Use the first ten laps for practice...triple on the last two. You good?"

Shane nodded, "Oh yeah...I'm good." They both smiled and Tom backed away.

106

The craziness of a Pro-level first turn has to be seen to be believed. TV doesn't do it justice. These bikes accelerate harder than any production car on the planet, slamming thirty 450s into turn one at mind-numbing velocities. Shane Pearson's velocity was best in class but Brady Hansen's was only half a bike length worse.

The two rivals exited the first turn level and swapped the lead four times on the first lap alone, pulling eight bike lengths over the mob fighting for third. Shane had no chance to even think about the backside berm, fighting just to keep Hansen corralled. The second lap flashed past with the same intensity and Shane once again found his hands full with a Medley Honda inches away on every part of the track. *Two laps down and I haven't even tried that early line in the backside berm*, was Shane's fleeting thought as he led Hansen across the line to start the third lap.

Tom had seen Shane miss the far-right entry two laps in row and discovered that he'd clenched his hands into fists. He relaxed and shook out his shoulders, knowing that getting uptight before his own main event wasn't the smartest move. *C'mon Shane…let him by and run second…*

The exact thought had occurred to Shane at almost the exact moment. Letting Hansen past wouldn't be too tough—the Honda was just about on top of the YZ-F. Finally, on the third lap of twelve, Shane tried Tom's line into the berm. But he forgot about fourth gear.

Half-way through the berm as the tire spun, Shane remembered the gear change. *Next lap...fourth gear...use the clutch half-way through.* He shut off his mind and focused on matching Hansen's pace through the rest of the lap...Hanson was on the edge, making mistakes here and there but riding through them with sheer desire...and big horsepower.

By the eighth lap Shane had gotten through the backside berm almost right once. *Two more laps to get it right...and better get it right because Hansen's going for broke.* In fact, the Honda had eked out a half-second lead and Shane still hadn't gotten the run-up to the triples perfect. The ninth lap was the best yet, the tenth lap practically perfect.

With two laps to go the crowd could be heard by both Hansen and Pearson. Hansen was fueled by the roar, Shane could hardly register it, his focus so intense on working out the triple while keeping Hansen in sight. Shane could see Hansen's aggressiveness ratchet up a notch...that actually calmed the Yamaha rider. He thought of Tom Hill at the ranch...going faster, smoother.

That was the key to tripling at the Colorado Fairs...smoothness off the backside berm...*not* spinning the tire, but gathering and gaining speed all the way through by balancing throttle against clutch against gearing to hit the face at a speed few could handle. Shane had a fleeting thought of Dragonback's fall-away. *I can handle it.*

On the eleventh lap Shane Pearson threw a triple on the back-straight of the Colorado Fairs. He literally flew over Brady Hansen... pictures prove it...landing in first and leading the beginning of the final lap. Bill Spencer led the crowd into a scream probably audible in Salt Lake City in response to one of the coolest things anyone had ever seen.

But Brady Hansen wasn't done. He'd seen Tom Hill triple there on the last lap of Senior practice and he'd thought about it non-stop since. *If he can do it, I might be able to do it,* was Hansen's thought after Hill had tripled. Now it was: *Pearson did it, I'm doing it.* Practice time was over.

The final lap saw two incredible riders circulate at the limits of their abilities. Each led for parts of the lap but Hansen bobbled and Shane led into the backside berm. The Yamaha swerved right and entered the berm early and relatively slowly. Hansen couldn't believe his luck and fired his Honda past, squaring off the corner and slamming the throttle open hard, spinning through third gear and catching fourth half-way to the lip of the triple. To give him credit, the Honda rider never faltered in his decision to become the fifth rider to triple at the Colorado Fairs. He left it pinned into and up the face, launching his CRF in an attempt at glory, history and the win.

He almost made it.

But *almost making* a triple and *making* a triple is similar to holding a live hand grenade or a double-dip chocolate-chip ice-cream cone. They might feel a bit similar and weigh the same, but one isn't as sweet. The Honda soared into the Colorado day and Hansen's body language and wide-open throttle gave a hint at what was to come: he knew he was short. Add to the picture of Hansen's strained body a Yamaha YZ-F450 soaring past, even higher.

As the bikes touched down, the difference between the hand grenade and the ice-cream cone became clear to all involved. Hansen's bike cased itself on the very tippity-top of the third jump and his race was over as the bike demolished itself. Even if the bike hadn't broken in two, Brady Hanson was done for the season. Broken ankles will do that to a motocross racer.

Shane saw it coming. Saw Hansen spin the tire, heard the late shift to fourth…saw the wisdom of Tom Hill's advice. *You gotta be ready to use the brakes on the lip of the jump if you don't get the exit perfect…if you spin or over-clutch or make a mistake and run third. If you don't go to the brakes, you'll overjump the doubles but not even come close to tripling.*

Shane cruised the remaining corners to take one of the most dramatic Fair wins in history. He was pulled off his bike by a mob of friends, family and fans, but his biggest hug was for his coach, Tom Hill. It was a giddy happiness…tripling at the Fairs, beating Brady Hansen, joining his brother as a Fair winner. In the laughter and excitement, Shane noticed Biganski standing with Tom's bike, giving him the thumbs up and a huge smile.

Tom's race is next, Shane remembered. *I'm going to the start with him.*

107

Shane didn't bother heading across the paddock to the Springs pit area, he just started his bike to catch up with Biganski, Tom, Teddy and Ken as they walked Tom's bike down to the Open Senior start. Shane couldn't go two feet without someone slapping him on the back or shouting congratulations and he was relieved to escape into the start area. He leaned his race winner against the cement wall and jogged over to the gang. Biganski had positioned Tom's bike on the starting gate and two spots away sat Paul on his 450, Preston by his side.

Tom stood behind his bike, next to Biganski and Ken. His head was bowed, eyes closed, chin on his chest. His small son stood on the other side, gazing around the starting area, holding his dad's helmet and gloves. The buzz of Shane's race endured. Energy, noise and emotion swirled around Tom Hill as the Senior Experts filed into the grid but his mind was locked into the memory of his two best starts, the throttle he used, the adjustments he made, the view of turn one. His mind ran a perfect start and amazing first lap, a track-record lap, a back-straight-triple lap.

Furious activity surrounded the thirty-five year-old rancher but he calmly raised his right hand and rested it on Biganski's shoulder...*my tuner, my wrench.* Tom Hill laughed, a prolonged chuckle submerged for fifteen years. Ken and Biganski smiled along...then they couldn't help but giggle. Shane caught the bug too, especially when they heard Teddy trying to stifle his own laughing. Who laughs on the starting line of a Fairs main event? Riders who love to race.

108

The Colorado Fairs starting area stretches the 450s into fifth gear before a tiny jump that leads into a huge left-hand, third-gear berm. The fans who had stood during Shane's race were back on their feet and Bill Spencer was building suspense, focused around Tom Hill's return to racing and the only Californian in the field, Paul Jupiter.

Spencer's prediction of a lightning start from Tom Hill was on the money. Hill fired his Biganski Yamaha over the gate and timed his second-to-third-to-fourth shifts perfectly, catching fifth about forty yards in front of the first little jump leading to turn one. His Yamaha had wheelied through the first four gears and gained Tom a ten-bike-length lead in the first nine seconds of the race. Picture-perfect.

Paul Jupiter was sixth and losing ground, soon to be eighth as the built Colorado 450s ran him down. Paul's start was good but straight-line acceleration punishes low horsepower and the Jupiter Yamaha slipped to tenth as the pack rolled off for the jump.

Then Jupiter was fourth: Will Iden never closed the throttle on his Kawasaki and catapulted his green bike over the jump and directly into the back wheel of Tom Hill. Hill had already entered the berm and was picking up the throttle to fire off the corner when the Kawi's front wheel pierced his spokes just behind the rear sprocket.

For the second time in Hill's career, his rear wheel exploded. Iden, Hill and two other riders hit the deck in a mangle of machinery and dirt. Paul Jupiter had a moment to register the crash before flashing underneath the melee, grabbing fourth place.

Bill Spencer and the entire Fairs crowd couldn't have told you who was leading the Senior main event because the focus of the words and eyes were on Hill. The rear-wheel strike had skittered his Yamaha 180-degrees and it lay facing backward on the track. Tom had been knocked sideways from the impact but managed to land on his feet before tumbling back into the berm. He was up in a flash and had his bike upright…still running.

Reality struck as Tom jumped on and started to release the clutch to get back in the race…the rear wobbled like an antique grocery cart on its worst day and Tom knew the bike wouldn't even finish the first lap. The desperation that Bill Pearson had seen at the Fairs had struck Tom Hill.

But Biganski's brilliance hadn't been dimmed. Tom heard his name shouted from the mechanics' signaling area fifty feet away… he looked up to see Ken and Shane screaming his name, motioning him over. Tom dropped the clutch and the Yamaha lurched across the track and into the signaling area as the few remaining spokes gave way and the wheel collapsed.

Tom barely caught the bike before it tipped and as he gained control, he looked up to see Ken and Shane holding Shane's 450 up as Biganski finished pulling the rear wheel. Biganski, Ken, Shane and Teddy had moved to the signaling area before the race started and Biganski had the presence of mind to bring Shane's 450 along. He originally asked Shane to grab it because the tuner didn't like his bikes sitting out in public for everyone to examine…but in the back of his mind he knew a backup bike was never a bad thing.

Or a backup rear wheel. The rules permitted pit stops, including rear-wheel changes.

Ken and Shane dropped Shane's 450 as the wheel came free, dashing to Tom's bike as Tom stepped clear. Biganski's 'emergency' tool kit made short work of the wheel swap and the pack of vet racers were just past half-way of the first lap as Big slipped the chain on calmly, deliberately...quickly. Biganski's ratchet snugged the axle nut as Tom stepped aboard and snapped out the kickstarter.

As the racer rose to boot his bike back to life, his twelve year-old son stepped in front of the 450 and caught his dad's eye. Teddy pointed to his head...*stay focused.*

Tom nodded, the bike fired, the new/used tire spun and caught. Spencer screamed, the crowd roared and the sound shoved the Biganski Yamaha off turn one like a kite caught in a tsunami. Hill tripled on the first lap and the crowd's roar intensified as Spencer fed the inferno. Tom Hill was back in the main, three-quarters of a lap down.

Paul Jupiter's shock of seeing his friend taken out was soon replaced with the challenge of holding fourth place against a horde of good riders on impressive bikes. He heard the ongoing roar of the crowd and Spencer's baritone filling the track and suspected the fuss was all about Tom. On the sixth lap, half-way through the race, Paul would have sworn that the crowd had intensified, moved closer to the fence, doubled in size. And it had. Hill was coming but Paul's fitness was beginning to pay off. He slipped into second place and his grimace could have been mistaken for a smile as he saw the leader get out of shape through the whoops.

Paul and Preston rode year-round in California...and the best workout for a motorcycle rider is to ride motorcycles. Paul took a deep breath and put in his quickest lap on the tenth go-around, arriving on the heels of the lead KTM with two laps to go. The

California imposter running a close second to one of the local favorites garnered his share of screams, whistles and shouts from the crowd, but the real noise for Tom Hill had never gone away. Paul now knew something big was happening behind him but his attention suddenly riveted on a single thought: *I've got to get around this KTM right now and hope I can outrun whoever is coming.*

Paul knew Spencer's dramatics and the crowd's reaction meant one thing: *It's Tom...I gotta go, NOW!*

Paul's mental order to *go, NOW* pushed his body to snap his YZ-F under the KTM in the same corner his son had passed the Medley Honda but Paul's move was borderline nasty. The Senior racer could feel the pull of the finish line just over a lap away, calling to him to push harder than he had ever pushed and that call put him near desperation. The win over Mann suddenly wasn't good enough. Jupiter wanted to be the guy who won two Fairs in the same year.

Beating Tom Hill never entered Paul's mind as he dug deep to gap the KTM and whoever the crowd was screaming for. As the final lap started, Jupiter knew he wasn't *beating* Tom Hill...*I'm just trying to outrun him for one more lap!* He felt like the bunny being pursued by the coyote and his fevered mind thought of the finish line the way the bunny thinks of his burrow. *Get there and you're safe.* The Senior racer from California pushed. The crowd thundered. Spencer boomed. Jupiter never looked back, his eyes searching for the finish line and the checkered flag.

And Paul Jupiter almost won both California and Colorado Fairs in one year. But Tom Hill tripled over him half a lap from the finish, launching the Biganski-prepped 450 into the air for the twelfth lap in a row, the twelfth time the crowd screamed as one voice. And the triple was just one of the awe-inspiring moves Tom Hill showed that sun-baked Colorado crowd that State Fair afternoon. The quiet rancher hammered through the whoops harder than anyone could believe, taking a different line every lap as he reeled in the best Senior riders in Colorado. And California. He seemed to defy gravity and physics and fans were hard-pushed to spot a flaw in Hill's twelve laps, including his impromptu pit stop.

Clearing the triple was a move Paul Jupiter had never seriously considered trying. Paul had always been comfortable in the air but the comfort had to be matched with nerve and talent. The elder Jupiter had spoken quietly with Tom about the triple after the final Senior practice, but Tom had told him what he had told Shane.

"I couldn't do it on a stock bike…it's a tough move." Tom never dissuaded his friend from trying it but he certainly didn't encourage him.

Paul had watched Shane experiment with the triple early, against Brady Hansen, watched the young racer go to the brakes before the jump every lap, gauging his drive off the berm, his speed. Paul saw the early berm entry, heard the clutch work in fourth gear, studied the successful attempt on the eleventh lap…but when he watched Hansen demolish himself and his Honda, his mind was made up. *If Tom says it's tough for him…I'll run hard and finish where I finish.*

Paul ran quick, getting within whispering distance of Andrew Short's lap record and a race win. He was the best of the rest, but Paul Jupiter was not Tom Hill on the racetrack. Few were, few will ever be. Even those in the crowd who knew nothing about motorcycles, had never even seen a race on TV, knew as they walked back to the fairgrounds that they had seen something magical when that guy on the Yamaha came from behind to win, running laps almost two seconds under the record. Bill Spencer had told them but they didn't need his words. *And those Pearson kids were good too…*was said more than once.

Rob Christopher thought so too.

109

Rob Christopher, sixty-six years old and virtually unknown in the Colorado Fairs paddock area, had come to the Fairs to help crew for his grandson Eddie Christopher, one of the 80cc experts who had qualified for this year's main event. Eddie had finished a creditable seventh in his Saturday race and his dad and grandfather decided to stay on and enjoy Sunday's racing. They'd walked through the midway, watched Eddie and his friends ride the rides, snacked on fair food...but the Christophers hadn't missed much practice, and none of Sunday's races.

Relaxing at a motocross race felt almost foreign to Rob Christopher. Not the racing, but the relaxing. Having a day to sit in the sun really appealed to the ex-Yamaha Motorsports Manager. He'd flown in from Orange County, California, where he and his wife enjoyed their retirement. Rob's previous twenty-five years had been spent in Cypress, California, at the headquarters of Yamaha US.

In his quarter-century at Yamaha Christopher had driven the company to the forefront of motorcycle racing in America. His decisions and actions formed the incredible race wins and championships Yamaha is known for. Racing was in his blood: watching his grandson run was a trip back to a time when he didn't have to worry about budgets, politics or next week's travel.

He had never truly retired. Guys like Christopher might leave Yamaha but knowledge like his was constantly asked for and imparted on the phone, e-mail and even the occasional lunch. He knew too much, had seen it all, could call anyone in the industry at any time and ask them anything. The ghost of Rob Christopher would always walk the halls of Yamaha because virtually every picture of every Yamaha champion adorning the walls of Cypress had come due to Christopher's work.

When Christopher heard Bill Spencer gushing about Tom Hill over the PA it caught his attention and triggered his memory... Rob had walked casually past Tommy Hill's pit at Anaheim in 1995 after Hill had qualified his old YZ for the main. Rob had looked the older 250 over quickly and labeled it the *quintessential privateer*. Tommy Hill looked fit and tough but those two labels fit every racer in the paddock.

Hannah had been in the war up front so Rob hadn't paid Hill much attention. After Hill's crash Rob had decided that Tommy's good run was just due to pure adrenaline and over-your-head-riding. He chalked it up to another kid hanging onto his bike long enough to race into the top ten, then quickly running out of talent and luck. Fifteen years had passed and the name Tommy Hill had never crossed Rob Christopher's mind again.

As he listened to Spencer he realized that Hill had quite a legacy in Colorado...and was spinning good laps. Christopher again ambled past Hill's pit area but this time the Colorado Springs operation impressed him to no end. *Better than we looked only five years ago,* he thought to himself. And there was Tommy...no Tom...Hill, looking fit and tough. Those two labels definitely did not fit every racer in the Senior class.

The Christophers watched Ken Pearson dominate the 250 Pro class and stood and screamed with the rest of the sun-drenched crowd as Shane Pearson tripled over Brady Hansen to snatch the Open pro class. The whole crowd cringed when Brady Hansen cased his Honda 450 but Rob Christopher had a moment of happiness as he watched the Honda destroy itself. He felt bad for Hansen but his twenty-five years of fighting against Honda couldn't be erased.

Rob admired Tom Hill's class-leading launch into turn one but grimaced when Iden cannonballed him. Spencer had established that Hill hadn't raced since Anaheim 1995 and Christopher recognized the cruel hand of fate in Tom's turn-one bad luck. Spencer's ongoing focus on the Hill/Iden crash kept Christopher's attention on them too.

"Hand me the binocs," Christopher said to his son.

"Well...whadya know about that?" Christopher muttered twenty seconds later, staring through the binoculars.

"What dad?" asked his son, also staring at the action in the pits.

"That really is Sam Biganski...wondered what happened to him," Christopher replied distractedly.

"Who?"

"Bike builder...tuner...out of California," Christopher explained to his son and grandson. "Must be up here working at that Springs Yamaha shop...no wonder the Pearsons won. That guy put together some pretty great stuff...did a lot of roadracers, got into motocross, Supermoto..."

Christopher was staring through the binoculars and saw a kid point to his head just as Tom fired his bike, nodded...and rejoined the race with a dazzling first turn exit. The ex-Yamaha manager flashed his binoculars back to Biganski and saw the tuner re-assembling his tools and getting the sign-board ready. *All business, as usual...that guy knows the business of winning.*

Christopher put down the binoculars to watch the race unfold but half-a-lap later he leapt to his feet with the rest of the crowd as Hill launched his bike to the moon and tripled on the back straight. As the pack thundered past three generations of Christophers, Rob never even looked at who was leading. His eyes were glued on Hill. When Tom smoked past half-a-lap later, Rob Christopher recognized the bark of a perfectly-tuned four-stroke motocross bike. A fast one.

As the second lap unfolded, Rob Christopher explained to his son and grandson what he knew about Biganski's cheating fiasco. He didn't interject any judgment on Biganski's guilt or innocence.

People in glass houses shouldn't throw stones. Three times during Christopher's career at Yamaha he had been forced to decide between rule-stretching (*my euphemism for cheating,* he thought to himself) and safety. Three times his group had tried to make a motorcycle do something it wasn't designed to do. He felt Biganski's pain when the hammer came down on him after Gray's second-place finish on the Supermoto Kawasaki…but he couldn't defend him to anyone. Yet he didn't convict him, either.

Hill's outright speed dazzled the crowd and sat Rob Christopher back on his heels. It seemed as if Hill rode on a different track than the Seniors he was streaming past…his track was smoother, the jumps were higher, the turns more banked.

"Eddie…just watch Tom Hill on that Yamaha…that's how you want to ride."

110

Tom Hill's Senior victory was the final race of the day and the Colorado Springs pit area had spread to encompass half the paddock...racers, racer-families and devoted fans brought their lawn chairs over with their coolers and even a few portable barbecues, setting up little camps of celebration. The area under the canopies was a mob scene and the crowning jewels of the entire affair were the Fairs trophies that sat on the five Yamahas under the tent. The Jupiters' bikes each held a second-place trophy, and three first-place awards sat on the two 450s and Ken's 250. The feeling that Bill Pearson had expressed at the Hill ranch only a few days ago had materialized and the dealership owner recalled his words as he slid the Jupiter barbecue out to light: *This is gonna be one heck of a state championship.*

Pearson lit the barbecue and when he turned around he jumped forward to grab Sam Biganski in a gigantic bear hug. Ken and Shane saw the move and before Sam could take a breath to scream, the three Pearsons had lifted him onto their shoulders and started to chant: *Biganski, Biganski, Biganski.* Three chants were enough for the crowd and more than three hundred people joined in. Tom Hill stepped to his bike, grabbed his trophy and thrust it into Sam's hands...the Pearsons bobbed up and down with the chant and Biganski laughed the true laugh of pure happiness...and then tears filled his eyes as he looked around at the crowd celebrating his work.

He'd left California with unfulfilled dreams...he'd just tuned the Pearsons and Tom Hill to Fairs wins.

Teddy Hill hung onto Biganski's pant leg as the Pearsons bobbed up and down and the crowd shrieked *Biganski!* The kid had never been happier...the joy came from the abject sorrow he'd felt when Iden had harpooned his dad. He had been standing next to Ken in the signaling area, looking forward to what he knew his dad could do, when the Kawi pierced his dad's rear wheel.

⊶•⦿•⊷

Teddy had felt his soul crumble as his dad's Yamaha came up wobbly and ruined...*the trick Bill Pearson played to get dad on Shane's bike, the ice-pack that froze Shane's knee, Henkle's video that showed a previous rear-wheel problem ruining a sixth-place Supercross finish, Biganski's hours of tricking-out dad's ride...*this and more flashed through his twelve-year-old mind as everyone realized that his dad's Yamaha was done.

But as sorrow flooded Teddy, action overtook Sam Biganski. The moment Tom went down, Sam dropped the signaling board and bent to grab his emergency tool box. Sam saw the rear-wheel immediately, even before Tom Hill realized the problem.

"Ken, Shane...get him over here, now!"

Biganski knew the rules prevented working on the bike on-track but Tom's crash was only fifty feet away. If he could get the bike here... Biganski had already whirled and run to Shane's 450 resting against the far-side wall of the signaling area. He slid to a stop on his knees behind the bike and within two seconds he had the wrench on the axle nut...spun the nut off... pushed the axle part way out...looked to see if Tom had heard Ken and Shane. He was wobbling over.

"Ken, Shane...lift this thing!"

They did, the axle slid out and the wheel was free...Ken and

Shane dumped Shane's bike and ran to Tom's, lifting it for Biganski to pull the damaged wheel and insert Shane's wheel.

Teddy had slumped against the signaling wall, distraught with grief, feeling his dad's loss like a physical pain. But Ken and Shane's yelling snapped him into real-time and he looked up to see Biganski on his knees behind Shane's 450. The next thing Teddy knew his dad was getting back on his bike and Teddy felt the turmoil swirling... like the water you'd feel if you jumped into the North Atlantic...in January. He saw his dad's usual calmness replaced with wide-eyed panic. Teddy knew that wasn't his dad, it was someone who had just been knocked down and was still frantic. The kid knew his dad didn't ride panicked...he stepped in front of the 450 and gave his dad the signal his dad had given him months ago at the Pueblo County Fair. When his dad nodded, his eyes were his own. Focused and intense.

———•((•))•———

Teddy bounced up and down with the Pearsons, Biganski holding the trophy over his head, the crowd celebrating him more than the media had berated him. The kid had a hold of Biganski's foot and the tuner looked down.

You're next, Teddy Hill...you're next, Biganski thought through the haze of the celebration. He'd seen the kid's talent, seen him lead Preston around the ranch track, never even trying, just running with the Californian using less than eighty percent of his 125's capabilities. The thought of this humble kid on a Biganski bike, a kid happy just to ride with his new friend Preston and didn't have to leave him in the dust, made Sam smile through his tears.

The Pearsons finally put Biganski down and the raucous chanting subsided as the racers enjoyed a Sunday night at the Fairs. Anyone who has ever felt the satisfaction of surviving a risk, doing his or her best, exploring new limits, knows how these racers felt on that Colorado Sunday evening, especially the racers under the Colorado Springs Yamaha tent.

Paul Jupiter glowed with his second-place effort, as did Preston. They had ridden to and beyond their limits, taking stock bikes into territory that nobody suspected they could reach—not in Colorado, anyway. The Jupiter men sat on both sides of Lori Jupiter and the Californians soaked in the scene, chanted for Biganski, snacked on the quesadillas that Brian Hill handed around and then enjoyed the prime rib Bill Pearson produced from their grill. The three Jupiters talked and dreamed…and planned.

The Colorado Fairs had changed their lives. To be more exact, meeting the Pearsons, Hills and Sam Biganski had changed them. The Hill ranch helped too and though Lori had never seen it, her boys' description of the place had her imagining her life-long dream of riding a horse in the west. Lori's purse held the highest-level mileage cards from three major airlines, she knew her way around New York City, Los Angeles, Paris, Amsterdam, Monaco…but as she sat in the darkening Colorado motocross pit, she couldn't remember being this happy in a long, long time.

Lori Jupiter couldn't wait to travel in the motorhome with Paul and Preston…couldn't wait to get down to Walsenburg and find a place to rent for the rest of the summer. *One month in Colorado with her men… Brian said we could ride Buck, Blossom and Flytrap anywhere, anytime.* Lori shook her head in disbelief that she might be riding horses across the mesas of a Colorado ranch the day after tomorrow! Judy Hill matched her smile from her seat next to Tom.

Lori Jupiter and Judy Hill had taken to each other the moment they met in Colorado Springs. Both were surprised that a woman leading the fashion industry would have anything in common with a woman running a ranch and working as a CPA in southeast Colorado…but each was surprised and pleased.

As the races unfolded and the two women from opposite worlds lived through the tumultuous ups and downs of the Fairs, Lori Jupiter found herself yearning for the simplicity of the life Judy Hill described. Yearning to take a vacation from fashion, ride a horse, eat a steak...be in Colorado. Paul Jupiter didn't know what to say when his wife proposed a month in Walsenburg because her idea put his feelings into words: he didn't want to leave, didn't want to go back to California yet.

Tom Hill smiled at the news in his stoic way but his heart sang and he couldn't help but give Paul and Lori a hug. Teddy and Preston whooped aloud and started making plans.

Epilogue

Darkness had overtaken the Fairs paddock and most racers had loaded up and idled out the gates. The Jupiter motorhome was packed with Hills, Pearsons and Jupiters…plus one Biganski…but the activities had wound down to quiet talk and more planning. Lori Jupiter had looked through a few Walsenburg real-estate sites on her iPad and passed it around to show everyone when she found a nice place for rent. She had two phone numbers jotted down and could hardly wait to call them tomorrow. Nobody was surprised at the Jupiter's decision to finish the summer in Colorado. It made perfect sense in so many ways.

A firm knock came on the door. Paul jumped to push it open. A grey-haired gentleman in a Yamaha jersey stood in the gravel and asked if he could speak with Tom Hill. Paul invited him in and Rob Christopher introduced himself, shaking hands with the men and nodding to the women.

"This is the winningest motorhome I've ever been in," Christopher began with a smile. "Whatever you guys drink, I think we should bottle it."

Then he surprised everyone present when he added, "Of course, you've got Sam Biganski."

"What do you know about our Sam?" Bill Pearson asked.

Christopher took a minute to describe what he had done for the last twenty-five years and Bill Pearson was nodding.

"I thought I recognized your name. You helped Shane when he came down to the Vegas Supercross…got him some brake pads, I believe."

"It was clutch plates," Shane corrected. "I still appreciate it…that was the best start I ever had!"

The chuckles died quickly. Why was Rob Christopher standing in a motorhome in Colorado?

He cleared his throat and turned to Tom Hill.

"Tom…that was quite a ride today. And at Anaheim fifteen years ago, at least before you crashed out. I guess I'm…"

"Sir, his wheel exploded just as he hit the front-straight jump…we have video to prove it!" Teddy's voice ripped through the motorhome and he strained forward like a bulldog on a leash.

Tom reached out and held his shoulder, gave it a pat…but nodded at Rob Christopher.

"It's true. I only found out last week…Paul here had a video that showed the wheel coming apart and finally collapsing. I quit racing after that…but decided to run this Fairs."

Christopher's eyes had widened at Teddy's retort, but a slow smile came over him as he heard the story. "But I'm guessing you never quit riding?"

Tom smiled. "Oh no…we have some land and ride a bit."

Everyone in the motorhome, except Christopher, just about choked with laughter that continued for almost a minute. Christopher looked around at the hilarity and couldn't suppress a smile.

"What's the joke?"

Judy Hill spoke up. "Mr. Christopher…there's a complete Supercross track at our house, courtesy of that crazy man right there," pointing at a grinning Bill Pearson. "And all these boys have been lapping that thing like lunatics to get ready for these Fairs." Judy paused, then added: "There aren't many days that a motorcycle doesn't get ridden somewhere on the ranch…so yeah, you could say Tom never quit riding." Nods and smiles all around told Christopher that these were his kind of people.

"All right…I didn't want to interrupt you too much. I'm here to extend an invitation to Shane Pearson and Tom Hill." The older man paused and looked at Shane and Tom in turn.

"Yamaha US wants you to represent them at the Anaheim Supercross next February."

A shocked silence quieted the motorhome for the first time all week-end. The air had been sucked from the lungs of everyone present...except Tom's dad, Carl. The old rancher stepped forward and extended his hand to Rob Christopher. The ex-Yamaha man clasped it and looked Carl in the eye. Carl spoke quietly but the words were clear and precise.

"Mister, I died inside when Tom quit racing but the economics of the time made ranch work the most important. You saw my boy ride, he's got something special, but I couldn't give him the support he needed. He'll be there in February."

Rob Christopher and Carl Hill shook again and they both turned to look at Tom. He nodded his ascent. He would be there. He had unfin-ished business.

"Shane?" Rob asked.

Shane had been watching but now he turned toward his dad. Bill Pearson's smile said it all.

"I'll be there...if I can bring Big."

It was Rob's turn to laugh. "Sam Biganski has been part of the deal ever since I bounced it off Keith Starr and Bob McCarty at Yamaha about an hour ago. He'll get two factory bikes and full access to every-thing we have."

All eyes went back to Shane.

Shane was nodding, a small smile playing on his face.

"And what about my slower, uglier brother Ken?"

Rob and everyone in the motorhome laughed but Rob could see the seriousness behind the question. This was a group of hungry racers but they had molded a fantastically successful approach to this sport...the mo-torhome, the pit area, the trailers, the bike prep...nobody in this motorhome was looking for a handout. These guys could qualify for a Supercross main event right now, Rob thought to himself, without my help.

Rob turned and looked Ken in the eye, then glanced at Bill Pearson, then back to Shane. "Your slow brother will run the Lights class at Anaheim on his own bike, but Sam will get full access to all our 250 parts and tuning info."

Sam Biganski cleared his throat and stepped out from behind Tom Hill.

"Ah, Mr. Christopher…when you talk about access, do you mean I'll get my hands on all your cylinder-head stuff and the new electronics? You mean all the new suspension pieces, links too?"

"That's what I mean. Bob McCarty said he'll get you anything you need."

Sam shook his head in disbelief. "Am I dreaming?"

"No…but you just won three Fairs, set the lap record and put two of your riders over that triple," Rob paused and looked around the motorhome. "It's not a dream, it's the way this sport has always been. This isn't car racing, where you buy a ride, this is bike racing where winning at the state level gets that rider a shot at the national level. I'm here to give you that shot. Deal?"

The Jupiter motorhome resounded with a single word: "Deal!"

The End

The Hill Ranch Racers
Glossary of Terms

Arroyo
A steep-sided mini-canyon formed by water but usually dry…until it flash-floods!

Berm
A banked corner on a motocross track. Sometime a berm is built by the track builders, but berms can also form naturally as the bikes' tires push the dirt to the outside of a corner.

Case It
Not a fun action! This means that the rider didn't jump far enough and lands on the very top edge of the jump, just short of the landing ramp. The term comes from the fact that the engine cases land on solid dirt with no help from the suspension. Ouch!

Cross Rut
Another not-fun action on a dirtbike. The front wheel gets caught in one rut and the rear wheel in another! Cross rutting often throws the bike off the jump sideways and out of control.

Cross Up
As the rider flies into the air off a jump, she tips the bike sideways and offsets that tip with her body.

Double or Triple Jump

Simply enough, a double or triple jump is two or three jumps in a row. But riders use 'double' or 'triple' as a verb too: "I'm going to double in that back section," meaning that the rider intents to launch off the first jump's launching ramp and land on the second jump's landing ramp.

Endo

Not good!! The word 'endo' comes from the term 'end over end'…as in: *The rider messed up the jump, landed on his front wheel and endo-ed.*

Four-stroke Engine

Most engines in our cars and motorcycles are 'four-strokes'. Fuel and air enter through an intake valve above the piston as the piston descends in the cylinder. That's one stroke. Then the piston comes up and compresses the mixture in the second stroke. Then the spark plug fires and the piston descends for the third stroke, and then the fourth stroke happens as the piston rises to push the burned mixture out the exhaust valve.

Holeshot

A holeshot is to accelerate your bike to the first turn first, as in, "That fast Medley Honda grabbed the holeshot."

Knack-Knack, Nac-Nac, Nak-Nak

As motocross freestyle was in its infancy, national-champion Jeremy McGrath threw a knack-knack off a jump and wowed the world… he basically stepped off the bike midair, leaving only one foot on the pegs. Also nac-nac, nak-nak.

Lost the Front

When riders use this term, what they've lost is the traction of the front tire. Sometimes the rider regains traction and keeps riding, sometimes the rider lies in the dirt and contemplates his loss.

Paddock

A paddock, or pit, is the area near a racetrack where the teams park and setup their tents, haulers, motorhomes and mobile workshops.

Quad

A quad is a four-wheeler and they come in all sizes and shapes, from ranch-work models to full-on racers.

Rev Limiter

A rev limiter is an electronic program in the ignition system that won't allow the engine to rev past a certain RPM. But there's a problem: Because it's electronic, it doesn't protect the engine if the rider downshifts and puts the bike into redline mechanically. Do that too often and it "gets expensive".

RPM/Redline

Revolutions Per Minute...how many times the crankshaft of an engine spins in one minute. Most motorcycle engines idle at about 1000 rpm and Grand Prix bikes spin to a maximum of 18,000 rpm. An engine's maximum rpm is called its *redline*.

Scrub

Yes, behind your ears but also a great way to keep your bike closer to the ground off jumps. The rider absorbs the suspension's energy with a quick flick sideways. The more the bike is on the ground, the more it can be accelerating or braking.

Starting Gate

A diabolical contraption that falls ***toward*** the rider and must hit the ground before the rider can launch her bike at the start of a motocross race. If the rider goes too early, the front tire is caught by the gate. You literally cannot jump the start of a motocross race!!

Tabletop Jump

A tabletop is the safest of jumps because the area between the launching ramp and the landing ramp is filled in with dirt. If the rider doesn't make it all the way to the landing ramp, that rider simply lands "on top of the table".

Thumper

A four-stroke, single-cylinder engine.

Torque

In the motorcycling world, torque is an engine's ability to pull without having a lot of rpm. If a bike "has no torque" it means that it must be revved high to make any power. If a bike is "torquey", it means the engine pulls hard at low revs.

Two-stroke Engine

As the piston in a two-stroke engine descends in the cylinder it uncovers the intake port and fresh air and gas enter, helping to push out the burned air and gas through the uncovered exhaust port. The piston then rises to compress the mixture and the spark plug fires it to produce a power stroke every time the piston rises. This makes two-stroke engines significantly more powerful than similarly-sized (normally aspirated) four-stroke engines. A two-stroke engine has poor emissions, but technology is working on that. If you've never ridden a well-tuned two-stroke, you're missing a huge thrill.

WFO

Wide Full Open…as in the throttle is pinned, cranked, buried.

Whoops

No, not "whoops I dropped my fork", but whoopdeedoos on a motocross track, a series of staggered bumps ranging in size and always getting worse as the laps go on.

Now…Get out there and ride!!!

About the Author

Nick Ienatsch is the chief instructor for the Yamaha Champions Riding School. He eats and breathes motorcycles and began writing for <u>Motorcyclist</u> magazine in 1984...and hasn't stopped since! You can find his words in Cycle World magazine, *cycleworld.com*, *ridelikeachampion.com* and on **fastersafer.com** as well as in the hot-selling Sport Riding Techniques. Nick lives with his wife Judy and their four American Mustangs in Colorado and Nevada...with too many bikes to count.

No matter where you are in your riding career, Nick's <u>Sport Riding Techniques</u> will improve your safety and enjoyment...and speed if that's what you're after!

CPSIA information can be obtained at www.ICGtesting.com
Printed in the USA
BVOW02s0856040216

435479BV00017B/18/P